WHATEVER HAPPENED
TO MOLLY BLOOM?

A selection of recent titles by Jessica Stirling

THE CAPTIVE HEART
ONE TRUE LOVE
BLESSINGS IN DISGUISE
THE FIELDS OF FORTUNE
A KISS AND A PROMISE
THE PARADISE WALTZ
A CORNER OF THE HEART
THE LAST VOYAGE
THE WAYWARD WIFE
THE CONSTANT STAR
WHATEVER HAPPENED TO MOLLY BLOOM?*

* *available from Severn House*

WHATEVER HAPPENED TO MOLLY BLOOM?

Jessica Stirling

severn
House

This first world edition published 2014
in Great Britain and in 2015 in the USA by
SEVERN HOUSE PUBLISHERS LTD
19 Cedar Road, Sutton, Surrey, England, SM2 5DA.

Trade paperback edition first published
in Great Britain and the USA 2015 by
SEVERN HOUSE PUBLISHERS LTD.

British Library Cataloguing in Publication Data

Stirling, Jessica author.
  Whatever happened to Molly Bloom?.
  1. Murder--Investigation--Fiction. 2. Police--Ireland--
  Dublin--Fiction. 3. Detective and mystery stories.
  I. Title
  823.9'14-dc23

ISBN-13: 978-0-7278-8440-4 (cased)
ISBN-13: 978-1-84751-555-1 (trade paper)
ISBN-13: 978-1-78010-602-1 (e-book)

All Severn House titles are printed on acid-free paper.

Severn House Publishers support the Forest Stewardship Council™ [FSC™],
the leading international forest certification organisation. All our titles that
are printed on FSC certified paper carry the FSC logo.

Typeset by Palimpsest Book Production Ltd.,
Falkirk, Stirlingshire, Scotland.
Printed and bound in Great Britain by
TJ International, Padstow, Cornwall.

PART ONE
The Detective

ONE

The bell of St George's tolled the hour of nine as Detective Inspector Jim Kinsella of the Dublin Metropolitan Police dropped from the tram and headed up into Eccles Street. It was a brisk, bright March morning with more than a hint of spring in the air and the city was lifting its head again after a dreary, rain-washed winter. Kinsella was glad to be out of the office, though why Store Street had requested assistance from G Division for what appeared to be an obvious case of domestic violence was puzzling.

On the steps of Number 7, a young constable in patrol uniform stood guard on the door. Tall, broad shouldered and fresh faced, a typical product of the Kevin Street Training Depot, he came to attention when he caught sight of the inspector. He did not, however, salute. Even here in the quiet backwaters of C Division the rank and file were still leery of drawing attention to a plainclothes detective who might be a target for nationalist desperadoes. A street whose lower reaches boasted only plain three-storey brown brick houses numbed by their own ordinariness was hardly likely to harbour a nest of volatile republicans but the inspector did not chide the young man for his caution.

'Kinsella,' he said. 'I believe I'm expected.'

'Mr Machin, sir, he's waiting for you inside.'

A Wexford accent, Kinsella thought, probably a farmer's son. He said, 'How long have you been here, Constable?'

'Short of an hour, sir.'

'Has the coroner arrived yet?'

'Not yet, sir.'

'Who was first on the scene?'

'It was me. I mean, I was.' The constable extracted a notebook from the side pocket of his tunic and read from it. 'At ten minutes to eight o'clock, nearing the end of my duty, I was approaching the corner of Lower Dorset Street from the north when a disturbance occurred in Eccles Street.'

'What sort of disturbance?'

'Shouting, a man shouting,' the constable answered. 'It was very loud and sounded . . . I don't have the word, sir.'

'Frightened?' Kinsella suggested. 'Angry?'

'More like wailing.'

'What did you do then?'

'I proceeded to the scene and found a man standing on the step of Number 7 Eccles Street, shouting at the top of his voice.'

'Was he coherent?'

'Sir?'

'Could you make out what he was saying?'

'He was crying, "She's gone. She's gone." That was all the sense I could get out of him.'

'How was he dressed?'

'In a grey tweed suit.'

'Did he have his boots on?'

'He did.'

'And a hat?'

'No, sir. No hat.'

On the step of the house next door a man hovered, half in and half out of the doorway. Behind him, hugging his back, was a boy of ten or eleven. Other doors were open too and curtains twitched in the windows of the houses opposite.

Kinsella ignored the curious neighbours. 'What did you do then, Constable . . .?'

'Jarvis, sir. Constable Jarvis. I calmed the gentleman best as I could and escorted him indoors.'

'Did he resist?'

'On the contrary, sir. He went of his own accord. He led me to a ground-floor bedroom where I found the body of a woman.' The constable paused. 'It was not a pleasant sight.'

'I'm sure it wasn't. Go on.'

'I entered the room to make sure the woman was no longer drawing breath, which she was not. The man was stood behind me all the while, moaning and wringing his hands. He kept saying, "Molly, Molly. I'm sorry. I'm sorry," over and over again. There was nothing I could do for the poor woman. She was beyond all aid. I put the man down into the kitchen, went outside and found a boy . . .'

'From next door?'

'Ay, sir. I dispatched him to Store Street police station. He returned promptly with Inspector Machin and Sergeant Gandy.'

'But no doctor?'

'No, no doctor.'

'What did you do with the prisoner . . . The gentleman, I mean?'

'I stayed with him in the kitchen.'

'Did it not occur to you to arrest him?' Kinsella asked.

'On what charge, sir? He says he was the one who found the body. I had no reason to suppose he was responsible.'

'Didn't he say anything to rouse your suspicions?'

'No, sir. He smoked a cigarette and, would you believe, put out meat for the cat. On Mr Machin's instruction Sergeant Gandy went to the Orphan School, where they have a telephone, and requested assistance from G Division.'

'Yes, I drew the duty,' Kinsella said.

'Mr Machin is still with the suspect, sir,' Constable Jarvis said. 'It don't be my place to say so but . . .'

'He's waiting for me, is that it?'

'He is, sir. He is.'

Twenty years back, in the darkest days of the Land Wars, Jim Kinsella and Tom Machin had been recruits together in the Kevin Street barracks where Jim's father had been a serving sergeant in the mounted troop. Paternal precedent had conferred no favours on young Kinsella. Conforming to the Metropolitan's rigid rules while living up to his pappy's reputation as a rough-riding martinet had been hard on him. Unlike his father, he had no stomach for recreational drinking, no affinity with horses or much interest in the competitive sports by which a recruit's mettle was judged. He was intelligent, diligent and ambitious for advancement, which, in the eyes of many of his cohorts, set him apart from the pack.

Now, in the spring of 1905, Kinsella was settled in G Division Headquarters in the lower court of the Castle and Machin, by a circuitous route, had wound up in the Rotunda Division where his progress up the ranking ladder had stalled.

They met in the narrow hallway and shook hands.

At six feet, four inches tall Kinsella towered over Tom Machin who had attained the Metro's minimum height requirement only by lifting his heels and combing up his quiff.

'You look well,' Kinsella said.

'Fit as a flea,' said Machin.

'Are you still plunging into the briny at every opportunity?'

Machin's fondness for sea bathing had been quite a joke in the old days. 'Much less often than I used to,' he admitted. 'The sea seems a lot colder than it did twenty years ago.'

'Most things are,' Kinsella said. 'Why have you sent for me?'

'I'd like you to take a look at a body before Slater turns up.'

'Why?'

'I prefer to be armed with something more substantial than guesswork prior to making an arrest.'

'Where is the body?'

'In the bedroom on the left.'

'And the husband? I assume he is the husband?'

'Bloom, yes, Leopold Bloom. He's downstairs in the basement kitchen with Sergeant Gandy. I've been staring at him for half an hour but the beggar is giving nothing away. I'm hoping you might have more luck with him than I've had.'

'Body first, please,' Kinsella said.

Stairs went steeply up from the hall. A closed door, left, concealed the living room and another room lay at the far end of the hall. The bedroom to which Machin admitted him was cluttered with furniture and the window screened by a blind. Filtered daylight gave the room a strange hazy air, like one of the veiled tableaux with which Lowry had closed his pantomimes back in the days when, as Kinsella's father was constantly reminding him, women were women and you could get blind drunk for fourpence.

Sprawled across the bed, the woman would have fitted perfectly into one of Lowry's tableaux; a motionless centrepiece in a rumpled nightdress displaying just enough limb and bosom to rouse an audience to whistles but not quite enough to bring down Lowry's curtain on charges of indecency.

Her position was languid and unnatural. Clad only in a night dress, she lay half on and half off the double bed, shoulders and arms resting on the floor, her feet entangled in the sheets, belly covered by a bedspread and her face tucked coyly into the crook of an elbow. Her hair, unpinned, spread over her bare shoulder and if it hadn't been for the pool of blood around her head you might, indeed, have thought she was posing.

'Is this how your constable found her?' Kinsella asked.

'Jarvis disturbed her just enough to feel for a pulse. He did admit to pulling up the bedspread to cover her parts, though.'

'To protect her modesty.' Kinsella nodded. 'We've all done that in our time. No one else clumping about in here?'

'Only me. I had Sergeant Gandy check the house from top to bottom, by the way, and the outhouse and garden. No signs of an intruder.'

'You think it's the husband, don't you?'

'He's the obvious suspect, of course,' Machin said. 'But certain factors don't quite chime. You've always had a nose for the unusual, Jim. See for yourself. See what you make of it.'

Kinsella squatted by the side of the corpse and eased the woman's head from the rug. A heavy blow had crushed her upper lip and driven it into her teeth and up into the base of the nostril, the flange of which was torn. The wound that gave Kinsella pause, however, had been inflicted on the socket of the left eye; a blow with a jagged object had gouged out the eyeball which clung on aluminous threads to her cheek. A splinter of some brittle material decorated with a tiny flower, possibly a forget-me-not, protruded from the spongy mass of the socket.

Scattered on the floor between the woman's head and the trailing bedspread were a number of small white fragments and three or four larger pieces. One of the larger pieces had a handle attached to it and another a spout.

Kinsella lowered the woman's head and got to his feet.

'Bludgeoned to death with a teapot,' he said. 'Now that's an original way to meet a sticky end. I don't see any sign of spillage so it's safe to assume the pot was not filled with tea.'

'You don't recognise her, do you?' Machin said. 'Weren't you and your good lady at the Glen Cree Reformatory dinner when Mrs Bloom sang in tandem with Bartell d'Arcy? Madame Marion Tweedy she styled herself then. I'm surprised you've forgotten. She had a voice, let alone a figure, that sent shivers down your spine. The story goes that if she hadn't married Bloom and popped a kiddie she might have made it to Milan.'

'Well, she isn't going to make it to Milan now,' Jim Kinsella said just as the coroner, Dr Roland Slater, bustled into the bedroom and said, as he always did, 'Well, what have we here?'

TWO

D ue process dictated that Bloom be conveyed immediately to Store Street station to make a formal statement. To gain a little more time with the suspect, however, Tom Machin sent Sergeant Gandy to round up a mortuary van while Kinsella and he went down into the half basement to allow the grieving widower a further opportunity to unburden himself before he was cautioned.

Bloom was hunched at the kitchen table listlessly stroking a cat that lay full length on the table top purring and licking its whiskers. Kinsella pulled out a chair and sat down. He took off his hat and placed it crown up on the table.

'What's his name?' he began.

'What?' Bloom said.

'The cat, his name?'

'It's a female: Pussens.' Bloom cocked his head and squinted out of puffy, red-rimmed eyes. 'What are you going to do to me?'

'We're just having a little chat, Mr Bloom.'

'Are you arresting me?'

From his stance by the stairs, Machin said, 'You haven't been charged with anything, Mr Bloom. We're waiting for transport to take you to the station to make a statement.'

'I was only gone for ten minutes, a quarter hour at most,' Bloom blurted out.

'Gone where, Mr Bloom?' Kinsella said.

'For meat, for breakfast.'

'Did you lock the front door?'

'No, I never do. I didn't think . . .'

'And you left Mrs Bloom, your wife, where?'

'Molly was in bed.'

'Asleep or awake?'

'Asleep.'

'So,' Kinsella said, 'you didn't have words?'

'Have words?'

'Exchange words. Speak to each other.'

'She was asleep. How could I have words with her?'

'Nothing then passed between you?' Kinsella said.

Bloom pursed his lips, full almost sensual lips braced by a spruce moustache sprinkled with a few grey hairs. His head hair, thinning a little from the brow, was glossy black and had probably received attention from the dye brush.

He wore a pale grey suit with a matching waistcoat and a shirt with a none-too-clean collar into which an unusually florid necktie had been inserted. Neither necktie nor collar had been loosened which may have accounted for the sibilant note in his voice, a thin, wheezing hiss that signalled either grief or defiance. We're not dealing with a slack-jawed bumpkin here, Kinsella thought. Machin's right: there is something fishy about the Jew, some aspect of his behaviour you can't put down to the idiosyncrasies of his race.

'No,' Bloom said. 'Nothing passed between us.'

'What sort of meat was it?'

Bloom's eyes opened wide. 'Begging your pardon?'

'The meat you bought for breakfast.'

'Calf's liver.'

'Where is it now?'

'I gave it to the cat.'

'All of it?'

'She was hungry. She hadn't been fed.'

'Didn't Mrs Bloom feed her?' Jim said.

As if colluding with her master the cat stopped licking and, stretching, yawned in the detective's face.

'Molly was very fond of Pussens.' Bloom spread the fingers of one hand and screened his eyes. 'She loved Pussens and Pussens loved her. Everyone loved Molly.'

Tom Machin raised a doubtful eyebrow while Mr Bloom, shoulders shaking, continued to sob.

Kinsella pressed on. 'When was the cat last fed?'

'I don't see what . . .' Bloom began then, with a watery sigh, appeared to capitulate. 'Last night, about half past ten.'

'Before you and Mrs Bloom retired for the night?'

'Yes.'

'How much liver did you buy this morning?'

'Two cuts. Seven pence worth.'

'Where did you buy your seven pence worth?'

'Dlugacz's. It's just around the corner in Dorset Street.'

'I was under the impression Dlugacz sold only the products of the pig,' Tom Machin said.

'I'm a Protestant,' Bloom said. 'I can eat what I like.'

'How do you cook the liver?' Jim Kinsella asked.

'For the love of God!' Bloom exploded, displaying as much temper, Kinsella reckoned, as a fellow like Bloom would ever display. 'What do my eating habits – she's lying – my wife is lying upstairs with her head bashed in and all you're concerned about is how I cook my breakfast.'

He rose abruptly, scraping back the chair.

Startled, the cat leapt from the table and with a haughty glance at Inspector Machin, raised her tail, stalked out of the door and vanished upstairs.

Kinsella said, 'There isn't much heat in the fire, Mr Bloom.'

Bloom glanced round at the stove, at the kettle, cold and inert upon the hob, at caked ash protruding from the rungs of the grate. 'Mrs Fleming used to do it. Clean it, light it, then when she had it going nicely we'd have breakfast.'

'Who is Mrs Fleming?'

'Oh,' Bloom said. 'She's gone long since. Our daily woman, she was. Molly didn't take to her.'

'Why didn't Mrs Bloom take to her?'

'Because she was old,' Bloom said. 'Molly never did take to any of our servants.' Collapsing on to the wooden chair, he buried his head in his hands and went back to sobbing once more.

Kinsella retrieved his long legs from beneath the table and got to his feet. He stared down at the crown of Bloom's head and, for an instant, felt almost sorry for the man. He had a strong suspicion that the fellow was lying but whether he had killed her or whether he had not, his wife lay dead upstairs and he, at this moment, must be struggling to come to terms with it.

'Take a moment to compose yourself, Mr Bloom,' Kinsella said, then, picking up his hat, went upstairs to talk to the coroner.

*   *   *

Roland Slater was a respected member of the medical fraternity who had been coroner for Dublin County and City for ten years and, barring unforeseen disasters, would hold the post for life. A garrulous little chap, now in his sixties, he wore an old-fashioned morning coat with beetle-wing tails, striped trousers and a shirt with a collar so stiff and tall that it reminded Kinsella of a slave ring. He was rarely seen, in or out of doors, without a scuffed leather valise attached to his fist and a silk hat perched on his frosty white hair.

He had laid the victim's body out not on the bed but on the patch of floor between the bed and a dressing table and had covered it with a sheet. He was wiping his hands on a striped towel when Kinsella knocked on the door post.

'I trust,' Slater said, looking round. 'that you haven't come to queer my pitch, Inspector. I know how you Metropolitan boys love to make mountains out of molehills. If Machin needs a warrant to arrest on suspicion of murder, I'll sign one here and now. Charge the fellow and trot him down to the station to make his statement. He can argue his case to the magistrate tomorrow. There's no question the woman was killed by two, possibly three violent blows to the face with what appears to be a heavy china teapot. The penetrative wound to the eye socket was almost certainly fatal but we'll leave it to an expert to decide on that. He isn't pleading innocence, is he?'

'He is,' Kinsella said. 'At least, he hasn't admitted guilt.'

'Do be careful how you handle him,' Slater warned. 'We don't want some nit-picking barrister insisting that his client's rights were infringed because we failed to follow the letter of the law. Blood on his clothing or person?'

'No obvious traces, no.'

'What's his story?'

'He says he left his wife in bed asleep while he went out to buy meat for breakfast. He was gone, he claims, no longer than a quarter hour. He returned to find his wife dead. He ran out on to the doorstep and shouted for assistance. One of Machin's constables, who happened to be nearby, responded.'

'I assume you'll speak to the butcher and the neighbours?'

'Machin's men will take statements, I don't doubt.'

'Damage to the door lock or evidence of forced entry?'

'Bloom left the door unlocked,' Kinsella said.

'How convenient.' Slater stuffed the towel into the valise and buckled the straps. 'It's as plain as the nose on your face that the fellow's guilty. Had an argument, lost his temper, struck her with a handy implement then ran shrieking into the street, appalled at what he'd done. He'll probably get away with manslaughter, particularly if she gave him cause. Women as celebrated as Marion Bloom . . .'

'Ah!' Kinsella said. 'You recognised her.'

'I may be knocking on in years, Kinsella, but I do keep in touch with what's going on in the city. Marion Bloom was one of our best-known concert sopranos. I heard her in the Ulster Hall in Belfast last August and she was superb.' He glanced down at the shrouded corpse and wrinkled his nose. 'Well, she's singing with the angels now, alas, and they, no doubt, will be glad to have her.'

'You will call for a post mortem, of course?'

'Haven't I just said so?' Slater said. 'What I'm not going to do is present the poor woman's corpse to an inquest jury. It'll be enough of a show as it is. Every damned hack in the country will be clamouring for copy. Well, the vultures will just have to make do with photographs. Beautiful woman, celebrated concert artiste slaughtered by a jealous husband, and a Jew to boot. Dear God, they'll have a field day.'

'Jealous husband?' Jim Kinsella said.

'Hah!' Dr Slater snorted. 'Not only are you a musical philistine, Kinsella, you don't even keep up with the gossip.' He tapped the side of his nose. 'Rumours abound, lad, rumours abound.'

'You mean Marion Bloom had a lover?'

'That's not for me to say.'

'Did Bloom know about it?'

'If he didn't he must be the only person in Dublin who didn't.'

'I don't suppose it would be proper for you to drop me a hint?'

'Certainly not.' Dr Slater adjusted his silk hat and hoisted the valise into his arms. 'You might, however, want to have a quiet word with Hugh Boylan.'

'Blazes Boylan?'

'Ah-hah! You've heard of *him*, I see.'

'Who hasn't?' Jim Kinsella said.

*   *   *

By the time the meat wagon arrived to convey Marion Bloom's body to the mortuary in Store Street quite a crowd of spectators had gathered to goggle at the goings-on. Nurses from the training house of the Mater Hospital, a couple of noviciate nuns on the loose from the Dominican Convent and the matron of the Protestant Female Orphan School, from whose office Sergeant Gandy had made his telephone call, rubbed shoulders with window-cleaners, milkmen, postmen, tradesmen and the Blooms' neighbours who, now that the cat was out of the bag, had cast discretion aside.

The deceased had been celebrated for a variety of reasons but piety wasn't one of them. Why Father Congleton from St Brendan's was invited not only to accompany the corpse from the house but to ride with it in the curtained wagon along with Dr Slater was a point worthy of discussion.

As soon as the doors at the rear of the wagon closed and the horse took two steps forward the buzz began.

'I thought she was a Jew?'

'No, he's the Jew.'

'Isn't he a freemason?'

'He's that too.'

'I never saw her at mass, did you?'

'I heard she was forbid the mass.'

'Who told you that?'

'Father Lafferty, I think.'

'Can't say I'm surprised.'

'She had a fine voice, all the same.'

'She'll be singing sweet enough in heaven, I'll wager, when they put the rope around his neck.'

'What? Are they saying he murdered her?'

'They're not taking him away for nothing, are they now?'

'Mr Bloom struck me as a quiet sort of gentleman.'

'Sure and aren't the quiet ones always the worst?'

'Is that him?'

'Ay, that's Bloom.'

Head lowered, hat slanted over his brow, a knitted scarf hiding half his face, Leopold Bloom emerged from the gloom of the hallway flanked by a constable and a bearded sergeant. He had been cautioned and charged with suspicion of murder under a coroner's warrant and would be held in custody prior to appearing before a magistrate to answer the indictment.

Unfortunately the police vehicle, a black van with no windows, had been delayed by a coal cart slewed across the mouth of Nelson Street. The brief hiatus allowed the two journalists who resided respectively at numbers 13 and 16 Eccles Street to sprint from their houses and, shouldering through the crowd, fire questions at the bewildered Bloom who, as an employee of the *Freeman's Journal,* they regarded as a colleague of sorts.

'Did you catch her in the act, Poldy?'

'Did she beg for mercy?

'Did you use an axe or a hammer?'

'What was Molly wearing? Was she in her nightclothes?'

'What were her last words, Poldy?'

'Did she beg for mercy?'

'Five quid for an exclusive statement, Mr Bloom.'

'I'll make that ten,' bawled a young man from the *Dublin Morning Star* who, to the chagrin of his peers, hurled himself from a hired cab and advanced on Bloom waving a fistful of notes. 'Ten, cash in hand, for your side of the story, Mr Bloom.'

'How about twenty for a thick ear?' Sergeant Gandy growled, giving the cocky young reporter a nudge with his forearm and, nimbly for such a large man, placing himself before the suspect. 'Stand back, all of you. Stand back.'

It was less the voice of authority than the appearance of six burly constables that caused the crowd, including the gentlemen of the press, to retreat while the constables formed a double line, like a guard of honour, from doorstep to pavement's edge and Mr Bloom, not bloody but certainly bowed, was hoisted up into the Black Maria and swiftly whisked away.

'How the devil did they get here so quickly?' Kinsella said. 'The Dublin grapevine is famously resourceful but the woman's only been dead for a couple of hours and they're already queuing up to see her hubby hanged.'

'They smell blood, that's all.' Tom Machin shrugged. 'We don't have too many murders in our fair city so naturally the press are all agog. I wouldn't want to be in Bloom's shoes if and when he's brought to trial.'

'Even if he pleads guilty,' Kinsella said, 'the Crown will still have to prove the case. It's not open and closed, by any means. If Bloom elects to stick by his story we'll be expected to collect enough evidence to convince a jury he committed the crime. On the other hand if we ignore the obvious and take Bloom at his word, the sooner we begin a search for an intruder, the better. I take it you're hastening back to the station?'

'I am. I'll have to rake up a jury for the inquest for one thing and that's never easy.'

'Please have your Super make formal application for G Division assistance. I doubt if there will be a problem on that score. I assume you'll put a constable to guard the premises but I'd be obliged if you'd let me have Jarvis as my runner for an hour or two, if, that is, he's willing to do an extra turn after night patrol.'

'Why Jarvis?'

'He's young enough to be keen.'

Tom Machin laughed. 'Oh, we're all keen here, Inspector. Do not be fooled by our side-whiskers and ruby red noses. Will one officer be enough for you?'

'For the time being,' Kinsella said. 'I'm going to poke about here while your whiskered loons are checking what passes for Bloom's alibi.'

'Precisely what are you hoping to find?'

'Evidence of motive,' Kinsella said. 'I gather from Slater that Mrs Molly Bloom was not as pure as the driven snow.'

'She did have a certain reputation for being how do they put it – "game". How game is a matter of conjecture.'

'Game enough to take on Blazes Boylan?'

'Hmm,' Tom Machin said. 'Now if I were a detective . . .'

'That's where you'd start?' Kinsella jumped in.

'Yes, that's where I'd start,' said Machin.

THREE

An interview with Blazes Boylan would have to wait. Jim Kinsella's first problem was to locate the house key. When he brought Constable Jarvis in from the step and took another look at the front-door lock it dawned on him that the key was nowhere to be found. It wasn't hanging on the little hook by the coats in the hall or anywhere obvious in the kitchen.

Kneeling, he examined the tin draft-plate at the bottom of the door and, swinging the door forth and back, listened to the loud click-clack the plate made against the sill of the step. He went into the bedroom at the hall's end, closed the bedroom door and called out to Constable Jarvis to do the same to the street door, close it and then open it again from the outside.

The sound was plainly audible, click-clack, in the back room.

He went out into the hall again, frowning.

'Mr Bloom did say he'd left the door unlocked, sir,' Constable Jarvis reminded him. 'Maybe the key's in his pocket still.'

'I expect that's it,' the Inspector said. 'If, however, Mrs Bloom was awake and heard the door plate rattle . . .'

'She'd think it was Mr Bloom going out.'

'Or coming in again,' Kinsella said.

'If it wasn't Bloom, though,' Jarvis said, 'she wouldn't know the difference. Do you wish me to look for the key, sir?'

'No, you're probably right and Bloom still has it. Besides, there's something else I need you to do for me,' Kinsella said. 'Is there a man on guard on the step?'

'Constable Fegan, sir.'

'Have the journalists gone?'

'I believe they have.'

'Good,' Kinsella said. 'I want you to find out where the woman who used to be Bloom's day maid lives. Her name's Fleming. Someone around here is bound to know her. If the worst comes to the worst try the greengrocer.'

Constable Jarvis grinned. 'Ay, Mrs Moody knows everyone's

business and she's not shy about sharing it. When I find Mrs Fleming shall I be fetching her back with me?'

'No, I only need to know where she's living now.'

'Right, sir,' said Constable Jarvis and so far forgot himself as to deliver a salute.

Kinsella watched the constable leave, then, closing the street door, stood alone in the hall and let out his breath. He'd been a Metropolitan copper for twenty-two years and a G-man for fifteen of them and he still couldn't shake off the excitement that possessed him at the start of an investigation.

He took off his hat and overcoat and hung them on the hook by the door, sharing for a moment the habits of Mr Bloom, then, rubbing his hands, he headed eagerly downstairs to the kitchen.

Fishwives had nothing on policemen when it came to gab and gossip and it was a rare treat for the lads of Store Street to entertain a genuine felon. It was all Superintendent Driscoll could do to deter them from sneaking down the corridor to the cells to peek at a prisoner who was already on the road to becoming famous.

Opinion as to Bloom's guilt was divided. Some of the lads were of the view that the suspect must be out of his nut to dispose of such a tasty armful as Mrs Molly Bloom who, if she'd been their wife, would have been brought to heel by nothing more drastic than a clout on the mouth followed by a damned good cocking. Others, more charitably inclined, argued that Bloom could hardly be blamed, morally at least, for blowing his top at his wife's goings-on.

It was given to Sergeant Gandy, a man of many talents – not least of which was his ability to sink four pints of black stout in under five minutes – to empty the prisoner's pockets, remove the prisoner's necktie, belt, scarf and boot laces and, while he was at it, check that Mr Bloom's clothing wasn't blood stained, though a few spots here and there would surely not detract from his claim of innocence.

On his return from the cell, Sergeant Gandy handed the items to Superintendent Driscoll who examined them carefully and found nothing more damning than a dribble of what smelled like mayonnaise on the necktie. Bloom's belongings, including a pocket watch, a house key, four shillings and eight pence, a picture postcard of Galway Bay, with no address or message on the back, and two soiled handkerchiefs, would be returned to him before his court appearance first thing tomorrow.

Slumped on a straw mattress on an iron cot with his collar sprung, waistcoat unbuttoned and trousers bunched in his fist, Mr Bloom resembled a tramp rather than a respected employee of the *Freeman's Journal*, for which newspaper, apparently, he sold advertising space. When Sergeant Gandy brought him a plate of buttered bread and a mug of tea, he stood up, then, to preserve his dignity, promptly sat down again. He put the mug on the floor between his feet and, pressing his knees together, balanced the plate on his lap and hungrily attacked the bread.

He chewed, swallowed, then, glancing up, said, 'Someone had better tell Milly.'

'Milly? Who's Milly?' Sergeant Gandy said.

'My daughter,' Bloom said. 'Someone had better tell her that her mother's dead.'

'Is Milly your only child?'

'The only one alive.'

'Where will we find her?' Sergeant Gandy asked.

'Mullingar,' Bloom answered. 'Coghlan's photographic shop in Castle Street.' Then, with a curt little nod, as if that was another item neatly ticked off his list, he folded a second slice of buttered bread and pushed it, whole and unbroken, into his mouth.

The doors on the top half of the kitchen dresser swung open at a touch. Plates, saucers and cups were arranged on the lowest shelf, together with egg cups, a salt cellar and a small jar containing black pepper. The middle shelf supported proprietary brands of tea and cocoa, a canister of lump sugar, a wicker basket cradling two wrinkled apples, a box of Beecham's pills and, towards the back of the shelf, a china milk jug and a sugar bowl, both decorated with tiny painted flowers.

Kinsella lifted out the jug and bowl, placed them on the apron of the dresser and, resting his hips against the table's edge, studied them thoughtfully. If, as seemed likely, the shattered teapot had been part of a set, who had taken it from the cupboard and why had he carried it upstairs? If the perpetrator of the crime *had* been consumed by a monstrous fit of rage, why would he trot all the way downstairs and select an empty teapot – a teapot, of all things – to serve as a murder weapon?

Stirring himself, Kinsella opened a dresser drawer and rattled through an assortment of forks, spoons and knives. A second drawer contained a carving knife with a serrated blade, two small knives of the sort used for coring fruit, a brass letter-opener and, scattered around the cutting implements, an assortment of buttons and bits of ribbon and a pair of vicious-looking pinking shears: weapons, in other words, galore.

He closed the drawers, placed the jug and bowl in the centre of the table and, pulling out a chair, hoisted himself up to fumble on the dresser's top shelf where he found nothing more incriminating than a bottle of brandy, unsealed, and a half-empty bottle of white port of the sort recommended for invalids and expectant mothers.

He climbed down from the chair, checked the cupboard in the base of the dresser – a pail, soap, wash-clothes, scrubbing brushes and a tousled old mop head – then, pausing only to light a cigarette, took himself upstairs to the living room.

The living room was cluttered with furniture: chairs, sofa, sideboard, bookshelves, two tables, a pier glass and a piano. He opened the piano lid and tapped two or three white keys. Unlike his wife, Edith, and all three of his daughters, he had no ear for music and couldn't tell if the piano was in or out of tune. On the scroll were three or four music sheets: 'Love's Old Sweet Song' was the only one he recognised. He closed the piano, crossed to the bookshelves and, pushing back the sofa, examined Bloom's library.

The books were mostly of the sort you might buy from the hawkers' carts down by the Merchant's Arch. They covered a queer old range of subjects, though: geology, astronomy, history, science, several works by J.A. Froude, 'Photography in a Nutshell', Shakespeare complete and illustrated, Dante ditto, Cosgrove's 'Dictionary of Dublin' – almost new that one – and a well-thumbed copy of Thom's massive Directory for 1901 with 'Property of the Freeman's Journal: Not to be Removed' stamped on the title page. Slotted horizontally on the top shelf were several novels of a sentimental sort and one title, 'The House of Shame', that looked as if it might be more to Marion Bloom's taste than her husband's.

Inspecting his books, Kinsella experienced a fleeing affinity with Leopold Bloom, for his head too was filled with ill-assorted scraps of information about how the world had come into being, how nature functioned and what role man had in shaping his own destiny.

He left the living room and crossed the hall to the bedroom.

The bed, minus a top sheet, and the fragments of the ornamental teapot had not been much disturbed.

The fireplace was flanked by a wardrobe and a wash stand with an empty cut-glass vase propped on its shelf. A chamber pot with a healthy quantity of urine in it was tucked half under the wash stand. The rackety old commode against the inside wall was no longer fit for purpose, it seemed. He moved to the dressing-table, the woman's domain: powder bowl, sable brush, tweezers, a jar of vanishing cream, a perfume spray with a puckered red rubber bulb, a pack of playing cards resting on a shoddily printed booklet entitled, not without irony in the circumstances, 'Your Fate'.

On a chair by the bed were stockings and stays and on top of a trunk at the foot of the bedstead other items of female clothing, including a petticoat. Kinsella pinned the clothing with a forearm and opened the trunk, which contained only blankets and sheets.

He turned his attention to the bed.

It was a very unusual bed, large and ugly, with metal rings along the rail that rattled when, knee on the mattress, he leaned to examine the stains on the wallpaper; stains made not by blood pumping from a wound but more likely from the weapon, the teapot, being brought down in a slashing arc.

Above the bed hung a framed, luridly coloured print of half-naked nymphs frolicking by the shores of a lake. Now, Kinsella wondered, did Bloom insist on hanging the titivating picture over Mrs Bloom's objections or did Mrs Bloom willingly capitulate in the belief that the picture was 'artistic'? One or other or both of the Blooms had, it seemed, a vulgar streak.

Something was missing, though. Bloom's nightshirt: there was no sign of Bloom's nightshirt. Stooping, he peered under the bed, then, on all fours, reached under the sagging springs and fished out a bolster which, at first sight, seemed unmarked save for a few dust balls adhering to the material.

He sat back on his heels and turned the bolster over to reveal a few faint patches the size, say, of a florin, and one larger patch not just damp but wet. With the bolster across his knees, he dipped a finger into the blood patch and brought out something hard and shiny which proved to be not a fragment of china but a broken tooth. He put the bolster on to the bed, removed a clean white linen handkerchief from his breast pocket, opened it out and carefully transferred the chipped tooth to the centre of the linen square. He folded the handkerchief in on itself, corner by corner, tucked it back into his breast pocket, gave it a pat to make sure it was snug, then, letting out his breath, got to his feet.

He had something, though he didn't quite know what just yet.

He would instruct one of Machin's men to collect the bits of the teapot in an evidence bag and take it to the station, but the little piece of Molly's tooth he would keep to himself for now.

Constable Quinn had the steadiest hand not just in Store Street but, by repute, in the whole of the Rotunda Division. He had been trained, by a knuckle-rapping aunt, to write a fair imitation of copperplate at high speed because the old bitch thought she was going to make a lawyer of him; an ambition that young Quinn, as well as his five brothers, three sisters, and his Da, a veteran of the Royal Irish Constabulary in Kilkenny, knew was laughable, though they were all too scared of old Auntie Nula to say so out loud.

Harsh though his aunt's instruction had seemed at the time, Constable Quinn was glad of it now. As the Superintendent's chief clerk he had a front row seat at all the dramas that were played out in the wood-panelled office with its plaques and photographs and the Division's collection of sporting trophies in a glass-fronted case behind the prisoner.

The prisoner, in turn, faced directly into the light from the tall south-facing window, a sergeant or duty inspector behind him and, on this particular day, Superintendent John George Driscoll seated across the table, smiling encouragement.

Neither Superintendent Driscoll nor Inspector Machin said

much, just a word now and then when it seemed as if Mr Bloom's soliloquy, as halting as Hamlet's, might dry up completely.

If the prisoner's story had been rehearsed it had not been well rehearsed or – the thought crossed Constable Quinn's mind – so well rehearsed that it made a nonsense of denial and became instead a lesson in the art of obfuscation.

It said much for Mr Driscoll's patience, or his guile, that he allowed the chap to drone on about the domestic habits of the Blooms, living and dead, and the sorrows that had been visited upon them since he'd met Molly playing charades – or was it musical chairs? – in the year of the short corn and how Mrs Bloom's father had served in the garrison on Gibraltar, a Major, no less, in the Dublin Fusiliers and had collected postage stamps as a hobby.

'Yes,' said Superintendent Driscoll at length. 'Quite!'

Mr Bloom, eyes downcast, paused, then, to Constable Quinn's surprise, said, 'Do you know, I once had a terrible dream . . .'

'I don't think dreams are relevant,' Inspector Machin said, 'unless you're pleading insanity.'

'No,' Bloom said. 'Really, I did. I dreamt I was on trial and all my friends and enemies turned up to bear witness against me. I shouldn't have been there in the first place, I suppose.'

'Been where?' said Inspector Machin.

'I went with a friend, a young friend. He got himself into a spot of bother with the drink. It's not a place I'm in the habit of . . .'

'You mean the Monto?' the Superintendent put in.

Bloom nodded. 'I have, on occasions, in the way of business, passed through the Monto.'

'This young friend . . .'

'He's gone now, gone abroad.'

'As a matter of interest what was his name?'

'Dedalus.'

'Simon Dedalus's boy?' the Superintendent asked.

'Yes,' Bloom answered. 'Do you know him?'

Constable Quinn's pen hovered over the foolscap. He had only a vague notion how to spell Dedalus but it had already dawned on him that three pages covered with Bloom's self-indulgent musings were about to be scrapped.

'When did this . . . this incident take place?' Mr Driscoll asked. 'I don't mean the dream, I mean your visit to the Monto.'

'Last summer,' Bloom answered and then, as if he had given too much away, instead of nothing at all, added, 'I don't suppose it matters now.' His shoulders heaved. 'Perhaps I should begin again.'

'Perhaps you should,' Superintendent Driscoll agreed.

Daguerreotypes of lean, severe-looking men with pointed beards did not seem an appropriate decoration for the walls of a young woman's bedroom. Kinsella assumed they were ancestral portraits foisted upon her by her father to remind her that she had exotic and possibly wealthy forebears hidden in the family tree. Until he'd opened the door of the room on the right of the hall, it hadn't occurred to him that the Blooms might have a family and Bloom, for some reason, had said nothing about children.

The narrow bed was battened down by a tightly tucked spread that released a cloud of dust motes when Kinsella patted it. The water jug on the wash stand was bone dry. There was no soap in the bowl or hairs in the brush on the ledge. The wardrobe had a few clothes in it but they, as far as he could make out, were just dainty little dresses that no one had had the heart to sell. Two pairs of shoes, very small and dainty too, rested against the fender of the tiled fireplace as if to tempt the child, like a changeling, to return. It required no great cerebral effort to deduce that Miss Bloom was no longer a permanent resident in the household.

He returned to the hall and went upstairs. What was Bloom doing living in such a large house? Why hadn't he rented out the upstairs rooms? There wasn't a stick of furniture in any of them, nothing save a flea-bitten mattress rolled up in a corner, a hideous oval mirror, cracked and fly-blown, and in the room to the front of the house, a weather-stained brown mackintosh hanging forlornly from a hook behind the door.

Outside, beyond the grimy window panes, the good folk of Dublin were going about their weekday business. He could make out the clatter of hoofs on cobbles, the yawping of seagulls, the croon of pigeons on the roof, a dog, a small dog by the sound of it, barking, and the shrill whistle of a locomotive from the Liffey branch line a half a mile away.

The click-clack of the door plate in the hall startled him.

'Jarvis?' he called out.

'Ay, sir, it's me.'

There being nothing upstairs to keep him, he was on the point of turning away when something skittered over the dusty floorboards like a tiny white mouse.

Hunkering, he picked up a ball of cotton wool, clean, fresh and white as a snowdrop, and, for no good reason that he could think of, sniffed it.

'Are you there, sir?'

'Yes, in a minute,' Kinsella said.

Scented, perfumed, not a medical smell; he sniffed again.

Lavender toilet water maybe? It smelled stronger than lavender but not oily or heavy. There were no smears on the cotton wool to suggest that it might be a simple lip salve. He was no expert in female fragrances but fortunately he knew someone who was. He opened a pocket in his waistcoat, dropped the ball of cotton wool into it and, as he'd done with the broken tooth, patted it into place before he went downstairs.

Jarvis was waiting in the hall.

'Did you find Mrs Fleming?' Kinsella asked.

'I did, sir. She resides on the second landing in the middle of the three isolated tenements in Union Court.'

'I know it,' Kinsella said. 'Between the back of the prison and the long wall of the engineering works. Did you speak with her?'

'No, sir. I did not engage the lady in conversation. I found out from a neighbour that's where she lives.'

'You must be tired, Constable Jarvis.'

'Well, I could do with a bite of breakfast, sir.'

'Can you hold out just a little longer, do you think?'

'Whatever's right for you, Inspector.'

'I'd like you to walk at an even pace from the front door to Dlugacz, the pork butcher's shop. Make careful note by your watch how long it takes and record the exact time in your book. Don't gallop but don't dawdle either. Understood?'

'Ay, sir. Understood.'

'After that, you may report to Store Street to sign off. Before you do, though, will you ask Inspector Machin to fetch up evidence bags and labels for the remains of the teapot, also both bolsters from the bed and the jug and sugar basin I've left on the kitchen table. Have you got all that?'

'I have, sir.'

'Tell Inspector Machin I'll drop by the station around one o'clock,' Kinsella said. 'Enjoy your breakfast, Constable Jarvis. I reckon you've earned it.'

'Ay, sir.' The young man grinned. 'I reckon I have at that.'

FOUR

Mr Henry Coghlan, known to all and sundry as Harry, was, by his own estimate, the best retoucher of photographic negatives not just in Mullingar or Westmeath but in the length and breadth of Ireland.

Buried in the darkroom at the rear of his Castle Street studio he could work miracles on the least likely subjects by skilled manipulation of matt varnish, finely powdered black lead, alcohol, ammonia and a penknife. If Mr Coghlan's wife, Biddy, ever harboured suspicions that photographic negatives weren't the only thing Mr Coghlan touched up in the dark behind the curtain she kept them to herself. He had certainly never laid a finger on any part of his young assistant's anatomy and Milly Bloom, the young assistant, considered her employer to be a perfect gentleman in all respects.

As a penniless young man on the doorstep of his career Mr Coghlan had manufactured a series of postcards depicting martyrs of the Republican Brotherhood, cards that had sold under the counter like hot cakes but would have meant a spell in prison if he'd been traced as the source. The stuff that boosted profits these days was a deal less treasonable and, though Mrs C still huffed and puffed, Harry Coghlan's sideline in prints of pretty little girls in fairy costume was well within the boundaries of the law.

Reverend Stephens, minister of the Presbyterian church next door to the shop, had had one of Harry's artistic prints bought for him by his scamp of a daughter. Going along with the joke,

he'd hung it in the vestry until a posse of prune-faced elders had
insisted he take it down and destroy it, an act of vandalism with
which Reverend Stephens had refused to comply. Instead he'd
put the picture up for auction at the annual church fete and had
watched it knocked down, after a frantic bidding war, at three
pounds, eighteen shillings, which was more than three pounds
over the price his daughter had paid for it, not including the
frame.

'All in a good cause, Mr Coghlan,' the Reverend chortled. 'All
in a good cause. I take it you're equally charitable to the poor
mites who pose for you?'

'Certainly, I am,' Harry Coghlan said. 'They're mainly servant
girls who slip down from Athlone on their day off. It suits them
to have a florin in their pockets and a free photograph of self
done up as May or July or . . . do you remember Peaseblossom?'

'A dream she was, indeed,' the Reverend said wistfully, 'with
her little wings sticking out.'

'Milly sewed the wings out of muslin. Clever with a needle
for a Dubliner. I'll use the wings again when I find the right
Cobweb.'

'Fair and slender and shining like the dew?'

'Exactly, Mr Stephens. Exactly.'

'Milly, I take it, is a trifle too – ah – robust for a Cobweb?'

'A little too down to earth. I can't see her as a fairy somehow.'

'As many things, Mr Coghlan, but as a fairy: no.'

Chaperoning the girls who offered themselves up to Mr
Coghlan's lens was one of Milly Bloom's less arduous tasks. She
never failed to be impressed by how well her employer treated
his youthful subjects, how patient he was with their shyness,
which, as a rule, disappeared as soon as they were in costume.
For the half hour or so it took to dress them, position them against
the painted backcloth, adjust the lamps and take the photograph
they were no longer unloved drudges but became the irresistible
charmers they'd always imagined themselves to be.

Milly was sure, even if Mrs Coghlan was not, that Mr Harry
Coghlan did not lust after young flesh or, for that matter, any
flesh that hadn't been hung on a butcher's hook. He saw the girls
as they saw themselves and was as delighted as they were by
their transformation.

He was less delighted by the fat wives and glowering sons and daughters of the family groups that made up his bread and butter, or by the couples who posed, bride seated, groom standing, in the studio and who, Mr Coghlan said, usually looked as if they were about to face a firing squad and not a life of bliss together. No, Mr Coghlan said, only half in jest, when it came to inspiring subjects he'd far rather have Archie Montiford's prize-winning bull, Zeus, or Lady Garrard's fox-hunter, Morning Meadow, which latter he'd tried not very successfully to photograph in motion using a giraffe tripod and a rapid rectilinear lens on full exposure.

Milly had no notion what the bull or the horse was thinking when the shutter clicked but she certainly knew how the girls felt. She'd been in front of Mr Coghlan's camera more than once and especially last September, when Mummy and Hugh Boylan had come down to visit the morning after Mr Boylan's concert party had performed in the Father Mathew Hall up the road in Athlone.

Mr Boylan had been very impressed by Mr Coghlan's work. He was on the verge of commissioning Mr Coghlan to 'do' her, Milly, as Titania or, better yet, Queen Mab, when Mummy had jumped in to remind Blazes that she was no longer his silly Milly but a grown woman and if he wanted a likeness it had better not be too revealing.

Consequently, she'd put on her tam, her short red jacket and long scarf and had gone outside into the autumn sunlight and posed before Mr Owen's cycle shop and Mr Coghlan had done a lovely composition with her seated astride a man's two-wheeler.

Hugh Boylan had said he would pay for three prints to be sent to his Dublin office and present one each to Papli and Mummy but Mummy had said, no, two would be enough, no point in wasting money. Mr Boylan had laughed and said 'Game ball, Molly,' whatever that meant, and had promised he would drop by the shop next time he was down in Westmeath, which would be in April for the Kilbeggan Handicap Cup in which he hoped to have a horse – half a horse, he said – running.

She'd seen Hugh Boylan once since then, up in Dublin in December. Mummy had been singing 'There is a Flower that

Bloometh', from *Maritana,* at the Traders' Association Christmas concert in the Belleville Halls. Half way through the song Papli, for no reason, had burst into tears. On the steps outside, after the show, Mr Boylan had patted Papli on the shoulder and had said something that had caused her father to leave hurriedly without waiting for Mummy or her.

She might have paid more attention to what was going on between Blazes and her father – who had never liked each other anyway – but she was still seething about the thing that had happened two nights before when her beau of the past year, Alec Bannon, and his so-called *bon ami,* Buck Mulligan, both drunk as lords, had tried to take liberties with her in a cab after a party at Kitty Loughlin's house, a party she shouldn't have gone to in the first place.

Mulligan had held her against the leather with his forearm while Alec had put his hand up her skirts and touched the front of her bottom and had said now was the time to see if she really had hair on it, saying, 'Stop bloody wriggling, Milly, and open your legs.' He would have stuck his finger inside her, too, if she hadn't screamed at the top of her voice and the jarvey hadn't stopped the cab, leaned down and asked if everything was all right down there. Mulligan, coarse brute though he was, had pulled Alec off and bundled him out of the cab and had paid the cabman to take her home, while Alec had staggered about on the pavement and called her filthy names, still shouting filthy names even as the cab had rolled off.

She'd been very upset by Alec's lewd behaviour and had longed to tell Mummy what had happened and ask her advice on what to do if he tried the same thing again. On arriving home, though, she'd walked in on one of her parents' rows. It took Papli all his time to open the front door and – shirt hanging outside his trousers – shuffle back along the hall into the bedroom and slam the door while she stood, trembling, in the hall.

When Pussens had crept upstairs to see what the fuss was about she'd carried the cat into her room and had told her all her troubles while the voices across the hall rose and fell, criss-crossing each other endlessly. Eventually, long after midnight, her father had blundered out of the bedroom and had gone downstairs into the kitchen to rattle pots and pans and, she imagined, console himself with toast and cocoa.

In the morning nothing had been said. When Papli had brought her tea in bed and had asked if she'd had a grand time at the party she'd said it had been fine, very nice, and had managed a smile, though he'd been on the way out of the door by then and hadn't even noticed.

It had been a relief to return to Mullingar, back to serving customers and filling in the negative book, which took great concentration, and be instructed in the mysteries of the camera and shown how to calculate exposure times.

She'd heard not a word from Alec Bannon, though he had family in Mullingar, out beyond the tennis ground, and when she'd bumped into his snooty cousin, Gladys, she was given the coldest of shoulders. She honestly didn't care if she never saw Alec Bannon again. She was too busy learning a profession and enjoying what the town had to offer and, now she was approaching sixteen, flirting freely with the boys in the cycle shop and giving sauce to Mr Coghlan who, within reason, didn't seem to mind. He called her an imp or his little minx, and upped her salary to twelve shillings and sixpence a week with three shillings deducted for board; and very good board it was, for Mrs C was a better cook than Mummy.

She continued to write to Papli but her heart was no longer in it. Papli said he might visit at Easter, if, that is, she couldn't persuade Mr Coghlan to give her time off to come home.

How could she tell her father, never mind her mother, that she didn't particularly want to come home? She'd written to Papli to explain that Easter in Mullingar was a favourite time for weddings and that Mr Coghlan, with the best will in the world, wouldn't be able to spare her even for a few days. She'd almost added that she was looking forward to seeing Mr Boylan again, if he did manage down for the Handicap Cup but, pondering, thought better of it and signed off with a kiss instead.

Shortly before noon on that March morning, five weeks before Easter, she was out in the front shop with a felt mat spread on the counter and a chamois leather, fresh from the bottle, in her hand. Polishing soft optical glass required care and she was flattered that Mr Coghlan had entrusted her with the delicate task. She had dusted the lenses with a camel-hair brush and was just about to finish off with a loosely rolled corner of the chamois

when the bell above the shop door tinkled and two men entered
from the street.

One was Constable Harris of the Royal Irish Constabulary,
broad shoulders blotting out the light. The other was Reverend
Stephens, uncollared, unhatted and unusually harassed. He came
forward to the counter and, to her surprise, sought her hand.

'Milly,' he said in a sombre voice, 'is Mrs Coghlan at home?'

'I believe she's upstairs,' Milly answered.

'And Harry . . . Mr Coghlan?'

Milly gestured to the door of the studio behind her.

'Best fetch him,' Reverend Stephens said, 'and the woman
too.'

Constable Harris nodded. Lifting the counter gate, he let
himself into the rear of the shop, knocked on the door of the
studio and, without awaiting an invitation, opened it and went
inside.

'What is it?' Milly got out. 'Is Mr Coghlan in trouble?'

'Milly, oh Milly.' Stretching over the counter, Reverend
Stephens looped an arm about her. 'It's news, sad news from
Dublin we've just received. I'm sorry to have to tell you your
mother has passed away.'

'Passed away?'

'Dead,' said the Reverend Stephens. 'I'm afraid she's dead.'

The display photographs of brides, grooms and family groups
danced and shimmered. Mirrored panels reflected splinters of
light with piercing clarity, then everything began to swirl like an
eddy in a stream and, still swirling, to blur and fade, then, for
the first time in her life, little Milly Bloom fainted dead away.

Kinsella crossed the canal bridge and approached the façade of
Broadstone station that stood out severe and imposing against
the skyline. He stopped at a stall in one of the porticos, purchased
a cup of coffee and paused to take in the view over the King's
Inns and the dome of the Four Courts before fishing out his
Memo Book and making note of his progress so far.

Paperwork was the bane of all departments in the DMP and
Kinsella was mindful that his every action had to be accounted
for at the day's end. He put the book away, swallowed the coffee,
took three puffs on a cigarette then, duly fortified, set off round

the back of the railway station in search of the lane that led down to Union Court.

There were much worse slums in Dublin, some close to where he lived in the old town. In his days as a patrol man Jim Kinsella had visited most of them. The Union Court tenements had originally been thrown up to accommodate extra hands in the engineering shops and coal yards of the Midland & Great Western, good solid dwellings for honest artisans that, like the artisans themselves, had fallen foul of progress and hard times.

Soot blackened the stonework and unrepaired eaves formed great green patches that made the buildings seem forbidding even in broad daylight. Several small children who were playing about the mouth of the stairwell stopped what they were doing and gawked at him and an old woman, dozing on a chair by a ground floor window, opened one eye and deliberately dropped a globule of spit in his wake as he went past.

An odorous staircase led to the second-floor landing where, drawing in a breath, he knocked on the peeling woodwork. If Mrs Fleming had found another post she probably wouldn't be at home. He was prepared to be disappointed but, no, the door opened, and a small, stoop-shouldered woman peered up at him out of the gloom. 'Are you the copper was asking about me?' she said.

'Indirectly,' Kinsella said, 'I am.'

'I tell you now we ha'na seen Eric in weeks.'

'I'm not here about Eric,' Kinsella said, then, 'Is he your son?'

'No son o' mine,' came a gruff voice from within. 'Lodger, Bastard hawked me only decent pair o' boots. Kill him I will he shows his face here again. Is it you the fella's after, Lizzie? What mischief have you been up to now?'

'Chance would be a fine thing,' the woman said ruefully and ushered Kinsella into the kitchen.

One room, cramped but clean: two beds, one tight to the gable wall, the other in a shallow alcove, a table, two wooden chairs, a stool and an armchair of sorts, very worn. The window was screened by a torn blind the colour of tobacco leaf. Under it was a wash-stand with a basin and jug and a small pile of dishes. On a grid over the fire a kettle steamed, the coals beneath it providing the room's only spot of colour.

Dressed in an undershirt and a pair of moleskin trousers, a

man crouched on the bed by the gable, legs tucked under him in the pose of an Indian Swami. He appeared to be about sixty, though a stubble beard and locks of dirty grey hair made it difficult to judge his age. Kinsella introduced himself.

'I knew you was a G-man,' the man said. 'You've got that smell about you. One o' the Castle crowd, are ye? One o' the Lord Lieutenant's anointed?'

'Stop it, Mickey,' the woman said, then, to Kinsella, 'He doesn't mean to give offence. His legs's bad this morning.'

'What's wrong with his legs?'

'Dead as mutton since me back got broke,' Mickey Fleming answered. 'Seven years near enough to the day since the load fell on me. We were puttin' in the tanks on Goulding's ground near the East Wall. Cracked me spine in two places. Lucky to be alive, they told me. Hah! Lucky, is it?'

Lizzie Fleming hurried to pull out a wooden chair and watched, frowning anxiously, as Jim Kinsella seated himself upon it.

'The gentleman isn't here to listen to your woes, Mickey,' she said. 'What is it we can do for you, Inspector?'

'I believe you were servant to the Blooms of Eccles Street, Mrs Fleming,' Kinsella began.

'Kicked her out, that cow.'

'Mickey, hold your rattle,' Lizzie Fleming said sternly, then, 'Yes, I was day maid to Mrs Bloom for near a year.'

'When did she let you go?'

'Friday before last Christmas,' the woman said. 'Why are you asking about the Blooms?'

Kinsella hesitated. 'Mrs Bloom was found dead this morning.'

Silence for a few seconds then a whistle from Mr Fleming. 'So he done for her at last. Can't say I'm surprised. Got what was coming to her, I reckon.'

'What makes you suppose Mrs Bloom didn't die of natural causes?' Jim Kinsella asked.

'You wouldn't be here if she had,' Mr Fleming answered. 'You don't rout out a G-man for natural causes. Foul play was involved, right? And that means old Bloom done her in.'

'There must be some mistake,' Mrs Fleming said. 'Mr Bloom wouldn't harm a fly. We used to have breakfast at the kitchen table when he wasn't in a hurry out.'

'While Madam lounged in bed like a bloody trollop.'

'Some days she didn't feel well.'

'She was always well enough to open her legs for *him*.'

'Him?' Kinsella spoke without inflexion.

'Boylan, Blazes Boylan,' Mr Fleming said. 'That fancy dan, that two-faced jackanapes. It was him got Madam Bloom to sack my missus.'

'You can't be sure o' that,' Mrs Fleming said.

'After you walked in on them, the jig was up,' said Mickey.

'What reason did Mrs Bloom give for releasing you?'

'She said I was too old to do the work properly.'

'Too old at fifty? Mother o' God, if she's as hale and hearty as you are, Lizzie, when she's fifty . . . well, that's a question we'll never see answered,' Mickey Fleming said. 'Strangled, was she?'

Kinsella was tempted to remind the fiery little fellow that he was the one asking the questions but he found the exchange between the couple illuminating and sought to encourage it.

'She was beaten to death,' he said.

'With a club?'

'No, a teapot.'

Mickey Fleming let out a hoot of laughter and covered his mouth with his fist. 'Pardon me. I thought you said a teapot.'

'I did. A big ornamental teapot painted with flowers. Do you recall seeing such a teapot in the Blooms' house, Mrs Fleming?'

'In the cupboard in the kitchen, yes. Mrs Bloom brought it home with her from her Belfast trip last summer. Mrs Bloom was very proud o' it. Wouldn't let me touch it.'

'Was it always kept in the dresser cupboard?'

'Not always,' said Mrs Fleming. 'When she was brought flowers she would have me put them in a dry vase in the bedroom and tell Mr Bloom to water them. She'd have him fill the teapot with water, fetch it up from the kitchen and fill the vase while she lay back on the bolster and watched.'

'And laughed,' said Mr Fleming. 'You told me she laughed.'

'She did, sometimes.'

'How often did you witness this occurrence?'

'Once or twice when I was clearing her breakfast tray. I offered to do it, to fill the vase, but she told me Mr Bloom loved flowers and was only too pleased to water them.'

'And was he?'

Mrs Fleming shrugged. 'You could never tell with Mr Bloom.'

'She barked, he jumped,' said Mickey Fleming. 'That's the long and the short o' it. He'd have licked her bum if she'd asked it of him. Maybe he did for all we know.'

'You seem to have a particular down on Mrs Bloom, Mr Fleming,' Kinsella said. 'Did you know her well?'

'Never clapped an eye on her in me life. How could I? I've been trapped in this rat hole for seven bloody years,' Mickey Fleming said. 'But I got ears. I hear everything Lizzie tells me and draw me own conclusions.'

Gossip and hearsay were not admissible evidence in any court of law, at least in theory. Kinsella let the crucial question hang for a little longer. 'Do you have children, Mr Fleming?'

'Three boys, two girls.'

'Where are they?'

'The little one's at school,' Lizzie Fleming said.

'And the others?'

'I sent them away,' said the man. 'Claire couldn't get off fast enough. She's up in Antrim, married to a Freemason. The boys go where the work is. Bristol for Alan. Glasgow for Bert and Willy.'

'You must miss them?' Jim Kinsella said.

'Ay,' Mickey Fleming admitted. 'I do.'

'All you did was quarrel,' Mrs Fleming said.

'It's the quarrelling I miss,' her husband said.

'Do they send you money?'

'When they can,' Mrs Fleming said.

'Not often enough,' her husband added.

'How do you manage?'

'She works,' Mickey Fleming said. 'She may not be much o' a wife but this I'll say for her, she's no shirker.'

'I take it you've found another post, Mrs Fleming?'

'With the railway.' Her husband answered for her. 'Tucks me up at half past ten, goes out on the tiles and comes home at six.' He laughed and added, teasingly. 'Says she's cleaning carriages up in the Gallant Street sidings. That's a tale and a half, that is. I think she's got a fella out there. Eh, Lizzie?'

'Surely not Mr Bloom?' Kinsella said.

'Never,' Lizzie Fleming said. 'Mr Bloom's a gentleman, in spite of what she thought. Always at him, she was, about his roving eye, jealous of every woman ever crossed his path. She was even jealous o' her own daughter. Milly was her daddy's darling and it hurt him sore to have to send her off to Mullingar.'

'Why *did* he send her away?'

'For her own good,' Mrs Fleming answered. 'He didn't want her to think less of her mother.'

'You mean he didn't want her catching her bloody mother with Boylan inside her,' Mickey Fleming said.

'Is that what you saw, Mrs Fleming?'

'Only once, only a peek. I didn't know he'd turned up early.'

'Mrs Bloom was with Boylan in the bedroom, I take it?'

'In the kitchen. On the table in the kitchen.'

'I'm glad I never had her shepherd's pie that night,' Mickey Fleming shook his head. 'On the bloody table! Jesus!'

'It *was* Hugh Boylan, though. You're sure of it?' Kinsella said.

'Ay, I'm certain.'

'And you saw them together in an intimate situation?'

Mrs Fleming nodded. 'I did, more's the pity.'

'Would you swear to it in court?'

'No, she would not,' Mickey Fleming jumped in. 'None of your tricks here, Mr G-man. You're not getting my Lizzie in court, no, sir, nor risk having her throat cut.'

'Throat cut? By whom?'

'Blazes bloody Boylan. Stop at nothing, that man.'

'How long after you saw Mrs Bloom and Mr Boylan together were you given notice?' Kinsella said.

'Half a day.'

'Didn't Mr Bloom object?'

'She didn't tell him till after I'd gone.'

'Did you tell Mr Bloom what you'd seen?'

'No, I know when to keep me mouth shut.'

'Wouldn't you like to help Mr Bloom by telling the court . . .'

'No court. No court. No bloody court,' Mr Fleming shouted. 'I been to court to sue for compensation and you know what the court gave me? Snap, bloody snap. You can stuff your courts up your backside, Mr G-man.'

If this had been an ordinary sort of interview he would have ordered the man to leave the room but that was hardly practical. Besides, he had what he came for, namely an eye witness who, under summons, might attest to Marion Bloom's adultery with Hugh Boylan and thus provide Bloom with an incontestable motive for murder.

'Has Mr Bloom been arrested?' the woman asked.

'He has,' Kinsella answered.

'Did he say he done it?'

'No.'

'He done it, he done. If he didn't do, who did?' Mickey Fleming shouted. 'You've got your man, Inspector. You don't need to go bothering my Lizzie no more.'

Mickey Fleming's interruptions were beginning to wear on Kinsella's nerves. He should, he supposed, feel sorry for the man and excuse his bitter tirades but it was Mrs Fleming who really elicited his sympathy. He got to his feet, thanked Mickey Fleming politely for all his help and made for the door.

Mrs Fleming followed him out on to the landing.

'Has Mr Bloom really been arrested?' she asked.

'He's been charged and held on suspicion.'

'He didn't do it, you know. He couldn't do it.'

'Couldn't do it? What makes you say that, Mrs Fleming?'

''Cause she wouldn't let him.'

It sounded glib and implausible, an emotional statement with no basis in fact. For all that, Jim Kinsella was tempted to believe that it might, just possibly, contain a grain of truth.

Lizzie Fleming glanced round, then whispered, 'Listen, if it'll help Mr Bloom, I'll do it. I'll give evidence.'

'A signed statement might be enough,' Kinsella said. 'I take it you'd be willing to slip down to Store Street police station, tell an officer there what you've just told me and let him put it in writing.'

'I would. Yes, I would.'

'Mrs Fleming,' Jim Kinsella said, sincerely, 'thank you for your cooperation. You really have been most helpful.'

He offered his hand and she took it. He felt the weight of it in his, a remarkably strong hand for the size of her.

'Lizzie,' came her husband's voice from within. 'Lizzie, I need the pot. The pot, Lizzie, I need the pot.'

'I've got to go,' she said, 'before he . . .'

'Of course,' Kinsella said and, releasing her, hurried off downstairs.

FIVE

Whoever was managing the Store Street barracks canteen these days was certainly doing a good job of it. The chop on Kinsella's plate came with piping hot gravy, braised cabbage and, according to the chalked board, Potatoes Dauphinoise, which, in the cook's interpretation, meant mashed with a sprinkling of garlic powder. Tom Machin settled for steak and kidney pudding and for the first ten minutes or so after the pair sat down there was little or no conversation. The arrival of tea things, including a brown glazed-earthenware pot, returned the officers' attention to duty.

Machin, doing the honours, held the teapot out at arm's length and studied it before, with a lift of the eyebrows, he filled Kinsella's cup. 'Well, that's one mystery solved,' he said. 'At least we know how the blessed teapot got from the kitchen to the bedroom.'

'Except there were no flowers in the vase,' Kinsella said.

'Can't say I noticed that,' Machin admitted. 'Might we assume the teapot was left in the bedroom? Or doesn't that fit your theory that Bloom planned the whole thing?'

'That isn't my theory at all,' Kinsella said. 'The truth of it is I have no theory, no judgement to make as yet. Is Bloom sticking to his story?'

'Like a limpet to a rock,' Tom Machin said. 'Driscoll gave him ample opportunity to stumble into a confession but Bloom was too shaken, or too cunning, to fall for it. By the by, it's Mullen who's holding court tomorrow.'

'You'll object to bail, of course?'

'I'm not sure I will.' Machin dropped two sugar lumps into his teacup and stirred with a spoon. 'There's precious little evidence to either support or undermine Bloom's account.'

'Request more time,' Kinsella suggested. 'Slater signed the warrant and that, surely, will boost your objection. I mean, we know what Mullen thinks of our coroner. No love lost there. Hasn't Bloom asked for a lawyer?'

'No.'

'He does know he's entitled to one, I suppose?' Jim Kinsella said, then promptly answered his own question. 'Oh, of course he does. No flies on our Mr Bloom. As it stands, it's his word against, well, ours, I suppose. Having a thumping good motive is certainly a start but on its own it won't bring him to trial.'

'Have you interviewed Boylan yet?'

'I haven't been able to find him. His office in D'Olier Street is locked and there's no sign of his secretary. None of his cronies seems to know where he's hiding.'

'Have you tried his home?'

'Not yet.' Kinsella blew across the surface of the tea in his cup and sipped tentatively. 'Bloom's alibi?'

'It holds up well. He bought two slices of calf's liver from Dlugacz about twenty minutes to eight o'clock. Dlugacz is sure of the time because he'd only just fetched down the shutters.'

'Did he notice anything odd in Bloom's behaviour?'

'He says not. Jarvis, at your suggestion, paced out the distance from Eccles Street to the shop: eight minutes. That's a sixteen-minute round trip. If we allow Bloom four or five minutes in the shop it adds up to just a shade longer than his first estimate, not enough to make a fuss about.'

'The neighbours, did any of them spot anything suspicious?' Kinsella said. 'Strange men in the street, anything at all?'

'A certain Mrs Hastings recalls bumping into Bloom as he turned into Eccles Street at about ten to eight. She wished him a good morning and received a good morning in return. All of which seems to confirm his story.'

'But no one saw him leave the house,' Kinsella said. 'No one saw him on the way to the butcher's.'

'What are you driving at, Jim?'

'We've only Bloom's word he spent the night in Eccles Street. If he didn't, where was he and who was he with? And if Bloom wasn't at home who can say who Molly might not have enter-tained, Boylan being the first name that springs to mind.'

'Or someone we don't yet know about?' Tom Machin said.

'Exactly. Anything in the noon editions, by the way?'

'A paragraph in the *Star.* Be a lot more in the *Telegraph* this evening, I imagine. Our noses are clean. Driscoll wasted not a moment in delivering a preliminary account of the investigation to the Castle, which should give the Assistant Commissioner enough to gnaw on for now. I wish I had more to go on: a strange man running away from the house; a scream; a glimpse of Bloom out and about before the witching hour of – what? – seven, shall we say?'

'Well,' Kinsella said, 'I do have something.' He reached into his top pocket, carefully withdrew the folded handkerchief, laid it flat on the table and opened the corners. 'It's not much but it may throw a little light on what went on in the bedroom this morning.'

Machin leaned forward.

'What,' he said, '*is* that?'

'It's a small piece of tooth belonging, I suspect, to Marion Bloom. Don't look so disappointed. Of course, her teeth were damaged by the blow. It's where I found it that's significant.'

'Where might that be?'

'On the underside of a bolster pushed beneath the bed. The bolster on the bed was soaked with blood but the bolster under the bed had only a few patches on it, plus this little piece of tooth. I suggest you put it in a jar and label it.'

Still frowning at the speck in the handkerchief, Tom Machin said, 'I still don't see . . .'

'It occurs to me that Marion Bloom may not have been killed by a couple of random blows from a teapot,' Kinsella said, 'and the bolster might have been put over her mouth to cover her cries.'

Tom Machin sat up. 'To finish her off, you mean?'

'Something like that.'

'In which case the action was murder, not manslaughter.'

'Let's see what the medical examiner comes up with. For all we know right now the poor woman might have been poisoned.'

'Or raped,' said Machin.

'Do you know,' Kinsella said, 'I never thought of that.'

*   *   *

When she opened her eyes her first thought was that she was safe in her bedroom in Eccles Street waiting for Papli to bring her tea. The ceiling was different, though. Her bedroom in Eccles Street had plaster cornices, not beams, and it didn't smell of cinnamon and coriander. Then the man-shape loomed over her and she was on the point of crying out when a sudden sharp stinging sensation shrivelled her nostrils, filled her mouth with the taste of sal volatile and caused her to suck in a great lungful of air.

'There, there,' Mrs Coghlan crooned from somewhere behind her head. 'There, there.'

She heard Mr Coghlan's voice, too, and that of Reverend Stephens muttering quietly but she couldn't make out what they were saying. Then she realised that the man-shape stooped over her was Dr Paterson from Greville Street, near the bank, where Mrs Coghlan had taken her last October to get a tincture to relieve her cramps.

Dr Michael Paterson was clean-shaven and had a long chin that, viewed from the underside, wagged weirdly when he spoke. He was young, or at least not old, and the blink of sunlight from the living-room windows made his ears appear transparent.

'Is it true?' she heard herself say. 'It's not true, is it?' She struggled to sit up. 'Tell me.'

The tinkling of a spoon in a glass was not an answer. Perched on the edge of the divan, Dr Paterson pushed the glass towards her lips and an oily liquid, bitter as aloes, trickled on to her tongue.

'That'll help,' the doctor said, 'as much as anything can.'

'Should we tell her?' Mr Coghlan said. 'I mean, is it wise?'

'She'll have to be told sooner or later,' Reverend Stephens said.

Dr Paterson stroked her brow and said, 'I'm afraid it is true, Milly. Your mother died this morning.'

'Oh, God! Oh, God!' Milly said. 'Poor Papli, poor, poor Papli.'

'Papli?' said Reverend Stephens.

'She means her father,' Mr Coghlan said. 'Who's going to tell her about *that* situation?'

'What situation?' Milly said. 'I've to get up, get home to Papli.'

'Would she like me to say a prayer?' Reverend Stephens asked.

'Not now, Reverend,' Michael Paterson replied.

'What are we going to do with her?' Mr Coghlan said.

'Keep her by us,' said Mrs Coghlan, 'at least for tonight.'

'Is there no one else?' said Reverend Stephens. 'A relative who might take responsibility? A friend of her father's, perhaps?'

'How many friends will he have now, poor devil?' Mr Coghlan said. 'Who'll take charge of the funeral arrangements, I wonder?'

'Oh,' said Reverend Stephens. 'Won't there be a post . . .'

'Hush,' said Mrs Coghlan brusquely, then again, 'Hush.'

Milly felt the liquid the doctor had given her slide down into her chest, burning and soothing at one and the same time. Her eyes watered worse than ever but she couldn't be sure if it was the medicine or if she was crying real tears.

There was something so unreal about all of it and, with tears running down her cheeks and Dr Paterson still perched on the divan beside her, she wondered if this was not the moment when she would swim up out of sleep to discover that it was nothing but a bad dream.

She closed her eyes in the hope that when she opened them again she would be lying in her own bed in her own house with Pussens curled up on her tummy, the smell of frying coming from the kitchen and Mummy shouting, 'Poldy, Poldy, something's burning, something's burning.'

'There must be someone we can contact,' Reverend Stephens said. 'Should I pop over to the house and telephone the police in Dublin on the off chance there's been a mistake?'

'If there had been a mistake they wouldn't have telephoned Constable Harris in the first place, would they?' Mr Coghlan said. 'On the other hand, I suppose he might be out on bail.'

'Who might be out on bail?' Milly said.

She opened her eyes as wide as they would go and, leaning into Dr Paterson's arm, sat up. She rubbed her wrist across her nose, a gesture that her mother would call unladylike, and then, with the same wrist, wiped her streaming eyes. 'Has someone been arrested?' she said. 'What's it got to do with my mother? Has there been an explosion? Did a bomb kill my mother?'

'Milly,' the doctor said, 'do try to keep calm. We've very little information so far and . . .'

Then a voice, a warm familiar voice, said, 'Excuse me for butting in. The shop door was open. I took the liberty of finding my way upstairs.'

'Who the devil might you be?' Reverend Stephens demanded.

'Hugh Boylan,' Blazes answered and shook the minister's hand. 'I've come to take Milly home.'

Luck was not on Bloom's side. Of all the stipendiary magistrates who administered justice in the County and City of Dublin, Patrick Mullen happened to be the one engaged in conducting hearings that session. Mr Mullen might have contrived an excuse for ducking the chore if the victim had been anyone other than Marion Tweedy Bloom and if he, Patrick Mullen, had not been a leading light in the Dublin Musical Society.

'Molly?' he cried. 'Molly's dead?' A question delivered with such profound horror that any half-decent lawyer would have declared Patrick Mullen unfit to judge the fiend who had allegedly done her in. In fact, Patrick Mullen had been only one of Molly Bloom's admirers and had known her rather less well than many another. He was, however, a man so dedicated to music that the untimely demise of any one of Dublin's songbirds affected him like a dagger to the heart.

'Bloom,' he said in a menacing baritone. 'Bloom, that ruffian,' though he had never met the man. 'How did he do the foul deed?'

'Split her head open with a teapot, apparently,' his clerk said.

Inured by a dozen years of dispensing Irish justice, Patrick Mullen did not seem to regard the mode of death as unusual. 'Where's the culprit being held?' he asked.

'Store Street police station.'

'Who issued the warrant?'

'Dr Slater.'

'Slater? Huh! On what grounds?'

'Suspicion of murder.'

'What does the prisoner have to say about it?'

'He claims he didn't do it.'

'Well, we'll just have to see about that, won't we?' said Patrick Mullen in a tone that boded ill for Bloom.

On the stage of the Lyric, the Gaiety or the brand new Abbey theatre an arc light would have isolated Hugh 'Blazes' Boylan and Milly Bloom while the others faded into shadow. Unfortunately the living room on the first floor of the Coghlan's house in Castle Street had no arc lights and Blazes Boylan's performance was, therefore, subjected to a noisy serving of tea.

Total concentration had long been Boylan's forte and had helped him through many a tricky situation. He had developed the ability to focus, eyeball to eyeball, on the person with whom he was engaged, as if he, or she, was, at that moment, the centre of Mr Boylan's world. Thus, seated on the divan with Milly almost but not quite on his knee, he imparted the circumstances of her mother's death and her father's arrest, punctuating the narrative with frequent pauses to allow the young woman to absorb the grim news, sip, as it were, by sip.

The final touch – the crusher Mr Coghlan called it – was the tear that trickled down Mr Boylan's cheek when, falling silent, he wrapped his arms around Milly and allowed her to shed buckets into the lapels of his chequered tweed morning coat.

'Lemon or milk, sir?' Janey, the Coghlan's servant, enquired.

'Oh, you've lemon, have you?' Reverend Stephens said.

'Fresh off the tree,' said Janey.

'I'll have the lemon with a dash of hot water, and two extra lumps,' the clergyman said then, with a lift of the shoulders and a sheepish grimace, glanced at the couple sobbing on the divan and whispered, 'Sorry, sorry.'

'Will the gentleman be taking tea too?' Janey bellowed.

To which Blazes replied, 'Only if you've nothing stronger.'

'Oh!' said Mr Coghlan. 'Ah! Yes, brandy. What am I thinking of? Brandy, it is. Coming right up.'

He hastened to the decanter on the sideboard, wiped a glass with his forefinger and poured into it a generous helping of the French stuff. He glanced at his wife, in search of her approval or, at worst, permission and, on her nod, tip-toed across the room to the divan and stood by while Mr Boylan extracted a mauve silk handkerchief from his breast pocket and, holding it to Milly's nose, let her honk into it.

'No brandy for the girl,' Michael Paterson stated.

Blazes Boylan said, 'Why not? What harm can it do?'

'Alcohol and chloral hydrate don't mix,' the doctor told him.

'You have this on good authority, do you?'

'He's a doctor,' Mr Coghlan apologetically pointed out.

'Is he?' said Blazes. 'I thought he was the boyfriend.' He snapped up a hand and removed the brandy glass from Harry Coghlan's grasp. 'Won't do *me* any harm, though, will it, Doctor?'

Dr Paterson paused, then, smiling thinly, said, 'Probably not.'

Blazes crossed one leg over the other and sipped. 'Much appreciated, Mr Coghlan. Thank you.'

Gratified, Harry retreated.

Tea cup and saucer balanced on the palm of his hand, Dr Paterson said, 'Are you related to Milly, Mr Boylan?'

'By blood? No, no. I'm an old friend and colleague of her . . . of Mrs Bloom. Known Milly since she was a tiddler. Haven't I, sweetheart?'

Milly sniffed and nodded.

'Where are you taking her?' the doctor said.

'To Dublin, to be close to her father.'

'He sent you to collect her, did he?'

'Well, no. How could he? He's incommunicado, shall we say, for the time being; just for the time being.' Blazes knocked back the brandy and put the empty glass on the floor behind the leg of the divan from which position, Janey, kneeling, retrieved it. 'Fact is, as soon as I heard the evil news my first thought was for Milly.'

'So you haven't spoken to Mr Bloom?' Mrs Coghlan said.

'Not possible,' Blazes said. 'Without conceit, however, I might safely claim to be the man Poldy would choose to break the news to Milly. Right, sweetheart?'

Obediently, Milly nodded and sniffed.

Dr Paterson said, 'How did *you* hear the news, Mr Boylan?'

'My profession brings me into contact with newspaper men, reporters and the like, and—'

'Precisely what is your profession?' Dr Paterson interrupted.

Blazes raised an eyebrow to indicate surprise that his name wasn't known in Mullingar. 'I've a finger in a number of pies. I lease out advertising space – hoardings, you know – and I promote things.'

'Things?' the doctor said. 'What sort of things?'

'I'm an agent for singers and musicians,' Blazes said, 'a bit of an impresario. I organise concert tours and do a spot of warbling myself. I also have a stake in the fisticular arts. Boxing, in a word.'

'And a horse,' Milly reminded him. 'Half a horse.'

'Ah, there you are,' Blazes said. 'Are you feeling a little better?'

'A little. I want to see my daddy.'

'And so you shall.' Blazes hopped up, extended a hand and hoisted Milly to her feet. 'There's a connection to Dublin at eighteen minutes after four. Why don't you wash your face, comb your hair and pack your togs, sweetheart. Perhaps Mrs Coghlan would be good enough to help you.'

The men watched Milly gather herself. Her lip trembled and she was shaky on her pins but she stiffened her knees, squared her shoulders and, still clutching Boylan's handkerchief, bravely followed Biddy Coghlan from the room.

Dr Paterson put his teacup, untouched, on the sideboard.

'If you want my opinion, Mr Boylan, which I'm rather sure you don't, Milly is in no fit state to travel. It would be better for the girl to stay here until she's less distressed.'

'I'm always open to expert advice,' Blazes said, 'but in this instance, Doctor . . .'

'Paterson.'

'Doctor Paterson, I feel Milly would be more comfortable at home in Dublin. No, comfortable isn't quite what I mean.'

'What do you mean?' the doctor said.

'Look, Bloom's in jug,' said Blazes. 'Chances are he'll be granted bail. Milly's the only thing he's got to hang on to right now.'

'What if he doesn't get bail?' said Mr Coghlan.

'Then Milly will stay with me,' Blazes Boylan said.

'With you?' Reverend Stephens put in. 'Well now, sir, that doesn't sound at all proper.'

'What sort of fellow do you take me for?' said Blazes indignantly. Then, tethering his high horse, he went on, 'Of course, you don't know me and you're right to express concern. Too many scoundrels in the world today. It's the times we live in, I

suppose. However, you may rest assured Milly will be safe in
my house; a house I happen to share with my spinster sisters,
ladies of strict moral principle who will stamp very firmly upon
any hint of hanky-panky.'

'There you are then,' Mr Coghlan said. 'All above board.'

'Besides,' said Blazes, 'it's what Milly wants that counts, and
what Milly wants is to return to Dublin.'

'For how long?' Michael Paterson asked.

'I have honestly no idea,' Blazes answered.

'Presumably until Mr Bloom is bailed,' Reverend Stephens said.

'He will get out, won't he?' Harry Coghlan asked.

'For sure, for sure he will,' Blazes answered.

'He didn't . . .' Mr Coghlan hesitated. 'I mean, you don't
suppose he actually . . .'

'Did it? No, no, no,' Blazes said. 'What possible reason could
he have for doing it?'

'In short, he's innocent?'

'As a new-born babe,' said Boylan.

SIX

The bar of the Belleville Hotel, with its marble table-tops,
mahogany panels and gilded mirrors, was a far cry from
the sour, smoky, piss-smelling dens where loud-mouthed
bigots were wildly cheered for their tawdry eloquence. Here, in
the Belleville's relative peace and quiet, a few of the gentlemen
of Dublin's fourth estate assembled to discuss matters of national
import and exchange racing tips. Horse flesh was not top of the
agenda that afternoon, though, for, with first copy duly posted
and the story gone cold, there was precious little for the boys
to do but sit tight, sup porter and theorise on who might have
done the dirty deed if justice miscarried and Leopold Bloom
was released.

The short odds were on Blazes Boylan, but Mr Flanagan, a
hack from the *Journal's* stable of reporters, professed to have
heard from a reliable source that Molly Bloom was not the first

mutilated female to be found in recent months and that the DMP
had been instructed by the Home Secretary to hush up the crimes
to avoid panic. Spurred by the gravity with which his peers
appeared to be treating his blathers, Flanagan predicted that before
the year was far advanced the gutters of Dublin would run red
with the blood of more slaughtered whores and virgins.

Jack Delaney nodded solemnly. 'An Irish Ripper? Now why
didn't I think of that? God, man, but I wish I had your imagination. There is, however, one small flaw in your premise,
Arthur.'

'And what,' said Arthur Flanagan loftily, 'might that be?'

'Bloom's wife was neither whore nor virgin.'

Robbie Randall, general dogsbody for the famously inaccurate
Advertiser, chipped in. 'Well, you know what they say: in the
dark all whores are virgins. Even murderers can't be right all
the time.'

'If we discover there's been a sudden run on painted teapots
then, by jingo, Flanagan, I'd say you're on to something,' said
Mr Palfry of the *Sun*

'How did *you* find out about the teapot?' Flanagan said. 'I
thought I had that on the q.t.'

'What did you fork out for the inside dope, Arthur?'

'Three bob.'

'Bargain. I paid five,' said Charlie Palfry. 'You, Jack?'

Delaney shrugged. 'Same: five.'

'Do you know, if we pooled together and put Gandy on salary
we could save our proprietors a fortune,' Palfry said. 'Jack, the
truth now, have you sprung the leak about the teapot in your
evening edition?'

Jack Delaney snorted. 'Sure and it's a gift wrapped in silver
for all of us but I'm not risking the spike for a fact so outlandish
it may not be true at all.'

'Gandy's usually reliable,' said Charlie Palfry.

'About as reliable as Arthur here,' Delaney said and the men,
all bar Flanagan, laughed. 'Besides, when you boil it down – if
you'll pardon the phrase – there's nothing particularly comical
about having your head stove in. Teapot, baton or billy club
you're still dead and it's still a crime against nature.'

'That's true,' Palfry conceded. 'But isn't there something in

Hebrew scripture that says taking a life with a teapot keeps the victim's ghost at bay?'

'Butter, that was,' Flanagan said. 'Butter in a lordly dish. Jezebel, I think, did in her hubby with a butter dish.'

'No,' Jack Delaney corrected him. 'It was Jael, wife of Heber the Kenite and, if memory serves, she did the actual deed with a hammer and a nail: Judges, chapter five.'

'Hark at the scholar,' said Robbie Randall. 'Judgement it'll be for Bloom whether it was a teapot or a butter dish he did it with. He'll swing like as not.'

'He won't swing,' Palfry said. 'He'll do a stretch of hard time and be back among us before you know it. Justification.'

Elbow on the bar, Jack Delaney lifted steadily his half full glass and gazed into the dark depths. 'Is it, though, the manifest destiny of women to be punished for adultery while men get off scot free? Now there's a subject for your next column, Palfry. Did Molly Bloom really think she could get away with putting the horns on her Poldy without ever paying the price?'

'Or did he relish it?' said Flanagan.

'Relish it? Relish what?' said Mr Randall.

'Nibbling nightly on a buttered bun.'

'Now that,' said Palfry, 'is a step too far even for you, Arthur.'

'Following in Boylan's wake,' Flanagan pressed his point, 'might not be so bad. At least Bloom didn't have to oil the lock before he fumbled for the key.'

Jack Delaney thumped his glass on the bar counter and, swinging round, squared up to the three at the table behind him.

'There,' he said, 'see what a joke you're making of it. It isn't a joke at all. How can we hope to strike a reasonable balance between tragedy and farce if you go on like that? There's a daughter – think of her – and a man betrayed who's now in peril of his life, and a woman cut down in the prime of her life lying dead on a slab in the mortuary. How can you sit here and make fun of their sufferings?'

'Because that's what our readers will do,' said Palfry.

'What our readers will shovel up,' Robbie Randall added. 'Adultery, a good-looking woman with a reputation for sharing her favours, a cucky . . .'

'And a Jew,' Flanagan intruded.

'To make no mention of a teapot,' Randall concluded. 'It's the teapot you can't get away from, Jack.'

'Stuffed her with a teapot.' Arthur Flanagan snickered. 'Puts a whole new slant on having one up the spout, eh?'

'I just don't find it funny,' Jack Delaney declared.

'No more do I,' said Jim Kinsella who, for the past couple of minutes, had been eavesdropping from a niche by the doorway. 'I've never found the sight of a mutilated corpse in the least amusing.'

The somnolent air stirred as the reporters pushed back their chairs and eagerly welcomed the inspector to the fold.

'What'll it be?' Hearty Mr Randall was first to offer.

'No, no, allow me to do the honours,' Mr Palfry insisted.

'All right,' Jim Kinsella said, 'I'll have a mineral water.'

'One mineral water, Meg,' said Mr Palfry and, cornered by his own generosity, was forced to add, 'and a top up for those in need.'

Jack Delaney rolled round the rim of the bar. 'Are you not an afternoon drinker, Inspector Kinsella, or are you still on duty?'

'On duty,' Kinsella said, 'I'm looking for Boylan.'

'*Still* looking for Boylan,' Delaney said. 'Has he not returned to his office yet?'

'No,' Kinsella said. 'Have any of you gentlemen seen him?'

'Meg,' said Palfry, 'has Hugh Boylan been in at all today?'

The barmaid poured mineral water into a slender glass and placed the glass on the counter. 'Haven't seen him and I've been on since ten.'

'Perhaps he's jogged off to Foxrock to feed his horse,' Flanagan said. 'Did you know he'd bought a half share in a filly?'

'Which half?' said Mr Randall.

'For sure it'll be back half, given Blazes' partiality for rumps,' said Flanagan. 'That's where he'll likely be, Inspector, at the stables in Foxrock.'

'Now we've solved your problem, Mr Kinsella,' Robbie Randall said, 'do you not have a tit bit or two for us?'

The Inspector studied the bubbles in his glass then, putting the glass to his lips, drank the contents in three swallows, barely pausing for breath. He put down the empty glass and said, 'My thanks for the refreshment, gentlemen. If Boylan does show up tell him I want a word with him. I'll be at the Castle offices until six or thereabouts.'

'Nothing,' Flanagan cried plaintively. 'Not a hint even?'

'It's a cruel world, Arthur,' Kinsella said, 'a very cruel world, indeed,' and headed for the door.

He'd gone no more than a few steps along the street before Delaney caught up with him. He wasn't in the least surprised to find the *Star* reporter hot on his heels. Blue eyes, fair curly hair, a broad grin: Delaney's trick was to disguise a conniving intelligence behind boyish candour. 'I know you're pressed for time, Inspector, so I won't beat about the bush,' he said. 'I've a fair idea where Boylan might be found and it certainly isn't Foxrock.'

'I didn't think it would be somehow,' Kinsella said.

'I'm not after money.'

'No, you're after – how do you lot put it? – the inside track.'

Delaney took his arm and steered him around the corner out of sight of the hotel's side door. 'If you'll answer me a couple questions, Inspector, I'll give you more than you think you need right now.'

'What questions?'

'Was the woman really murdered with a teapot?'

'Go on,' Kinsella said.

'Is Bloom the only suspect?'

'What do I get in exchange?'

'I can tell you where Hugh Boylan was last night and where he might be right now.'

Kinsella hesitated. 'Yes, it was a teapot,' he said at length, 'and Bloom is currently our only suspect. He'll appear before the stipendiary tomorrow morning. Now it's your turn.'

'Boylan was down in the Monto until close to midnight.'

'How do you know this?'

'Because I saw him there.'

'Where precisely?'

'In the street outside Nancy O'Rourke's,' Delaney said. 'What's more he wasn't alone.'

'Really? Who was with him?'

'Leopold Bloom.'

'Really?' Kinsella said, sharply this time. 'What were Bloom and Boylan doing together?'

'Arguing, by the look of it.'

'Were blows exchanged?'

'Not that I saw. I had no reason to linger,' Delaney said. 'I bumped into him again by chance this morning.'

'Boylan?'

'Yes, Boylan. He was on the way to his office.'

'What were you doing across the river in D'Olier Street?'

Delaney grinned. 'Looking for Boylan. There, I'll admit it.'

'Time?'

'Coming up for eleven,' Delaney said. 'I wanted to ask him if he knew Mrs Bloom had been found dead. He said he didn't.'

'How did he react to the news?'

'He gave every appearance of being shocked, more so when I told him Bloom had been charged with her murder. He turned white as a sheet and put a hand against the wall to stop himself falling down. Then he said, "I'd better go and fetch Milly," and, looking flustered, hurried off. Milly's Bloom's daughter, isn't she?'

Kinsella nodded.

'Flanagan says she has a job in Mullingar. Is that true?'

Kinsella nodded again.

'Then that's where you'll find Boylan,' Delaney said. 'I'll lay odds he's on his way to Mullingar to fetch the girl.' He cocked his head and squinted up at the G-man. 'Now why do you think he would do such a thing?'

'Search me,' Kinsella said.

Even late on a weekday afternoon the trains that ran through the junction at Mullingar were crowded. They were loading cattle into wagons in one siding and a squad of militia, weary and travel-stained, were crammed into the carriages of the eighteen minutes past four train to Dublin.

Blazes had had the foresight to spring for first-class tickets for himself and Milly and they shared a compartment with a prosperous-looking old farmer and a young, whey-faced woman who, by her sober garb, might well be on her way to or from a convent and who, after a swift disapproving glance at Blazes, went back to reading her Testament.

Blazes put Milly's suitcase on the rack and settled the girl into

a corner seat. She seemed dazed, numbed perhaps by the stuff the
quack had ladled into her while peeking down the front of her blouse,
for which breach of Hippocratic etiquette Blazes could hardly blame
him. If there was one thing you could say about Milly Bloom – and
there were many things you could say about Milly Bloom – she
was very much her mother's daughter in face and figure if not, thank
God, in temperament.

He hadn't known Molly back in her Gibraltar days but he
didn't doubt that she'd driven the garrison's subalterns mad. In
one fit of post-coital nostalgia she'd told him how she'd once
shaken the peg of a bashful young naval lieutenant and pulled
him off into her handkerchief. It didn't take much imagination
to envisage Molly at Milly's age in the heat of a Mediterranean
summer tugging away on the tools of blushing adolescents in
white ducks or, for that matter, pressing her bubs against any
man she wanted to take a rise out of. Why she'd ever fallen for
a man like Bloom was beyond him, and beyond her too if her
reticence was anything to go by.

When he'd asked her what she'd ever seen in Bloom she'd
thrown a tantrum, had kicked him out of bed and told him he
was only half the man her husband was. But when he'd turned
up at her door four days later with a shilling's worth of roses
and a tray of chocolates, she'd given him a slap and told him
he'd better come in before someone took a photograph for the
Chronicle and, five minutes later, had been riding him as furi-
ously as Hardy bringing Sceptre home down the straight at
Doncaster.

Molly was dark, of course, all over dark, while Milly was fair,
all gilded curls and eyes as mauve as his silk handkerchief; an
inheritance from ancestors back down the line, probably. She
already had a chest on her, without the sag that had marred poor
Molly's udders latterly.

He looked over Milly's head at fields stabbed by spears of
crimson light. They were travelling east, the sun dipping behind
them, which was why he couldn't see the shadow of the train or
the smoke from the locomotive billowing over bridges and hedges.
Sad light: sad time. He glanced at Milly who was looking from
the window too. He couldn't imagine, not for the life of him,
what was on her mind right now. She was no longer a silly Milly,

filled with pep and childish gaiety. She might never be his silly Milly again, he thought despondently.

The old farmer had fallen asleep, chin on chest, and the would-be nun, if that's what she was, was deliberately ignoring him. He drew Milly closer, tidied the folds of her coat to keep her warm and put an arm about her shoulder.

'He will get out, Blazes, won't he?' she murmured.

It was the first time she'd ever called him Blazes to his face, a sign not only that she was growing up but that she wasn't afraid of him, which, for his purposes, was all to the good.

'Of course he will, sweetheart.'

'You'll get him out, won't you?'

'I will, Milly. If I have to move heaven and earth to do it, I will.'

Mercifully, she seemed to believe him and, resting her head on his shoulder, sighed and, soon after, fell asleep.

SEVEN

Superintendent Smout approved his report, the duty inspector signed him off and, buttoning his overcoat and tugging on his hat, Kinsella stepped out into Lower Castle Yard.

The sandstone and granite parapets of the Castle's towers were tipped pink by the setting sun but the streets below were already in shadow. He was tempted to leg it along Dame Street to have one last go at tracking down Hugh Boylan but if Delaney's information was correct and Boylan had gone to Mullingar to fetch Milly Bloom the chances were that he wouldn't be back yet. He might slip out for an hour after supper, for Boylan lived in Sefton Street not much more than a mile from Kinsella's home in Escott Place.

On being posted to G Division, Kinsella had been obliged to reside within the ward and his wife's uncle had put them up in one of his shabby properties near Christ Church Cathedral, rather too close for comfort to the dark and dirty heart of old Dublin. Blood being marginally thicker than water, though, the uncle had

charged them a reasonable rent that had remained unchanged
even when Jim's circumstances improved.

From outside, the narrow, three-storey building with its cluster
of ornate chimneypots and steep-sloping roof looked quaintly
down-at-heel, like an illustration from a child's fairy book. At
one time, it had been the residence of some ecclesiastical dignitary
but its glory days were long past. Apart from replacing rotting
window frames and painting the rusty railings in front of the
postage stamp sized garden, Jim had done nothing to improve
the house's outward appearance for, crowded into the decaying
tenements that flanked the narrow alleys nearby, lived the poorest
of the poor, not all of them entirely honest, and the Inspector
was too downy a bird to advertise his gentility to potential thieves.

Edith had done a marvellous job of furnishing the rooms and,
with never more than one servant to help her, ran as tight a ship
as a man could wish for. Being married to a policeman was not
an easy lot but his wife rarely chided him for his erratic hours
or the solemn moods that came upon him when an investigation
was going badly. And if that wasn't enough virtue for one woman,
she even put up with his father, Robert, who had lodged with
them since his retirement nine years ago.

Jim's spirits rose when he opened the squeaky iron gate, saw
the light in the hallway through the thick triangular glass at the
top of the door, heard one of the girls practising her scales on
the piano and glimpsed in the window of the dining room Edith
helping the maid, Noreen, lay the table for supper.

He used his key to let himself in and, as always, was greeted
with savoury smells from the kitchen mingled with floor polish
and a faint flowery air he could only put down to his daughters'
fondness for scented soap and toilet water. He removed his overcoat and hat and was on the point of going into the living room
when Daisy, the youngest, came clattering downstairs, calling
out, 'Grandpa, he's home. Daddy's home,' and his father thumped
his stick on the first-floor landing and shouted, 'About time, too.'

Edith emerged from the dining room, followed by Noreen.

Oldest daughter, Violet, popped her head round the door of
the living room and blew him a kiss while middle daughter,
Marigold, abandoned her scales and broke into a grand march
that he thought might be from 'Entry of the Gladiators', though

he couldn't be sure. Edith kissed his cheek. 'You're just in time, dear. Soup will be on the table in five minutes.'

'Good, that's good,' he said, then, 'I may have to pop out after supper, I'm afraid, but I shouldn't be much more than an hour.'

'That's what they all say,' his father bawled from half way down the stairs. 'Next thing you know it's dawn and the bed's still empty. Is it this murdered woman in Eccles Street? Blossom, is it?'

'Bloom,' Jim Kinsella said. 'I assume you read it in the evening papers. I'm not quoted, am I?'

'Who'd want to quote *you*?' his father said. 'Where's the key?'

'In my pocket, where it always is,' Kinsella said and watched Edith, throwing up one small exasperated hand, follow the maid along the passage to the kitchen.

His father, impatient as always, gave him a prod with his walking stick to hurry him on and trailed him into the living room.

'Edith tells me Mrs Bloom was a singer,' his father said.

'Yes, she was. Quite well known.'

'Well, I've never heard of her.'

'Oh, Grandpa,' said Marigold, glancing up from her music, 'you've never heard of *anyone*.'

'I have. I've heard Lettie Le Mond sing on the stage at Lowry's, which is more than you've ever done.'

'What did she sing?' said Violet.

'Something about the moon.'

'Are you sure it wasn't something about Ireland?'

'Perhaps it was. Ay, perhaps it was.'

Distracted by the sight of his son fitting a key into the lock of the cabinet in which his, Robert Kinsella's, badges, ribbons and medals were displayed, he conceded the point without argument. Licking his lower lip, he watched Jim remove a quarter bottle of Jameson's whiskey from among the decorative plates together with two glasses, each of which had a shamrock engraved on the bottom.

Jim uncorked the bottle and carefully measured out a thumb's length of the golden liquid into the glasses.

'Don't break the bank,' his father said sarcastically. 'Here, what the devil are you doing?'

'Joining you.'

He gave a glass to his father, corked the bottle and locked it away in the cabinet, then, picking up his own glass, held it out between finger and thumb.

'The road to ruin, Pa,' he said.

'The road to ruin, it is,' his father said.

The glasses clinked rims lightly. Marigold, giggling, improvised a snatch of the 'Sailor's Hornpipe' and Violet, in mock horror, called out, 'Mother, he's at it again.'

He waited until they were all seated at the long table in the dining room and Edith was dishing out broth from the big tureen before he brought the little ball of cotton wool from his vest pocket.

He didn't want to tempt the girls into asking questions about the grisly murder in Eccles Street, though Edith said they were much more savvy about the nasty side of his profession than he gave them credit for. He squeezed the cotton ball gently between finger and thumb and waited for someone to notice what he was up to, which, naturally, didn't take long.

'Have you been bleeding?' Violet asked.

'What? No.'

'I thought you'd missed your chin with the razor again,' his oldest said, nodding at the pinch of cotton wool. 'What is it then?'

'I know,' said Marigold. 'It's a clue, isn't it, Dad?'

He tried to laugh it off. 'What makes you think it's a clue?'

'Because of the way you're holding it,' said Marigold. 'Shall I fetch your magnifying glass?'

'I don't think that will be necessary,' Jim Kinsella said. 'However, before you go mad with the pepper pot, Vi, I wonder if I might borrow your nose for a moment?'

'My nose?' Violet self-consciously prodded her snoot. 'What's wrong with my nose?'

'Not a thing,' Jim said. 'It's a very fine nose, a very sensitive nose, in fact, which is why I'd like to borrow it.'

'Huh!' said Violet, not sure whether she'd been complimented or insulted. 'Oh, very well. Borrow away.'

He rose from the chair and, leaning across the plates, offered the little white ball to his daughter without releasing it.

She drew back. 'It doesn't have blood on it, does it?'

'No, no blood. Can you identify the fragrance?'

Edith stood at the head of the table, ladle in hand, watching intently. Noreen, by the door, watched too. Even Grandpa, who was usually too occupied with his food to notice anything much, scowled across the table as Violet brought her nose to the cotton ball and inhaled. She sniffed again, then sat back and shook her head.

'Don't tell me you don't know what it is?' she said.

'Should I?' Jim Kinsella said.

'It's *my* perfume. I wear it every time we go out.'

'You've been found out, Daddy,' said Daisy, chin on hand. 'You gave Vi a bottle last Christmas.'

'Does it have a name?' the inspector asked.

'Halcyon Days,' said Violet. 'Oh, do stop blushing. Don't think I don't know Mama bought it for you.'

'Where?' The inspector glanced at his wife. 'Smely's?'

'Winterbottom's,' Edith said. 'On Sandymount Road.'

'Why there?'

'It's the scent Violet wanted. Winterbottom's was the only shop in Dublin that had it in stock.'

'Why is it so difficult to find?'

'It's imported from America,' Violet informed him.

'Is it now?' Daddy Kinsella said, 'Is it, really?' and, tucking the cotton ball safely into his vest pocket, passed his plate down the table to claim his share of the broth.

It was still daylight when they arrived in Broadstone railway station. They made their way down the platform, across the shallow forecourt and out through the lofty colonnades. Blazes carried her suitcase in one hand and gripped her arm with the other as if to protect her from the buffeting wind. Even after Blazes had bundled her into a cab and they were clipping down Constitution Hill she nursed an irrational fear that Papli would come looking for her and that she should be back at the station waiting for him.

Broadstone station was the last place she'd seen Papli. He'd walked her up from Eccles Street at the end of the Christmas holiday under a leaden winter sky that, like a cauldron lid, had trapped the din and stink of the railway yards. He'd kissed her on the brow as if he was saying goodbye for ever. He'd pressed two half crowns into her gloved hand in spite of her protests and had waited until she'd found a seat in a third-class carriage and the locomotive was making steam before he'd turned away; another hat and overcoat vanishing into the crowd.

'Where have they taken her?' Milly asked.

'Who?' said Blazes. 'Oh, you mean . . . well, to the mortuary.'

'May I see her?'

'No,' he said softly. 'No, sweetheart. She'll be kept there safe and sound until we can arrange the funeral.'

'My father will do that.'

'If he can't,' and Blazes, 'then we'll do it between us.'

'Where is Papli now?'

Blazes rubbed his blunt chin. 'They'll be holding him in Store Street or possibly the Castle until a magistrate hears his case.'

'When will that happen?'

'Tomorrow probably.'

'And then he'll be released.'

'I don't doubt it,' said Blazes dubiously.

Milly slumped against the cab's musty upholstery. It had finally dawned on her that she would never be able to go back to the home she'd left ten months ago, for it was her mother's strident presence that had given the house life, just as it had enlivened all the other houses they'd stayed in after her baby brother had died.

Familiar streets yielded to those less familiar. The cab crossed the O'Connell Street Bridge. She glimpsed the Liffey, like a ribbon of steel, and the smoke of the barges crawling upon it.

The cab veered left and, a few minutes later, drew up outside a building with huge wooden letters pinned high up on the facade. Before she could take her bearings, Blazes had her out on the pavement and tripping up three shallow steps and through an open door into a hallway as dark and echoing as a mausoleum.

'Hughie,' said a female voice from out of the gloom, 'where on earth have you been?' A second female voice piped in, 'Who's this you've brought home? Another of your fallen women?'

The gas light in the long hallway was so dim that it took Milly a moment to make out the figures who stood, like basalt pillars, one on each side of a wide staircase that soared up into inky blackness.

'No, Maude,' Blazes said. 'This is Milly Bloom, Marion Bloom's daughter. In case you haven't heard the news . . .'

'We have,' said Maude. 'Very sad.'

'Very sad,' echoed the other sister, Daphne, and stepping out of the shadows, placed a hand on Milly's sleeve. 'Come, child, let me show you to your room.'

The wooden letters half way up the face of the building had been stripped of gilt by wind and weather. Three letters swung from their pegs and two more were missing, which gave the sign – *Ancient Order of Rechabites* – an inappropriately tipsy appearance that suggested that the Rechabites had moved their tents to a more salubrious location. The printed card posted in the pavement-level window, *Rooms Let to Distressed Gentlewomen,* seemed more the ticket, though why any gentlewoman, distressed or otherwise, would wish to sleep under the same roof as Hugh Blazes Boylan was more than Kinsella could fathom.

Any notion that stragglers from a Friendly Society might still be lurking behind the weathered door was dispelled when, in response to Kinsella's tug on the bell-pull, the door swung open to reveal an overbearing woman dressed in a cross-buttoned Norfolk jacket and green pleated skirt so out of date that not even his father would have considered it fashionable.

The Norfolk jacket growled, 'We're closed.'

'I'm not looking for a room,' Kinsella said.

'You're looking for charity, aren't you?'

'No, actually . . .' Kinsella groped in his pocket for his warrant card and, a split second before the door closed, found it and thrust it up into the woman's face.

'Police,' he said, growling too. 'Detective Inspector Kinsella.'

The woman reared back, swung round and called out in a voice that reverberated through the catacombs like the whinny of a coalman's nag, 'Hughie, what have you been up to now?'

'Caretakers,' Hugh Boylan explained as he escorted the inspector along the hallway towards a sliver of light beneath the staircase. 'My sisters are still associated with the Ancient

Order, which isn't so ancient as all that. When the whole shebang upped and moved to splendid new halls off Sackville Street we – my sisters – volunteered to keep this place in decent trim until the lease expires.'

'The card in the window?'

'Lodgers?' Boylan shrugged. 'A perquisite, you might say.'

'How many women are lodging here at present?'

'Nary a one, as it happens.'

Boylan had betrayed no surprise at Kinsella's arrival on his doorstep and had personally escorted the inspector into the house. He was clad in flannel trousers, a floral waistcoat and a linen shirt, the sleeves of which were held up by garters. A table napkin was tucked into the vee of his waistcoat but, in spite of his casual attire, he still managed to appear dapper.

He paused in the corridor outside the lighted room. 'We're just finishing dinner. I assume you know I have Milly Bloom here? If you failed to fish out that titbit of information then you can't be much of a detective. Which of my loyal friends shopped me?'

'Delaney of the *Star.*'

'Hmm,' Blazes said. 'Just because I sent my secretary home for the day and closed the office it wasn't my intention to be – what? – furtive. My first thought was for the child.'

'How is she?'

'Stricken and confused,' Blazes said. 'On the other hand she did manage to tuck away a decent bite of supper. One of the advantages of being sweet sixteen, I suppose, is a hearty appetite.'

'How much does she know?' Kinsella said.

'No more than I do,' Blazes said, 'which, frankly, isn't much more than I read in the paper.'

'Does the girl know her father stands accused of murder?'

'Oh! Has Bloom been formally charged? That's new.'

'He's being held on suspicion.'

'No other suspects?'

Kinsella refrained from answering. He said, 'Bloom will appear before a magistrate tomorrow morning. Given the serious nature of the felony the hearing will be closed to the public and I doubt if he'll be granted bail, but if the girl wishes to see her father afterwards I'll arrange it.'

'Kind of you to come all this way to tell her, Inspector,' Blazes Boylan said. 'Shall I bring her out or will you . . .'

'I'll have a word with her where she's most comfortable,' Kinsella said. 'Then, Mr Boylan, I'd like a few words with you in private.'

'By all means. Anything you wish to know – any way in which I can help – I've nothing to hide,' said Blazes, still unfazed, and pushed open the door to the dining room.

EIGHT

Milly Bloom was three months short of sixteen. She seemed older, though, more of an age with Violet than Daisy, Kinsella thought. She was certainly no skinny child, no whimpering waif crushed by grief. She was seated at an oval table, napkin in hand, with the remains of supper spread before her. The room, unlike the entrance hall, was lit by electricity. A crystal chandelier, adapted to take four glass bulbs, hung directly over the table but there were also lamps on the mantelshelf above the fireplace and, in a corner, a standing lamp placed before a head-high draft screen. There were no pictures on the walls and no additional furnishings. Kinsella suspected that at one time the room had been used as a meeting hall.

The woman who'd opened the front door to him was almost as tall as he was and the old-fashioned outdoor jacket and pleated skirt made her seem even more imposing. She was, he guessed, in her mid forties, eight or ten years older than her brother. The other woman in the room was somewhat younger. She wore a tea-gown decorated with faded lace.

Boylan introduced his sisters: Maude, the taller; Daphne, the younger. He stationed himself behind Milly's chair and, leaning down, whispered into her ear. It occurred to Kinsella then that however composed Milly Bloom might appear to be she was probably still fragile and that the questions he'd planned to ask her were too leading to put to her here and now.

He took off his hat, pulled out the chair that Boylan had vacated and seated himself.

Milly Bloom stared at him, waiting for him to speak. She tossed down the napkin and touched a hand to her sandy-blonde curls. Her eyes, he noted, were a beautiful shade of blue and not free of tears.

'Why have you arrested my father?' she said.

Blazes Boylan and his sisters nodded in unison as if the young woman spoke for all of them.

'He's only a suspect, Milly,' Kinsella said.

'Miss Bloom, if you please.'

'My apologies. Your father was found at the scene.'

'He lives there, don't you know,' Milly Bloom said. 'Of course he was found at the scene. It's because he's a Jew, isn't it?'

Caught off guard, Kinsella glanced at the sister, Daphne, as if hoping that she might provide an answer, but all he received was a flinty glare.

He said cautiously, 'Isn't your father a Protestant?'

'He converted,' Milly Bloom said, 'but he's still a Jew in everyone's eyes. Is that why you have him in jail?'

'The law acknowledges no such prejudice, Miss Bloom.'

'The law is nothing but a collection of prejudices, Mr Kinsella,' Maude Boylan said, 'put together by the English ruling class.'

The inspector ignored her. To Milly Bloom, he said, 'A magistrate will decide if there's a case to answer.'

'And is there?' Hugh Boylan put in.

Kinsella hesitated. 'There may be, yes.'

The young woman toyed with her hair once more. Clinging on to the last vestiges of her self-control, she displayed an obstinate determination not to give in to emotion.

'Where was my mother . . . I mean, where was she found?'

'In her bedroom.'

'How did she . . .?'

'A blow to the head. She was struck down with a teapot.'

Her lip trembled and tears welled up in her eyes. 'A teapot? Mummy's special teapot?'

'What was special about it?'

'It was a gift from Mr Boylan.' Milly Bloom looked round at her guardian for confirmation. 'After the tour?'

'Something a little more lasting than a bouquet of flowers to remember us by,' Hugh Boylan said.

'Us?' Kinsella said.

'The party, the concert party.'

'I see.' Pushing back the chair, Kinsella got to his feet. 'May I have a word with you alone now, Mr Boylan?'

'My father would never lay a finger on Mummy,' Milly Bloom blurted out. 'He loved my mother. I'll tell that to the magistrate. I'll make him believe me.' She reached for the napkin and held it to her face. 'Papli wouldn't do such a horrid thing. Never.'

Daphne Boylan reached across the table and patted the young woman's hand. Blazes said, 'If you'll give me a moment to fetch a jacket, Inspector, we'll go next door.'

'Why can't you talk to him here?' said Maude.

'Hughie has no secrets from us,' said Daphne.

Either Hugh Boylan's sisters were blind and deaf, which patently wasn't the case, or they had their heads planted in the sand. It wasn't a question of what they knew about dear Hughie's double life but what they would be prepared to admit to knowing.

Kinsella had no desire to spar with the Boylan clan, not with Miss Bloom sitting there with her ears flapping. He would leave it to Machin to take statements from the Boylan sisters. Perhaps the sight of a uniform would intimidate them, but he doubted it.

He said, 'Have you any other questions for me, Miss Bloom?'

She shook her head and held the napkin to her face once more. Her eyes were still dry, though, and she had about her the same watchful mien he'd detected in her father that morning.

'We'll talk again soon,' Kinsella promised and, with a polite nod to the hawk-eyed sisters, allowed Boylan to usher him from the room.

The room Boylan had chosen for the interview was nothing much more than a dusty storeroom containing an odd assortment of chairs and side tables and an old grandfather clock; no fireplace and no electrical light. He offered the inspector a choice of brandy or port but Kinsella would have neither. Something told the inspector that however shallow Boylan might appear he was no fool and in dealing with him, man to man, he would need all his

wits about him. Boylan turned up the gas jet that protruded from
the wall then dug a bottle of brandy and a glass from inside the
clock case and, after a final, 'Are you sure?' to Kinsella, poured
himself a snifter. He flicked dust from a chair and gestured to
Kinsella to be seated while he, glass in hand and thumb tucked
into the top pocket of his waistcoat, strolled round the store with
the swaggering air of a landed gentleman.

'My haven,' he said. 'My refuge from domestic travail. You
might suppose a man's home would be his castle, but it's not so
in my case. My castle is my office in D'Olier Street and, I daresay,
the city of Dublin itself.' He drank from the glass. 'Gentlewomen?
No, not at this season of year. We had a few last summer, strays
passing through town, but my sisters are not welcoming. We've
no servants, you see. Maude won't countenance another woman
doing what she can do perfectly well for herself. The sight of
my sisters on hands and knees scrubbing floors or splashing about
in laundry tubs fairly raises my hackles but they, like all women,
are stubborn creatures, recalcitrant as camels. Not that I've much
experience of camels, mind.' Another sip of brandy, then, 'I didn't
think he'd do it. I honestly didn't believe he had it in him. Goes
to show, you can never judge a book by its cover or a man by
the face he presents to the world.'

'Bloom, you mean?'

'Who else?' Blazes Boylan said. 'I was convinced Molly had
him on a leash, and so, indeed, was she. In all honesty I thought
he didn't mind.'

'Didn't mind what?'

'My potting the meat for him.'

'Good God!' Kinsella exclaimed.

'Come on now,' Boylan said, 'don't pretend you're shocked.
It was no secret Molly was hot stuff. For a woman of her attrib-
utes, not to speak of appetites, she needed more than Bloom
could provide. Once she'd sampled the real thing she just couldn't
get enough of it.'

'When did the affair begin?'

'June, last year.' Blazes sighed. 'By Jesus, I thought she'd drain
me dry that first time. She came and came like a geyser, and—'

'Was she in love with you?'

'She was in love with my cock, if that's what you mean, but

the other thing? No, I doubt it.' Blazes refilled his glass. 'What she liked in me were all the things she hated in herself. She was as randy as I was in my glory days but she didn't dare admit to it.' He sighed and, lifting the glass, toasted an invisible presence. 'Damn me, if it hadn't been for Bloom I might even have married her.'

Kinsella attempted to interrupt but Boylan, with barely a pause, was off again. 'At first Molly was nothing to me but a bored wife with an itch begging to be scratched. Then, God help me, during that autumn tour, I got the taste of her. We were two of a kind, as close as makes no matter.' He smiled and clicked his tongue in his cheek. 'Every evening it was "Love's Old Sweet Song" on stage or platform and in the hotel bed every night more of same. Coming home to Dublin was hard on both of us. Believe it or not, I was jealous of Bloom, though Molly assured me, on her Bible oath, she never gave him more than a rub and a tickle.'

'Did you believe her?'

'What choice did I have?' said Blazes. 'She jumped on me eagerly enough two or three afternoons a week. We were hard at it down in the kitchen when the servant walked in. She didn't even flinch, my Molly, didn't miss a stroke.'

'Bloom didn't visit you on the concert tours?'

'No, he kept well away. Deliberately, I reckon.'

'How long have you known the Blooms?'

'Too many years to count.'

'A friend of the family, might you say?' Kinsella asked.

The irony was lost on Boylan. 'I suppose you might say that. He seemed suddenly weary as if all that strolling about had caught up with him. He seated himself on one of the chairs, planted his elbows on his knees, peered into the brandy glass and gave the liquid a swirl.

'Now,' he said, 'when did I first meet Molly? Would it be 1890? Yes, 1890, at the races at Leopardstown. What was I, twenty-three? She came down with Josie – I don't recall her other name – and Bloom. Josie and Bloom were making sheep's eyes at each other. Molly was mad at him so I thought I'd chance my arm with Molly. But she wouldn't wear it. Bloom worked for Hely's, the stationers, then. I gave him an order for paper and we did business on and off. But Molly, no, I didn't bump into her again until I stood in for D'Arcy at a church soiree. She was carrying the kiddie she lost, Rudy, and—'

Before Boylan got completely carried away on a wave of nostalgia, Kinsella intervened. 'I find it difficult to believe it took a man like you close to fifteen years to get what you wanted?'

'You mean, Molly out of her stays?' Blazes looked up, grinning. 'Oh, we sniffed each other like dogs but the time was never quite ripe for her.'

'What changed her mind?'

'I don't know.'

'Were there others in the meantime, other men?'

'Rumour was she had a fancy for Simon Dedalus's boy but he was far too young for her and everyone knew it. Anyway, he scuffed off to Paris in the fall.'

'Any others you can put a name to?'

'Fellow called Gardener, a solider. He died of a fever in the Transvaal five or six years back, I think. My father knew of him but my father won't say a word about the war since everyone called him a traitor for selling horses to the English and, by the by, raking in a packet in the process.'

'Where is your father now?'

'Cork; but he won't talk to you.'

'Why not?'

'He thinks all coppers are shite.'

'He's not alone in that opinion,' Kinsella said. 'Where were you last night, Mr Boylan?'

'Sure I knew you'd get around to it sooner or later,' Blazes said. 'I was here at home, in bed.'

'Will your sisters confirm it?'

'They'd better,' Blazes said, adding, 'ay, they will, they will.'

'And you didn't leave the house after midnight?'

'For what reason?'

'To visit Mrs Bloom, perhaps.'

'With Bloom at home? No.'

'Bloom wasn't at home,' Kinsella said. 'What's more, neither were you, Mr Boylan. I have a witness—'

'He's lying.'

'I have a witness who saw you outside Bella Cohen's—'

'Lying, lying, I swear he's lying.'

'—who saw you arguing with Leopold Bloom at midnight outside Bella Cohen's.'

Boylan shook his head vigorously. 'No, I tell you. No.'

'What was the argument about?' Kinsella said. 'Were you arguing about Mrs Bloom?'

'Fact is, I was nowhere near Bella Cohen's last night.'

'For God's sake, Boylan,' Kinsella said, 'you're not some grubby young soldier indistinguishable from all the other grubby young soldiers who invade the Monto after nightfall. You're known to every publican and brothel-keeper in Dublin. If I found one witness without even trying don't you suppose I won't find others?'

Blazes blew out his cheeks, fluttered his lips and surrendered. 'It wasn't Bella Cohen's,' he said. 'It was Nancy O'Rourke's and it wasn't midnight. It was half past eleven at the latest. I was coming out just as Bloom was going in. We weren't arguing. We were sharing a joke. I'd had a skinful, you see.'

'Was Bloom drunk too?'

'Bloom doesn't drink. Glass of wine now and then when someone else is paying, never the hard stuff.'

'So,' Kinsella said, 'you knew Mrs Bloom was alone?'

'Ah now, you're not going to catch me on that one, Mr Kinsella. I picked up a cab, poured myself into it and was home here on the stroke of midnight. If you doubt my word ask Maude. She it was who let me in and helped me through to my bed.'

'Were you surprised to meet Bloom at Nancy O'Rourke's?'

'To look at Bloom you'd think butter wouldn't melt in his mouth but he's just as big a rascal as the rest of us. He mightn't be able to raise the flag with his wife but, by God, he loves his nights upstairs with Nancy's girls.'

'Did Molly know about this . . . this hobby of his?'

'She had her suspicions.'

'You didn't tell her, did you?'

'I'd hardly be one to grudge Bloom his pleasures, would I? Of course, I didn't say anything to Molly. If Leo needs a tickle with a pandybat on his bare bum to get it up, it's no business of mine.'

'Is that what goes on upstairs in O'Rourke's?'

'Among other things,' said Blazes. 'See, now you've tricked me into giving Bloom an opportunity as well as a motive.'

'On the contrary,' Kinsella said. 'If Bloom wasn't tucked up with his wife in Eccles Street last night, his claim she was killed by someone else gains credibility.'

'By someone else? I hope you don't mean me?'

'Now why would you think that, Mr Boylan?'

'What reason in the world would I have for killing Molly?'

'Perhaps you were tired of her?'

'If I had been, I'd just have walked away. Fact is, I wasn't tired of her. I liked her. I enjoyed her. Oh!' said Boylan, ruffled now. 'Do you think I might have done her in because she was throwing *me* over? Na, na, Inspector, that's a woman's trick, not something a man would do, not a man like me anyhow.'

'Where's your room, your bedroom?'

'What?'

'In which part of the house?'

'Two doors down off the corridor. Why?'

'And your sisters sleep where?'

'Upstairs.' Blazes clicked his tongue in his cheek again. 'I see. You think I slipped out, don't you? Slipped out and went all the way over to Eccles Street to beat Molly Bloom to death with a teapot?'

'That may not have been your intention.'

'Good luck to you, fella,' Blazes said. 'You'll not be finding a cabman in the whole of Dublin who'll swear he took me back to Eccles Street in dead of night. I was home here in bed, too bloody pickled to tie me own bootlaces let alone stagger half way across town to murder someone with a bloody teapot.'

Blazes drank off the contents of the brandy glass, placed the glass on one of the tables and, hoisting himself to his feet, began to pace the room once more. 'Bloom did it,' he said. 'You know it and I know it. Bloom's your man, Inspector. As for me, well, I'd no motive for doing Molly in, no motive and no opportunity. And I have – what is it you call it? – an iron-clad alibi.'

'Which your sisters will no doubt support.'

'Too deuced right, they will.'

Kinsella slapped his hands to his knees and got up. 'Well, Mr Boylan, I think you've answered all my questions, most of them anyway. I can't guarantee you won't be bothered again, however.'

'No,' Blazes said, with a nod of acknowledgement. 'I'm the third party, like it or not. Bloom, me, and Molly. I'm as much

to blame as he is, I suppose. Poor bitch. What a price to pay for
a bit of pleasure, eh?'

'Yes, indeed,' Kinsella agreed.

He watched Boylan open the door and turn off the gas. In the
whisper of light from the corridor he looked larger than he really
was, not the big man that some folks believed him to be but a
shadow, a huge shadow cast by a trick of the light.

'What are you going to do with the girl?' Kinsella asked.

Boylan's head whipped round. 'Pardon?'

'Milly Bloom, what will you do with her?'

'Keep her here,' Blazes said, 'at least until things are settled.'

'Is she amenable to that arrangement?'

'Doesn't have much choice, does she?' Blazes said. 'Anyhow,
taking care of her kiddie is the least I can do for Molly now.'

'And Bloom?'

'Yes, Bloom too,' said Blazes.

NINE

It was not unusual for lay magistrates to regard the laws of
evidence as more of a lawyers' fad than an essential cog in
the machinery of justice. In certain rural areas professional
rules were looked upon as restrictions, artificial and pettifogging,
and no match for sturdy common sense when conflicts in judgement arose.

Patrick Mullen was no uneducated lout from the bogs, however.
He had trained at the Inner Temple and had been for several
terms Chairman of the Dublin Quarter Assizes. The hearing over
which he presided early that Friday morning was, for all intents
and purposes, conducted on model lines in obedience to every
statute on the books and all the latest amendments that came
over from Westminster by the boatload.

Inferior men might incline against a defendant on grounds of
race or creed or even an inability to soar over a five-bar gate in
pursuit of a fox. But the prejudice that Patrick Mullen harboured
was nothing if not original: namely that the accused had robbed

Dublin of a musical star, which, even for a nut like Mullen, was pushing it more than somewhat. When all was said and done, Marion Bloom had been no better than a half-decent soprano whose popular appeal had relied as much on her heaving bosom as the timbre of her voice; yet so obsessed with music-making, in all its multifarious forms, was old short-sighted Paddy, that Bloom's goose was cooked before he even stepped through the courtroom door.

Bloom had chosen to defend himself, or, rather, not defend himself, by sleepwalking through the proceedings. The police, on the other hand, were keenly represented by Crown solicitor, Fergus Menton, a young turk from an old-established firm who nursed a grudge against Bloom on behalf of his uncle, John Henry Menton, who, in a time long gone, had been defeated, on the bowling green of all places, by said Leopold Bloom, an insult that had not been forgotten and would never be forgiven.

Patrick Mullen was only too well aware that the onus of proof in any felony lay on the prosecution: if the evidence did not make the guilt of the defendant clear beyond reasonable doubt then the defendant must be discharged. Fortunately for the magistrate's personal prejudices a number of irregularities were already attached to the case, irregularities that would validate his inclination not to dismiss Bloom but to throw him, as it were, to the wolves. Not least of these trifles was the fact that the warrant had been signed by the coroner. Mullen was confident that, if the worst came to the worst, he could emulate Pontius Pilate, bind Bloom over to be held without bail and let cocky Dr Slater advance the charge at the inquest.

The hearing began with the Crown solicitor reading the charge. This was followed by testimony from a DMP inspector, a hairy-faced sergeant and a young constable. In the absence of a legal adviser, Mr Bloom was permitted to make a short statement. Bloom's statement was so resigned and defeatist that Patrick Mullen felt almost sorry for the chap who, if he'd slaughtered some tone deaf citizen who couldn't tell an A sharp from an E flat, would have received the benefit of magisterial misgiving and walked away free.

As it was, Patrick Mullen elected to bind the defendant over until the findings of the coroner's inquiry became known and recommended that until then Mr Bloom be kept in a holding cell in Store Street and not banged up in Kilmainham or, God help him, the Mountjoy. For this compassionate gesture bare-headed Mr Bloom, kneading his hat in his hands, thanked his lordship before being led out into a corridor where, true to his word, Inspector Kinsella had brought Milly to meet him.

On seeing her father metaphorically in chains Milly burst into tears. Moved by his daughter's distress, Bloom did likewise. He clasped Milly to his breast and hugged her. When Sergeant Gandy stepped in to separate the sobbing couple Kinsella caught him by the sleeve and drew him off down the length of the corridor to allow Bloom and his offspring a few moments to grieve in private.

At the far end of the corridor, where a heavy double door opened out into the street, Blazes Boylan chatted to Tom Machin, while outside on the courthouse steps a noisy crowd of reporters fought to catch a glimpse of Bloom and be first to offer a bribe to Blazes to give them access to the girl.

Kinsella watched the Blooms, father and daughter, from the corner of his eye. He didn't quite know what he expected to see, what odd little telltale might be revealed in the meeting.

As a father himself he felt sorry for the girl, and for Bloom too, yet there was a flinty bit in his heart – or was it his head? – that protected his objectivity. He had dealt with weeping women and pulverised children too often in the past, with men who could ornament their plight so convincingly that you would stake your life on their innocence if it hadn't been for the blood on their hands. He knew well enough that the guilty could easily appear innocent and the innocent guilty and that guilt itself was a two-faced god.

It did not escape his notice that just as they parted Bloom slipped something into his daughter's hand and that she whispered something into her father's ear. Then came the telltale: a flick of Milly Bloom's head, a turnaround glance to see if the stealthy exchange between herself and her father had been noticed.

'Take him out the back way, Sergeant Gandy,' Kinsella said.

'What about the gurl, sir?' Gandy asked.

'No, leave the girl to me.'

He watched, coldly now, as Bloom was wrenched away from

his child and, slouch-shouldered and splay-footed, hastened off down the length of the corridor that connected the courts to a door in the rear of the building where a prison van was waiting to convey the prisoner safely back to Store Street.

Milly came towards him, a handkerchief held to her nose. Her fingers were closed not only around the corner of the handkerchief but around whatever it was that Leopold Bloom had given her. Her cheeks were wet, the tears undoubtedly genuine, but she was just too young, too lacking in cunning to hide her unease.

Kinsella glanced down the corridor. Machin had gone. Blazes Boylan was standing with feet apart, head raised, like a stag catching the scent of a stalker on the wind, not alarmed yet, not even anxious, but alert.

'Miss Bloom?' With three neat steps of which his dancing daughters would have approved, Jim Kinsella put himself directly in the girl's path. 'May I see what you have in your hand?'

Saying nothing, she held up her left hand and opened it.

'The other hand, please,' Kinsella said.

He watched her fingers close, thumb pinching the corner of the handkerchief as she took it from her nose, her pinkie, ring and index fingers curled into her palm.

'It's just a handkerchief.' She held it dangling like a stinking fish, before him. 'It's not . . . not awfully clean.'

'That doesn't matter.'

She slid her gaze from Kinsella to Boylan who, hesitantly, had begun to move down the corridor towards them. Then, left with no option, she dropped the handkerchief into the inspector's hand. Her hand, the right hand, edged towards the pocket of her short red overcoat. Kinsella caught her arm below the elbow.

'Take your paws off me,' she squealed.

Indignation cut no ice with Jim Kinsella. He could hear Boylan's heels on the marble, clattering. He snared her wrist and, quite gently, rotated it. Her fingers flared to expose the object that for some reason she'd tried to hide.

'It's a key,' Milly Bloom said. 'Just a key.'

'A key to what?'

'Our house,' the girl said, tossing her curls. 'Papli gave it to me so I can get in. He needs a clean shirt and collars. Stockings and drawers. His black tie, too. You can't stop me fetching his things.'

'No,' Kinsella said, slowly. 'No, I can't, but . . .'

'I'll go with her,' said Boylan, a little breathlessly. 'I'll make sure she doesn't see anything she shouldn't. The house hasn't been sealed by the coroner, has it?'

Kinsella had no idea if Slater had had No 7 Eccles Street sealed after Marion Bloom's body had been removed, though he rather doubted it.

'Send a copper with us, if you like,' Boylan said. 'Inspector Machin has no objection. It's his responsibility, after all.'

'When do you intend to make the visit?' Kinsella asked.

'More or less at once,' Blazes answered. 'All right, sweetheart?'

'Yes,' said Milly. 'Do let's get it over with.'

'Are you sure you're ready for this, Miss Bloom?' said Kinsella.

'As ready as I'll ever be,' said Milly.

Kinsella wasn't in the least surprised to find Assistant Commissioner Archibald Harrison Murphy O'Byrne, CB, CBE, MVO, occupying the only padded chair in Superintendent Smout's office on the half landing off the stair in Lower Castle Yard. The office was cramped at the best of times but with Rotunda Division's Superintendent Driscoll and Inspector Tom Machin also present it was all Kinsella could do to squeeze through the door and find a corner in which to stretch out his legs.

The Assistant Commissioner, Driscoll and Machin were smoking cigarettes and Smout had his pipe going full blast. The atmosphere in the office was as thick as a November fog. Jim's eyes immediately began to water, a minor inconvenience that didn't deter him from accepting one of the Turkish cigarettes that Archibald Harrison Murphy O'Byrne, who liked to pretend he was just one of the boys, offered him from a scrolled silver case.

'Passed the buck, did he?' the Assistant Commissioner said. 'I can't say I'm surprised. Between thee and me, gentlemen – and let it go no further – a certain stipendiary magistrate is all too good at that. He has little or no patience with the pace

of the work of detection. Your predecessor, Smout, the revered
John Mallon, was never done reminding our magistrate friends
that the four essentials for a policeman are truthfulness,
sobriety, punctuality and extreme caution as to what you tell
your superiors.'

Although they had heard the old chestnut many a time before,
the officers laughed dutifully.

'Now, Kinsella, where are we?'

Jim Kinsella wafted smoke from his face. He was not deceived
by the Assistant Commissioner's affability, nor did he suppose
himself to be on a par with the great John Mallon when it came
to low down and dirty detective work. That said, he *had* solved a
dozen tricky cases from the Murder File without the aid of informers
and had a reputation for spotting leads so slender that they were
invisible to the more myopic members of the constabulary.

He said, 'If it isn't murder, sir, then it is, as it stands,
manslaughter. If he shifts his position a little towards the truth,
the suspect, Bloom, could claim he lost his temper with his wife
and struck her down on a violent impulse. Candidly, it would be
difficult, if not impossible, to prove otherwise.'

'But,' Machin put in, 'Bloom admits to no such thing, sir.'

'I've read his statement,' the Assistant Commissioner said.
'He's a queer fellow all round, is our Mr Bloom. Do you agree,
Kinsella?'

'I do, sir,' Jim Kinsella said, 'but he's not, in my opinion,
aberrant or perverse. Far from it. I think he's very sharp and
logical, and, with due respect, may be playing us for fools.'

'And if he is?' said Superintendent Driscoll.

'Then he's guilty of murder, not manslaughter,' Kinsella said.

'His version of events being that his wife was murdered by an
intruder in the quarter hour it took him to shop,' said Mr O'Byrne.
'Have you uncovered anything to indicate another party was
involved, apart, that is, from the wife's lover, what's his name?'

'Boylan,' Kinsella said.

'I take it this Boylan person *was* the woman's lover?'

'He freely admits it, sir,' Kinsella said. 'He's proud of it, in
fact. I'm rather hoping that pride might be his downfall.'

'His downfall?' The Assistant Commissioner raised a bushy
eyebrow. 'Do you mark Boylan as a suspect?'

'Too soon to say that, sir.'

'Then you must apply yourself, Inspector,' the Assistant Commissioner said. 'I don't suppose I need remind you that it may be neither Bloom nor Boylan and that someone as yet unknown to us is skipping about Dublin laughing up his sleeve.'

'Can I take, sir,' Superintendent Smout put in, 'that you wish G Division to continue with the investigation?'

'Quite definitely,' Mr O'Byrne said. 'The death of a woman may not threaten the security of the nation but it is, nonetheless, murder, and murder, last time I looked, is a crime and bringing criminals to book is your business, is it not?'

He ground out his cigarette in the ashtray on Smout's desk and got briskly to his feet. He was a portly man, slab-cheeked and jowly, but had long ago learned how to balance on the tight-rope between ceremony and effectiveness.

'Gentlemen,' he said, 'I'll leave you to it. Do keep me up to the minute on your progress. The Commissioner is less than enthusiastic about receiving his information from the *Journal* or the *Star.* Inspector Kinsella, a word with you before I go, if I may.' And before any of his officers could leap to open the door for him, Mr O'Byrne opened it himself and ushered Kinsella out before him and down the short flight of steps on to the pavement.

'Now, tell me, Inspector,' said Mr O'Byrne, '*is* Bloom a Jew?'

'Jewish by blood but a convert to Protestantism.'

'I see. And the woman, the victim, was she a Jew too?'

'What she was isn't entirely clear,' Kinsella frowned. 'Is there a point to your question, Mr O'Byrne?'

'I wonder how aware you are of the mutual estrangement between Jews and Irishmen. The Jews, it's said, understand the Irish but little and the Irish understand the Jews even less. Bloom has the misfortune to be both. Tread carefully, Kinsella, please. I doubt if the Castle will appreciate criticism from the Anglo-Jewish press who, without doubt, will be following the case closely.' He slapped his folded gloves lightly against Kinsella's chest. 'Mark you, the Castle doesn't appreciate criticism from *any* quarter if it can be avoided. You will be at the inquest, won't you? Monday at eleven at the new building in Store Street, I believe?'

'That's correct,' said Kinsella.

'I do hope Bloom isn't sent for trial, though I fear Slater will do his best to see that he is,' the Assistant Commissioner said. 'What a dilemma it will put us in if Bloom's found guilty of murder.' He grunted ruefully. 'I mean, if he's one part Jew and two parts Irish which part do we hang first?' Another friendly tap with the folded gloves. 'Do your level best to see it doesn't come to that, Inspector. Do try to save Bloom from himself.'

'Indeed, I will, sir,' Kinsella promised, though at that exact point in the investigation he was not at all sure that he could.

TEN

I t was no coincidence that Constable Jarvis arrived on the doorstep of No 7 Eccles Street just five minutes before Boylan and his fair-haired companion showed up. With Mr Driscoll's consent, Tom Machin had switched Jarvis to day duty on the off chance that Kinsella would need him again, which, as it turned out, Mr Kinsella most certainly did.

Constable Jarvis had barely returned to Store Street police station after his appearance in the magistrate's court before the duty inspector summoned him to the telephone and he found himself talking or, rather, listening to Inspector Kinsella who, it seemed, was now in charge of the case. The inspector's instructions were not as specific as orders barked by a parade ground sergeant or, come to think of it, by his termagant older sister, Breda, who bullied him something dreadful, but Jarvis was a bright young chap and understood exactly what was required of him.

Boots and buttons shining in the pale spring sunshine, he joined Constable Fegan, who was guarding the crime scene from inquisitive citizens, just in time to catch his breath before Blazes Boylan, driving a hired gig, navigated the corner and reined up at the kerb in front of the house.

'Move along now, move along,' Constable Fegan advised in a surprisingly mild tone of voice. 'Nothing to see here.'

Blazes ignored him, jumped down, secured the rein and, with a flourish, handed Miss Bloom to the pavement.

Constable Fegan, who sported a black beard and bristling moustache that gave small children the vapours, planted his fists on his broad hips and, less mildly this time, said, 'Move along now like you've been told or I'll be having to do it for you.'

'Don't you know who I am?' said Blazes.

'I don't care if you're Herod the Great,' said Constable Fegan. 'Shift that cart double quick or I'll have you in my notebook.'

Constable Jarvis knew that the man and the girl had been given permission to enter the house but he liked watching his colleague's temper rise, and said nothing. The girl was very pretty and not lacking a figure but her red coat and daft tam were unsuited to mourning. She wasn't daunted by Fegan's beard or his snarl. She brushed past Boylan and holding up a key between finger and thumb wagged it in the constable's face.

'It's my house,' she said. 'You've no right to refuse me entry to my own house, so make way, please.'

Constable Fegan wasn't used to being sauced by young females. 'N-name?' was all he could think of to say.

'Bloom,' the girl answered, stretching it to three syllables as if she were talking to a foreigner or an idiot. 'Mill-lee Bloo-om.'

At which point Constable Jarvis prudently intervened and led the couple indoors.

It crossed Kinsella's mind that he might drop by his house, wheel out his bicycle and ride down to Sandymount Road. It wasn't much more than a couple of miles from the Castle, though, and, with a fresh breeze blowing, he decided to stretch his legs and walk.

Soon, he had the sea in sight; a long, blue-grey plain scalloped by white horses as far out as the eye could see. He loved the salty tang on his tongue, the nip of salt air in his sinuses and the slap of the wind on his cheeks. He'd often been here with Edith and the girls, even oftener on his trusty old boneshaker, tail up and snout to the breeze, pumping away at the pedals, all on his own and never happier.

According to Edith's mother, in the good old days the appearance of bathing boxes on the Strand had been the first sign that summer was on the way but, with Easter falling late this year,

Dublin's Sunday dippers would wait awhile to romp in the briny. Even if bathing boxes had still been in fashion they wouldn't have survived the waves that rolled in with the high tide and blossomed, booming, into sheets of white spray when they met the slope of sand and the rocks at the root of the wall.

On reaching the shop on Sandymount Road, Kinsella realised he'd visited it once before, six or seven years ago, in search of a snip of bandage to wrap round Marigold's finger when, so she'd claimed, she'd been bitten by a crab and, sniffing bravely, had insisted on immediate medical attention before all the blood in her body drained away through the all but invisible wound.

Flanked by an ironmongers and a news agents, Winterbottom's window struck a colourful note. It was dressed not just with the trademark display of three glass carboys filled with rainbow liquid and urn-like jars with black-letter Latin names but also with a row of pastel bathing caps and a phalanx of jade green bottles optimistically labelled *Tropical Sun Stroke Reliever.*

Kinsella opened the door. The bell above it tinged.

The shop smelled of menthol and rosewater with an undercurrent reminiscent of sulphur. Through a curtain behind the counter the pharmacist made his appearance, accompanied by a puff of smoke. To Kinsella's disappointment the smoke was nothing more arcane than pipe tobacco and Mr Winterbottom carried in his hand neither crucible nor lightning rod but only a cup of tea.

In his fifties, smooth-shaven and balding, a cream-coloured linen smock tied over his waistcoat, the chemist slid the teacup under the counter and rubbed his pudgy hands.

'Good afternoon, sir, and what can I do for you?'

Kinsella said, 'I'm looking for a particular perfume.'

'For a particular lady?' said Mr Winterbottom archly, with further rubbing of the hands. 'Of course.'

'She's partial to – let me see – Halcyon Days, would it be?'

The pharmacist's face fell. 'Oh, that one. I'm sorry, sir, we're clear out of Halcyon Days.'

'Really! That's a blow!' Kinsella said.

'We should have stock in again by Easter.'

'Must be popular,' Kinsella put in.

'It is, very popular. Many girls will have no other. It falls within their means, you see. Cheaper than French but,' Mr Winterbottom added quickly, 'just as good.'

'Ah women!' Kinsella said. 'Once they get something to their heads nothing will shake it. It was recommended to my daughter by some of her friends down this way. Perhaps you know them?'

Beginning to smell a rat and with no sale in the offing, the pharmacist answered guardedly. 'Perhaps I do.'

Kinsella leaned an elbow on the counter. 'I don't suppose you've many men buying perfume?'

'Not many, no.'

'If you did you'd remember them?'

'Here, what's your game? You're not after scent at all. You're a detective, I'll be bound.' Mr Winterbottom rose to his full height which, Kinsella estimated, put him just short of a par with Machin. 'My Drug Book's up to date, and those pills was never proved to do harm to nobody.'

'Perfume is all I'm interested in, Mr Winterbottom,' Kinsella said. 'Specifically which of your customers buys Halcyon Days.'

The pharmacist wiped a bead of sweat from his temple. 'I . . . I sell in confidence. If you are a copper, I need to see your card.'

'Quite right.' Kinsella put his warrant card on the counter. 'Can't be too careful these days. Tell me about the gentlemen who buy American perfume.'

Mr Winterbottom had pushed the boat out as far as he dared. With barely a glance, he shoved the card back at the Inspector.

'They don't,' he said. 'Truth is, I've never sold one bottle of that stu , , , of Halcyon Days to a man.'

'All right,' Kinsella said. 'What about girls?'

'What about them?'

'Are they local?'

'They're just ordinary young women, or not so young women, come to think on it.'

'A name or two would be useful,' Kinsella said. 'They're not in any trouble, Mr Winterbottom. I'm investigating a theft and have to show I've been thorough. Names, I need just a few names to flesh out my report.'

'Meg Cooke, Anna Morris, Davina, her cousin,' said Mr Winterbottom. 'There's the other one, Edy something, but I ha'n't seen her since last summer. She never bought but one bottle.

Came in mostly for baby ointment. She was with the cheeky one, tall girl, all legs and lip who never spent more than a shilling on soap and lip salve. Her name, what was her name? Chrissie . . . no, Cissy. Father's a drunkard, so I've heard.'

'None of them regular purchasers by the sound of it.'

'No,' said Mr Winterbottom regretfully. 'Not regular enough.'

'Well, that's enough to be going on with, I think.'

'You didn't write it down.'

'I have it up here.' Kinsella tapped his forehead. 'Thank you, Mr Winterbottom, you've been most—'

'Oh, yes!' The pharmacist exclaimed. 'What am I dreaming of? The cripple. She buys regular, has done for a year or more. Halcyon Days is her favourite. Recommended in a lady's magazine, she told me. Alluring, she says, as if anything could make her alluring. No girl now, poor soul. Twenty-four, if she's a day.'

'What's her name?' Kinsella asked only out of politeness.

'Gerty,' the pharmacist said. 'Gerty MacDowell.'

Kinsella thanked him once more and, ten minutes later, was riding back to town on a tram, cursing himself for having squandered the best part of the day on a wild goose chase.

Blazes didn't know quite what he hoped to find in No 7 Eccles Street. He also had a suspicion that Kinsella had told the copper to keep a close eye on him. Copper or not, there was something unnerving about entering Molly's house now Molly was gone. The sense of guilt that enveloped him was almost overwhelming. Everything was exactly the same as it had been last time he'd stepped into the hallway and, try as he might, he couldn't shake off the suspicion that Molly might be waiting for him behind the closed door of the bedroom, spread out, spread-eagled and demanding his manly attentions.

If it was bad for him, it must be terrible for Milly. He prayed she wouldn't go all hysterical. Blood drained from her cheeks and she clung to his arm as if her life depended on it when the policeman, hand raised, said, 'Not the bedroom, Miss. I have my instructions: not the bedroom.'

'But that's where Papli keeps his shirts,' Milly complained.

'With the officer's permission,' Blazes said. 'I'll fetch 'em.'

'But you don't know where they are,' said Milly.

Blazes met the constable's eye. The copper hesitated, nodded, stepped forward, snared Milly by the arm and, using no more force than necessary, prevented her darting past him while Blazes, seizing the opportunity, opened the bedroom door and slipped into the room. With Milly's plaintive cry, a wavering note around the range of middle C, ringing in his ears, he closed the door behind him.

He waited motionless, backside pressed against the door knob until the sound of the girl's distress died away, then placed his hat on the lid of the old commode and, steeling himself, turned to face the rumpled bed and bloodstained wallpaper.

Bolsters and one sheet had been removed but as far as he could make out nothing else in the room had been touched; the chamber pot beneath the wash stand still had Molly's piss in it. He willed himself to the dressing table and surveyed the jars, bottles and brushes with which Molly had fought off ageing; meaningless now, reduced to a smatter of blood on the wall above the bed, the same bed in which she'd bucked and sweated, hair unloosed, lips stretched as she urged him to pummel her, pummel her and bring her off again. He sighed and closed his eyes for a moment then, remembering why he was here, pulled himself together.

He slid out the drawer of the dressing table where Bloom's linen was kept; three shirts, three vests and four pairs of drawers. He took out a shirt, a vest and two pairs of drawers not long back from the wash by the smell of them. He laid them over his arm and fished out a starched collar and from a small box that had once housed Beecham's pills, two studs and a pair of cuff links.

Three neckties were rolled up and stuffed into a corner. The black one was stringy and, he noticed, stained on the tip as if it had been dipped in tomato soup. He furled it tidily, balanced it on top of the clothes on his arm then, having seen enough, hurriedly left the room before it smothered him with its memories.

The constable was leaning against the wall close to the door of the bedroom. He pulled himself upright and, without being invited, relieved Blazes of the armful of clothing.

'What?' Blazes said. 'Do you think I'm stealing them?'

'Just being helpful, sir, that's all.'

'Where's the girl? Where's Miss Bloom?'

'Gone to look for her cat.'

'Gone where?'

'Next door. I think they have him there.'

'Her,' Blazes said. 'The cat's a female. What are you going to do with the clothes?'

'Find something to put them in. Is there a bag or suitcase we can use, do you know?'

'No, I don't know,' Blazes said. 'Try the kitchen.'

He couldn't blame the copper for obeying Kinsella's instruction to record everything removed from the house. He had no doubt that at some stage the items would be listed and he'd be obliged to sign for them, or perhaps it would be left to Milly or even Bloom, but somewhere down the line someone would demand a signature, for that was the way it was when you were dealing with a system hog-tied by rules and regulations.

He watched the constable go off downstairs. The instant the uniform disappeared, he flung open the door of the living room and went in. He still didn't know what he was looking for but if Bloom did have something to hide chances were he'd plant it somewhere where Molly would never think to look.

Molly had been possessed of a suspicious nature and a deal of natural cunning but she was no match for her husband when it came to guile. Blazes didn't doubt that she'd raked through drawers, poked into cupboards, lifted cushions and carpets and emptied Bloom's pockets in search of evidence that her hubby was up to something so shameful that it would give her a stick to beat him with when it came to recriminations.

Blazes knew the living room like the back of his hand. He'd even shifted furniture around at Molly's request to make room at the piano back last June when they'd begun their regular 'rehearsals' for the concert tour. God, he thought, that voice, that lovely voice that blended so well with mine, pitch perfect and sweet without being cloying. He blinked, surprised again by sentiment and the realisation that he'd never again sing 'Love's Old Sweet Song' or 'The Moon Has Raised Her Lamp' with Molly or hear the angelic clarity of her 'Ave' ringing out in church or hall.

Inside the piano, inside the stool? Far too obvious. He cast his gaze around the room from mantelshelf to armchair to sideboard. No, not the sideboard. He heard the front door open and Milly's heels tapping on the hall floor. Not the sideboard but perhaps the bookcase. He vaulted the arm of the sofa and began hauling the books forward, tipping them down so that he could peer into the tight-packed pages from the top.

Bloom's books, bound black and brown, bruised blue and acid green, thick and dull, closed and impenetrable as far as Molly was concerned. How often had he heard her sneer at Bloom's books? Dust-catchers, she'd said, full of useless knowledge without a good story in any one of them, sneering because she was intimidated by all the things her husband knew that she didn't.

Blazes had no more affinity with books than Molly had had. Dumpy little volumes of M'Call's Racing Chronicle and the annual records of bloodstock sales lined his office shelves and his bedside cabinet at home was crammed with nothing more substantial than boxing magazines and theatre programmes.

In the hall, voices: Milly's shrill; the copper's soft, male, and placatory. Dante, no. Shakespeare, no. Spinoza, dense as a doorstep, no.

Four or five volumes at a time, he worked down the shelves, irked by his own conceit in thinking that he could outsmart crafty old Bloom. Astronomy, geology, J.A. Froude's – whoever the devil he was – *Nemesis of Faith* and *English in Ireland* and *The English in the West Indies* and . . . there! He tugged out the volume and pushed the others hurriedly back on to the shelf. Four thin sheets of paper, typed upon, were folded between the pages.

My dearest, naughty darling.

My own, my one true love.

Martha.

Martha? Never mind Froude, who the devil was Martha?

'You all right in there, sir?' the constable enquired.

Blazes shook the sheets from between the pages and stuffed them into his inside pocket just as the copper appeared in the doorway, Milly, the cat in her arms, behind him.

'I'm looking for a book to keep Mr Bloom amused over the weekend,' Blazes said. 'No law against that, is there?'

'None as I know of, sir,' the copper said. 'Have you found one?'

'Hmm.' Blazes displayed Froude's volume on the West Indies. 'This should take his mind off things.'

'He's read that one,' Milly said.

'Then,' said Blazes, 'he can read it again.'

'Are you finished here?' the copper asked.

'I am,' Blazes said. 'Milly, how's puss?'

'She missed me, can't you tell?' He watched Milly hug the scraggy creature. 'Olly says he'll feed her until Papli comes back.'

'Olly?'

'Oliver, from next door.'

Bending, Milly released the animal who shot off through the half open front door as if, Blazes thought, she couldn't get out of this haunted place fast enough. 'Is there anything you need from your room?' he asked. 'I mean, clothes or shoes?'

'I've nothing black,' Milly answered. 'Not a thing to fit me.'

It was on the tip of Blazes' tongue to suggest that some of her mother's clothes might be trimmed and taken in but he realised just how heartless that would seem and, with a smile, said, 'Well, sweetheart, we'll just have to go shopping, won't we?'

Bloom's clothes were wrapped in brown paper and tied with string like a parcel ready for the post. Blazes took the book and wedged it securely under the string.

'Do you have everything you came for, sir?' Jarvis asked.

'Oh, yes,' said Mr Boylan. 'I think we're all done here.'

There being no hacksaws, rasps or sticks of dynamite concealed in the parcel, Mr Driscoll gave Sergeant Gandy permission to take Bloom's clothes, minus wrapping paper and string, down to his cell, together with the book that inspection had shown to be free of poison pills and coded messages.

It was still broad daylight, a pleasant, if gusty, spring afternoon. Patches of blue sky showed amid scudding white cloud in the high barred window of the holding cell.

Bloom was seated on the side of the iron cot. His bits and pieces had been returned to him after his appearance in the magistrate's court but, having no reason to feign respectability, he had left off his boots, coat and collar and with hands on his knees and face angled up to the light from the window looked, Gandy thought, more like a dirty Hebrew than ever.

The plate on which his midday dinner had been served had been licked clean and placed, with his tea mug, on the floor by the cell door where Gandy kicked them on entering.

Bloom looked up.

'Clothes,' Gandy said. 'Keep 'um clean for Monday.'

'Monday?' Bloom said.

'Coroner's Court, Monday.'

'Oh!' Bloom said. 'Right you are.'

'Where do you want them put?'

'Here on the bed will do.'

Smirking, Gandy held out the neatly folded bundle and dropped it deliberately to the floor.

Bloom, without apparent irony, said, 'Thank you.'

Gandy stood before him, big belly thrust out, and, gripping Bloom by his shirt, hoisted him, unresisting, to his feet.

'I thought I told you to keep 'um clean,' he said.

'Yes,' Bloom said. 'My fault entirely.'

'Then pick 'um up.'

'By all means,' said Mr Bloom

Stooping, he scooped up his clothing from the floor. He knew what would happen next and was prepared for it but the force of Gandy's knee ramming into his rump caught him by surprise. He pitched forward, the bundle clasped to his chest, then, drawing up his legs, scrambled on to the mattress before Gandy could strike again.

'Sorry, Sergeant,' he said. 'I won't be so careless next time.'

'See you don't then,' Gandy said, nonplussed by Bloom's lack of reaction. Picking up the plate and tea mug, he went out of the cell and closed and bolted the door.

Bloom groaned, kneaded his backside and examined the bundle of clothing that Milly had fetched from home. He lifted the drawers and held them to his nose, smelling the fresh aroma of the wash upon them, a smell that Molly had loved. He could see her still, his drawers pressed to her nose as she inhaled, not his smell, of course, but the clean odour of soap suds. Then, he noticed the book. He let out a cry, snatched it up and thumbed frantically through its pages. He leapt to his feet and, gripping it by the spine, shook it so violently that the binding ripped.

Dropping the book, he hurled himself against the cell door and pounded on it with both fists.

'Gandy,' he roared. 'Machin. Get me a lawyer. Quick.'

PART TWO
The Lawyer

ELEVEN

Far and wide had Councillor Nannetti travelled in the company of Mr McCarthy, the City Architect, to study Anglo-Saxon methods of dealing with the dead. He had no interest in burial mounds, quaint country churchyards, sprawling urban cemeteries or newfangled crematoriums which were still, thank God, prohibited in Ireland. What Councillor Nannetti hoped to build, to Mr McCarthy's design, was a mortuary of which Dublin could be proud.

The site of the old city bakery and flour mill had fallen vacant. Here, according to the Councillor's way of thinking, was an ideal location not only for a mortuary but also for a coroner's courthouse. In no time at all, by Dublin standards, bakery and mill were gone and a dignified sandstone building had sprung up in their stead, conveniently close to Store Street police station. In fact, the cell in which Mr Bloom presently languished was separated from the place where his wife lay, though Bloom knew it not, only by a horse doctor's yard and short stretch of pavement.

Inspector Kinsella, together with the coroner, his deputy, a clerk, an anonymous medical officer and Miss Milly Bloom, entered the mortuary building in Store Street on a cloudy Monday morning a couple of hours before the courtroom opened its doors to jurymen, reporters and those members of the public who had queued since dawn to secure a seat in the gallery.

Miss Bloom had exchanged her redbreast coat and tam for a black tailored coat and skirt and a hat of similar material, worn without a veil. Whatever pretty penny it had cost Blazes for the outfit had been money well spent, Kinsella reckoned, and whoever – one of the sisters, perhaps – had dressed Milly's hair had done a grand job, for Miss Millicent Bloom, pale as a lily and hollow-eyed, was no longer a girl but a woman full-blown in her grief.

There was a brief but rancorous altercation with Mr Boylan who had expected that he too would be allowed to view the body of the deceased. Dr Slater was having none of it. It fell by default to Jim Kinsella to offer Milly his arm, which, rather to his surprise, she accepted without protest.

Tense but otherwise composed, Milly followed the official party along the echoing corridor and down a short flight of steps to the plate glass window beyond which, discreetly slotted in chilly pigeon-holes, the bodies of Dublin's dubious dead were filed.

Dr Slater, hatless for once, paused.

'Are you prepared, Miss Bloom?' he asked.

Resolute and mature, Milly answered, 'I am, but I've no intention of saying goodbye to my mother through a sheet of glass like she's an item in a shop window.'

'Fair point.' Dr Slater nodded to his deputy who knocked upon the window and signalled to the mortuary attendant to open the door and allow Miss Bloom, with Jim Kinsella at her side, to enter the mortuary proper.

It was all very cool and antiseptic in the gelid light from the skylight. Molly had been placed on her back, every part of her, save her head, covered by a spotless sheet. A saddle of polished wood raised her head at a slight angle, as if she were watching the door for her daughter's arrival.

Against the nether wall, a second draped table supported the body of a young man, identity unknown, who had been fished from the mouth of the Liffey only that morning. In a nook left of the door was a deep stone sink and a trolley bearing cutting instruments and coiled rubber tubes which, Kinsella thought, showed a degree of carelessness on someone's part, for mortuary and post-mortem room were, or should have been, chambers separate and distinct.

Milly tottered forward to the table and looked down on her mother's face. Clerk, medical officer, and mortuary attendant positioned themselves behind the table facing Miss Bloom while Dr Slater, his deputy, and Jim Kinsella stood by her side.

The post-mortem had been carried out by Dr Benson Rule, a qualified demonstrator in St John's teaching hospital and recently appointed pathologist to the County and City of Dublin. He would be summoned to appear in court later that morning to explain his findings to the jury.

Rule or his assistant had done a first-class job of repairing Molly's damaged features. The thin black lines of stitches were visible, of course, blemishing her beauty, but her eyeball had been replaced, nostril and lip sewn up and a pad of lint inserted in her cheek to fill out her sunken mouth. With eyelids closed and her long, dark lashes covering the worst of the scars she appeared almost serene.

'Miss Bloom,' said Slater gravely, 'is this your mother, Marion Tweedy Bloom?'

'It is,' Milly answered. 'My mother, yes.'

'There is no doubt in your mind?'

'No, of course not.'

'Have you seen enough, Miss Bloom?'

'A moment longer, if you please,' Milly said then leaned over and kissed the corpse on the brow. 'Mummy,' she whispered. 'Oh, Mummy, what have they done to you?' In tears, she let Jim Kinsella lead her away.

Mr Bloom had barely downed a last spoonful of lumpy porridge and still had flecks of oatmeal adhering to his moustache when the door thumped open and a young man in a narrow four-button morning coat, striped trousers and spats burst into the cell with glad-hand extended. Bloom's first inclination was to pass the lad his empty bowl but in spite of his flamboyant appearance there was about the stranger something that discouraged levity.

Glossy brown locks rimmed his collar and bounced softly when he dipped his head and invited Bloom to shake his hand. 'Bloom?' Before Mr Bloom could answer, he rattled on with his introduction. 'Neville Sullivan, partner in Tolland, Roper and Sullivan. I believe you have need of our services.'

Bloom put down the bowl, wiped his fingers on his trouser leg and shook the lawyer's hand.

'I'm not sure I can afford your services.'

'Um, yes, the matter of cost is always a concern.' Sullivan brought up a shiny new valise and propped it on the cot. 'I'm here only to offer advice, to ensure that your interests are protected in the coroner's court. No more, sir, no less and, for the time being at any rate, no fee.'

Bloom, still standing, said suspiciously. 'Who sent you?'

'Did you not ask for a solicitor?'

'Yes, on Friday.'

Mr Sullivan flipped the tail of his morning coat, seated himself on the bed, and reached for the valise. 'We are, relatively speaking, but piglets in the legal sty, Mr Bloom. It occurs to me, shamelessly mixing my metaphors, that Tolland, Roper and Sullivan may have been the last port of call or, to put it another way, the bottom of the hopper. Sit, do, please sit.'

Bloom lowered himself on to the bed beside the solicitor who, still talking, opened his valise and pulled out an accordion file.

'Superintendent Driscoll, I believe, cornered our senior partner, Mr Tolland, after church last evening and suggested we might assist in your defence. I have' – he let the file spill from his hands – 'barely had time to scan your statement and the list of witnesses the coroner intends to examine.'

'Are you sure Boylan didn't hire you?'

'Boylan? Great heavens, no. Now, about your statement . . .'

'Which one?' said Bloom.

'Oh!' Mr Sullivan paused. 'You made more than one statement to the police, did you?'

'Two.'

'How many did you sign?'

'One . . . the second one.'

'Um.' Mr Sullivan shook his chestnut locks again, a habit vain enough to be irritating. 'I don't have a copy of the original and, since it wasn't signed, the police are under no obligation to give me sight of it. Do you recall what you said in it?'

'I rambled a bit, I'm afraid. I wasn't quite myself.'

'Understandably,' Neville Sullivan said. 'Now, this intruder? You didn't actually *see* an intruder, did you, Mr Bloom?'

'No.'

'The existence of an intruder in your house is speculation on your part, is it not?'

'I was only gone out for twenty minutes.'

'Speculation,' Sullivan went on, 'upon which the police have singularly failed to act.'

'I didn't do it. I didn't murder my wife.'

'The police are convinced you did,' Sullivan said. 'So convinced, in fact, that they've ignored all other possibilities.

Now, it doesn't matter what I think. Indeed, if pressed, I'd be inclined to agree with the constabulary which' – another toss of the head – 'is why I'll do everything possible to keep you from being sent to trial.'

'You mean, you think I'm guilty?'

'There's no evidence to the contrary,' Mr Sullivan said. 'I mean, no evidence being offered to the contrary. The distinction is not as subtle as it may seem. Where, Mr Bloom, are your witnesses?'

'I have none.'

'You've the butcher, for a start, and this woman mentioned in police depositions – Mrs Hastings – whom you encountered in Eccles Street on the morning of the crime.'

'I'd forgotten about her.'

'Fortunately, she hasn't forgotten about you,' Sullivan said. 'The coroner, bless his heart, has seen fit to summon both the butcher and the woman to balance your account. Now, tell me, has anyone thought to inform you that you do not stand before a coroner's jury as a prisoner and no charge is preferred? No, I thought not. However, the magistrate, for reason beyond fathom, has passed the onus on to the coroner, possibly because he believes Dr Slater was presumptuous in issuing an arrest warrant in the first place.'

Neville Sullivan played another silent tune on the accordion file and bestowed on Mr Bloom a smile that while very white and pretty was not particularly reassuring.

'Let's be blunt, Bloom: this is a case of homicide,' he continued. 'It requires no medical expertise to deduce from the nature of her injuries that your wife was struck down by the hand of another. The coroner's jury will be expected to bring forth a verdict of wilful murder and the coroner will issue a fresh warrant committing you to be tried at the Assizes.' Another pause, a faint smile. 'However, the presentation of the written statement of the jury, if it contains the subject-matter of accusation, is equivalent to the finding of a grand jury and you, I'm afraid, may be tried upon it alone.'

'Then I'm as good as hanged,' said Bloom.

'Not for manslaughter.'

'I'm not clear on the difference,' said Bloom.

'Malice aforethought,' Mr Sullivan said. 'In other words, was the violent act committed on an irrational impulse or planned in advance of commission? The line betwixt the two can be exceeding fine. Lacking witnesses, the decision usually hangs upon the credibility of the accused. Incidentally, any statement you choose to make in the coroner's court will not be under oath.'

'Are the witnesses examined under oath?'

Young Mr Sullivan, who had been whistling through his guide-lines more or less by rote, stared at Mr Bloom as if he, Mr Bloom that is, had suddenly grown horns. 'Why do you ask?'

'Is Boylan . . . Hugh Boylan on the list of witnesses?'

'I don't believe he is.' Sullivan scanned a sheet of paper attached to a more formal-looking document. 'The name doesn't appear anywhere.' He stared at Bloom again. 'Does this man have something against you?'

'No, but I have something against him,' said Bloom.

'And what might that be?'

'He's stealing away my daughter just as he stole . . .' Bloom bit off the tail of the sentence. 'What, Mr Sullivan, can you do to ensure I'm released on bail?'

Sullivan hesitated. 'If the jury are unconvinced by the facts put before them they may find there is no case to answer and it would be left to the coroner to dismiss you or, on his own judgement, hand you up for trial at the assizes. In the latter event the granting of bail would be a formality.'

'What if I were to admit to manslaughter?'

'What are you saying, Mr Bloom?'

'Would I be released on bail before sentencing?'

'No, you would not.'

Bloom frowned. 'I'm afraid I don't understand the mechanics of the law.'

Neville Sullivan let out his breath and punished a curl that threatened the integrity of his brow. He studied Bloom for a moment longer, slapped his knee and jumped to his feet. 'Fortunately for you, Mr Bloom, I do,' he said. 'Now, have you fresh linen and brushes for your suit and shoes?'

'Yes, I have.'

'Good, I'll send someone along with hot water, a razor and

soap. In court you must appear to be just what you are, sir: a thoroughly respectable gentleman.'

Bloom rose and shook the lawyer's hand.

'Thank you for your advice. I have sore need of it, it seems.'

'That you do, Mr Bloom,' said young Mr Sullivan. 'That you do,' then hurried out of the cell and loped off down the corridor like a hound on the scent of a hare.

Roland Slater had served his time conducting inquests in draughty halls and the odorous back rooms of public houses, places where the respect due to a coroner and the traditions of a court that could trace its history back to Edward I was scant to nonexistent. He was eternally grateful to Councillor Nannetti for providing him with a courthouse that befitted the dignity of the office and had promised the Councillor that if he, Joseph P. Nannetti, ever decided to run for mayor of Dublin, he, Roland Slater, would be right behind him.

Slater was no vinegary bachelor creeping home at night to a cold supper and a colder bed. He had a plump, jovial wife and two married sons who were as fond of music and gossip as he was, plus six tuneful grandchildren and another little minim on the way.

In all aspects of life, Dr Slater was a happy man, though, it must be said, never happier than when poring over the multitude of forms that attached themselves to the office of coroner and happiest of all when he took his seat in the big green-leather chair and heard Mr Rice, his court officer, proclaim, 'Oyez, Oyez, Oyez,' to set the inquisitorial ball rolling.

Seated on the coroner's right were fifteen jurymen, good and true, in a raked box two rows deep. Below them, facing the not-too-lofty witness box, was the coroner's clerk, Mr Devereux. To Slater's left was a long table for counsellors, solicitors and the parties they represented and, directly in his line of sight, benches for the press, the court officer and officers of the Dublin Metropolitan Police. Last, and most definitely least in Roland Slater's view, up there, facing him, was a gallery for friends and relatives of the deceased and, of, course, the usual curious representatives of the great unwashed.

The elected foreman of the jury, George Conway, a bookbinder by trade and formidably well read, was fully aware of both the law and his rights. If Dr Slater thought for one moment that the jury would agree to be palmed off with photographs of the handsomest corpse ever to grace the Store Street mortuary he had another think coming.

After the calling of the jurors and a lengthy swearing in, Mr Conway gathered his flock and waited patiently for Mr Rice to lead them off to view Mrs Bloom's remains through the mortuary's plate glass window. If any juryman was roused by the sight of the woman's voluptuous body naked beneath a sheet he kept his feelings to himself as the procession wended down the narrow corridor and, in due course, filed back into the courtroom.

In the interval, Dr Slater seized the opportunity to remind the gentlemen of the Press that they were forbidden to publish anything about the inquest until after a verdict had been reached and that he, backed by the full weight and majesty of the law, would be down on them like a ton of bricks if they did.

Tom Machin leaned into Kinsella and murmured, 'Slater loves all this blarney, you know. Look at him, puffed up like a toad.'

'He's only doing his job,' Kinsella said. 'Give the beggar his due, Tom, he does keep everyone in order. What do you make of Bloom's choice of legal council?'

'Young Sullivan? He wasn't Bloom's choice. Driscoll took it upon himself to dig up an advocate on Bloom's behalf.'

'He looks like a boy,' Kinsella said.

'He is a boy,' Tom Machin said. 'He's the most junior of junior partners in Tolland's firm and this is his first criminal case.'

'Is that the best Driscoll could do?'

'Better a young warhorse snorting for recognition than some tired old nag who's only interested in filling his feedbag. However, yes, he's the best Driscoll could find on short notice.'

'Bloom's certainly getting his moneys worth by the look of it. Sullivan hasn't stopped talking since they sat down.'

'Instructing his client, I believe it's called,' Machin said and, with the coroner giving him stern looks, folded his arms and sat back.

TWELVE

'What,' Slater began, 'is your name?'

'Leopold Bloom.'

'Where do you live?'

'7 Eccles Street, Dublin.'

'What is your occupation?'

'I am employed by the *Freeman's Journal* to sell advertising.'

'Have you seen the body that the jury have viewed?'

'I have.'

'Do you recognise the deceased woman?'

'I did. I mean, I do.'

'What was her full name?'

'Marion Tweedy Bloom.'

Roland Slater had been through this rigmarole a thousand times. He had the pace off pat, deliberate enough to allow the clerk to record every word but not so studied as to irritate the jury. Neither threat nor tedium evident in his tone, he addressed the witness in a manner more avuncular than theatrical.

'What relation was the woman to you?'

'She was my wife.'

'Where did she live?'

'With me in 7 Eccles Street.'

'Did she have an occupation?'

'She sang professionally from time to time but had no regular employment other than that of housewife.'

Whether following Sullivan's advice or his own inclination to be infernally polite, Bloom answered with just the right note of deference. He fixed his gaze not on the coroner or the jury but on the nib of the recorder's pen as if to watch the story of his life being written under his nose.

'And your wife's age?'

'Thirty-four last birthday.'

'What would you say was the general state of her health?'

'Very good. Excellent, really.'

'Mr Bloom, when did you last see your wife alive?'

'About half past seven on the morning of 9th March.'

'Can you be more precise?'

'She was still in bed, still asleep.'

'I mean,' Slater said, 'as to time.'

'I left the house about . . . I returned about ten minutes to eight. No, that's right, if not to the minute: half past seven.'

'She was in bed and asleep when you left the house?'

'She was.'

'You left the house for what purpose?'

'To buy meat at Dlugacz shop in Dorset Street.'

'When did you return to number 7 Eccles Street?'

'At ten minutes to eight.'

'And what, Mr Bloom, did you find?'

'I found her . . . found my wife dead in bed.'

'How can you be sure she was dead?'

'She wasn't breathing.'

In the rear of the gallery some fool tittered. Dr Slater hoisted himself up by his arms and, half standing, glared at the culprit. With evidence regarding the instrument of death – a teapot – looming, the warning that he would brook no levity in his court was timely. He lowered himself slowly back into his chair and continued. 'How could you be sure that your wife wasn't breathing, Mr Bloom?'

'Because she was lying out of the bed with her face bashed in.' No hint of laughter now just a general in-suck of breath, a sound as sibilant as sand blowing across a dune.

'What did you do then?'

'I ran out into the street and called for help.'

'And was help forthcoming?'

'A constable came running round the corner. I took him into the house and showed him . . .' Eyes still fixed on the recorder's pen, Bloom paused. 'I showed him the body.'

'Very well, Mr Bloom. One final question for now. Was the body of the woman discovered in the bedroom of number 7 Eccles Street that of your wife, Mrs Marion Tweedy Bloom?'

Bloom lifted his head and flicked a single glance up at the

gallery before meeting the coroner's eye. 'It was, sir. Yes, it was.'

'Thank you, Mr Bloom. You may . . .'

George Conway, jury foreman, was on his feet immediately. 'Coroner Slater, we have questions for this witness.'

'I'm sure you do, Mr Conway, and you'll have ample opportunity to put them, just not at this sitting. The primary purpose of the session is to establish the identity of the deceased and cause of death. Mr Bloom's statement will be read to you later. Any questions the jury may have will be answered then. To eliminate all possibility of error or deceit in the matter of identification,' Slater went on, 'the deceased's daughter, Miss Millicent Bloom, viewed the body before witnesses this morning. Miss Bloom is in court and may be brought forward without subpoena, but not under oath, if you require it. Miss Bloom has been resident in Mullingar for the best part of a year and hadn't seen her mother since Christmastide. I would respectfully suggest that the young woman is unlikely to contribute anything material to our inquiry. Do you wish me to bring Miss Bloom before you, Mr Conway?'

'No, sir, we do not.'

'Very well,' Slater said. 'Stand down, Mr Bloom.'

Kinsella watched the anguished husband descend from the witness box and, groping a little, seat himself at the table beside his solicitor. Sullivan laid a hand on Bloom's shoulder but whether the gesture was one of congratulation or commiseration was difficult to determine.

'Mr Rice,' said Slater, 'summon the next witness, if you please.'

'Who is it, Jim?' Machin whispered.

'The pathologist, Benson Rule.'

'Ah! Now we're beginning to get somewhere.'

'At long last,' said Jim.

Benson Rule was a small man in his late twenties, clean-shaven and lean-cheeked. His brow was creased by a brooding frown that seemed fitting for a gentleman who whittled away at corpses for a living. He stood ram-rod straight, chin up, glanced down only occasionally at his notes and arranged each page with hands so tiny that they were almost swallowed up by his cuffs. He repeated the oath in a light, crisp baritone, stated his name and credentials and, without further preamble, plunged in.

'On the morning of March 10th I made a post mortem examination of the body of the deceased in the presence of Mr Thomas McGurk, mortuary attendant, and Stephen Flaherty, student of medicine at St John's Hospital, who acted as my assistant. The body was that of a mature, well-built and well-nourished woman in her early thirties. Muscles and organs had passed through the rigor stage and were relaxed. The process of decomposition, though slight, had already commenced. I would say that she had been dead for upwards of thirty hours but I can be no more accurate than that.'

Kinsella looked up at the gallery, at Milly Bloom. She was slumped over, only the crown of her hat showing. Boylan, stooped too, talked to her in whispers. Behind Milly, a row back, two men, one in his fifties the other considerably younger, also appeared to be concerned about the young woman's welfare, the elder even going so far as to offer a handkerchief.

Bloom, by contrast, remained impassive, as engrossed in Rule's grisly report as if he were listening to a lecture on Schopenhauer or the canals of Mars.

The woman's limbs and torso, Benson Rule explained, were unmarked, her injuries confined to jaw, mouth, nasal passage and eye socket. Central incisor and lateral incisor were broken, the left canine tooth loosened from the gum. The left nostril was torn. Coagulated blood was present in the nasal passage and glottis but there was no rupturing, bleeding or bruising of the larynx. Fragments of china were extracted from the gum of the upper jaw and the lining of the cheek, indicative, Rule said, of a blow to the mouth with a heavy object.

Here Slater saw fit to interrupt. 'In your opinion, Dr Rule, were the injuries to the mouth severe enough to cause death?'

A curt and unequivocal, 'No.'

'Now, the heavy object: what, in your opinion, would constitute a heavy object? An iron bar, say?'

'Not a solid object but one prone to shatter on impact.'

'Like a bottle or a vase?' Slater hesitated, took in a breath, and added, 'Or, let us say, a china teapot?'

'A large china teapot, yes.'

No one in the courtroom uttered a sound.

Slater said, 'A large china teapot similar in shape and size to the pieces found by the woman's bed?'

'Yes.'

'May I take it, Dr Rule, that the fragments embedded in the victim's mouth matched the pieces of teapot found at the scene?'

'They did.'

'For the record, would it be fact, not opinion, to state that a large china teapot was the weapon used to deliver the fatal blow?'

'It would.'

Slater sat back in the green-leather chair with the relieved air of a man who has just missed stepping in dog dirt.

In the gallery Milly Bloom's face reappeared, mouth open, thumb resting against her teeth. At the solicitors' table Bloom moved not a muscle while an officer of the court, on cue, brought out a canvas evidence bag, opened it with great care and displayed first to Benson Rule and then to the men of the jury two broken pieces of floral china, one with a handle, the other a spout.

'Would you say, Dr Rule,' Slater pressed, 'that these are pieces of the very weapon with which Mrs Bloom was killed?'

'I would.'

'Have you examined them?'

'I have.'

'Your findings, please?'

'I found distinct traces of blood on each of the pieces.'

'The victim's blood?'

'I believe it to be so.'

Mr Rice, the court officer, placed the canvas bag upon the solicitors' table and laid gently the two pieces of teapot upon it. Mr Bloom, motionless save for a lazy roll of the eyeballs, surveyed the jagged objects with no sign of revulsion, barely of interest.

'Now,' Slater went on, 'if the blow to the mouth was not the cause of death, Dr Rule, what was?'

'The blow' – Rule lifted his right arm, closed his fist and fashioned a stabbing thrust from which the jurymen and even some folk in the gallery instinctively recoiled – 'to the eye.'

'The blow,' Slater said, 'to the eye?'

'That is correct.'

'In your opinion, Dr Rule, was this a single blow or one of a series of blows?'

'Based upon my observations, the likelihood is that it was a single blow, that the weapon, the teapot, shattered on first impact – the blow to the mouth – which formed a sharp edge. The penetrative wound to the eye socket – the orbit – was certainly not caused by blunt force.' The doctor glanced at his notes. 'I may say with a degree of certainty that no more than two blows were struck *in toto*.'

'On what is that judgement based?'

'The absence of attendant bruising or laceration in the region of the face and neck. I would say two blows, the first delivered in a swinging arc with the teapot intact: thus.' He demonstrated with a sudden swish of the arm that, once more, had the jury flinching. 'Followed at once by a thrust with the broken pot which now had a sharp penetrative protrusion.'

'Do you have other evidence for this assumption, Dr Rule?'

'I do. There were no bruises or lacerations on the victim's hands, wrists or forearms which strongly suggests that she did not have time to defend herself and that the first blow was unexpected and the second blow, the fatal one, followed instantly.'

The coroner looked at the jury with a faint, patronising smile. 'A roundhouse right followed up by a jab?'

'In a manner of speaking,' Dr Rule said, agreeing, though the deepening of the furrow that cleft his brow indicated that he did not approve of sporting analogies. 'The damage was entirely to the left side of the victim's face which would suggest that the attack was conducted from a position in front of the victim with the pot held in the right hand.'

'An attack from the rear would not be feasible,' Slater pointed out, 'given that the woman was in bed when the assault took place and the bed was fast against the wall.'

'I have not seen the room, so I cannot say,' said Dr Rule.

'Nor have we,' Mr Conway announced.

'Oh!' the coroner exclaimed. 'Don't tell me . . . I mean, do the jury wish to see the room?'

The jury nodded.

'Very well,' the coroner said, stifling a sigh. 'I will see to it that the jury are conducted to number 7 Eccles Street under police supervision first thing after recess. Will that be satisfactory?'

The jury, with some enthusiasm, nodded again.

'Now, Dr Rule,' the coroner said, 'will you please continue.'

For the next ten minutes the courtroom was treated to what amounted to a lesson in the structures of the human skull, orbit, frontal bone, lachrymal ducts, ophthalmic artery and all. Rule's depiction of the detached eyeball hanging by a thread, followed by a lengthy dissertation on ganglia, muscles and nerves, was in danger of becoming dreary until, once more, he demonstrated just how the eyeball could be plucked out by a motion akin to that of scooping a soft-boiled egg from its shell, a gruesome mime that had several ladies in the gallery reaching for their smelling salts and some of the jurymen swallowing hard.

It was during this latter charade that Neville Sullivan raised his hand to catch the coroner's attention.

The coroner frowned. 'Mr Sullivan?'

'May I ask a question of the witness?'

'You do know that you are not allowed to cross-examine?'

'I do, sir,' Neville Sullivan said. 'However, I have a question that is pertinent and to which, I'm sure, the jury would appreciate an answer.'

'What is your question?'

Neville Sullivan left the solicitors' table and took up a position below the witness box. Looking up at Dr Rule, he said, 'Did the blow that penetrated the eye socket cause injury to the brain?'

Benson Rule considered his reply. 'No, sir, it did not.'

'No bruising to the lobes of the pre-frontal area, no discolouration; nothing of that nature?'

'None that I found.'

'Intracranial swelling, perhaps?'

'Mr Sullivan,' the coroner warned.

Again Benson Rule hesitated. 'No, none.'

'I take it that the brain was excised?'

'Now that is enough, Mr Sullivan,' the coroner snapped.

Mr Sullivan bowed to the expert witness and sat down again. He exchanged a glance with his client, tidied his hair and missed the superior little smile that played at the corner of Rule's lips.

'Dr Rule,' the coroner said, 'pray continue.'

'On proceeding to an examination of the victim's reproductive parts' – a phrase guaranteed to take the jury's mind off brains – 'I found no evidence of recent intercourse. However, the condition of the vagina and cervix prompted me to open the pelvic cavity and examine the uterus.'

Sullivan swung round, first to Bloom and then to glare at the doctor in the box above him.

'At ten weeks an embryo is generally recognised as having evolved into a foetus,' Benson Rule said.

'Sweet Jesus!' Tom Machin murmured.

'A foetus, so formed, was found in the victim's womb. It was, as far as I can tell, healthy, though, of course, no longer a living thing.'

The cry from the gallery was audible throughout the courtroom but the coroner, swiftly identifying its source, offered no reprimand and, in the pin-drop silence, Milly Bloom's unchecked sobs rang out with heartbreaking clarity.

'Are you saying the woman was pregnant?' the coroner asked.

'Without doubt,' Benson Rule answered. 'Close to the end of the first trimester, ten or eleven weeks along.'

'Christmas?' Tom Machin whispered.

'Early December,' Kinsella whispered back.

'Do you think Bloom knew?'

'Of course Bloom knew. The question is, did Boylan?' Kinsella said just as the coroner fished a watch from his pocket and declared, 'Gentlemen, time for a break, I think. We will adjourn for thirty minutes after which the jury will assemble here to be conducted to Eccles Street.'

'By cab?' said Mr Conway.

'On foot,' said Dr Slater.

THIRTEEN

Dr Michael Paterson wasn't particularly tall or muscular and had none of the not-quite-feminine good looks of young Neville Sullivan. He had a blunt chin, thin upper lip and eyes of an indeterminate shade of grey. He was a quiet man, a listener not a talker, and no competition for the voluble rabble who gathered about Miss Bloom in the hall of the coroner's court.

This irksome swarm included not only Hugh Boylan but also Malachi Mulligan, Alec Bannon and Kitty Laughlin's middle brother, Finn. As cocky sober as they were in their cups, they offered Milly their condolences with all the heartfelt sincerity of Republicans saluting the Union flag.

'Who the devil are they?' Harry Coghlan asked.

Michael Paterson shrugged. 'Students, probably.'

'What're they after?'

'Miss Bloom's virginity, I imagine,' Michael Paterson said. 'For all their idealistic chatter about art and aesthetics, they don't really have much on their minds but drink and fornication.'

'Was it that way in your day, too?' Mr Coghlan asked.

'Not so much of the "my day," please. I don't have one foot in the grave just yet, in spite of practising in Mullingar.'

They leaned against the wall close to the ornate faux bronze fitment that contained not holy water but cigar butts and tobacco ash and watched Milly Bloom struggling to cope with her admirers.

Mourning garb didn't suit her, though it certainly made her more grown up, Michael Paterson thought. In his professional capacity he'd watched her blush and fumble for euphemisms to describe the discomfort that nature foisted monthly upon females. He had provided advice as well as a herbal tincture to soothe Milly's cramps. He'd met her thereafter at summer galas and church soirees and had seen her blossom into a lovely, carefree young woman. It saddened him to see her now, flattened by life's ugly realities and robbed of much of her innocence.

'Milly didn't have an inkling about her mother's pregnancy, you know,' Harry Coghlan said. 'If she did, I'm sure she'd have let something slip, if not to me then to Mrs C. What a time the poor lass is having of it. One thing after another. I wonder if she'll ever come back to Mullingar?'

Not if Boylan has anything to do with it, but Dr Paterson kept this thought to himself. It hadn't taken him long to see through Boylan's unfettered arrogance, the self-serving confidence that came with a bit of money and the admiration of shallow men and women. Boylan was no longer all that young, however, and, possessively rather than protectively, was doing his best to keep the antlered herd at bay.

'I rather regret we made the trip,' Harry Coghlan said. 'I thought Milly might need our support but it appears she has her own crowd here in Dublin.'

'I'm not too sure it is her crowd,' Michael Paterson said.

'At least she's being well looked after by that Boylan chap,' Mr Coghlan said. 'I suppose if her father does go to jail she'll stay on with Boylan and his sisters.'

Dr Paterson kept his thoughts on that matter to himself too. He said, 'If the jury's being carried off to inspect the scene of the crime we might have time to slip out for a bite to eat.'

'I'm not averse to that,' Harry Coghlan answered but before the pair could move towards the door, Milly caught sight of them and, pushing through the crowd, scurried across the hall.

Dr Paterson removed his hat. 'Miss Bloom.'

Mr Coghlan, hatless too, said, 'How are you bearing up, lass?'

Milly said, 'As well as can be expected, I suppose. It's awfully nice of you both to come all this way for me.'

'I hope you don't think we're snooping?' Mr Coghlan said. 'It was Mrs C's idea, really. When I said I'd shut up the shop for a day Michael kindly offered to accompany me.'

'I'm glad to see you, so glad to see you.' Milly glanced over her shoulder. 'Blazes – Mr Boylan – has been very kind, but the others . . . I can't think what they're doing here unless, as you say, it is just snooping.' She put a gloved hand on Harry Coghlan's arm. 'I don't mean to imply . . .'

'Of course, you don't.' Mr Coghlan gently patted her hand. 'I want you to know, Milly, there will always be a place for you in Mullingar and we all look forward to having you back.'

Milly began to cry.

Mr Coghlan said, 'I'm sorry. I didn't mean to upset you.'

'It's only me being silly again,' said Milly and to show there were no ill feelings, far from it, went up on tiptoe and kissed his cheek as Hugh Boylan advanced from one direction and Inspector Kinsella from another.

'We meet again,' Blazes said.

'It seems we do,' said Michael Paterson.

There was no offer of a handshake.

'Just up for the day?' Blazes asked.

'To see our girl,' Harry Coghlan answered.

'Your girl?' said Blazes, frowning.

'My employee,' said Harry. 'I mean, my employee.'

Before Mr Coghlan could dig another hole for himself Inspector Kinsella stepped up to the little circle and Milly introduced him to her friends from Mullingar.

Inspector Kinsella said he was pleased to see Miss Bloom had made new friends in Mullingar. Mr Boylan said he and her old friends from Dublin were about to spirit her off for a spot of lunch in the Belvidere, if time permitted. Inspector Kinsella said he'd arranged for Miss Bloom to meet privately with her father in the office of the clerk of court.

Milly promptly said goodbye.

For a second or two after her departure the men did not speak. There was more animosity than awkwardness in the silence for it was clear that Mr Boylan cared no more for Dr Paterson than Dr Paterson cared for him.

'Lunch?' Mr Coghlan at length suggested. 'Perhaps you can recommend some place nearby, Mr Boylan?'

'No, I can't,' said Blazes curtly and, turning on his heel, went off to join the young men who, hooting at some filthy witticism, were already heading for the door.

Neville Sullivan had a sweetheart. Like it or lump it, he was stuck with Alfred Tolland's daughter, the price he'd had to pay for a junior partnership. Engagement was in the offing and marriage inevitable but, if you put a gun to his head, young Neville would admit that he didn't really mind being cornered. Sarah Tolland, three years his senior, was quite a beauty and by no means lacking in brains and he, in spite of his airs, graces and splendid head of hair was merely the son of a humble Inspector of Schools from County Fermanagh.

The first thing that struck him about Bloom's daughter was how mature she seemed, aided, no doubt, by the stiff, tailored bombazine that emphasized her bust. Her cheeks were flushed and her eyes more starey than starry, in spite of which he experienced an unexpected chug of desire when she first entered the room. She paid him such scant attention, however, that his ardour quickly cooled and he stepped hastily to one side to let her embrace her father.

The embrace was oddly restrained, as if they were distant cousins who hadn't seen each other in years. They kept the table between them, Bloom leaning over it, the girl meeting him half way; a brusque kiss to the brow, a one-armed hug, and Bloom sat down again. Neville Sullivan leapt to draw out a chair for the girl but Kinsella beat him to it. He watched Miss Bloom tuck her rustling skirts around her bottom and carefully sit down.

Bloom said, 'Where did you get that dress?'

Milly said, 'Don't you like it?'

Bloom said, 'Did Boylan pay for it?'

'What if he did?'

'I don't want you taking things from Hugh Boylan, Milly.'

'Why not?'

Bloom said, 'You're too young to be taking things from men.'

Milly said, 'Mr Boylan isn't any man. He was Mummy's friend. Who else is going to take care of me? You? You couldn't even take care of Mummy.'

Oh, my! Neville Sullivan thought, it's dawned on her at last that her father's tale of an intruder is bunkum and he might actually be guilty. He slid a pace to his right and brought both Bloom and the girl into clear view. Bloom's jet-black hair sprayed across his forehead almost covering one eye and, with lips pursed, his moustache seemed about to disappear up his nostrils. His sullen dark eyes glittered not with tears but with anger. He offered his daughter no reprimand, no rebuttal.

Milly went on, 'Why didn't you tell me?' Fists on the chair back, Kinsella inclined forward, eager to catch Bloom's reply. Bloom said nothing. 'You *must* have known, Papli. Surely you must have known about the baby.'

'Papli' was an unusual endearment, Neville Sullivan thought. Why not Pappy or even Poppy; Sarah Tolland called her father Poppy, however inapt. He'd heard that Bloom's father had hailed from Hungary and wondered if Papli was Hungarian for father, or if it was Yiddish or, more likely, a contraction held over from childhood.

'Another Rudy,' Milly went on. 'Another Rudy, and you said

not a word. Did you think I'd object to having a brother or a sister now I'm grown up?'

Bloom said, 'You're staying with him, aren't you?'

'Yes, I am. Don't fret yourself, his sisters are there too.'

'Daphne and Maude?'

'Oh?' said Milly, a little taken aback. 'Do you know them?'

Bloom's cheek twitched, almost a smile. 'Many years ago. The Reckless Rechabites. Nothing reckless about them now, I imagine. Where's Boylan?'

'Outside.'

Bloom glanced up at the Inspector. 'May I speak with him?'

'No,' Kinsella said.

'Not even a word?'

'Not even a word.'

To Milly, Bloom said, 'What's he been telling you about me?'

'He says he's going to get you out of here by hook or by crook.'

'Is that what he says? Well, I don't doubt he means it.' Bloom looked up again. 'I thought someone mentioned tea?'

'I believe it's on its way,' Kinsella said.

'See if you can hurry it along, please,' Bloom said. 'And take Mr Sullivan with you.'

'I don't think that's allow—' Neville Sullivan began.

Kinsella interrupted him. 'You want a little time alone with your daughter, Bloom, is that it?'

'What do you say, Inspector? Five minutes?' The crinkled half smile again: 'I'm not going to bolt.'

'You wouldn't get far if you did,' Kinsella reminded him, then, taking Neville Sullivan by the arm, led the lawyer out of the office and left Bloom to appease his huffy daughter as best he could.

Up in the gallery they were eating sandwiches and drinking soda pop from sticky brown bottles. The din floating down from above was deafening. The consumption of alcohol was forbidden, court officers were strict on that point, which didn't, of course, prevent some wily boozers nipping from hip flasks and quarter bottles.

The hall below had emptied a little but the stairs were crowded with examples of Slater's great unwashed, some sitting, some standing, almost all smoking, the air thick with tobacco smoke and countless variations of rich Irish brogue.

If she hadn't been so tall – and alone – Kinsella wouldn't have given her a second glance. He had more to occupy him than ogling girls, especially ten-for-a-penny not quite working girls in from the suburbs for the show. She *was* striking, though, not just because of her height, curly black hair and full lips. Something in her pose gave him pause: confident and just a little insolent, shoulders resting against the wall at the bend of the stairs, looking down her nose at him. When he hesitated, drawing Sullivan up by the elbow, she turned her face away, hiding it with one long-fingered hand as if she were playing peek-a-boo which, Kinsella thought, was patently ridiculous.

He moved quickly on, steering the lawyer along the corridor into the all-but deserted courtroom.

Slater, his deputy and clerk were closeted in the coroner's office, fortifying themselves with a lunchtime snack. Tom Machin had hastened off to find a police van for the jury's trip to Eccles Street for it was the DMP's responsibility to ensure no juryman was 'lost' during the excursion and the route from Store Street passed too many pubs to take any chances.

Once inside the courtroom, Kinsella released Sullivan's arm. 'I require a private word with you, counsellor.'

'Is that all?' Neville Sullivan said. 'Thank God. I thought I was being arrested. Speaking of which, you're taking a frightful risk leaving Bloom without a police guard. He may not be presented as the accused but he's still in custody.'

'On suspicion,' Kinsella said.

'Suspicion my backside,' Sullivan said. 'You've nothing worth snuff to charge him with. Your case is circumstantial, all circumstantial. You haven't one shred of evidence to prove Bloom did anything wrong.'

'And you haven't a shred of evidence to prove he didn't.'

'Impasse is not a word you'll find in any book of law. Besides, I'll have him out on bail on a writ of *habeas corpus* in a trice.'

'I'd prefer it if you didn't,' Kinsella said. 'I've lost felons who were as guilty as sin to lawyer's writs before now.'

'So you think Bloom's guilty, do you?'

'In fact, no, I don't. I think he's shielding someone.'

'Shielding someone?' Neville Sullivan said. 'Um, yes, now that might explain why the stubborn fellow won't plead to manslaughter.'

'There's no other suspect,' Kinsella said. 'If you don't offer a reduced plea on the back of a confession, the best you can hope for is a fresh warrant handing him up for trial at the April assizes.'

'What are you driving at?'

'If Bloom didn't do it, as he claims, then someone else did,' Kinsella said. 'My guess is that Bloom knows who that someone is, and I would very much like to find out.'

'Wouldn't we all,' said Sullivan. 'Go on, do.'

'Slater's no fool. He knows perfectly well the case against Bloom is creaky and he won't let it go as it stands. For reasons of pride, mainly, he wants to send Bloom to the assizes with a noose round his neck. Yes, I know: whatever happens Bloom won't hang, but one week in jail compared to a life stretch is not to be sneezed at.'

'A week?'

'I'm asking Slater for an adjournment.'

'The devil you are!'

'This is your first criminal case, is it not?'

'What if it is?' Sullivan said.

'In High Court circumstantial evidence carries a great deal more weight than it does here,' Kinsella said. 'I have witnesses not on Slater's list who'll testify that Bloom had motive as well as opportunity, a motive strong enough to lead to a murder conviction.'

'You're bluffing.'

'One pregnant wife with a lover?' Kinsella said.

'She had a lover?'

'See what I mean, Mr Sullivan. If you think I'm bluffing about the weight a High Court jury will give to motive then I suggest you ask your mentor, Mr Tolland. God knows, he's sent enough men to the clink on the strength of not much more than rumour.'

Sullivan cocked his head. 'What *do* you want, Inspector?'

Kinsella held up a forefinger. 'One week's adjournment, which I'm certain Slater will concede. One week's adjournment without resistance from you and with Bloom still in custody.'

'Bloom will never accept. He's keening for bail.'

'In which case, all he has to do is tell me whom he's protecting or plead to manslaughter and take his chances at the assizes. One uncomfortable week in Kilmainham in exchange for a chance to walk out of that door a free man in seven days' time, that's my offer.'

'You can't guarantee a dismissal.'

'No, I can't,' Kinsella admitted. 'I can't even be sure I won't unearth proof that Bloom committed the crime. I am, however, acting on the premise that he didn't.'

'Um,' Sullivan said. 'I need a little more than that, sir.'

'I have a lead, several leads.'

'Will you tell me what they are?'

Kinsella shook his head.

Sullivan said, 'Do they involve the lover?'

'They may do.'

'And I thought Alfred Tolland played things close to the chest,' Sullivan said. 'Still, I suppose secrecy comes as second nature to the men of the detective division. Well, I'm prepared to trust you, Inspector, but, frankly, I doubt if my client will.'

'Then it's up to you to convince him.'

'All right,' Neville Sullivan said. 'One week.'

'One week is all I need. Believe me, it'll be better for all concerned if this case goes no further than the coroner's court.'

'Do you think I'm incapable of steering Bloom's defence before a bench of High Court judges? Is that it?'

Kinsella grinned. 'In a nutshell, Mr Sullivan.'

Neville Sullivan saw the joke. He laughed. 'Do you suppose I'm capable of finding someone to fetch my client a dish of tea?'

'I do hope so,' Kinsella said. 'And one for the little girl too.'

'The little girl?'

'Miss Bloom.'

'Oh, yes, of course,' said Neville Sullivan. 'Listening to your pappy denying that he murdered your mother must be thirsty work. Where's the kitchen in this warren?'

'I honestly have no idea.'

'Some detective you are,' Neville Sullivan said and, with a toss of his handsome head, went off to find an officer to fetch the Blooms some tea.

FOURTEEN

Pussens had wisely abandoned No 7 and had taken up residence next door. She sat now in the ground-floor window on a ledge shared with a shabby castor oil plant and watched impassively as Sergeant Gandy and two constables herded fifteen good, grumbling men and true from the back of a horse-drawn van, lined them up on the pavement and attempted to call the roll. She, the cat, had no inclination to leave her cosy perch for a chilly pavement and, recognising no friendly faces in the crowd, just an array of heavy, tail-nipping boots, soon lost interest and, with a yawn, stretched out under the drooping leaves of the castor oil plant and fell asleep.

Sleep was the last thing on Sergeant Gandy's mind. He was furious at being handed an additional duty, his temper frayed by snivelling jurymen who, to hear them clatter on, had been treated worse than cattle and were sore and hungry after a journey that had lasted all of ten minutes.

Deprived of lunch, a stealthy pint or two and an opportunity to sell 'inside' information, most of it fabricated, to a bunch of gullible journalists, Sergeant Gandy was in no mood to cosset his charges.

In a voice rasping enough to strip lichen from a rock, he shouted out the names of the jurors while the constables arranged the men into groups on the step of the so-called house of death to await the arrival of Inspector Machin, who had elected not to share the over-crowded police van but, as befitted a person of his rank, travel by tram instead.

'Lyons?'

'I'm here.'

'Tarpey?'

'I thought we was bein' fed first.'

'No, Mr Tarpey, you're not being fed,' said Gandy. 'You're here to view the crime scene and you've only yourselves to blame. Gregory? Mathew Gregory?'

'Sah.' Gregory answered with a sarcastic salute that added fuel to the sergeant's smouldering temper. 'Where do you wish me to put meself?'

'Over there, out of my way,' snarled Gandy. 'MacDougall?' Answer came there none. 'MacDougall? Where the devil's MacDougall?'

Any sort of street theatre inevitably drew a crowd and the arrival of a police van outside the Blooms' house was no exception. Twenty or so citizens heard the whiskered sergeant shout, 'MacDougall, you bugger, will you answer your bloody name?'

Johnny MacDougall, a meek little chap, had toddled off to find a place to empty his bladder. He appeared, unabashed, from the steps that led down to the Blooms' cellar door still fumbling with the buttons of his fly.

'Now did I hear you callin', Sergeant?'

Gandy's nostrils flared. He bit his lip and in a menacing tone enquired, 'Are you John MacDougall?'

'The same.'

'Then, Mr MacDougall,' the sergeant seethed, 'will you kindly get your arse over there before I kick it for you?'

'All in order, Sergeant Gandy?' Tom Machin breached the ring of spectators in the nick of time. 'No trouble, I trust?'

'Winding up the roll call, sir,' Sergeant Gandy replied while behind his back the jury smartly reassembled itself into three groups of five without any help from the constables.

'Good, very good,' Tom Machin said. 'Now if you'll just unlock the door, Sergeant, we'll get on with it.'

'I ha'n't got a key, sir.' The sergeant patted his pockets with big red-knuckled hands. 'Haven't you?'

'No, I have not.'

'You must have, sir.'

'I tell you I haven't.'

Quick to sense confusion, the jury muttered and shuffled.

Foreman Conway asked, 'Is there a problem, officer?'

'No, damn you, there's no problem,' Sergeant Gandy shouted and, tossing jurymen right and left, surged up to Bloom's front door and, grabbing the handle in both fists, wrenched and tore at it with all his might. Then, sheepish and breathless, he looked round.

'It's locked, Mr Machin.'

'I know it's locked, Sergeant,' the Inspector said.

Mr Conway said, 'I do hope we're not going to be kept waiting out here in the cold while you sort this out.'

'Didn't you retrieve the key from Miss Bloom?' said Machin.

'Miss Bloom?' Gandy said. 'She's got it, has she? What the hell is she doing with our key?'

'It's her house,' Machin patiently explained.

'Are there no other doors? There must be other doors,' Mr Conway put in.

'There are, but they're both secured,' Tom Machin said.

'Well,' said Mr Conway, very reasonably, 'if we're going to be kept out here for long might I suggest we repair somewhere for something to drink. At the city's expense, of course?'

'Oh, no, you don't,' said Gandy

Stepping back, he aimed his boot at the door and struck it a massive blow with his heel. The draught plate rattled, the door panel cracked and the crowd on the pavement cheered.

Thoroughly incensed now, the mainstay of the DMP's tug-of-war team was not about to be defeated by a bloody door. He let out a lion's roar and drove his boot directly into the lock which resisted the first blow and the second but yielded, with a squeal of metal against wood, to the third.

The door of the house of death swung slowly open.

'There!' Gandy said and, grabbing Mr Conway by the shoulder, yanked him into the hallway. 'Happy now?'

Whatever had passed between Mr Bloom and his one and only had brought no fresh tears. The young woman was stiff and steely when she emerged from the clerk's office and with barely a nod to Mr Sullivan hurried off to join her friends from Mullingar who, it seemed, had not deserted her in favour of refreshment after all.

On the table in the clerk's office was a little brown teapot, milk jug, sugar basin and two cups and saucers. There was also an oval plate of tinned-salmon sandwiches cut into dainty triangles. Bloom was smoking a cigarette he'd scrounged from the court officer but hadn't touched either the tea or the sandwiches.

Sullivan drew out a chair, seated himself and filled two cups from the little pot. 'Better eat something, Bloom. We've a long afternoon ahead, I fear.'

Bloom looked up. 'Where's Kinsella?'

'He has business of his own to attend to,' Sullivan said. 'You're stuck with me, Leopold. Have a sandwich, do.'

Bloom pinched the cigarette between finger and thumb and blew smoke. 'I know what Kinsella's game is. He wants me to plead guilty to manslaughter and sweep me under the carpet. He doesn't think I'm important enough to bother with.'

'There, Mr Bloom, you're wrong. If anyone wants your case swept up and brushed aside it's Coroner Slater. May I have one of your sandwiches?'

Bloom nodded, watched the lawyer bite into the soft white bread and saw, greedily, the moist pink salmon flesh squeeze out at the corners. He took a last puff on the cigarette, dabbed it into the ashtray and reached for the sandwich plate.

Sullivan said, 'Inspector Kinsella wants your case held over. If you agree, he'll press Slater to adjourn the hearing for a week or so to give him time to prove your innocence.'

Bloom tongued bread into his cheek. 'If I am innocent.'

'Aren't you?' Neville Sullivan said, then hastily added, 'No, no, don't answer that.'

Bloom swallowed, smiled. 'Is it more difficult to defend a man who may be innocent than a man you know to be guilty?'

'In coroner's court, no,' Neville Sullivan said. 'In front of assize judges it's nigh impossible.'

'And why might that be?'

'Because we'll be up against seasoned Crown prosecutors who'll strip our witnesses bare in cross examination and fetch in witnesses of their own to swear that you and your wife were at loggerheads over her pregnancy.'

'What if I were to tell you, Mr Sullivan, that I didn't know Molly was pregnant?'

'I find that just as hard to believe as will a jury.'

Bloom sipped tea and reached for another sandwich.

'I assume Boylan will make an appearance in the witness box at some stage,' he said. 'Knowing Blazes, he'll manage to convince the jury he begged Molly to divorce me and let him make an honest woman out of her. Love's eternal flame. Sentiment always wins the day in the end.'

'I haven't spoken with Hugh Boylan yet, so I can't predict what he'll say or do. He isn't on Slater's witness list, though that doesn't mean he can't be called if you think it would help.'

'Help who? Help me? Fat chance of that,' Bloom said. 'Blazes Boylan never helps anyone but himself. He's taken Molly from me and now he's after Milly.'

'He's far too old for Milly.'

'Don't you believe it,' Bloom said. 'Boylan's motto: a man's only as old as his penis. Anyway, he's only thirty-five or -six and that's not old these days.'

'Well, I can't apply for a court order to prevent Boylan from consorting with your daughter without evidence he means to harm her. Am I to take it that Boylan was your wife's . . . I mean to say, that he and your wife had an intimate relationship?'

'I thought you were aware of it,' Bloom said. 'God knows, Boylan's not shy when it comes to bragging about his conquests.' Another sandwich went to his mouth. He paused, then said, 'Whichever way he tells his story he'll be the hero and I'll be the cucky, a poor impotent Jew man who couldn't satisfy his wife.'

'Kinsella thinks you're protecting someone?'

'Oh, I am,' Bloom said.

'May I, as your lawyer, ask who that might be?'

'Molly,' Bloom said. 'I'm protecting Molly.'

'Her reputation, you mean?'

'She had the swagger and the voice and that was well enough for most folk.' Bloom put down the half-eaten sandwich and rubbed the tip of his nose with his thumb. 'The best I can do for Molly now is leave her with that.'

'What about your daughter?'

'What about her?'

'Aren't you concerned about her future?'

'I'll see Milly right whatever happens.' Bloom picked up the half-eaten sandwich and brought it to his lips then, as if his appetite had suddenly deserted him, dropped it back on to the plate. 'If Slater calls an adjournment will he let Molly be buried?'

'Oh, yes.' Neville Sullivan nodded. 'He'll issue an Order for

Burial at the end of the session. Have you given any thought to funeral arrangements?'

'She'll be buried at Glasnevin,' Bloom said. 'Rudy's there waiting for his mama in our plot out towards Finglas.' Bloom rubbed his nose again. 'I've told Milly what I want done and' – he shrugged – 'Boylan may as well make himself useful. We'll all be buried there in time, all of us together, turning to dust together. Can you get me out for the funeral?'

'If you insist I'll press for a parole. But Kinsella thinks, and I agree with him, that the ends of justice will be better served if you agree to remain in custody.'

'The ends of justice being what?'

'Your unconditional release.'

'What if I don't agree?'

'Then Slater will send your case up for trial at the April assizes whatever verdict the jury reaches today. It may appear to you like a false promise but Kinsella's on to something.'

'What?' said Bloom, warily.

'He won't say. I'll be ready to wave a writ for *habeas corpus* if there's any undue delay. You, meanwhile, will spend an unpleasant week in Kilmainham.'

'And the alternative is what? Admitting to manslaughter?'

'No, the alternative is a trial before High Court judges under a new warrant. Both strategies involve risk, Leopold. I won't deny it.'

'What do *you* think I should do?'

'If you agree to let Slater call an adjournment and don't insist on bail then your statement to the police will be read out to the court and I'll refuse to let you be questioned by jury or coroner, which I'm fully entitled to do. The police will appeal for more time to advance their enquiries, other witnesses, such as they are, will be bound over and the inquiry will be suspended.'

'And Boylan won't be called?'

'No.'

'Are you sure Boylan won't be called?'

'Absolutely.'

'In that case,' Bloom said, 'let Kinsella have his way.'

The jurors returned to the courthouse at 1.48 pm, not much enlightened by their tour of the house of death and grumbling because they hadn't been fed. The coroner, who had been fed, placated them by announcing that he intended to detain them only long enough to read a statement by Leopold Bloom followed by a request from Superintendent Driscoll of Rotunda Division that his officers be granted more time to gather evidence, after which he, the coroner, would formally bind over witnesses and jurors to appear in seven days' time, instruct Mr Rice to proclaim an adjournment and send the jurors home. There being no dissent from the jurors, proceedings closed at twenty-eight minutes after two o'clock, and the courthouse emptied.

By ten to three Dr Slater was seated in his office filling out the Order for Burial while his clerk gathered depositions and recognizances to file for safekeeping. Having said farewell to Milly Bloom, Harry Coghlan and Michael Paterson were sitting down to afternoon tea in the lounge of the Belleville before catching a train back to Mullingar. Inspector Kinsella was on his way to Lower Castle Yard to log the day's events and Tom Machin was organising transport to convey Bloom to Kilmainham jail to sample the austere life that awaited him if his gamble went horribly wrong.

FIFTEEN

There was nothing remotely sensual in the care Maude Boylan devoted to dusting the plump curves of the two near-naked nymphs who guarded the staircase. According to Daphne, the figures, representing Prudence and Chastity, were fashioned from finest translucent alabaster and had been painted over with dark green paint only to preserve them from Dublin's abrasive fogs. In Maude's view, however, they were naught but a couple of chubby adolescents slathered with thick green paint to disguise the fact that they were cheap plaster casts left over from the days when the house had belonged to a demented tea-broker who, according to local legend, had been found hanging from a hook in his bedroom with *the* most enormous erection and a blissful smile on his face.

In memory of, if not respect for, the dear dead demented, Maude polished off her daily round by flicking each protuberant buttock with her feather before, chuckling to herself, she lugged bucket, mop and duster along the passageway to the kitchen to get down to the really serious business of scrubbing floors, sinks and lavatory pans.

What brother Hughie made of the statues the sisters never inquired. It hadn't escaped their notice, though, that some of the girls Hughie had smuggled into his room in his shaping years had borne more than a passing resemblance to the pair in the hall and, if young Milly Bloom was anything to go by, his tastes hadn't changed much.

'She's a child, Maude, a mere child.'

'That,' Maude said, 'she's not.'

'Fifteen,' said Daphne, 'is not a woman.'

'Mother was married at fifteen,' Maude reminded her.

'No,' said Daphne, 'Mother was pregnant at fifteen and married at sixteen before she knew which end was up.'

'Well,' said Maude, rinsing her mop at the sink, 'I doubt if Hughie has marriage on his mind. He's resisted so far and I see no reason to suppose if he ever does decide to take the plunge it'll be to a penniless waif.'

'Is she penniless?'

'Of course she is,' said Maude. 'She's Bloom's daughter and when did Bloom ever have two farthings to rub together?'

Daphne paused in the act of dicing carrots. 'Hughie wouldn't marry a Jew, would he?'

'The girl isn't a Jew. Her mother wasn't a Jew and Leo converted years ago. In any case, if Hughie's mind is made up then it wouldn't matter if the girl were a Hottentot.'

'I'm thinking of the bloodline,' said Daphne.

'The bloodline!' Maude scoffed. 'What bloodline? We're mongrels, my dear. If Papa hadn't invested his horse profits in the Friendly Society we'd all be in the workhouse by now.'

'Surely not Hughie.'

'No,' Maude conceded, 'possibly not Hughie.'

A saucepan of minced beef spluttered on the stove. Daphne

finished chopping and tipped the carrots into the pan. 'Why has he brought her here, Maude?'

Maude was scouring out the mop pail with a bristle brush, her broad back bent over the task, her muscular arm, bare to the elbow, pumping. 'Guilt,' she said. 'Conscience, if you prefer it.'

'Hughie doesn't have a conscience.' Daphne popped the lid on the saucepan and turned down the gas. 'Where is Milly, by the way?'

'Resting,' said Maude. 'She's putting on a brave face but what happened in court today really upset her. I gather Bloom's been sent to Kilmainham to cool his heels while the investigation gathers steam. I rather thought it would be over by now.'

Daphne leaned on the dresser and folded her arms over her small, hard bosom. She looked down the length of the kitchen, which, like so many of the rooms in the house, suffered from a paucity of light. The door to the yard was open, though, and an arc of daylight framed her sister at the sink.

'Maude, do you think he killed her?'

'Bloom?' Maude did not look up. 'I greatly doubt it.'

'If he didn't . . .'

Maude flushed the pail with a gush of cold water and rounded on her sister. 'Say it, just say it. Very well, I'll say it for you: why did a detective come knocking on our door? Isn't it obvious even to you, Daphne, that our brother was more to Molly Bloom than her concert manager?'

'I'm not altogether blind, Maude. I knew something was going on.' Daphne said. 'Is it because he and Molly Bloom were . . . were friends that he's looking after her daughter? If so, I'd call that charity, not conscience.'

'Call it what you like,' Maude said, 'it doesn't alter the fact that Hughie's a suspect.'

'What!' Daphne exclaimed. 'Hughie was here at home with us and drunk into the bargain.' She paused, blinking nervously. 'He was, wasn't he? At home with us?'

'Of course he was,' said Maude.

Daphne, not convinced, dampened a washcloth under the tap and wiped the chopping board while her sister poured hot water from the kettle into the gleaming pail. 'I feel sorry for her,' Daphne said. 'Child or not, she's lost her mother and her father's in jail.'

'You're too soft by half,' said Maude. 'Milly is Molly Bloom's daughter and you know what a conniving creature Molly Bloom was when she wasn't much older than Milly.' She hefted the pail from the sink, dropped into it a pellet of lye soap and gave it a shake. 'Look how badly she treated Leo and what a dance she led him.'

'Especially after she lost the little boy,' Daphne said.

'Yes, that's true. A kind of revenge, I suppose.'

'On Leo? Why?' said Daphne. 'The little boy was his too. In any case, I really can't imagine what all this has to do with Milly or, come to think of it, our Hughie.'

'It's murder, my dear, cold-blooded murder. The police are exploring all avenues of inquiry, isn't that how the *Journal* puts it? Naturally, they want to talk to Hughie. As long as we stick to our guns we've nothing to fear.'

'Stick to our guns? What do you mean?'

Maude lifted the pail, toted it down the length of the kitchen to the water closet that faced into the yard, placed it on the flagstones and returned to pick up the mop.

Loitering by the sink, Daphne held the mop at arm's length. 'Hughie *did* come home that night, didn't he, Maude? You *did* let him in and help him to bed, didn't you? That's what you told the policeman.'

'Yes, I did,' said Maude, 'and if that G-man comes calling again that's what you'll tell him: Hughie was home by midnight, drunk as a lord, and we *both* helped him to bed.'

'Now that you mention it,' said Daphne, blinking once more, 'of course, we did,' and handed her sister the mop.

It was just as well that Mr Bloom arrived in Kilmainham jail inside a Black Maria and did not see the prison walls close around him. He was hauled from the back of the van and hustled through two doors and down a short corridor by a couple of prison guards who clearly had no notion who he was. He had no reputation as a hero of the cause, hadn't blown up a post office or stabbed a member of the English parliament. He was a milk-and-water Home Ruler who had once booed Joe Chamberlain at a public meeting but he was no staunch citizen of the underground elite. Consequently no one cheered when, after booking, he was led

across the floor of the Great Hall and up the spidery iron staircase
to the first floor gallery, carrying his blanket, pot, mug and spoon.

Mr Bloom had never thought of himself as anything other than
an ordinary man struggling to earn a crust and snatch a little
pleasure in the passing. But here, in the vast, vaulted East Wing
of Kilmainham jail, he realised he was, in fact, invisible. He
doubted if the jailers even knew he wasn't a convict but a prisoner
on remand and, unlike the other short-term inmates in this cathedral of confinement, had been found guilty of no crime.

For seven days he would be a captive of his own conscience,
locked alone in a white-plastered cell with a window too high
to reach and nothing to do but dwell on his grief, his fears and
fantasies and, in the darkest hours of the leaden night, remember
the good times with Molly and plan for the better times ahead.

It was many a year since Blazes Boylan had last had the shakes.
The fit came upon him out of the blue or, more accurately, out
of the dusk for now that the sun had set, D'Olier Street was
filled with shadows. He had never liked the half hour when day
was not quite over and night had not begun. Even he, famed for
his self-assurance, was prone to brooding and, on that evening
in particular, had begun to question not if but when he had lost
his way.

If chance hadn't taken him into the tailor's shop on Eden Quay
a year back in September he wouldn't have bumped into Bloom
who was there to have his trousers altered. They'd been neighbours once, briefly, Boylans and Blooms, in a tenement in
Clanbrassil Street. Later, he'd flirted with Molly, to no good
effect, when she hadn't long been married. But then the Blooms
had become nomads moving from one address to another and
eventually he'd lost touch with them, which had been no excuse
for Bloom pretending not to recognise him that day in the tailor's
shop.

'Boylan, Blazes Boylan, man. Don't say you've forgotten me?'

'Ah, yes, of course. Boylan.' Bloom had shaken his hand
limply. 'How are your sisters?'

'They're well. And Molly, Mrs Bloom?'

Soon Bloom and he were drinking in the Bleeding Horse
Tavern and, as sure as night follows day, he'd met up with Molly

again. The DBC restaurant just round the corner in Dame Street; Bloom, Molly and he together once more, dormant urges stirring. Tea again, Molly and he, Bloom absent. Then, after his big win on the Keogh fight, a splash dinner at his invite, and soon after that, the dance. Walking home by the Tolka in the dark afterwards, he'd squeezed her hand and, thereafter, she and he and Bloom were, all three, entwined.

He spent an hour organising Molly's funeral, calling through the open glass-panelled door to Miss Dunne to clear his calendar for Friday. Yes, all of Friday. He telephoned the intimation to both the *Journal* and the *Morning Star* in words that conveyed nothing of the circumstances, nothing of the pain and guilt. Then, suddenly drained, he slumped back in his chair.

When he reached out to switch on the electrical lamp his hand shook. He raised his other hand, the left, and watched it shake too. His knuckles rapped uncontrollably on the desktop, drumming a ragged rhythm. He clamped left hand over right and pressed his forearms to the wood, his brow dappled with cold sweat. For a stark moment he thought he was about to drop dead at his desk.

'What's wrong, Mr Boylan? You don't look well.'

Dull, dumpy Dunne in her baggy blouse and creased black skirt, peered down at him through her horn-rims as if he were a cockroach or a beetle. For a split second he almost expected her to crush him with the heel of her hand. Then, thanks be to God, he was breathing again and the cold sweat was replaced by a flush of embarrassment at being caught in a moment of weakness.

'Shall I fetch you a glass of water?' his secretary asked.

'Gin,' he answered. 'You know where the bottle is.'

'Water would do you more good.'

'Just get me the bloody gin, will you?'

He watched her pad away, broad bottom registering disapproval. Twenty-eight, or was it -nine? As much a virgin as the day she'd been born, moon-faced Miss Dunne was wedded to her Underwood typewriter, too plain to poke and too valuable to sack.

He heaved himself to his feet, rolled unsteadily around the desk to the window and gazed down at the street below. Solicitors' clerks, chaps from the news depot, women released from bondage in the Gas Company offices or the Army & Navy Stores, all bustling home or heading for a snort at the Star & Garter or an early dinner at the Red Bank Oyster bar. The very thought of tackling an oyster right now rendered him queasy.

When Miss Dunne came up behind him with a tumbler of gin and tap water, he plucked the glass from her thick fingers and took a long, uninterrupted swallow.

'Battley's want the poster on Renwick Street corner renewed for another three months, beginning on the 7th. What'll I tell them, Mr Boylan? Is the rental rate the same?'

'Summer rates apply from April.' He drank another mouthful of watery gin, hardly tasting it. 'You should know that by now, Miss Dunne.' Surprised that she'd brought the bottle from the cupboard above the filing cabinet, he held out the tumbler and let her pour him another niggardly inch. 'Put the quarter's costing in a letter and I'll sign it before I go.'

He turned again to the window and drank once more. The gin tasted better without tap water. He felt his nerves steady, his vigour return. The woman's reflection hovered in the window glass, motionless, bottle in hand.

'What?' he said. 'What is it now?'

'Those letters on your desk . . .'

'What letters?'

'The typed letters . . . Martha.'

Blazes swung round. 'Have you been prying again?'

'They're lying open on your desk Mr Boylan, and they're typed,' Miss Dunne said. 'Do you . . . do you want me to file them?'

'No, they're private.'

Motionless still, the bottle held up like a fisherman's catch, she asked, 'Where did you get them, Mr Boylan, those letters?'

'None of your damned business.' Annoyance was almost as restorative as alcohol. He waved her away. 'Go on with you, back to your machine.'

To his amazement, she stood her ground. 'They're not yours, are they? I mean, they weren't sent to you?'

'Of course they're not mine.'

'Mr Boylan, will you not tell me who he is?'

'Who who is?'

'Henry.'

My dearest, naughty darling.

My own, my one true love.

Blazes experienced another thump below the heart, a sensation unconnected with panic or annoyance or the thought of a salty oyster slipping down the length of his digestive tract. He kept his excitement in check, hidden from his secretary.

Graciously he said, 'Tell me, Maureen, why do you ask?'

'I'm just . . . just curious, Mr Boylan, that's all.'

He finished the gin and handed her the glass. Bottle in one hand and tumbler in the other she was powerless to fend him off. He planted a hand on her shoulder and, sticking his big Roman nose into her face, enquired, '*You're* not Martha, by any chance?'

Her mouth opened wide enough to show a chalky white tongue and small stained teeth. He could smell onions on her breath and the perfume she sometimes wore, stale now at the day's end. Her hair was as coarse as horse tail but, for an instant, he wondered what it would look like unpinned and if she, five years his secretary, was really capable of spanking a man's bare backside while clad in nothing but a pair of lacy French knickers and a sailor's hat.

'No,' she said. 'No, no, no.'

He rubbed his nose against hers in an Eskimo kiss that knocked her spectacles sideways. He slipped his hand from her shoulder to her breast. 'Wouldn't you like to be?' he said. 'Wouldn't you like to be Martha, whoever she is, and spank Henry's botty?'

Again: 'No. No, no.'

She held her arms out from her sides, balancing tumbler and bottle, and pressed her chest into his hand. If she hadn't been wrapped in winter woollens he might have felt her spinster's heart beating against his palm.

'Does reading other people's mail excite you, Maureen?'

She shook her head, sending her spectacles slanting across her cheek. With a forefinger, Blazes tipped the spectacles into place on the bridge of her nose and peered through the convex lenses into her dark brown eyes.

'Don't you fancy it?' he said. 'I mean, what Martha says she does to Mr . . . to Henry? I wonder what *he* does to *her*? Do you think he spanks her too? Would you like that, Maureen, to have a man put you across his lap and lift your skirts?'

'Stop it,' she said. 'Stop it, please.'

'What a naughty girl you are, Miss Dunne,' said Blazes, grinning. 'I can't tell you who Henry is, or Martha, but I can tell you where to find a bit of that sort of stuff, if that's your fancy.'

'It's not,' she said stiffly, 'my fancy at all, Mr Boylan.'

She didn't sway or ask him to remove his paw from her breast. A twitch behind his fly buttons, nothing serious, nothing rampant; he'd been without intercourse for more than a week now and talking saucy even with dumpty Miss Dunne reminded him of it. He wondered what sort of price she'd be willing to pay to have her answer but, before that thought could take root, pushed her away.

She was dogged, that he would say for her.

'Where *did* you find those letters, Mr Boylan?'

He lied glibly but unimaginatively. 'I bought them from a fella in a pub for the price of a couple of pints.'

'What was the fella's name?'

'I don't remember. I don't think he mentioned it.'

'What pub was it?'

'Look, that's enough. I've more to do than prattle about dirty letters. If you're so all-fired curious, you can read them. And if that doesn't open your eyes to what you've been missing, nothing will.' He stepped to the desk, picked up the top sheet of one of Bloom's letters and waved it. 'Here, take it away and read it.'

'You didn't buy them in any pub, did you?' Miss Dunne said.

Temper rising, he said, 'Are you calling me a liar?'

Fearing for her job, she backed down. 'I'm sorry. I'm just not myself these days, Mr Boylan.'

'None of us are, none of us are,' said Blazes. He held up the letter. 'To read or not to read, Miss Dunne?'

'I think . . . no, it's not for me that sort of thing.'

'Too hot for you, is it?' said Blazes, anger giving way to complacency. 'Right-o, right-o. Type up the Battley letter and then you can go home.'

She held her ground for a few seconds longer. He could read nothing into her expression through the convex lenses that made her brown eyes seem so large and trusting. He felt foolish for even considering that she might be Bloom's mysterious lover. Surely not even Bloom would be desperate enough as to take up with a woman like Maureen Dunne.

'Will that be all, Mr Boylan?'

'Yes,' said Blazes. 'That will be all for now.'

She placed the gin bottle on the desk, the tumbler too, switched on the electrical lamp and with one last glance at the letters waddled off back to her Underwood.

SIXTEEN

S arah Tolland could not understand why her intended found her father so intimidating. He was and always had been sweet natured, considerate to clerks and servants and patient to a fault with her mother who, Sarah had to admit, could be a little capricious now and then. He doted on her, his daughter, sole product of his loins, and had made it abundantly clear that any man who sought her hand would have to match her in wit and intelligence but if he fulfilled those criteria he would be treated as a surrogate son and drafted into the firm to give it a much-needed boost.

Roper, at eighty, was well past his prime and he, Alfred Fitzgerald Tolland, while not exactly decrepit, was knocking on somewhat. In a city that housed more lawyers than rats in its sewers, competition for legal business was fierce and stamina and zeal were required to keep the fees rolling in, points made plain – in the nicest possible way, of course – to young Mr Sullivan as soon as Sarah decided that he was the man for her.

The desk in Poppy Tolland's chambers was larger than a papal sarcophagus, a great slab of dark mahogany polished to reflect light from the box window or, at this hour of an evening, the glow from the lovely old oil lamp that Mr Tolland still retained, though the building had recently been wired for electricity.

A lesser man might have used the desk as a prop to power, but that wasn't Poppy Tolland's style. He was, in size and shape, no Great Dane, no wolfhound or husky but more like a little fox terrier trained not to hop about and snap, a comparison that went by the board, however, when he donned his robes and squared up to opposing counsel.

The oil lamp cast reflections not only upon the desk but also on the glass-fronted bookcases that lined the walls, cases filled with calf-bound volumes in which were recorded every jot and tittle of the statutes of English law and the decisions rendered there under. The lamp's glow also shone in Poppy Tolland's pince-nez, an affectation intended to make him appear more affable, which, at least in Neville Sullivan's view, it singularly failed to do.

'Toast,' said Poppy Tolland, after listening to Neville's account of events in the coroner's court. 'You realise you have him on toast.'

'I didn't, um, no, I hadn't quite realised that,' Neville confessed. 'I take it you mean Bloom?'

'Heavens, no. Slater.'

When conducting interviews in his office it was Mr Tolland's habit to hunch behind his desk and show the client or, in this case his protégé, just the glint of his eye-glasses and a crown of gingery hair. He spoke from behind his hand and you rarely saw his lips move, a habit that made his pronouncements, however prosaic, seem profound.

'The coroner,' said Mr Tolland, 'done wrong.'

'Beg pardon?' said Neville.

'Not to put it too finely, Roland buggered up.'

'Oh?' said Neville. 'Really? I mean, *really*?'

It was possible that Poppy Tolland allowed himself a dimple of self-satisfaction at this point but if he did it was hidden by his hand. He said, 'Do you suppose I'd send you into battle armed with nothing but a slingshot and a pebble? Bloom should not be in prison. Indeed, he shouldn't have been charged in the first place. Any magistrate other than Paddy Mullen would have dismissed the case instanter. Now, can you tell me why?'

'Lack of evidence,' Neville suggested.

'Forget evidence. Apply your knowledge of the law at its most fundamental level.'

'The arrest?'

'Precisely. Go on.'

'The police from C Division turned up without a medical

examiner,' Neville said, 'and the detective from G Division, Kinsella, arrived before the coroner. Some time before the coroner according to the logs. Slater took it upon himself to issue an arrest warrant, which he's qualified to do, of course, but by that time Bloom had been in police custody for the best part of an hour.'

'Doing what, do you suppose? Playing whist?'

'Being questioned before he'd been charged,' said Neville.

'Or, I suspect, without being cautioned.'

'How can I extract that admission from the policemen, let alone Slater, when I'm not permitted to cross-examine?'

'It's simple, Neville. Feed your questions through the coroner on behalf of the jury. Didn't you pull that one today?'

'I did,' said Neville, surprised. 'Yes, come to think of it, I did.'

Poppy Tolland's head rose and his smile became visible. 'There you are. Irregularities in the manner of arrest. Questioning before charge and without caution. No medical examiner brought to the scene. Paddy Mullen must have been in a state of torpor not to dismiss or, so a little bird told me, furious at Bloom for doing in a well-built soprano.'

'I shouldn't have agreed to an adjournment, should I?'

'No, you made the right decision, Neville,' said Poppy Tolland. 'Kinsella's no fool. He knows you've high cards in your hand and can play them at any time. He wants our client off stage for a reason and I'm curious as to what that reason may be. Has Bloom requested parole to attend his wife's funeral?'

'Oddly, no.'

'Does he know he's entitled to apply?'

'I'll be surprised if he doesn't,' Neville said. 'I've come around to thinking that Mr Bloom is at least one step ahead of us.'

'Has he raised the matter of our fee?'

'I told him what you told me, that there's no fee for our services in the coroner's court.'

'Did he seem relieved?'

'He didn't seem bothered one way or the other.'

'What does he do for a living?'

'Sells advertising for the *Journal*,' Neville answered. 'Rather hand to mouth if you ask me.'

'Yet Mr Bloom appears to have no concerns about money. What, Neville, might that suggest to you?'

'Either a nest egg or a windfall.'

'And what might the nature of that windfall be?'

Neville stroked his flowing locks for several seconds to encourage inspiration and then, sitting upright, said, 'Life insurance. A policy on his wife's death. Good God!'

'Upon which,' said Mr Tolland, 'he can make no claim until he walks out of court free and clear of all collusion in her death.'

'If he does stand to profit from her death,' Neville said, 'it's small wonder he won't plead to manslaughter. Is there anything we can or should do to clarify this situation?'

'Oh, yes,' said Poppy Tolland. 'Find the bloody policy and find it bloody quick.'

Conveniently situated for trams, omnibuses and Abbey Street's commercial offices, the Sunnyhill Hotel had become an affordable refuge for professional women of a certain age. It currently housed a nest of self-supporting typists who, best efforts notwithstanding, had so far failed to find a man willing to take them on.

None of the 'girls' who gathered in the parlour while waiting for supper to be served would ever see twenty-five again. Spinsters to a man, they weren't committed to the single life on principle but, like Boylan's Miss Dunne, had slipped gradually into what might best be described as an illogical state of ever-hopeful resignation.

Maureen Dunne and her friend, Anne-Marie Blaney, who worked in the head office of the Hibernian Bank, had adjacent rooms on the Sunnyhill's second floor. They each had a room with a window that looked out on the drying green, each an identical bed, dressing table, wash-stand and chamber pot, for Mr Flaherty, proprietor of the hotel, had purchased the furnishings in a job lot from the now-defunct Harp of Erin Club in Kildare Street.

It was left to the ladies to decorate the rooms according to taste and wherewithal, to add the feminine touches that softened the general institutional frowziness and made the shabby old place seem like home. Miss Dunne, for instance, had adorned her bedroom with a cheery floral print bedspread from Clery's basement sale and a baize-covered draught screen that Mr Boylan had found for her to which she'd attached postcards from far-flung places that she knew she would only ever visit in her dreams.

Miss Blaney, a year or two older than her friend, had settled for Moroccan-stripe curtains and, in lieu of postcards, had strewn the narrow mantelshelf and every spare inch of her dressing table with gewgaws presented to her, usually on parting, by a covey of discerning gentlemen who having sampled the starter had, as it were, no wish to order the entrée.

It was not that Miss Blaney was ugly or had allowed her figure to run to seed or even that she lacked an aptitude for the easy congress that gentlemen found appealing in a companion. Anne-Marie's flaw, if such it was, was eagerness, a passionate eagerness that some men found alarming and others positively terrifying. Whatever you desired, Miss Blaney hinted, she was willing to provide, asking nothing in return save a wedding ring and a lifelong commitment to pander to her every whim, an offer that even the sappy lads who drifted in from the country did not consider a bargain, no matter how you sliced the pie.

The burnt-toast smell of the gas fire was comforting, the bedroom warm. A gas mantel in a scrolled glass globe suffused a cosy glow and threw upon the wall the bulky shadow of the typewriter that for the best part of seven months had been Anne-Marie's lifeline to Henry Flower. She'd purchased the machine at auction and had lugged it back to the Sunnyhill by cab for the blessed thing was bigger than the Blarney Stone and weighed a ton but, for half a year, had seemed like the best investment she'd ever made and worth its weight in gold.

Planted on a stout knee-high table the machine took up a great deal of space. The only way Anne-Marie could operate its keys was to kneel before it and, in that prayerful position, woo her hesitant correspondent, Henry Flower, with ever more racy promises. In letter after letter she had exposed her longings without inhibition or fear that Henry would think ill of her or, when they finally came face to face, that he would necessarily hold her to the more *outré* aspects of their paper relationship.

After half a dozen letters had been exchanged, c/o the Post Office in Westland Row, Anne-Marie had come to regard 'Henry' as more of a father confessor for sins not yet committed than a potential husband. In any case, he'd made it plain from the first that he was married – no deception there – and that what he wanted from 'his Martha' were all the things his staid and ailing wife would not countenance, which admission, naturally, set Anne-Marie's mind racing and fired her imagination.

She had first encountered Mr Flower via an advertisement in the *Irish Times* in which he'd called for a smart young lady typist to aid him in his literary work. She, though she knew it not, had been but one of forty-four women to respond – three from the Sunnyhill alone – and had been flattered, nay, ecstatic, when Mr Flower had personally answered her pseudonymous application. Literary work had gone by the board, never mentioned, and Mr Flower had soon become her guardian angel and bashful lover and, when the mood was upon her, shivering in her shift, a swarthy, unscrupulous brigand who would stop at nothing to have his wicked way.

Secure behind her *nom-de-plume*, Martha Clifford, she'd sent him pressed flowers, then motto cards with hearts stencilled on the back and at length, at his request, a small lock of hair snipped, she broadly hinted, not from her head but from elsewhere on her person. The hair, it seemed, had done the trick though whether, by then, she really wanted the trick done was another matter altogether. '*Meet me*,' he'd written, '*at the north corner of Merrion Square at half past twelve o'clock on Wednesday. If this time is not suitable to you, my darling, tell me one that is, and where.*'

Running then like mad along Nassau Street past the College Park and the Gallery in her half hour dinner break, jumping up to see if he – who? – was there and finding no one, no man loitering expectantly. Throughout the afternoon, pecking at her typewriter in the bank managers' office, she'd blamed herself for arriving five minutes after the half hour, and that night in the Sunnyhill she'd knelt on the rug and rattled off page after page of apology begging Henry's forgiveness for her tardiness.

Seven long days she'd waited for a reply. Convinced that Henry had gone forever and she would never hear from him again she'd taken her friend, Maureen Dunne, into her confidence, seeking not so much reassurance as sympathy.

And then: '*Do not berate yourself, my sweet girl. It was my fault or should I say the fault of my employer who sent me out of town on an errand at the last minute. I am sure you will understand. I could think of no means of letting you know. How hurtful it must have been for you to find me wanting in my promise. It is I who must beg your forgiveness. Shall we say Sunday at one o'clock at the Poolbeg Street entrance to the Theatre Royal, off Hawkins Street? I will be wearing a grey suit and will carry a flower to show you who I am.'*

'Don't go,' Maureen Dunne had advised.

'Oh, but I must. I must.'

It had rained that Sunday, as it often did in Dublin in October.

Although she'd found shelter under the theatre's glass awning, she'd been soaked by that time. She'd waited an hour then stalked angrily off towards the rain-lashed quays and then, spinning round, had returned to the rendezvous and had waited another twenty minutes before, bladder aching and nose running, she'd trailed back to her room in the Sunnyhill where she'd thrown herself on the bed and wept until Maureen had brought her tea and fruit cake and, without once saying 'I told you so,' had helped her change into dry togs and take stock.

'It's all very well,' Anne-Marie had said, tearfully, 'being given the heave-ho by a man to whom you've almost surrendered your all but to be jilted by a man you've never clapped eyes on is the ultimate slap in the face.'

'I think,' Miss Dunne had said, 'you're well out of it.'

'I do believe I am,' Anne-Marie had said. 'To hell with him.'

Then another letter from Henry had arrived in her post box.

'What can I do, my darling girl, but throw myself at your feet and abase myself. I deserve a whipping for what I have done to you. I deserve every sort of punishment you can mete out on me. It is not for worlds I would hurt you so and leave you standing. My wife was taken sudden ill and a doctor had to be called to attend her . . .' etcetera, etcetera, etcetera.

'He's playing you fast and loose, Anne-Marie,' Maureen Dunne had said. 'The man's a cad. Ignore him.'

'That's what I intend to do,' Miss Blaney had agreed. But after the ladies of the Sunnyhill were all asleep, the muffled chatter of a typewriter had echoed in the corridor as 'Martha Clifford' had hammered out one last desperate plea for 'Henry' to grant her an opportunity to find ecstasy in his arms.

The third and final time had been the worst of all; Christmas not far off, the streets of the city bustling, a few flakes of snow falling, the lights of the shops bright lit in the gloom. *We'll meet outside Webb's, the Tailor and Outfitter, along in the Corn Market*, Henry had written, his choice of location unexplained.

She'd purchased a new scarf and had trudged out tingling with excitement and had waited again an hour, pretending to study the display of mackintoshes in the window. An unseen band nearby had played seasonal melodies, cornets ringing in the melancholy air, but the stink of pubs and brewery warehouses had eventually overwhelmed her and, more depressed than she'd ever been in her life, she'd given up and had crossed the bridge to Rossiter's Tearooms and ordered a pot of tea and an almond finger and had eaten it alone at a window table looking out at the gentlemen passing, wondering, still wondering, if one of them was he.

A final letter, brief and bleeding, tapped out on the machine at midnight: 'Henry, what do you want from me?' But the question was never answered and not another word did she hear from her lover, Henry Flower, whose identity remained a mystery.

'I know who he is,' said Maureen, closing the door behind her.

Combing her hair at the dressing table, Anne-Marie swung round. 'Who?'

'Your Mr Flower.'

Indifference is not easy to feign. 'Oh! Really?'

Maureen placed a gentle hand on her friend's shoulder and kissed the top of her head. 'I'm sure – almost sure – it's Bloom.

'Bloom?'

'Leopold Bloom, the murderer.'

'Maureen, that's not funny.'

Miss Dunne retreated as far as the bed and seated herself upon it, hands folded in her lap. 'Mr Boylan has your Martha letters. I saw them, two of them, on his desk. He says he bought them in a pub but he's a fibber. He's been at the court all day and he's got Mr Bloom's daughter staying in his house and that's all just too much of a coincidence, don't you think?'

'Are you sure my Henry isn't your Mr Boylan?'

'Boylan doesn't need to write letters to find women. I mean, he'd never have let me see them if he had.'

Anne-Marie put down the comb and studied her pallid face in the mirror. 'What,' she said at length, 'does he look like?'

'Bloom? I've only seen him once or twice. He's . . .' Maureen paused judiciously. 'He's personable enough,' she said, then added, viciously, 'for a man who slaughtered his wife.'

'Are you sure it's the same Bloom?'

'Anne-Marie, for heaven's sake!'

'Where is he? Where have they taken him?'

'Kilmainham I think Mr Boylan said.'

'To hang?' said Anne-Marie.

'No, the trial's not over. Anyhow, it isn't a proper trial. It's the coroner's thing and they're only holding him on suspicion.'

'He's innocent. I know he's innocent,' said Anne-Marie. 'And if he isn't innocent, perhaps he did it for me.'

'Did what for you?' said Maureen.

'Got rid of his wife. Got rid of her to have me.'

'Anne-Marie! Anne-Marie! He stove her head in with a teapot.'

'To be with me, yes.' Anne-Marie rose from the stool at her dressing table and cried, 'Yes. Yes, to be with me forever.'

'Calm yourself, Anne-Marie, please,' said Maureen Dunne coolly. 'There's no guarantee that your . . . that Bloom committed the crime. Tell me, did you keep any of his letters?'

'All of them.'

'Where are they?'

'In a shoebox under the bed. Perhaps I should destroy them.'

'No,' Miss Dunne said quickly. 'Don't do that.'

'Why ever not?'

'They may come in handy one of these days.'

SEVENTEEN

Half past seven was a ridiculously early hour to be considering retirement but candles were rationed. Besides, his eyes ached from reading the tiny print in the battered Bible that was the only book he was permitted to have in his cell. He was on the point of blowing out the candle and undressing for bed when the door opened and the priest popped in.

'Mr Bloom.' The priest offered his hand and, given the slightest encouragement, Bloom thought, might have offered him a cuddle too.

'Mr Bloom, or may I address you as Leopold? It is Leopold, isn't it?'

'It is,' Bloom said. 'What can I do for you, Father?'

He expected a platitudinous answer but the priest surprised him. Still gripping Bloom's hand, he said, 'You wouldn't happen to have a smoke on you, by any chance?'

In fact, Bloom had seven Player's Weights in a packet tucked into his vest pocket, a gift from Sullivan. The packet had been ignored by the jailers, tobacco being one luxury prisoners were allowed. He was by disposition respectful of the clergy, even priests, and his hesitation was fleeting.

'Only tiddlers, I'm afraid.' Tugging the packet from his pocket, he tapped out one of the small cigarettes. 'Help yourself.'

The priest plucked the cigarette from the packet, stuck it in his mouth, jogged the tip in the candle flame and gratefully inhaled. He let smoke trickle down into his lungs and then, with a cock of the head and a click of the tongue, said, 'Thanks be to God for that. Most kind, Mr Bloom, most kind. The blessed jailers wouldn't cough out for a Catholic even in his hour of need.' He inhaled again. 'You're in for murder, aren't you?'

'Suspicion thereof.'

'How long did they give you?'

'Seven days.'

'Only seven days? You must have murdered an Englishman.'

'I'm accused of murdering my wife. I didn't, of course.'

'Think yourself lucky. The kiddie four cells down got three weeks for swearing at a policeman. He pleaded guilty, of course.'

'If you've been sent to persuade me to plead—'

'Nothing of the sort. I'm an arm of the church not the Lord Lieutenant's toady.' He watched Bloom slip the packet of precious cigarettes into his pocket then, pinching with finger and thumb, he removed the Player's from his lips and held it out.

'Your turn, I believe.'

Bloom peered at the moistened paper. 'Sanctified, is it?'

'Holy spit, the very best kind.'

Bloom laughed and the priest laughed with him and, saying not a word, they finished the smoke between them down to the last shred.

'I see you've been reading your Bible?' the priest said. 'How far have you got along?'

'Leviticus.'

'Ah, the third book of the Torah.'

'I'm not a Jew, you know, not now.'

'Once a Jew always a Jew, as it is with us Catholics.'

Bloom seated himself on the cot. In the flickering light of the candle the priest seemed incredibly young, hardly more, Bloom thought, than a stripling. He rested his shoulders against the corner wall, stretched his legs at forty-five degrees and crossed his ankles.

'Are you really a priest?' Bloom asked.

'What else would I be? I'm Father Joseph O'Grady. Rosie they called me at the seminary, before I was appointed a parish.'

'Which parish?'

'St. Mary, Donnybrook.'

'Oh!' said Bloom.

'I see you know it.'

'Not,' Bloom said, 'intimately.'

'Perhaps you're more familiar with Sandymount?'

'I do enjoy a stroll by the sea from time to time,' Bloom admitted. 'Isn't there a priests' house beside the church? Is that where you put up?'

'It is. With Father Conroy and the Canon. I was born and raised in Irishtown so it's uncomfortably close to home.'

'I didn't think that was allowed. I mean, being allocated a parish so close to home.'

'I doubt if I'll be there long,' said Father O'Grady. 'I've indicated to Father Conroy that I'm interested in mission work. Africa would suit, or India. It isn't what suits me, however. It's what suits the Church.'

'Of course,' said Bloom, waiting.

'My cousin's a doctor.'

'In Africa?'

'In Dublin. Perhaps you've heard of him: Willy Wyatt.'

Bloom shook his head. 'Can't say I have.'

'Truth is, he isn't quite a doctor yet, but he soon will be. Calls himself Will, now, not Willy. He rides for Trinity in the bike races.'

'No,' Bloom said. 'The name means nothing to me.'

'He lives in the terraces on Tritonville Road. There's quite a clan of us down that way. The Wyatts are the Protestant branch of the family but we don't hold that against them.'

Bloom licked his upper lip. 'I'm not sure what all this has to do with me. I've told you, I don't know them.'

'I spent a lot of time with my cousins when I was growing up, and with the local girls. Friends we were, good chums. Still are, I suppose, in spite of my collar.'

Bloom shifted his weight from one buttock to the other. 'You aren't one of Kilmainham's regular chaplains, are you?'

'An occasional visitor, shall we say?' the priest replied. 'I offer comfort to prisoners from time to time. The governors are very gracious about it, very encouraging.'

'How *do* you offer prisoners comfort?' Bloom enquired.

'I intercede with God on their behalf and ask Him to forgive them their sins in the name of Jesus Christ, our Saviour, and His Holy Mother, the Virgin of virgins.'

'Do you hear confessions?'

'That I do not do, unless they're on their deathbed which they never are, not here at any rate.' Father O'Grady continued without pause, 'Have *you* anything you'd like to tell me, Leopold?'

'Why don't you explain why you're really here,' Bloom said, 'then I'll think about trading confidences.'

'Ah, yes, I heard you were sharp.'

'Who did you hear that from?'

'An old chum of mine. Chum of yours, too, I believe.'

'One of your parishioners?'

'She is. She is, indeed.'

Bloom lay across the width of the cot and rested the back of his head against the wall. 'This parishioner of yours, is she conscientious in her observances and devotions?'

'She is.' Father O'Grady paused, then said, 'I assume we're now reading from the same page? Mr Bloom – Leopold – I must ask you a direct question to which, I hope, you'll give me a direct answer.'

'Ask away.'

'Have you taken advantage of Miss MacDowell?'

'Miss MacDowell?'

'Oh, come now. You don't buy a young woman soap – lemon soap, wasn't it? – and then pretend you've forgotten her. Gerty MacDowell of Sandymount.'

Bloom sighed and capitulated. 'If you mean, as I think you do, have I taken advantage of Gerty's trust, the answer is no, I have not.'

'She's very emotional, very impressionable. Easily swayed.'

'Do you suppose I don't torment myself with that knowledge every night in life,' Bloom said.

'Torment yourself?' said Father O'Grady.

'Is it pity, I ask myself, or is it affection.'

'Or lust?' the priest said. 'You're a married man, Leopold.'

'I was.'

'Yes, quite!'

Bloom squinted up at the priest. 'If you're asking what there is between us in a carnal way,' he said, 'the answer is nothing. A kiss – more than one kiss – but that's all. I wouldn't do it, not to her. How much did Gerty tell you?'

'She's infatuated with you, that much is obvious,' the priest said. 'What's less obvious is what you have to offer a woman so much younger than you are when you're not free to marry.'

'I am free to marry,' Bloom reminded him. 'You haven't answered my question, Father O'Grady: what did Gerty tell you?'

The priest detached himself from the wall and shook one leg and then the other to loosen his calf muscles. He said, 'When I was very young I'd take Gerty on my back and run with her into the waves. She'd shriek with delight and cling on to me with bare legs and arms. I thought then, as you do when you know no better, that one day I would marry Gerty MacDowell and we'd live in a house on the strand and be happy ever after. That, however, was before she became a cripple and ashamed of her infirmity.'

'It's not her fault. She took a tumble on Dalkey Hill and broke her foot. The bones were badly set by some ham-fisted quack,' Bloom said. 'Her damned father wouldn't pay for surgery and the result is that awful limp.'

'What, Leopold, did you promise her. A new foot?'

'No, only to take care of her.'

'How were you going to do that when you already had a wife,' Father O'Grady said, 'a wife and a daughter?'

'My daughter's settled in Mullingar and my wife . . .' Bloom sighed and spread his fingers. 'My wife had her own life.' He hesitated, then added, 'Her career as a singer, I mean. They no longer had need of me.'

'You wanted someone to care for you, is that it?'

'No,' Bloom said, 'I wanted someone to care for.'

'I see.' The priest said and, reaching into his pocket produced a plain brown envelope. 'Well, this is for you, from Gerty?'

'Have you read it?'

'No. I've been compromised enough as it is,' said Father O'Grady. 'Aren't you going to open it? What if it requires a reply?'

Bloom nodded and, with the envelope held low between his knees, carefully opened it and unfolded the sheet of notepaper it contained. Printed in tiny, meticulously formed letters in violet ink the message read, *'What ever happens, dearest, I will always love you. P.S. The suitcases are safe.'*

'Tell her,' said Bloom, 'I understand.'

'Is that it? Is that all?'

'Gerty will know what I mean.' Mr Bloom rose from the cot and held out his hand. 'Thank you for coming.'

'I didn't do it for your sake.'

'I know.'

The handshake was less prolonged this time and there was no indication that the priest might wish to hug him.

'Goodnight, Mr Bloom.'

'Goodnight, Father,' Bloom said and, to save Rosie O'Grady the trouble, hammered on the cell door to summon the jailer.

EIGHTEEN

'Here's a mystery for you,' Jack Delaney said. 'If Bloom converted to the Protestant faith to marry Molly, why is she being buried in Glasnevin? Is there a Jewish section somewhere, or what?'

'Bloom has a family plot,' said Martin Cunningham, one of Leopold's loyal friends. 'It's over by the Finglas Road so we've quite a hike before us.'

'Not so much of a hike as the pall-bearers,' said Neville Sullivan. 'This plot, who's buried there?'

'Bloom's mother and his infant son,' said Mr Cunningham.

'What about his father?'

'Ah, no,' Mr Cunningham said. 'His father took his own life. He lies in Ennis. Bloom attends a vigil there every year.'

'What was he, the father?' Jack Delaney enquired.

'Came over from Hungary years ago,' Mr Cunningham informed him. 'Family name was Virag. He changed it by deed.'

'Very wise of him,' Delaney said. 'Jew, I take it?'

'He was, poor chap,' said Mr Cunningham.

'Do you pity him for being Jewish,' Neville Sullivan said, 'or for taking his own life? I assume the two are not connected?'

'Not in my mind,' Mr Cunningham said curtly.

Dawdling a half pace ahead of the others, Kinsella glanced over his shoulder. 'In Bloom's mind, do you think?'

Martin Cunningham said, 'To be sure old Rudolph is never far from Bloom's thoughts. The sadness was stirred up in him again when he lost his own little boy ten or eleven years back.'

'Is he on watch, Inspector?' Neville Sullivan asked.

'Watch?'

'My client, on suicide watch in Kilmainham?'

'Oh, I doubt if Bloom intends to do away with himself,' Jim Kinsella answered. 'I think he'd consider it cowardly.'

'And illegal,' Delaney put in. 'By Crikey, a man can get ten years hard labour for doing himself in.'

Mr Cunningham politely smiled. He was employed as an official in the Works Department of the Castle and, as such, had a nodding acquaintance with Kinsella but he clearly didn't approve of Delaney.

It was a day of low cloud, cool but not cold. All four men wore dark overcoats, suits and black neckties. They had met by chance, not arrangement, by boarding the electric tram car in the vicinity of the Pillar all bound in the same direction.

'I promised Bloom I'd attend,' Neville Sullivan said apologetically. 'He wants me to make note of who's here.'

'It'll be in the paper, won't it?' Mr Cunningham said.

'No,' Delaney said. 'It's *sub judice.*'

'Nonsense!' said Mr Sullivan. 'It's no more *sub judice* than fly in the air. It's not as if you're publishing the names of the jurors.'

'Exactly what I told my editor,' said Jack Delaney. 'But he's cagey, very cagey since we ran foul of the courts last year. By the way, apropos my previous question, who's calling the tune today?'

'Boylan, I believe,' Kinsella said.

'Why isn't Leo here?' said Mr Cunningham. 'In the name of common decency wouldn't parole have been in order?'

The lawyer said, 'Bloom chose not to request parole.'

'Couldn't face the funeral, I expect,' said Jack Delaney. 'One way or the other he just doesn't have the neck, is my guess.'

Martin Cunningham opened his mouth to defend his old friend but closed it again promptly when the coffin appeared from the direction of the Finglas Street gate which, with its noble granite piers and a view of the O'Connell tower, was as beautiful an entrance as the departed could hope to pass through.

The men removed their hats and stepped back to allow the grave-diggers' cart to pass. The cart was preceded not by a priest but by a vicar in flapping black robes. He led the mournful procession at a brisk pace past the mortuary chapel into the avenue that curved like a bow between monuments and gravestones back towards Finglas. There was nothing much to Finglas save the proximity of the cemetery and a couple of uninspiring spires. Off to Kinsella's right, across the Tolka, the handsome old mansions of Glasnevin village peeped from the ridge, just visible through a forest of marble and a network of branches.

Kinsella had only been to a couple of funerals here, Catholic colleagues who had died not bravely in the line of duty but of wasting illnesses that had carried them away too soon. His mother, two aunts, three uncles, a niece and cousin were all interred at Mount Jerome across the Liffey at Harold's Cross. For some reason he couldn't quite put his finger on, he felt less comfortable here than there, where his ancestors awaited his arrival.

Behind the coffin, walking fast, came a straggle of mourners, headed by Milly Bloom, all in black, clinging to Boylan's arm. It was rare for women to attend funerals. The Inspector wondered how much argument Boylan, or his sisters, had put up to dissuade the girl from flouting tradition. None at all, maybe, given that, Bloom excepted, Milly was Marion Tweedy Bloom's only living relative, at least the only living relative anyone knew about.

She walked, the girl, with head unbowed, hat bobbing. She did not glance at the men as the cortege passed but kept her eyes on the coffin; no shoddy affair knocked up out of knotty pine but good sturdy wood polished to a silky sheen. Brass handles, too, Kinsella noted, that tapped a rhythm on the side panels as the cart lurched after the striding clergyman; no lullaby but a march for Molly and the child curled like a caterpillar in her lifeless womb.

There were fewer mourners than Kinsella had anticipated. His wife had predicted that Dublin's choristers would turn out in force but for once Edith was wrong.

He recognised D'Arcy's horsy features and wax moustache, another man he could not put a name to, a barrel-chested baritone if memory served him, and, walking alone, a lanky downcast man in a scruffy knee-length mackintosh, who may or may not have been a singer too. He looked in vain for the boozy crew from the *Journal* or some of Milly Bloom's slavering suitors but they had all steered clear, he reckoned, because of the taint of murder, a taint that would follow Poldy Bloom, whatever a jury decided, all the days of his life.

The grave had been opened on a little slope of ground with only a few monuments in the row. One small white stone, stained by lichen, held hands with a granite slab that settling earth had tilted inwards as if it were listening for the sound of the infant,

Rudy, whimpering in his sleep below. Now here was Molly, a woman given over more to nature than to God, with a hired Church of Ireland minister to commit her body to the ground and her soul and the soul of the unfledged wee thing within her, Bloom or Boylan made, into the presence of an all-seeing God who, Kinsella was sure, wouldn't judge her too harshly.

'I take it,' Delaney said in a whisper, 'you're on duty? What are you looking for here, Inspector? The phantom intruder?'

'What are *you* looking for, Mr Delaney?'

'What I'm always looking for: a good story.'

The grave-diggers unloaded the coffin from the back of the cart. Several wreathes had been tucked into the cart and they were taken out and laid on the grass too. The minister, still anxious to get on with it, instructed Milly and Boylan where to stand. The minstrel mourners formed a hesitant half circle, two rows deep, and allowed the clergyman to bully them into position.

Kinsella, Delaney and Sullivan kept to the rear, intruders themselves after a fashion. Mr Cunningham, round-shouldered, stood in front of them and answered Kinsella's quiet questions without turning his head.

'The old fellow in the coat with the astrakhan collar?'

'Dillon,' Mr Cunningham muttered. 'Old friend of Molly's father, the Major. Has a house in Terenure where Bloom and Molly first met.'

'And the young man, the boy?'

'One of the widow Dignam's lads.'

'Why is he here?'

'Bloom took care of Mrs Dignam after her husband died. Not many of Paddy's so-called friends gave a toss.' Mr Cunningham spoke into his chest but Kinsella could hear him clearly enough. 'Mrs Dignam thinks highly of Mr Bloom. The boy's attending in her stead, I fancy, since he's head of the household now.'

Kinsella shifted his shoes on the grass, moving an inch closer to Martin Cunningham's shoulder. 'Bloom and Mrs Dignam . . .'

'No, nothing of that nature,' said Mr Cunningham. 'Bloom's a conscientious sort of chap. He made sure Dignam's insurance was paid out promptly and he visited the family as often as he could.'

'Where does Mrs Dignam live?'

'Tritonville Road, I think, or thereabouts.'

'Really?' Kinsella said, then, submissive as schoolboy, shrank into silence under the stony gaze of the vicar who was about to begin the committal.

From the moment Blazes had helped Milly into one of Kelleher's musty cabs and closed the door he'd become aware that soon after the funeral he must address the question of what the devil he was going to do with her if Bloom was sent up for trial at the April Assizes.

In the tailored black outfit Milly looked less like a foal and more like a filly or, add a year or two, a healthy brood mare while he, in striped trousers, frock coat and silk hat felt more like a decrepit stockbroker than a young dandy. Even so, if Molly hadn't been riding in the hearse ahead of them he might have squeezed an armful of supple young flesh just to allay the dread that had undermined him ever since Bloom had stumbled unexpectedly on Molly's battered corpse.

The corpse had been dressed and coffined in the mortuary room, which, Blazes had learned, was not uncommon after post mortems, something Corny Kelleher knew how to deal with, even if he did not. He'd paid sweet for Kelleher's services and the fee for the minister who Maude had persuaded to do the honours. Damned, though, if he was hiring cabs for Bloom's cronies who, given a half chance, would drink his bank account dry in Dunphy's afterwards. In any case, as Daphne had been at pains to point out, certain elements in society regarded a murder victim as being almost as abhorrent as a suicide and would stay away on principle. Being a man of absolutely no principle Blazes hadn't known what his sister was blathering about until the hearse drew up at the gates of the cemetery and he saw how scant the crowd was.

Wrapped up in such thoughts, Blazes kept his eyes down and head bowed as the service progressed through its dreary ritual. God knows, he'd heard enough sermons as a boy when Maude and Daphne had dragged him to St Michael's or St Catherine's or all the way out to All Saints' in Phibsborough to listen to some obnoxious preacher shout the odds about

hellfire and the gruesome fate that awaited fornicators, mastur-
bators and the Papist heretics who were intent on bringing the
Union down.

It wasn't until the coffin, expensive brass handles and all,
was lowered into the pit that Milly reeled a little. He, in the
same moment, experienced a compelling urge to turn on his
heel and, leaving Milly in the lurch and Molly in the grave,
head at the double for Dunphy's to drown his sorrows with
four or five whiskeys before the hounds of hell caught up
with him.

'Blazes,' the girl whispered, 'are you all right?'

'Fine, fine, perfectly fine, sweetheart.'

Looking up, Milly gave him her arm to lean on while the first
rattling hiss of in-fill, like someone pissing pebbles, came up to
meet him from the grave.

'Mr Boylan, you really don't look well,' Dr Paterson said.
'Are you feverish? Here, let me . . .'

'Keep your blasted hands to yourself,' Blazes snarled. 'There's
nothing wrong with me that a pint of porter won't cure.'

'He's upset, that's all,' Milly Bloom said soothingly. 'He didn't
have much to eat at breakfast.'

And too much to drink last night, Michael Paterson thought.
He didn't care much for Hugh Boylan but as a registered medical
practitioner he was obligated to tend the sick whether they were
citizens of Mullingar, Dublin or roaming the surface of the moon.
To judge by his pallor, trembling hands and the manner in which
he slurred his words, slight but detectable, Milly's guardian angel
was either about to have a stroke or throw an uncontrollable fit
of rage, possibly both. Two fingers on the pulse in Boylan's neck
would shed light on the state of his blood pressure but he had
no wish to rile the fellow and risk becoming involved in an
unseemly squabble.

He glanced over at the vicar who was glowering down his
snoot at the delay or perhaps hanging on to see if he could collect
another fee for burying Boylan too, double up.

Milly said, 'Can you walk, Blazes? If not I'll send for . . .'

'Of course I can bloody walk,' Boylan said. 'No, sorry, not
your fault, not your fault. If you could just give me a hand, sweetheart. Once I'm on my feet . . . breath of fresh air . . . *wooo!*'

He rose unsteadily from the tumulus, groped for the shaft of the digger's wheelbarrow with one hand, Milly's hand with the other and hoisted himself to his feet. He plucked at his necktie and collar. He was vaguely aware of mourners gathered in bewildered little groups along the path. He knew the beggars were waiting for drink, but Maude had assured him that this was no ordinary funeral and that such niceties would not be expected.

Milly and the Mullingar doctor had moved away from the graveside and, facing each other, only inches apart, were engaged in earnest conversation. He took a pace towards them but his knees buckled and, stepping back, he seated himself on the end of the wheelbarrow and waited for his head to clear.

Milly said, 'It's very kind of you to come, Dr Paterson. I didn't expect to see anyone from home today.'

Michael Paterson said, 'Home?'

'I mean Mullingar. Mr Coghlan's house.'

Dr Paterson smiled. 'Harry had too many bookings or he'd have been here too. He told me to be sure to pass on his condolences.'

Milly paused. 'Dr Paterson, may I ask you a question?'

'By all means.'

'The baby in my mother's belly, did he . . . did it . . .'

'Suffer?' Michael Paterson said. 'No, Milly. It was too undeveloped to be aware of anything. It would be gone as suddenly as a candle snuffing out,'

'I see,' said Milly. 'Thank you.'

'Milly,' the doctor said, 'how are you?'

'Better than I thought I'd be. How long will I have to wear mourning?'

'It's usually a year for widows but in your case I think a month or perhaps two will be enough. Mrs C will keep you right on that score.' He hesitated. 'Unless your father is released, as well he might be, and you decide to stay in Dublin.'

'No,' Milly said firmly. 'Whatever happens, I will not be staying in Dublin. Will you be in court on Monday?'

'Harry and I will be there if you need us,' Dr Paterson said. 'Your friend, Mr Boylan, seems to have recovered.'

'What's wrong with him?'

'Nervous exhaustion by the look of it,' Dr Paterson said. 'Not uncommon in men of his age.'

'I'll take him home and let his sisters look after him.'

'Will you be able to handle him on your own?'

'Oh, I can handle Mr Boylan,' said Milly with a little grimace.

She put out her hand, palm up and cradled Dr Paterson's hand, palm down, just as Blazes called out crossly, 'Milly, help required.'

NINETEEN

Although they'd taken his watch, along with his other possessions, Bloom was conscious that the hour of final parting was at hand. He had lain awake since just after dawn watching the band of grey daylight on the cell wall grow ever larger until, before the clink of breakfast trays sounded on the galleries, he'd risen, washed in a basin of cold water and dressed with extra care.

Shaving water would be delivered – lukewarm and scummy – and a razor blade which would be removed after he'd used it but, unlike meals, the timing of that order of prison business was erratic and he feared he might have to keep his vigil with a day's growth of beard and his moustache untrimmed. He would have a brief period of respite from the sight of four walls when he, with the other prisoners on the gallery, was shuffled downstairs to the long trough to empty his slop bucket and rinse it under a gushing tap, but that sordid exercise in sanitation apart he was faced with another long day alone with nothing to do but grieve for Molly.

He knew what they'd say, those erstwhile friends of his. They'd say he was a coward not to demand parole, that guilt had kept him away from the graveside but, oh, how their opinions would change if ever the truth got out.

If Molly had taken up with anyone other than Hugh Boylan, if, after that first midsummer 'rehearsal' in Eccles Street, she hadn't fallen asleep with a stupid smile on her face, he might have swallowed the remnants of his pride and forgiven her. When

Boylan's four o'clock appointments became regular events, however, he realised that meekly surrendering to Molly's cupidity was a mistake.

Why, though, did it have to be Boylan? Boylan, that braggart, that dolt, that swaggering donkey with his fat wallet and ever swollen cock, who strutted about Dublin and told everyone who cared to listen who he was ploughing and how parched Molly had been and how Bloom, the cuckold husband, could do nothing but stain the sheets with his impotent tears.

In June, when the affair began, he'd had Dublin to distract him, his jaunts, his voyages about the city, knocking from Pillar to Post Office; Martha's naughty letters, poor Paddy Dignam's funeral up there in the Prospect where at half past ten this morning Kelleher's hearse would carry Molly's body and Blazes' bastard to Glasnevin to rest beside his mother and little Rudy.

Molly, Boylan, Dignam; the strand that connected them was not, as Molly might have it, Fate but a word he'd read somewhere or had discussed with young Dedalus in the kitchen in Eccles Street with Molly lying, sated, upstairs. Still dwelling on what the word might be, he seated himself on the side of the cot and, hands clasped between his knees, prepared to surrender himself once more to tears.

Then the clink of a key, the clack of the bolt, the cell door opened and the jailer, McGonagall, rasped, 'On your feet, Bloom, you've got visitors.'

'Visitors? Who?'

'Your sisters.'

'My sisters?'

'Up from Bantry.'

'I don't have— I mean, how kind of them to make the trip.'

'Since they're country ladies the Governor's stowed them in the Lawyers' Room. You've a half hour, Bloom. Get a jig on.'

He grabbed his coat, fastened his collar then, pausing, enquired, 'What time is it now, please?'

'A quarter after ten,' McGonagall told him. 'Jig-jig.'

Kelleher's horse-drawn hearse would be en route from the mortuary to Glasnevin, Boylan and Milly following in a carriage. He should be with Milly, consoling her. Instead he was being hustled down a metal staircase to greet sisters he didn't have.

He had no opportunity to take his bearings. The jailer marched him across the vast hall and through an unlocked door that led to a long passageway with an arched window at the far end. They turned left. The jailer unlocked an ancient iron gate and off they went along a corridor flanked by scarred wooden doors to emerge at length in a waiting area.

When the jailer drew up before a varnished door with a stencilled sign saying 'Lawyers' Room' Bloom could contain himself no longer. Brushing past the jailer, he threw open the door and barged into the room. Tall windows admitted a flood of daylight: a table, three chairs, two occupied. Two women, one of whom he recognised, the other a total stranger, leaped to their feet.

If McGonagall hadn't pulled him back Bloom was certain the taller of the women would have flung herself upon him and smothered him with kisses.

'Henry,' she cried at the pitch of her voice. 'It's Martha.'

'Oh, Christ!' said Mr Bloom, and promptly turned to flee.

The boy was young, almost certainly still at school, but his Ma had sent him out alone to act a man's part and, even now that the ordeal was over, he maintained an air of gravity that mimicked maturity.

He was not long out of short trousers, Kinsella guessed, but had picked up from someone, an uncle probably, a neat trick with hand-me-downs that were a shade too long and baggy to fit his skinny shanks. Kinsella watched the boy pluck at the trousers with forefingers and thumbs and, in the act of being seated, hitch up hems and square creases as if he'd been wearing a borrowed suit since birth. The Inspector almost expected him to haul out a pipe, stuff it with ropey black tobacco and puff away like a coal-heaver but young Master Dignam fished a pineapple chew from his coat pocket and settled for that instead.

Riding the top deck of an electric tramcar was no longer the thrill it had once been apparently. The boy appeared to be quite blasé about the wonders of 20th century engineering. He sucked on the sweet, stared dully at the houses flying past and, when Mr Cunningham leaned across the seat and addressed him, took several seconds to respond.

'Pardon me, young man,' said Mr Cunningham without a trace of condescension, 'aren't you Paddy Dignam's lad?'

The boy turned his head slowly, eyelids heavy. Kinsella wondered if he'd been thinking of his father and his last trip to Glasnevin. He could hardly have been affected by Mrs Bloom's passing, given that he'd almost certainly never met the woman.

The boy sniffed and shifted the sweet into his cheek.

'Yus.'

'I was a friend of your father's,' Mr Cunningham said. 'I don't know if you remember me. I'm Martin Cunningham.'

The boy did not answer.

Kinsella said, 'How's your mother doing these days? Is she managing?'

'Yus.'

'Now,' said Mr Cunningham, 'which one are you?'

'Patrick.'

'Your father's first born. Ay, of course. I didn't recognise you in that fine suit. I take it your ma gave you a day off school to pay the family's respects to Mr Bloom's wife?'

Again: 'Yus.'

Delaney had gone off to the pub with three or four other mourners, Bartell D'Arcy and the barrel-chested baritone among them. Neville Sullivan, with apologies, had sprinted off to find a cab, while he had followed the boy and, accompanied by Martin Cunningham, had boarded the tram just behind the lad.

'None of Mr Bloom's other friends from Sandymount turned up, unfortunately.' Kinsella threw the remark casually into the pot.

Not a nibble from Patrick Dignam.

'Perhaps Mr Bloom doesn't have any friends down your way,' Kinsella suggested.

Patrick Dignam said, 'Ma says he never done her.'

'Done who?'

'Her, the wife, never done her in.'

'What about your sisters?' Jim Kinsella asked. 'Do they think Mr Bloom done her in?'

'I never listen to what they say,' Patrick answered.

'Sisters!' said Jim Kinsella. 'I have my share of those.

Forever moaning about something and stinking up the house. Do *your* sisters spray themselves with all sorts of stinky stuff, Patrick?'

Patrick looked at him blankly, or so at first it seemed. It should have occurred to Kinsella that when it came to scandals involving sex schoolboys were just as alert to every bit of gossip as adults. He watched the boy's expression turn sly. He brought the pineapple sweet on to his tongue and, curling his tongue around it, sucked noisily for a moment.

Then he said, 'Me sister's chum, Gerty, does. She stinks.'

'Gerty?' said Mr Cunningham. 'Who's she?'

'Mr Bloom's mot.'

Master Dignam watched to see what effect the gutter word would have on the two curious gentlemen. He was ready to duck if one of them aimed a slap at his ear the way Uncle Barney would have done. It was, Kinsella realised, the word that the boy feared might offend, not its implication.

'Who says she's Bloom's mot?' Kinsella asked.

'Mrs Stoer. I heard her and Ma talking about it. Ma says it's the best thing ever happened but I heard from Caffrey that Gerty got a kicking from her old man for going out with Mr Bloom.'

At that age being the centre of attention was more important than discretion. Young Master Dignam, repository of dark schoolyard secrets, looked smug.

'What else did you hear, Paddy?' said Kinsella.

'Heard Mrs Stoer say he done the wife in for Gerty.' A manly, world-weary shrug. 'Can't see as how he would, though.

'Why not?' Kinsella asked.

'You wouldn't catch me doing it with a blooming crip.'

'Gerty's a cripple, is she?'

'Lame as a three-legged donkey. Mrs Stoer says he's stuffing her. Ma says he's not.'

Mr Cunningham sat back, appalled.

Kinsella said, 'Gerty: does she have another name?'

'MacDowell,' said Master Dignam. 'My stop. I gotta get off here for the connection.' Balanced with the agility of youth against the lurching of the tram, he rose to leave. 'You won't say I said nothing, will you, if you see me ma?'

'Our secret,' Kinsella promised and watched his youthful

informant leap down the twisting steps, drop to the pavement and, hitching up his baggy trousers, swagger off.

McGonagall, the jailer, had taken a stance in the waiting area outside the open door. From that angle he could observe the prisoner and his visitors but even with his big elephant ears flapping could not make out much of the conversation.

'Oh, Henry, how could you do this to me?' said Anne-Marie.

'My name's not Henry, it's Leopold.'

'The least you can do is answer her,' Miss Dunne told him.

'Did Boylan send you?' Bloom asked.

'It's none of Mr Boylan's business,' Miss Dunne replied.

'Was I so ugly you couldn't even bear to speak to me?'

'I was delayed,' Bloom said. 'Three times, delayed.'

'In case you've forgotten,' Miss Dunne said, 'Mr Boylan's attending your wife's funeral this morning.'

'I thought you'd be taller. Your writing sounded taller.'

'Penmanship is not a gauge of . . .' Bloom began then, leaning across the table, said, 'What *is* your name, by the way?'

'Anne-Marie Blaney. Oh, Leopold, did you do it for me?'

'Do what for you?'

'Get shot of your wife.'

'Jesus!' Bloom formed a Y with finger and thumb and cradled his brow upon it. 'Oh, Jesus!'

'It doesn't matter to me if you're a Catholic. I'll convert.'

'He isn't a Catholic,' said Miss Dunne. 'He's a Jew.'

'A Jew! You didn't tell me he was a Jew.'

'I did,' said Miss Dunne, 'but you weren't listening.'

The odd thing was that he actually found 'Martha' attractive in a grotesque sort of way. She was older than he'd imagined her to be, closer to forty than thirty, with broad, open features and a full-lipped mouth. Strong shoulders supported an impressive bust. He didn't doubt that the intimate details of what her stays contained had not been exaggerated. He suffered a disturbing vision of her naked, carpet-beater in hand, a mental image that might even have tempted him to cast prudence to the wind a half year ago.

Seated with 'Martha' before him in the flesh, however, his imagination faltered. He saw in her a different kind of nakedness, emotional not physical, and experienced a wave of regret for the weakness that had almost led him astray.

'I'm a Protestant,' he heard himself say, then, taking a firm grip on his scruples, added. 'Not that it matters a jot.'

'It matters to me, Henry . . . Leopold. After all we've meant to each other I'm willing to forgive you.'

'Forgive me what?' Bloom said. 'For being a Protestant?'

'Your transgressions.'

'Eh?'

'Now, now, Anne-Marie.' Miss Dunne tapped her friend's arm. 'You promised you wouldn't let him upset you.'

Bloom drew himself up in the chair. Though he didn't feel particularly threatened by doting Anne-Marie, Boylan's secretary's intentions were patently malicious. He said, 'Whatever you may have heard to the contrary, or whatever you may choose to believe, I did not murder my wife, not even to be with you, Miss Blaney.'

'She was sick, she was ailing. She couldn't give you what a man needs from a woman,' Miss Blaney said. 'You told me so yourself.'

'Bare-faced lies,' said Miss Dunne. 'False promises.'

Bloom, risking rebuke, said, 'You lied to me, too, Anne-Marie.'

'I gave you my heart, Henry, and you trampled on it.'

'Which,' Miss Dunne said, 'is why we're here.'

Bloom said, 'Blazes won't be too pleased when he finds out his telephone has been left off the hook. And you, Miss Blaney, what will your employers say when you fail to turn up at your desk this morning?'

'I'm sick,' Anne-Marie said.

'Heart-broken,' Miss Dunne said. 'Her health's been undermined by your cruelty. I've read your letters.'

'So Boylan *is* behind it. I *knew* it.'

'Mr Boylan has nothing to do with it,' Maureen Dunne said. 'We're here to inform you that Miss Blaney has preserved all your letters and intends to present them to an appropriate authority at the first opportunity unless—'

'Unless what?' said Bloom. 'Unless I promise to marry her? Are you barking mad? I'm jugged up on a murder charge. Do you think a few saucy letters will make any difference?'

Miss Dunne said, 'How will a breach of promise case sit with the judges in a court of Assize? Ask yourself that one.'

'What,' Mr Bloom said, 'do you want from me?'

'Two hundred pounds,' Miss Dunne said promptly.

'In the name of God, woman, I don't have two hundred pennies, let alone two hundred pounds. Where do you think I'll find that sort of money?'

'Sell your house.'

'I don't own the blessed house. It's rented.'

'Sell your furniture, your clothes,' Miss Dunne said. 'Borrow from your wealthy friends for all I care. Two hundred pounds is the price of our silence. Isn't that right, Anne-Marie?'

'It is, Henry. I'm sorry to say, it is.'

'And what's the price of *my* silence,' said Bloom after a pause.

'Your silence?' Anne-Marie said, puzzled.

'Do you think you're the only one who keeps letters?' Bloom said. 'There are two sides to every correspondence and, by Gum, Anne-Marie, your letters to Henry Flower are a blessed sight more interesting than mine. Racy isn't the word for it. I'll bet the tufts of hair you sent me would fetch a few quid in the right quarter too. Frankly, I'm surprised you've any hair left down there.'

'Have I not suffered enough?' Miss Blaney said, 'Surely you wouldn't subject me to more humiliation?'

'For two hundred pounds I would,' Bloom replied. 'Where do you work? A lawyer's office, a city merchant's, a bank, perhaps? It shouldn't be too difficult for my lawyer to find out. Imagine how you'll be treated when a selection of your letters, even without the curls, arrives on your employer's desk. You'll be a laughing stock, an object of derision, and lucky to find another job in Dublin.'

'Maureen, is that true?'

'No, he's bluffing.'

'Am I?' Bloom said. 'You, I gather, have had sight of the letters Blazes stole from me. Well, I've dozens more like them, dozens and dozens, each more explicit than the last.'

'Two hundred pounds or we go to the police.'

'Wait,' said Miss Blaney. 'Maureen, wait.'

'Where are these letters, may I ask?' Miss Dunne said.

'In safe keeping,' Bloom said. 'If the detectives couldn't find them, or bloodhound Boylan either, rest assured they're well beyond your reach. But if one letter of mine – of Henry Flower's – turns up in court be in no doubt I'll produce Martha Clifford's replies. I'm sorry, Anne-Marie, but my life's at stake and I can't afford to be a gentleman. I suggest you burn them.'

'If I do,' Anne-Marie said, 'will I ever see you again?'

'Considering that I may be found guilty of murder,' Bloom said, 'I think it's highly unlikely, not to say inadvisable. Burn my letters and forget Henry Flower ever existed.'

'He's doing it again,' Maureen Dunne said testily. 'He's seducing you, Anne-Marie, don't you see?'

'I loved you, Leopold, and you let me down. Why didn't you keep our rendezvous? Were you afraid?'

'Yes,' Bloom said. 'I was afraid I'd fall in love with you.'

'It's not too late,' said Anne-Marie Blaney. 'You're free now, free to marry, free to . . . to love me.'

'Or murder you,' Maureen Dunne put in.

Bloom sighed. 'Miss Blaney,' he said, 'if I had money I'd give it to you willingly. I have no money and, whatever the court decides, no future in Ireland. If I'm released then I'll be gone, vanishing as if I had never been, as if you'd never known me . . . or Henry Flower.' He sighed again. 'What I will have, what I will take with me, is the memory of our friendship.'

'I'll do it. I'll do it for you, Leopold. I'll . . . I'll burn them.'

'Anne-Marie! Are you blind and deaf?' said the strident Miss Dunne. 'He's conning you again *and* fleecing me out of two hundred pounds into the bargain.'

'You?' Bloom said. 'What do you have to do with it? Are you so in thrall to Hugh Boylan you can no longer recognise love?'

'Doomed love,' Anne-Marie amended.

'Exactly,' said Bloom, sweating a little. 'A love that might have been between two ships that passed in the night.'

'Blather, pure blather,' Maureen Dunne said.

'You believe me, Anne-Marie, don't you?' Bloom said.

'Yes, Leopold, I do. I believe you.'

'Then you're a bigger fool than I took you for, Anne-Marie Blaney.' Miss Dunne scrambled to her feet. 'Don't think you've heard the last of this, Mr Smug. I'll teach you to trifle with a woman's affections and throw her over like . . . like a piece of orange peel.'

'Did you really keep all my letters?' Anne-Marie asked.

'I did. I did, indeed,' Bloom answered. 'Every last one.'

'If, by some miracle, you escape the gallows,' Maureen Dunne said, 'the day you step out of that court you'll be hearing from us with a writ for breach of promise.'

'No, he won't,' said Anne-Marie. 'My word on it, Leopold. You won't hear from either of us again.'

'It's more than I deserve,' said Bloom humbly.

'Too bloody true, it is,' said dumpy Miss Dunne.

Anne-Marie Blaney said, 'It was my fault as much as yours. You didn't treat me very well but I was wrong to open my heart to you, a stranger. I'm glad we met, though. A lifetime of wondering would have done me no good at all. It's best for both of us if we let Henry and Martha rest in peace.'

Bloom stifled a whoop of relief. He rose with as much dignity as he could muster and bowed. 'Thank you, Miss Blaney. From the bottom of my heart, I thank you.' He hesitated, then, going the whole hog, took her hand in his and bussed her knuckles. 'Goodbye, Martha, my dearest. Goodbye.'

'Goodbye, dearest Henry.' She paused. 'Forever.'

Bloom turned discreetly away to hide his emotions while McGonagall showed the ladies out into the yard and pointed them in the direction of the tram stop on the O'Connell Road.

The jailer lingered for a moment at the door to watch the older woman link arms with the younger and wondered what they could possibly be saying and why, when they reached the pavement, the tall one in the feather boa and blue toque gave a merry little skip.

'Well,' said Miss Blaney, 'that was a lucky escape, I must say.'

'What?' said Miss Dunne. 'Why?'

'Now I've met him,' said Anne-Marie Blaney, 'I don't fancy him at all,' then, to the bewilderment of jailer McGonagall, gave another little skip just as the tram arrived to carry them away.

One of the perils of being the junior partner in Tolland, Roper and Sullivan was that you were expected to juggle a dozen clients at once and, for the sake of the fees, let alone your own reputation, keep them happy while their cases bogged down in legal limbo.

It was not, therefore, all fun and games and coroner's courts for young Neville who, immediately on his return from Glasnevin, had to deal with a delegation from a Dutch shipbuilder whose contract to build a suction dredger for the Dublin Dockyard Company had been blocked by an upstart geologist from the Port Authority who was concerned about rising silt levels which, as Neville and several irate Dutchmen tried to point out, was exactly the problem the dredger was designed to solve.

The geologist became more recalcitrant and the Dutchmen more irascible as morning gave way to afternoon and the large scale tidal maps that Mr Oram, Neville's clerk, had spread about the office were in danger of being ripped to shreds.

It was into this melee that Miss Sarah Tolland – with some egging on from Mr Oram – intruded.

If there was one thing Poppy Tolland's daughter was good at it was pouring oil on troubled waters; Lord knows, she'd had enough experience arbitrating between her father and her mother over the years. Good manners dictated that she apologise and retreat but common sense prompted her to hold her ground and, it being past lunch time, swords were sheathed, a truce declared and, with Neville's promise to convene another meeting soon, both parties repaired to the Parador to continue the argument over beef steaks, apple charlotte and a bottle or two of burgundy.

Closing the door of the office with his heel, Neville kissed his intended's ear, her neck and finally her lips with a fervour that owed more to gratitude than passion.

'Thank God, darling,' he said. 'I thought I'd never get rid of them. Billing's one thing but bull-headedness is quite another.'

'Is there no resolution in sight?'

'Absolutely none.'

'Can it be taken to arbitration?'

'Civil court? It may come to that. If not I may just have to . . .'

'Resign?' Miss Tolland said.

'Elope,' said Mr Sullivan.

When Miss Sarah Tolland smiled the effect was nothing short of dazzling. 'I'm not averse to that,' she said, 'but I would prefer to have lunch first, if it's all right with you.'

'Sound idea,' Neville said. 'A little fizz to wash away the taste of silt and graveyards would go down a treat. I have' – he consulted his pocket watch – 'one hour and twenty-two minutes before my meeting with a market gardener who feels he's been diddled over a load of horse manure.'

'I'm sure Poppy would have something to say about that,' Sarah said. 'Speaking of which, I didn't drop by just to scrounge lunch. Father asked me to give you this?'

Neville took the envelope and turned it over suspiciously, as if he expected it to explode in his hand. 'What is it?'

'Poppy's not going to confide in a mere blood relative, especially a female. Perhaps if you open it . . .'

'Um, yes, of course,' said Neville and, with his thumbnail, slit the seal of the envelope and tipped out a printed card – *Mercury Life Assurance Society, Established 1888, Unusually Low Premiums on Family Life Policies and Endowments. Dublin Office, 18 Smile Street. Secretary for Ireland, J.F. Leonard* – across which in heavy pencil Mr Tolland had scribbled, 'Bloom.'

'How on earth did he track it down?' said Neville.

'Ah,' said Sarah, tapping not her own nose but Neville's. 'Poppy, like God, moves in mysterious ways. Is it of use to you?'

'I'll say,' Neville answered. 'Smile Street? Is there such a street in Dublin or is it made up?'

'I've never been entirely sure that Dublin itself isn't made up,' Sarah said, 'but, yes, I know where Smile Street is. It's a tiny street off the bottom of Amiens Street, not far from the courthouse.'

'Hardly the Equitable Life then?'

'Hardly,' Sarah agreed. 'Are you going there now?'

'No, I'm accompanying a beautiful woman to lunch,' said Neville gallantly. 'Tomorrow will do. I assume the Mercury does business on Saturday.'

'If it does any business at all,' said Sarah and, adjusting his necktie and handing him his hat, steered him away from the office before he could change his mind.

TWENTY

Miss Gerty MacDowell was hastening home from Irishtown down the length of Tritonville Road. Dusk now, or almost so. A stiff easterly layered the sky above the Bay with turbulent clouds, within which the beams of the lighthouse flickered in sullen flashes.

The lamps along the road were being lighted and the lamps in the houses too. Walking as fast as her legs would carry her, Gerty passed gardens and hedges shawled in shadow. In spite of traffic on the road, kiddies playing on the pavement and the familiar tea-time troupe of men and women returning from work, she felt exposed. The foot was dragging and the straps of her shoe would be scuffed if she didn't slow down. She was all too aware of the man behind her, a big man in a belted mackintosh and brown fedora who had picked her up somewhere shy of London Bridge Road and had dogged her footsteps every since.

It wasn't the first time in the past week she'd felt as if she was being followed. She'd told Cissy and Cissy had tried to laugh it off but hadn't quite managed. Cissy too had lost her – what was the word Poldy used? – her insouciance and took everything, or nearly everything, seriously these days.

She knew it couldn't be Father O'Grady. He'd dropped in mid-morning when she'd been out in the back hanging sheets in the hope it wouldn't rain. He'd come out to her – her mother watching from the window – and had told her he'd seen Mr Bloom and had given him her note and Poldy had said, 'I understand,' which was all the reply she'd needed and had made her feel much better.

She glanced over her shoulder. The man was still there, matching his step to hers, slowing when she slowed and starting up again when she did. She wasn't far from home. She could see the privet hedge that her father never cut hanging over the pavement, leaves rustling in the wind in the lamppost light. She was cramping, her calf cramping. She had to stop, just had to and, hand braced against the wall in front of the house painter's house, she did.

The man padded up behind her and then around her so she couldn't escape. Tipping back his hat and stooping, he looked into her face and said, 'Miss MacDowell, is it? Miss Gerty MacDowell? Inspector Kinsella.' He politely took off his hat so she could see his face. 'Dublin Metropolitan. May I have a word with you?'

She felt blood rush to her cheeks, swayed a little and rested her bottom on the wall, not caring if her skirt got soiled. She had her breath back but her heart had gone to the races and she needed the wall for support.

'I'm sorry,' he said. 'I didn't mean to alarm you. I thought it best to catch you before you reached home. If you wish we can go to your house and have a chat there.'

'No,' Gerty got out. 'Here.'

Kinsella could readily understand why Bloom found her attractive. She was pretty in a pale, china-doll sort of way. She had blue eyes and stencilled brows that gave her face definition and what his daughter, Violet, would call feminine mystique. She had beautiful hair, short cut, dark brown and wavy, and wore just exactly the right sort of little hat to show it off. The navy skirt was stride cut, he noticed, and her blouse not just clean but spotless. He pondered her age: six or seven years older than Milly Bloom, probably thirteen or fourteen younger than Leopold: twenty-three or -four would be his guess.

'Do your parents approve of your friendship with Mr Bloom?'

'I don't know what you're talking about.'

'Don't you read the newspapers?'

'No.'

Mr O'Shea, one of her father's boozing friends, went past, stepping wide of the policeman, and slid an inquisitive glance at her. It was all up with her now. Even if the policeman didn't take her off to jail she'd have to answer to her father. There would be more shouting, more raging, another excuse for him to stamp out of the house to drink away money they didn't have.

In the window of the living-room of the painter's house behind her a light went on. She knew, without looking round, that Mrs

Gorman, the house painter's wife, would be squinting to see who was sitting on her wall.

The detective put on his hat and, crouching slightly, said, 'If you're going to lie to me, Miss MacDowell, I'll have to escort you to the police station, and you wouldn't want that would you? So, I'll ask you again: your friendship with Leopold Bloom, do your parents know of it?'

'Who told you about Leopold? Was it Cissy?'

'No,' Kinsella said. 'Whoever Cissy might be, it wasn't her.'

'Leopold and I aren't . . . we don't do what married people do. Mr Bloom would never take advantage.'

'He's a gentleman, in other words?'

'He is, he is.'

There was a rhythm to questioning, a beat like the beat in music, like the tick-tock of the metronome on top of Marigold's piano. All he had to do to get Miss MacDowell to answer his questions was find the right tempo.

He said, 'How long have you known Mr Bloom?'

'Since August.'

'Where did you meet?'

'At Mrs Dignam's.'

'Where does Mrs Dignam live?'

'Newbridge Avenue.'

'Is Mrs Dignam a friend of yours?'

'She's a widow. My mother sent me round with a fruit pudding to give the children a treat.'

'Mr Bloom, what was he doing there?'

'Making sure Mrs Dignam received her insurance money.'

Darkness was settling quickly and the east wind had a keen edge. The young woman shivered. Jim Kinsella resisted an urge to cut short the informal interview and let her get off home. He was curious about the circumstances of that first meeting, though, and how the affair had progressed.

He said, 'Did Bloom visit your house?'

'Once, just once, before Christmas. My father tried to throw him out but Poldy wouldn't leave. He said he had nothing to be ashamed of. My father said did he think we were low life and he could do what he liked with me. Poldy flew into a temper and told my father off good and proper. After that, we met outside.'

'How often?'

'As often as we could.'

If I press her too hard she'll break, Kinsella thought. He could pull her in but he didn't want to do that just yet.

He said, 'Did Mr Bloom give you presents?'

'Yes, soap.'

'Soap?'

'Lemon soap, for Christmas, in a lovely box.'

'Perfume, did he give you perfume too?'

'No, he said he liked the scent I wore.'

'What sort of scent do you wear, Miss MacDowell?'

'Halcyon Days it's called.'

'My daughter likes that one. I think she gets it from Winterbottom's.'

'That's where I buy mine too,' said Gerty MacDowell.

'Were you ever in Mr Bloom's house?'

Curtly: 'No.'

'Did you ever meet Mr Bloom's wife? I assume you knew he was married?'

The question gave her pause. He wondered what they talked about, Bloom and she, or if Bloom saw in her a blank slate upon which he could draw his own pattern.

'He told me he was married. Anyway, Mrs Dignam knew he was married. She told me he was unhappy at home and it wouldn't be wrong to be friends with him provided I didn't . . . you know. If I didn't do it I could still go to confession and take the mass.'

'And Mr Bloom's wife?'

'I never met her.'

'Did Mr Bloom ever talk about her?'

'Now and then. Not much. I'm sorry she's dead. Poor woman to pass like that.'

'You're sure you never visited number 7 Eccles Street?'

Again curtly, too curtly: 'No, never.'

She waited for him to ask again, to browbeat her into revealing the truth. Poldy had told her she must say nothing to anyone until his trials were over and, if a jury found him guilty, must forget she'd ever known him. Thoughts of Poldy in prison, thoughts of never seeing him again filled her with dread. The only person she'd told about that night was Cissy. She hadn't even told Father O'Grady.

She said, 'Have you seen Poldy— Mr Bloom today?'

'No, not since we left court.'

'Didn't he get out to go to her funeral?'

The Inspector shook his head. 'He didn't request parole.'

'Were *you* there?' she asked. 'At Glasnevin?'

'I was,' Kinsella answered.

'Were there wreathes?'

'Yes, several.'

'And flowers?'

'No, no flowers.'

'Poldy told me she loved flowers. Did anyone sing?'

Kinsella shook his head again.

'Poor woman,' Gerty MacDowell said. 'Poor woman, though she had only herself to blame, I suppose.'

'What makes you say that?'

'I don't know. I just said it.'

She stamped her foot, the lame one, not, he thought, petulantly but to ease a cramp. He wondered if she'd been born with the deformity or if an accident had caused it. Without that blemish she'd probably have been married by now.

She was shivering again, white-faced.

'All right, Miss MacDowell,' he said. 'I think that's enough. You've been very helpful.'

'Have I?' She seemed surprised. 'How?'

'Every crumb of information is useful.'

'Will he . . . will Poldy go free?'

'I believe there's every chance of that happening.'

'Oh!' She smiled for the first time. 'Oh, that would be the answer to all my prayers. Thank you.'

'Thank *you*, Miss MacDowell.'

Tipping the brim of his fedora, Jim Kinsella nodded and headed off in the direction of the tram stop, leaving Bloom's naive little ladylove to limp off home for her tea.

If she'd still been living in Eccles Street Milly was sure it would all have been too much and she'd have collapsed under the strain. In her year away from home, however, her outlook had changed.

Dublin was no longer the hub of her universe. Even so, all the lovely things that had made her childhood a happy one should have counted for more than they did. She'd loved her mother, though not quite as much as her father. She recalled how when Mummy was being what Papli called 'unreasonable' he would slip away with his little Milly to ride on a tram-car or stroll round town and was never ashamed to be seen holding her hand or, when she was small, carrying her on his shoulders like a sack of potatoes. But Papli too had changed. During those first weeks in Mullingar she'd wondered if she'd been sent away as a punishment or because she'd become, to use one of Mummy's favourite expressions, 'an inconvenience'.

Papli had explained that he'd arranged for her to train to be a photographer so she'd have a career to fall back on and wouldn't have to marry just any Tom, Dick or Harry. She hadn't really believed him and her first thought on learning in court that Mummy had a baby inside her was that she'd been packed off to make way for a new Rudy or another little Milly, which, of course, was impossible; she'd been in Mullingar for fully eight months before the baby had even been conceived.

The way her mother had met her end would have disturbed her more if the weapon had been a dagger or a pistol. That was the way heroines died in all the plays and operas she'd ever seen. Being murdered with the painted teapot of which her mother was so proud seemed more like a comic sketch than anything else. Seeing her mother laid out on the slab in the mortuary had shocked her, though. But self-control was expected and the funeral had been a brave show on her part. It had pleased her no end to see Michael Paterson from Mullingar there, *her* friend, not one of her father's cronies or her mother's admirers but someone who'd come from the country to pay his respects to *her,* and no one else.

The one thing of which she was certain was that Papli would never strike a woman. Her father had too much respect for women. Besides, he'd loved her mother and had never laid a hand on her that she'd ever seen. What sustained her was the conviction that her father was innocent and that, in due course, the police would lay the intruder by the heels. Meanwhile, she'd few qualms about letting Mr Boylan take care of her. Blazes had not only been her mother's friend but also her manager and, according to Papli, had more than cleared his feet, financially, out of their engagements.

Shaky and sour in mood, Blazes had insisted on returning to his office immediately after the funeral. He'd sent her on by cab to his sisters' house where Daphne made a great fuss of her and, seeing that she wasn't totally beside herself, had suggested they might go out for lunch and do a little shopping. Maude had elected to stay at home for the upstairs rooms needed dusting and someone had to do it. Over lunch in the Dame Street DBC, Daphne had asked her all sorts of questions about the funeral. Milly had answered as honestly as possible, but when Daphne had quizzed her about her mother and father and other personal matters, she'd taken refuge in a shower of crocodile tears that had put an end to Daphne's prying.

As soon as they got back from the outing, Milly had gone to her room to shed a few more tears, genuine this time, and, slipping off her shoes and top clothes, had lain on the bed and had fallen asleep.

She had no idea of the hour, whether it was early or late. For a confused moment, she imagined that the wan light in the window might be dawn and not the last vestiges of that awful day.

She stirred and sat up.

The figure of the man beside the bed was indistinct. For a split second she thought it might be Dr Paterson and her heart gave a little bump in her chest. Then she saw it was only Blazes, coatless, collarless and with his waistcoat unbuttoned.

'You really are beautiful when you're asleep,' he said.

'What time is it?'

'Coming up for half past six.'

'I'd better dress. Is dinner ready?'

'No, sweetheart,' he said. 'Not just yet.'

A faint wisp of smoke curled around him. She smelled his cigar before he brought it to his lips. With languid deliberation he put out his tongue, sucked on the end and filled his mouth with smoke.

He said, 'You didn't tell Daphne about me, did you?'

'No,' Milly said. 'I thought you wouldn't want me to.'

'No sense in making a fuss.' Blazes inhaled again. 'You look so like your mother, like Molly.' He picked a fleck of tobacco from his tongue. 'She would be proud of us this day, Mill, for giving her a grand send-off.'

'It didn't strike me as especially grand.'

'Respectful, then. Call it respectful.'

He shuffled closer to the bed. 'God,' he said in a voice thickened by cigar smoke, 'you really have grown up down there in the country, haven't you? You're going to make some man very happy one of these days.'

She recalled Buck Mulligan pinning her down and Alex Bannon's hands all over her. There was no love, no affection in them or, she realised, in Hugh Boylan. She reached for the bedspread and pulled it up to her chin just as the bedroom door flew open.

'What do you think you're doing, Hughie?'

Unperturbed, Blazes blew a stream of smoke in Maude's direction. 'Making sure our guest's all right.'

'I'm sure she'll be a lot better without you breathing all over her,' Maude Boylan said. 'Dinner's in half an hour so come away and let her get dressed.'

'By all means,' said Blazes – the old insolent Blazes – and, puffing on his cigar, sauntered from the room and closed the door.

Night fell and with it Mr Bloom's spirits. 'Martha Clifford' and Boylan's typist showing up together out of the blue had reminded him just how cramped Dublin could be and how everyone seemed to know everyone else's business.

After his panic subsided, the meeting in the Lawyers' Room had turned out to be quite entertaining. Martha, or, rather, Anne-Marie had piled it on just too thickly. Beneath the gush he'd sensed disappointment and in the speed of her departure a note of finality. As for the hobble-hipped, melon-breasted Miss Dunne, quick thinking on his part had thwarted her ham-fisted attempt at blackmail. Even for a share of two hundred pounds, Anne-Marie Blaney wouldn't risk her secret desires being dragged into the limelight to titillate every leering tippler from here to Bantry Bay.

Barring the two he'd carelessly left inside the Froude, he'd kept none of Martha Clifford's letters and still couldn't fathom what Boylan had been searching for in the Eccles Street bookcase or what possible use the rogue might make of two mischievous letters from a woman unknown. He could see no logic in it, no angle by which Boylan might benefit, save to furnish the Crown with a motive for murder which, thanks to Boylan himself, the Crown already had in trumps.

Looking back, he realised that he should have stopped writing to naughty Miss Clifford far sooner than he did. It had never really been his intention to board the merry-go-round with Martha or to tease her with false promises. He was not, by nature, cruel the way Boylan could be cruel or, now and then, Molly. He should have broken off with Martha Clifford when his affection for Gerty became too insistent to ignore but the epistolary romance had seemed harmless and unreal in contrast to his feelings for Gerty MacDowell, which were all too real and not at all harmless. It was close to Christmas before, giving himself a shake, he had said farewell to his over-eager correspondent once and for all, having no more need by then of the tawdry thrills that Martha offered.

Back in June he could not, of course, have known that he would ever encounter face to face the little charmer, Gerty, who'd so roused his ardour on a warm, summer evening on Sandymount beach, flirting with him and showing him her stockings from a safe distance. It had shaken him to bump into her again a few weeks later in, of all places, Mrs Dignam's front parlour.

On seeing him in the doorway, Gerty had blushed peony-pink.

'Oh! she'd said. 'Oh! Oh!'

In that ghastly moment of recognition guilt had united them. Before she'd known who he was she'd flashed her frillies on Sandymount sands and he'd responded by spilling his seed via a hand in his trouser pocket, all without a word exchanged between them. Transparent stockings covered a multitude of sins and he hadn't twigged she was lame until she got up to leave.

'I don't believe you know Miss MacDowell,' Mrs Dignam had said. 'A pleasure to make your acquaintance, Miss MacDowell,' he had courteously replied, while cursing himself for failing to realise that his friend, Mrs Dignam, and the tempting little puss from the beach might be neighbours.

From the moment of first meeting, Gerty had offered him not just respect but love. He, in return, had smothered his base instincts. There would be time enough for 'that', as Gerty called it, when, nominally at least, they were man and wife and had put Dublin far behind them.

Squatting on the cot in his cell in Kilmainham he couldn't shake off the memory of the last months of his marriage or of the passion Molly had aroused in him when he and she had been young. Now it was over, all over. Molly was at rest in the family plot hard by the railings of the Finglas Road. And where's your horse-cocked lover now, Molly, he thought, when you need someone to mourn for you? Tipping his boater to some other slut, like as not, or helping our daughter to a bowl of broth in the haunted hall of the Rechabites while his sisters look on askance.

Molly, Molly, I can do no more for you now than light my prison candle and pretend it never happened.

So, alone in the darkness, Mr Leopold Bloom lit the candle stump, blew out the match and, quite without conscience, wept for the wife he'd killed.

TWENTY ONE

Neville would surely have been able to locate Smile Street, short though it was, but he was too gallant to object when Sarah volunteered to be his guide, mainly, she said, to ensure that he didn't stray off the straight and narrow and find himself in Montgomery Street and at the mercy of all sorts of wild women.

One wild woman, Neville assured her, was quite enough to be going on with, thank you, but he would, nonetheless, be only too pleased to have her company on what was, after all, an enquiry that involved neither ethics nor etiquette.

The Mercury's Dublin headquarters were situated in a shabby building squeezed between a shop that sold gas ovens and the premises of a sanitary engineer. The step at the entrance was unwashed and the two narrow street-level windows too, though each was draped inside with heavy brocade curtains that reminded Neville of his one and only visit to a brothel, to which he'd been dispatched by Mr Roper to draft a will for one of the madams who was slowly succumbing to tumours in an unmentionable spot.

The door had brass hinges that uttered not a squeak when Neville leaned upon them and, ushering Sarah before him, quietly entered the Mercury's bijou hall.

'Carpet.' Neville worked his foot into the Axminster. 'Good quality at that.'

'Parlour palms and a lovely coleus too,' said Sarah. 'My goodness, someone's keen on their potted plants. I do hope they're properly watered.'

'Assiduously, ma'am, I assure you,' said a voice from the stairs. 'Every morning, me and me little watering can. Are you a botanist, by any chance?'

'Alas, no.' Sarah peered up into the half light. 'I'm Miss Sarah Tolland and this is Neville Sullivan, soon to be my husband.'

'Oooo, customers,' said a female voice from upstairs. 'Put the bottle away, Jono, and spread the welcome mat.'

'Definitely not the Equitable,' Neville whispered in Sarah's ear as a small, apple-cheeked gent in a chequered tweed lounge suit danced down the staircase and, with a sweep of the arm, said, 'Step this way, folks, and ignore me good lady who hasn't learned no proper manners yet.'

Neville had dealt with insurance agents before but Mr J.P. Leonard bore no resemblance to the stiff-necked actuaries who staffed the imposing buildings on Dame Street or west of the Four Courts. He looked more like a market trader than a person skilled in the intricacies of finance, an image endorsed by his uncultured accent and unruly grammar. Sarah seemed quite taken with him, though, and, smiling, followed him into a ground-floor room decorated with yet more potted plants.

'Cheese here,' said Mr Leonard with an airy wave at foliage creeping up the wall. 'Aspidistra there, and that' – he paused lovingly by a large blue pot – 'is a Florida Strangler, a variety of fig dashed hard to cultivate indoors. You won't find many of 'em in Dublin, I can tell you.'

Tearing himself away from the display, he popped behind a tall desk and, placing both hands upon it like a counter jumper from Walpole Brothers, said, 'Now, what can I do for you good folks? Fire, Theft, Life, Endowment? We have policies to suit all requirements and can trim the premiums to the purse. Please, be seated.'

He waited politely until Sarah eased herself into an armchair upholstered in what may have been buffalo hide and Neville, less comfortably, on to a spindly object with gilded arms. Mr Leonard took his place in a swivel chair behind the desk and, sitting upright, cocked his head and invited Neville to state the nature of his business.

Sarah said, 'Frankly, Mr Leonard . . . if you are Mr Leonard . . .'

'In person.'

'Frankly, we hadn't expected . . . I mean, you are the Mercury's Irish Secretary, are you not?'

Mr Leonard chuckled. 'Not impressed? No, I knows what it looks like. It looks like all this stuff is flash and we takes your money and vanish at first sign of a claim. Ireland, says my employer, is a country in which no man's honesty goes unchallenged.'

'Who says . . . said?' Neville asked.

'Mr Rothschild.'

Sarah and Neville piped up in unison. 'Rothschild!'

'Well, he ain't exactly a genuine Rothschild. He's a Goldstein. But he's hooked to the bankers by marriage. This here is just one of his little ventures. Me and the missus was shipped over from the Liverpool office to test the waters.'

'Jews,' said Neville. 'You're Jews.'

'Do you have something against Jews, Mr Sullivan?'

'By no means,' Neville said. 'It does, however, explain . . . um, certain facts. Does Mr Goldstein hale from Hungary?'

'He does, indeed,' said Mr Leonard, then, with a little admonishing wag of the forefinger, 'Bloom sent you, didn't he? You aren't here to buy a policy. You're – what? – Bloom's attorney?'

'How did you know that Mr Bloom sent us?' Sarah asked.

'I done ten years with the Mercury in Liverpool as a false claims inspector and there's nothing – I mean nothing – you can teach me about fishy business. You, Mr Sullivan, can't expect me to help you clear Bloom's name. It's not in the Mercury's interests to see Bloom walk free.'

'Ah-hah! So Mr Bloom does have a policy with your company?' Neville said. 'May I have sight of it?'

'Can't be doing that unless you've a signed letter giving you the right. Have you got such a letter?'

'No, I have not,' said Neville.

'Really, Mr Leonard,' said Sarah, with a little *tut*, 'I see no reason to bother Mr Bloom with incidentals at this difficult time.'

'Difficult as in locked up,' said Mr Leonard, affability fraying at the edges. 'Mercury clients are guaranteed confidentiality when they signs on the dotted.'

'What they are guaranteed and what they are legally entitled to,' said Neville, 'are not quite the same. It wouldn't bother me in the slightest to have the coroner summon you as a witness, Mr Leonard. Then, under oath, you'd be obliged to reveal the terms of Bloom's policy and, I might add, a great deal about the fly-by-night nature of Mercury Life Assurance.'

'We ain't no fly-by-night.'

'Of course you're not,' said Neville smoothly, 'but by the time I get through with you in court you'll be commercially tarred and feathered – if you take my meaning – and lucky if you can sell life insurance to Methuselah.'

Mr Leonard twitched his mouth to one side and then the other.

'Nope,' he said, at length 'I don't intimidate that easy. I been in many a witness box before now and I can talk double-Dutch with the best of 'em. Do *you* take *my* meaning, Mr Sullivan?'

Neville opened his mouth to stiffen the threat but only got as far as 'Um' before Sarah intervened. 'Now, Mr Leonard,' she said, 'what say we remove Mr Bloom's name from discussion and you simply sell my fiancé and me a life insurance policy.' A tilt of the eyebrow and a dazzling smile. 'I'm sure you've a standard form you can offer us.'

'Crafty,' said Mr Leonard. 'Very crafty, Miss Tolland. You'll want the same sort of policy as your friend Mr Bloom, I suppose?'

'Mr Bloom? Never heard of him,' said Sarah, still smiling. 'A

basic life policy in which a husband benefits on the death of a
wife would suit us admirably.'

Mr Leonard drummed his fingers on the desk. 'Or,' he said,
at length, 'you might be interested in our special family policy.'

'Family policy?' said Neville. 'What sort of terms are offered
on a family policy or, to put it plainly, who benefits?'

'Issue,' said Mr Leonard.

'Issue?' said Neville.

'Children,' Mr Leonard said. 'Kiddies. Husband insures his
life and that of his wife on a joint policy to make sure when he
or his wife pop off the pay-out goes straight to the children.'

'Hold on,' said Neville. 'Do you mean to say that if either the
father or mother dies the children receive the pay-out and the
surviving spouse gets nothing?'

'Plenty of women don't want their hubby to drink the money
away and there are hubbies who distrust their wives so much –
wives with a fancy-man, say – they leap at the chance to provide
for their kiddies and leave nothing but a poke in the eye for the
spouse.'

'What if the children are too young to receive benefit?' Sarah
Tolland asked.

'Mercury invests the money until every child alive at the time
of the parent's death reaches sixteen, then we pays out equally
to each of the little blighters, male and female, to give the child
or children a nest-egg to make a start in life.'

'And rake in a tidy profit for Mr Goldstein in the process,'
said Neville. 'How many of these special family policies have
you sold since you opened the office in Dublin?'

'Twenty or thereabouts.'

'Good Lord!' said Neville. 'What's the average pay-out?'

'Any sum you care to name, depending on the premium. It's
no penny a week scheme, I admit.'

'What's the average sum insured?' said Sarah.

'Three to five hundred pounds.'

'I can readily understand why the Mercury would prefer my
client to be found guilty,' said Neville. 'If Mrs Bloom died at
the hand of an unrelated assailant the daughter stands to collect
as soon as she turns sixteen.'

'That's right.'

'How much?' said Sarah. 'Three hundred?'

'Five, in fact.'

'When did Mr Bloom take out the policy?' Sarah said.

'December,' said Leonard. 'That's all I'm saying. If you want a copy of the policy, I'll need authorisation from Bloom.'

'One last question,' Neville said. 'Am I to understand that Mr Bloom took out a policy that would benefit his daughter and not himself. Only one policy, no other?'

'No other with this company,' Mr Leonard replied.

'Mr Leonard,' said Sarah, 'you've been exceedingly generous with your time. Thank you.'

'I'm surprised Bloom didn't let on his daughter was the one to benefit,' said Mr Leonard. 'Even if he's locked up, I can still do Mr Bloom a special little endowment policy. Sixpence a week mounts up over twenty or twenty-five years, believe me. He could wind up a rich old man.'

'I'm sure Mr Bloom will be gratified to learn that Mercury Life Assurance has his financial interests at heart,' said Neville.

'Just so long as he doesn't swing,' said J.F. Leonard.

'Really?' Neville said.

'Oh, yer,' said Mr Leonard. 'If he swings all bets are off.'

Neville Sullivan and his beautiful bride-to-be were partaking of an early lunch in the Metropole Grill in Prince's Street. One of Sarah Tolland's most endearing traits, as far as Neville was concerned, was her fondness for eating heartily. He loved to watch her wading into oxtail soup or scoffing a plate of ribs, for he cherished the unscientific notion that a female who approached dining with such enthusiasm would be equally enthusiastic when it came to satisfying her clandestine appetites too.

'Good?' he asked, as she bit the head off a shrimp.

'Delicious,' Sarah answered and, ladylike, dabbed her lips with a napkin. 'How's the rarebit?'

'I've tasted worse.'

Another shrimp fulfilled its destiny. 'Are you pleased, Neville?'

'What? With the rarebit?'

'With the result of our visit to the Mercury?'

'I suppose I am.'

'I assume you'll have no scruple about summoning Leonard to the witness box if the case goes to the Assizes?'

'None whatsoever,' Neville said. 'Heaven knows, we'll need every scrap we can muster if the Crown rolls out the heavy brigade.'

'Poppy will powder his wig and lead, you know.'

'I sincerely hope so,' Neville said. 'If a coroner's jury brings home a verdict of murder what hope will Bloom have in High Court?'

'Can't you persuade him to plead to a lesser charge.'

'He won't plead to any charge,' Neville said. 'It's acquittal or nothing. And now we know why. Five hundred pounds will provide his daughter with a head start in the marriage stakes. How long Bloom will hold out, though, remains to be seen.'

Fork poised, Sarah said, 'Doesn't it strike you as odd that Bloom bought a joint policy in the first place. Mercury Assurance is hardly where one would begin to look for special life cover.'

'How did your father find out where the policy was housed?'

'Poppy? Knowing how devious my father can be, he probably narrowed the field just as we've done and took an educated guess that happened to be right.' Sarah scoffed the last shrimp, delicately licked dressing from the corner of her lips and pushed the dish away. 'The other point that's interesting is why Bloom took out the policy in December?'

'Perhaps,' Neville said, 'he thought *he* might die.'

'Oh, you mean that someone might try to kill *him*?'

'Yes,' said Neville. 'But who?

'The lover, what's his name? Boylan.'

'Even in a darkened room it's highly unlikely anyone would mistake Molly for Leopold. He hates Boylan, you know. Bloom, that is,' Neville said. 'He thinks Boylan's after Milly, his little girl.'

'That's disgusting.'

'I agree,' said Neville. 'Boylan will be even keener on Milly when he finds out she has five hundred pounds in her account. Of course, for that to happen Bloom will have to walk free.'

'What are his chances, Neville? Fifty-fifty?'

'Better than that,' Neville said. 'The police have no other viable suspect so far. In terms of prosecuting the case through the courts the Crown is faced with trying to prove a negative, not so much that Bloom did it as that no one else could have.'

'Except the phantom intruder.'

'Who,' Neville said, 'may be a figment of Bloom's imagination.'

'And then again may not,' Sarah Tolland said.

TWENTY TWO

From the police station in Store Street a short walk across Talbot Street carried you to Montgomery Street and the heart of the district known to every Dubliner as the Monto, where girls and their pimps plied the oldest trade. Kinsella had nothing but sympathy for the girls, but the madams were another matter, for even the lowest among them rarely suffered a black eye or broken nose, let alone the welts and bruises that the girls endured to keep their mistresses in gin and jewellery and their sons at fancy English schools.

Over the years the tide of fortune had shifted forth and back across the streets of Monto. The flash houses now were not in Purdon or Gardiner Street but a few hundred yards to the west where, in Upper Tyrone Street, squeezed between the Penitents' Retreat and Byrne's Square, three high-class brothels vied for trade.

If your taste ran to a spanking by henna-haired girls in sailor suits then plump Bella Cohen would make you welcome. If you fancied something a little more exotic involving girls from foreign climes then Ida Freemantle would see you right. If, however, all you wanted was a buxom lass from County Clare or a wicked wee witch from Sligo to sing you a ditty and pour you a glass while you waited to take her upstairs, then Nancy O'Rourke's was the place to go.

The door was polished oak with gleaming brass fittings and the light in the transom outlined the owner's name: A.G. O'Rourke. Once you knocked on that door there was no pretending you'd mistaken it for a house that catered to lascars and navvies.

The boys who guarded the hall admitted you on the strict under-
standing that you would not only behave like a gentleman but
pay through the nose like one.

Mrs O'Rourke was not above inviting uniformed constables
into her kitchen for a glass or two but the appearance of a G-man
on her doorstep brought a frown to her powdered brow. She was
enough of a realist to acknowledge that the servants of the Crown
could close her down for any one of a dozen reasons and having
'One-Lamp' Keelie Martin or granite-jawed Joe Forgan refuse a
detective entry was just begging for trouble.

On Keelie's muted whistle Nancy rushed from the parlour and
scooted across the wood-panelled hall. Unlike her neighbour,
Bella, Mrs O'Rourke was slim, pretty and fairly well preserved.
She wore a pale blue tea gown with a high lace collar to hide
the first signs of turkey neck and carried in her hand an ivory
wand with which she directed her girls hither and thither without
having to raise her voice.

'Inspector Kinsella. What a delight it is to see you again. How
many years has it been? Too many, I fear. Now, tell me, is it
business or pleasure brings you here this dreary evening?'

Her topknot barely came up to the middle of Kinsella's chest
and the tilt of her head upward and the upward roll of her sea-
green eyes made her appear winsome. She tapped his shoulder
playfully with the tip of the wand and Jim Kinsella, in spite of
his antipathy to whoremongers, was courteous enough to take
off his hat.

'Business, I'm afraid, Nancy, just business.'

The tip of the wand transferred itself from the G-man's shoulder
to the madam's less than imposing bosom. 'With me? What have
I been up to that brings a handsome fella from the Castle knocking
on my door?'

Behind Kinsella, Joe of the granite jaw chuckled, amused by
his employer's oratory. Keelie Martin had already slipped outside
to warn off potential customers who may not wish to come face
to face with an officer of the law.

'Is Blazes here tonight?' Kinsella asked.

'Blazes? I don't believe I know anyone of that name.'

'Oh, Nancy,' Kinsella chided, 'how can you have forgotten
Blazes Boylan? Big chap with a straw boater and a fat wallet.'

Nancy's chesty laughter had much the same effect as a giggle. She wagged the wand and said, 'How remiss of me to forget Mr Boylan. Ay, of course, I remember him now. No, he's not here tonight. Just the other evening Claire was saying we hadn't seen Mr Boylan for quite some time.'

'How long is "quite some time"?'

Before Nancy could reply a young bare-legged blonde clad only in a shift appeared on the stairs that led down to the hall. She was followed by a portly middle-aged gentleman whom Kinsella recognised as an alderman from the Mansion House ward. On seeing the detective the girl faltered, the alderman piled into her and, for a second or so, it seemed that the pair might come tumbling down to land in a heap at Kinsella's feet.

'The other stairs, girl, the other stairs,' Mrs O'Rourke yapped, then, snaring Kinsella by the belt of his raincoat, dragged him after her with all the force of a small shunting engine. 'We'll be more comfortable in the parlour, I think,' she said and hauled him into the front room.

Velvet curtains draped the windows. A glass-fronted cabinet held bottles and glasses and a glittering chandelier hung from the ceiling. In the window alcove a young woman in an evening gown and elbow-length gloves was seated at an upright piano, playing a lovely old Irish ballad. Her complexion was as white as milk, eyes dark as brambles, lips red as cherries. She smiled and continued playing and, for a wistful moment, Jim Kinsella almost forgot that he was happily married, the father of three daughters and an officer in the Dublin Metropolitan.

'She'll give you anything your heart desires,' Jack Delaney said. 'Her repertoire is remarkably extensive.' He glanced at the sheet on the music scroll, reached down and turned the page. 'What will it be, Inspector? Bach, Chopin or "The Leg of the Duck?" You know that one by heart, don't you, Alicia, my love?'

However refined Alicia might appear, when she opened her mouth there was no disguising her Ulster accent. 'Sure an' do I not now,' she said and, grinning, chanted a few bars of the bawdy song.

There was no one in the parlour apart from the girl and Jack Delaney. The room contained two leather armchairs, a long sofa and a chaise longue upon which was draped a snake-like black stocking and a pair of French knickers, a tasteless addition to the décor. Nancy, darting, stuffed the offending garments behind a cushion in the hope that the copper hadn't noticed them, which, of course, the copper had.

Jim Kinsella wasn't particularly surprised to encounter the *Star*'s reporter and had an uncomfortable feeling that Delaney already had the answers to the questions he'd come here to ask.

'Alicia,' said Nancy O'Rourke, with a twitch of the baton, 'take Mr Kinsella's coat then make yourself scarce.'

Alicia rose gracefully from the stool and closed the piano lid.

'Thank you, Alicia,' Kinsella said, 'but I'll hang on to my coat. I won't be stopping long.'

'What about you, Jack?' the girl asked.

'I am stopping,' Delaney answered. 'So keep the custard warm.'

The girl laughed and left the parlour via a curtained alcove that screened the dressing-room and main stairs.

Jim Kinsella seated himself on the sofa and, with a rueful shake of the head, said, 'You seem to pop up everywhere, Delaney. Is this one of your regular haunts?'

'Singing lessons twice a week. Isn't that right, Nancy?'

'Keen as mustard on his doh-ray-mees,' the madam confirmed. 'Will you be having a glass of something, Inspector?'

'Claret, if you have it,' Kinsella said, adding, 'Isn't that Mr Bloom's tipple?'

'Come now,' Delaney said. 'Nancy isn't going to fall for anything as obvious as that. Why don't you just ask her if she knows Poldy Bloom?'

Nancy opened the cabinet, took out a decanter and three glasses, filled the glasses and delivered one each to Delaney and Kinsella, who waited until she returned to sit by him before he said, 'Tell me about Leopold Bloom.'

The woman glanced at Delaney who said, 'It's the man's job, for God's sake. Gird your loins, Nancy. Tell him what he wants to know. I mean, Jesus, it's not as if you're betraying your country.'

'Bloom,' Nancy O'Rourke said, frowning. 'That blackguard. He shattered a chandelier in Bella's house next door.'

Delaney said, 'Bloom didn't smash Bella's crystal. It was that idiot Dedalus, Simon's lad. Bloom offered to pay for the damage.'

'All I know of Bloom I got from Bella,' Nancy said. 'Sly, Bella thought him, and mean. Said he'd pay for the broken chandelier but never a penny has she seen. She'll not get a farthing out of the beggar now, him being in prison and all. Is the wine to your liking, Inspector?'

'It is,' Kinsella said tactfully.

'Only the best for my gentlemen,' said Nancy.

'Bloom wasn't one of your gentlemen?'

'Certainly not. Old miser.'

'Unlike Mr Boylan.'

'Oh, yes, my ladies do like *him*.'

'All the ladies like Blazes,' Delaney put in. 'It's rumoured he has the biggest appendage in Dublin. Would that be true, Nancy?'

'How would I be knowing a thing like that?' the woman said without the flicker of a smile. 'The girls like him 'cause he slips them a few pennies extra behind my back. Anyhow, what do you want with Blazes, Inspector? I thought you were after Bloom?'

'Boylan was putting it to Bloom's wife behind Bloom's back.'

'That Tweedy bitch. I don't know what he ever saw in her,' Nancy O'Rourke said. 'The baby, was it his?'

'I doubt if the woman herself knew who the father was.'

'Blazes put two of Bella's girls up the spout. He admitted to nothing, of course,' Nancy said, 'but he paid for one to lose it.'

'I thought Mrs Cohen took care of that sort of thing.'

'What sort of thing?' said Nancy guardedly.

'Terminations.'

Beneath the powder her cheeks reddened as if the word offended her. 'That's women's business.'

'But Boylan made it his business, didn't he?'

'I do not discuss my gentleman's affairs.'

'Bloom's not one of your gentlemen.'

'That's a fact,' said Nancy. 'Bloom wanted to rent a room for an hour or two. One of my rooms, I ask you. Does he think I run a boarding house here? He wanted a room to be with his fancy woman, I expect.'

'Did you see Bloom with a woman.'

'I did not.'

'I want you to think carefully before you answer,' Kinsella

said. 'Bloom and Boylan had a barney just outside your door. When did it take place?'

'Last Wednesday.'

'At what hour?'

'What, do you think I was standing in the street?'

'What time, Nancy?'

'About half past eleven, I think.'

'Not midnight?'

'No, earlier.'

'How drunk was Boylan?'

'He was half seas when he turned up here. I had a full house and he was angry at that. He had one drink then I asked him to leave. He went quiet enough. I saw him out myself. Bloom was waiting in the street.'

'Bloom wasn't with Boylan in the house then?' said Kinsella.

'I told you, Bloom isn't one o' my gentlemen,' Nancy O'Rourke said. 'He dropped in on Bella now and then but after she kicked him out I don't know where he went for his fun.'

'Did you see either Boylan or Bloom again that night?'

Nancy shook her head. 'Never saw either of them since.'

'Why did Bloom want a room in the Monto when Dublin's filled with hotels and boarding houses?' said Delaney. 'If Bloom had a woman on the side then this is the last place he'd want to bring her. And what was Bloom doing in the Monto apart from the obvious. Will you fetch Boylan to the witness stand?'

'That's not for me to decide.' Kinsella finished his wine, handed the glass to Mrs O'Rourke and, to the woman's relief, got to his feet.

'Oh, are you leaving us?' she said, rising too.

'I won't outstay my welcome,' Kinsella said, 'particularly as Alderman Keogh will be anxious to get home to his wife.'

She looked up at him, winsome again, and smiled.

'Ah, you're a sharp tack, Inspector, so you are now.'

'That I am,' Jim Kinsella agreed. 'That I am,' and, with a nod to Delaney, allowed the skinny little whore-mistress to show him out.

If it hadn't been for the gout he'd have caught her by the hair but the table was between them and the best he could do, summons in one hand and stick in the other, was bring the stick down on the table and send the dishes flying. Her mother let out a scream. Her mother knew what was behind the summons.

If it hadn't been for her mother she'd never have had the courage to leave in the first place. Her mother had told her it was her only chance, her father so bad with the drink even an office job would soon be beyond him. So she'd stifled her fears, packed a bag and slipped out to meet Poldy at the gate at half past one o'clock on a dark March morning, saying goodbye to Tritonville Road forever. Four hours later she was back, praying to St Joseph her father wouldn't hear her scratching at the kitchen door. When it all came out in the newspapers next day, he'd sneered and told her what a filthy old Jew bugger Bloom was and wasn't she lucky not to be the one lying dead with her head stove in. Full of himself, griping about the pain in his foot with no thought for the pain in *her* foot or the pain in her heart, off up town to the office, crawling to the pub afterwards to brag how he'd saved her from a fate worse than death at the hands of a Jew who, by God, should be drawn and quartered not just hanged.

Then the summons arrived by Saturday afternoon post just as her mother was binding his foot. She opened the sealed letter and would have slipped it to her mother if he hadn't snatched it from her hand. 'A summons, by God in Heaven! What have you done now, Gert? What have you done to me now?' And he grabbed the stick and tried to catch her by the hair and she crawled under the table and across the floor and flew upstairs into her room with him roaring at her mother to catch her.

She cowered in her room, panting, that electric feeling in the roots of her hair and listened to him cursing and the thump of the stick as he crept upstairs, just another tosspot ruined by the drink. Then, remembering that Poldy was in jail and depending on her, she threw open the bedroom door and caught him, crouched, three steps below the landing and, lifting her skirts, stepped over his head and big, ugly bottom and picked her way down to the foot of the stairs where she turned and said, very clear and very loud:

'Sod you, Daddy. Sod you.'

*   *   *

Cissy and she sat side by side on the wall by the gate of the
Caffrey residence, arms entwined. Cissy's young brothers were
in bed but not asleep. Mrs Caffrey had gone round to visit Mrs
Dignam and Cissy's father had volunteered to pop into the
MacDowell house and offer his gouty friend an arm to lean on
as they made their way to the Sandymount Arms. Gerty had
helped her mother sweep up the broken dishes then she'd planted
her foot on the hearthstone and had called her father a name or
two and warned him that if he so much as raised a finger to
either of them she would see to it that her friend, Inspector
Kinsella of the DMP, got to hear about it and she wouldn't be
the only one receiving a summons to appear in court, only in his
case it wouldn't be as a witness.

'What did he have to say to that?' Cissy Caffrey asked.

'Nothing,' Gerty answered. 'He huffed and puffed and put on
his boots and when your dad arrived went out with him without
saying a blessed word.'

'You'll be for it when he comes home with a skinful, though.'

'Let him try,' said Gerty. 'Just let him try.'

Cissy tugged the shawl over her friend's shoulders, fumbled
a bashed cigarette from the top of her knickers and, with a kitchen
match struck against the wall, carefully cupped her hand over
the flame and lit the gasper. She drew smoke through parted lips
and passed the cigarette to Gerty who, without a moment's hesitation, took it and inhaled.

She no longer gave a toot what the *Lady's Pictorial* had to
say about women who smoked. Devotion to the advice offered
by the columnists in the *Lady's Pictorial* had done her no
good, apart from keeping her up-to-date with fashion. Poldy
had told her smoking cigarettes was all the rage with women
in London and considered very sophisticated. He'd even let
her have a puff at one of his cigars, though that, she had to
admit, had not been pleasant for cigars didn't taste nearly as
nice as they smelled.

She allowed smoke to drift through her nostrils the way Poldy
had taught her, then handed the cigarette back to Cissy.

'Are you really going to court on Monday?' Cissy said.

'What choice do I have? You get fined if you don't show up.'

'What'll you wear?'

'Nothing too bright,' said Gerty. 'I've got that waterfall skirt with the tucks I put in around the hips.'

'It hides your legs, though.'

'Poldy's not going to be looking at my legs.'

'Has he really not snapped your garter yet?'

'I told you. He's a gentleman. We've agreed to wait.'

'You won't have to wait long if he gets off. As soon as he's out of mourning he can marry you fair and square then you can do it all night and all day. By the way,' said Cissy, 'has he told you what he's going to do about his daughter?'

Gerty shook her head.

Cissy went on, 'She's only fifteen, they say. Well, by jiminy, you could have fooled me with a kiss and a biscuit. They were all round her like flies, the College mob, though I didn't see your Willy there.'

'He was never my Willy,' Gerty said.

'More's the pity, eh?'

'I'd rather have Leopold than a dozen Willy Wyatts.'

'You might not say that, dear, if your man's found guilty. Now don't you be telling me you'll wait for him. God, you'll be dead before he gets out of prison.' Cissy took a final puff at the wilting cigarette. 'You wouldn't be silly enough to marry him if he really did it, would you, Gerty? Surely you wouldn't marry a murderer?'

'My bag's still packed,' said Gerty, ignoring the question. 'As soon as Poldy's free we'll be off to Liverpool.'

'What's Mr Bloom using for cash?'

'He has plenty of money.'

'Then why's he living in rented in Eccles Street?'

'You're not being very helpful, Cissy. Are you jealous?'

'You know, dear, I am. Dead jealous.' Cissy could lie with the best of them. 'I should have given him an eyeful of *my* knickers on the beach that night and it might have been me instead of you was off to Liverpool.'

'Is Edy jealous too?'

'You know Edy. She's jealous of our cat.' Cissy flicked away the remnants of the cigarette. 'I'd best go in, see what mischief those imps are up to.'

'Cissy,' Gerty said, 'will you come with me to court?'

'What about your ma?'

'I don't want her there. It'll only bring on her megrim.'

'And he won't go, I suppose.'

'Not him, no.'

A hug, a kiss on the cheek: 'Yes, dear, I'll be there.'

'Monday then?' said Gerty.

'Monday it is,' Cissy Caffrey promised and, filled with apprehension, watched her love-sick friend limp off along the pavement home.

PART THREE
The Intruder

TWENTY THREE

A t precisely half past ten on Monday, 20th March, before the crowd in the gallery had properly settled, Mr Rice read the proclamation of the adjourned hearing and tolled off the names of the jurors, all of whom, thank heaven, had shown up again.

Coroner Slater proceeded to read out a summary of evidence taken at the first hearing, laying emphasis on the conclusions reached by Benson Rule in respect of the condition of the deceased and the injuries inflicted upon her. That done, he paused, and glanced at the foolscap page upon which his clerk, Mr Devereux, had listed the names of witnesses who, on police advice, had been summoned to appear before the court. Below each name the clerk had attached a brief note on how the witness might be expected to contribute to the narrative of events.

First into the box was Otto Dlucgaez, pork butcher of Upper Dorset Street, who confirmed that Leopold Bloom, a regular customer, had entered his shop at twenty minutes to eight on the morning in question and had exited again some four minutes later.

'What did he purchase?' the coroner inquired.

'Two slices of calf's liver.'

'I thought you were a pork butcher.'

'I cater to all tastes, your lardship.'

'Was it usual for Mr Bloom to ask for calf's liver?'

'He liked all the organs. Sheep's kidney was his favourite.'

'Really?'

'He liked gizzards, too, and—'

'Thank you, Mr Dlucgaez. I think that's enough.'

The mystery of why Bloom had bought calf's liver in preference to pork having been satisfactorily put to bed, Dlucgaez was replaced in the box by Mrs Norma Hastings, who claimed Mr Bloom as a neighbour.

Elegantly coiffed and dressed for the occasion, Mrs Hastings was thwarted in her attempt to turn her account of a fleeting encounter with Bloom into a three-act opera by the coroner's curt dismissal and returned to the benches more than somewhat abashed by the brevity of her appearance in the spotlight.

Bloom had been brought up from Kilmainham early that morning. He had undergone a stiff examination from his counsel, Neville Sullivan, in respect of a certain insurance policy. An argument of sorts had ensued and the accused and his legal representative did not appear to be on speaking terms when they entered the courtroom and took their seats at the defence table.

Bloom's moustache was untrimmed, his hair greasy, his trousers creased and his collar wrinkled. Gone was the cool, watchful fellow of a week ago. He had about him now a deflated air and was by no means cheered to discover Miss Gertrude MacDowell's name on Sullivan's copy of the witness list.

Indeed, it was all he could do to raise a smile when Gerty gave him a wave from the second row of the witness benches and when she blew him a kiss he covered his face with the flat of his hand and turned his head away.

'What's *she* doing here?' he hissed.

'She's been summoned as a witness.'

'I can see that, damn it. Did you fetch her?'

'Not I,' Neville said. 'Kinsella found her, no thanks to you.'

'She knows nothing, I tell you. Send her away.'

'Can't be done, Bloom. It's out of my hands.'

'Elizabeth Fleming to the stand, please,' the court officer called.

Hand still screening his face, Bloom whispered, 'What is this? What's happening? I thought we had an arrangement. Who else is on the list? Is Boylan on the list? He is, isn't he? Look, he's there on the benches, grinning like an ape.'

'Mr Sullivan,' the coroner said, 'is your client unwell?'

'No, sir,' Neville said. 'We're just having a bit of a tiff.'

'Well, I'd be obliged if you'd tiff in your own time, Mr Sullivan. May I continue with this witness?'

'By all means, sir,' Neville Sullivan said and scowled at his agitated client to silence him.

Roland Slater was proud of his ability to cut through fustian. He had read Kinsella's summary of the police investigation and

firmly believed he was on top of the case at last. He wasn't
oblivious to the lapses in procedure that might allow Tolland's
protégé to raise troubling issues if the jury sent Bloom on to the
Assizes. Here and now, however, he was the conduit through
which all police evidence must pass and, as such, he intended
to piece together for the jury a feasible estimate of what had
happened on the morning of March 9th in the blood-stained
bedroom in Eccles Street.

The witness, Mrs Fleming, answered his questions as to who
she was, where she lived, how she was occupied – railway carriage
cleaner – and stated that her relationship to the Blooms had been
that of day-maid. Impressed by the woman's demeanour, Slater
removed his foot from the heavy pedal and addressed her gently.

'Now, Mrs Fleming, I must ask you for an opinion based
on the things you heard and saw in the Blooms' household
during the period of your tenure. I would point out to the
members of the jury that such evidence should not be treated
as hearsay and will enter into your deliberations as evidence
directly related to a possible motive for unlawful killing. Are
we clear on that point, gentlemen?'

Foreman Conway glanced right, left and behind and, on behalf
of his fellow jurors, stated, 'We are.'

Mrs Fleming's coat covered a blouse that had been washed
and patched almost beyond repair. The skirt too had been damp-
pressed and ironed once too often and the coat, a cheap half-length
garment, had the musty sheen of respectable poverty. Only the
hat, a plain black straw, added a modicum of dignity. The woman's
eyes were tired but in the shaft of morning light from the courtroom window she seemed, the coroner thought, to show an
intelligent awareness of what was required of her.

'Were you well treated by your employers, Mrs Fleming?'

'I was not ill-treated, sir.'

'Did you enjoy your spell with the Blooms?'

'I did, sir, until the end. Near the end.'

'Mrs Fleming, is it correct that you were dismissed from
employment a few days short of Christmas last year?'

'Sure and it is, sir.'

'What reason were you given for the severance?'

'None, sir, none really.'

'Were you accused of dishonesty, perhaps?'

'No, sir, not that.' Lizzie Fleming paused and looked down at her hands. 'She said I was too old for to do the work.'

'Mrs Bloom said that, did she?'

'Yes.'

'Had Mrs Bloom complained about your inability to do the work required of you before that day?'

'No, sir. She groused sometimes but it wasn't no more than a bit of grumbling like you'd expect from any mistress.'

'Did it come as a surprise when you were suddenly dismissed?'

Still looking down at her hands, Lizzie Fleming said, 'No, sir, it did not. I . . . I saw things I was not supposed to see.'

'Quarrelling between Mr Bloom and Mrs Bloom?'

'I never heard raised voices, if that's what you mean. Never saw a raised hand neither. It was something else.'

'No need to keep us guessing, Mrs Fleming,' Roland Slater said. 'What was it you saw that, in your opinion, led to your dismissal?'

A deep breath and then, 'I saw Mrs Bloom in the company of another gentleman.'

'Where?'

'He came to the house.'

'So he was known to you?'

'Yes. He came regular to the house. For rehearsals.'

'A fellow singer, then? A professional singer like Mrs Bloom?' the coroner said. 'What harm is there in that, Mrs Fleming? Mr Bloom did not, I assume, object to this arrangement, given that it was Mrs Bloom's piano that was used for . . .' Then, as if the significance of the word had just occurred to him, he interrupted himself. 'What do you mean by company, Mrs Fleming? Please explain.'

'Doing what they shouldn't be doing,' said Lizzie Fleming.

'Kissing?' said Slater. 'You mean kissing?'

'It was worse. She had him inside . . .' Lizzie Fleming might live with one of the earthiest men in Dublin but candour had its limits. Flushing, she shook her head, at a loss to describe the act she'd witnessed.

'Am I to understand that what you saw isn't fit to talk about in public?' the coroner said.

'No, sir, it's not.'

'It was, however, an act of sexual intercourse?'

'It was.'

'Where did this act take place?'

'In the kitchen. He shouldn't have been there. He came early.'

Someone in the gallery guffawed. Roland Slater ignored the interruption and went on, 'Are we to take it, Mrs Fleming, that the man friend of the deceased came at the same appointed hour for every visit?'

'Four o'clock. I was always gone by then.'

'Except on that one unfortunate occasion when the gentleman arrived early,' the coroner said. 'Did Mrs Bloom see you?'

'She did.'

'Did she say anything to you about the incident?'

'No, sir, not a word.'

'And you, did you tell Mr Bloom what had occurred?'

'I did not,' said Lizzie Fleming.

'You were dismissed from Mrs Bloom's service; when?'

'Next morning – Friday – soon as Mr Bloom went out to work.'

'Are you in no doubt concerning what you saw in the kitchen?'

'None, sir.'

Crouched at the table by the coroner's chair Mr Devereux, the clerk, wrote in a neat, speedy hand, never more than a phrase or two behind. Dr Slater allowed him a moment to catch up. When Devereux gave him the signal by glancing up, however, the coroner did not sustain the obvious line of questioning.

'Now, Mrs Fleming, let us turn to another matter.'

Mr Conway was on his feet instantly. 'We have questions, sir.'

'I expect you have,' said Roland Slater. 'I will seek answers on your behalf shortly. Meanwhile, Mrs Fleming, will you be good enough to tell the court where the tea things, including the teapot, were kept.'

Milk jug and sugar bowl, duly labelled, had been placed upon the evidence table, together with two pieces of the broken teapot. Dr Slater, leaning forward, dabbed a forefinger at the objects to draw the woman's attention to them.

'Those,' he said.

'The jug and bowl were in the dresser in the kitchen. I never saw them used,' Mrs Fleming said. 'I'd've known if they'd been used 'cause I'd have had to wash them. The teapot was never used for making tea. It was a gift from Mrs Bloom's man friend.'

'What *was* the teapot used for?'

'Watering flowers – filling the vase – in Mrs Bloom's bedroom. Mr Bloom did it for her whenever there were flowers.'

'It would not be stretching imagination to conclude that the teapot might well have been left in Mrs Bloom's bedroom after Mr Bloom had watered the flowers?'

'No, sir, it wouldn't.'

'The friend who gave Mrs Bloom a gift of painted china and the man with whom Mrs Bloom was engaged in sexual dalliance are one and the same, I take it?'

'He is, one and the same.'

'Is that person in court today?'

'Ay, sir.'

'Do you know his name, Mrs Fleming?'

'It's Mr Boylan.'

'Would you point him out.'

'There. That's him.'

Blazes hoisted himself up to display his profile first to the jury and then to the gallery. Shame, he seemed to be saying, was not a virtue to which he would make pretence. If he'd been wearing a hat he might have tipped it to acknowledge the interest his entry into the case aroused in the crowd.

'Are you absolutely certain that Mr Boylan is the man you saw engaged in intimacy with Mrs Bloom?'

'Ay, it was him, sir,' Lizzie Fleming said. 'I'll swear it was.'

Being neither a fool nor entirely ignorant of sexual matters, Milly was not surprised by Mrs Fleming's revelations. Blazes' reactions to being exposed as a philanderer, however, made her flesh creep. She could not, as yet, bring herself to deal with her mother's role in the affair or imagine Mummy in Hugh Boylan's arms or doing that other thing.

Disgust swiftly gave way to anger, anger that she'd been taken in by Hugh Boylan's concern for her welfare and, in spite of all the harm he'd done, that he still had the gall to pose.

Driven by rage, she shot to her feet and, holding on to her hat, leaned over the gallery rail and screamed, *'You pig, Hugh Boylan, you filthy pig,'* then sank back into her seat and wept, while Dr Paterson, an arm about her shoulders, comforted her as best he could.

It took the court officers several minutes to quell the furore that Miss Bloom's outburst caused. In an atmosphere of restless speculation, the coroner asked the jury, 'Are there any further questions you wish me to put to this witness?'

Mr Conway was too discreet to press Mrs Fleming for details as to what precisely she had seen Marion Bloom doing with Mr Boylan. He said, 'It might be useful to learn how often the gentleman visited Mrs Bloom and when the visits began.'

'Mrs Fleming?' the coroner said. 'You may answer?'

'It would be once a week or twice,' Lizzie Fleming said.

'When was the first time Mr Boylan visited Eccles Street?'

'June of last year, just before Mrs Bloom went off on a singing tour with him . . . with Mr Boylan, I mean.'

Mr Conway said, 'Did Mr Bloom accompany his wife on any of these engagements?'

'Mr Bloom stayed at home in Eccles Street, though he might have gone to concerts in Dublin,' said Lizzie Fleming. 'I can't speak about those.'

'Mr Sullivan, do you have anything to say,' Roland Slater asked, 'bearing in mind that you have no *locus standi* in this court.'

Neville got to his feet and, with a hand on his client's shoulder, presumably to hold him down, said, 'I'm mindful of the coroner's courtesy. With permission, may I put a question to the witness as to the deceased's state of mind.'

'State of mind, Mr Sullivan?'

'I'm curious as to how the deceased coped with what appears to be a deception of several months standing and to establish, for the jury's benefit, if Mrs Bloom's manner was furtive or did she flaunt . . .'

'Flaunt?' Slater interrupted. 'Have a care, Mr Sullivan.'

'I bow to your discretion, sir,' Neville said, then, changing tack, 'Would it be permissible to ask the witness where the flowers in the vase in the bedroom came from?'

Conscious of the jury's interest, Roland Slater relayed the lawyer's question to the woman in the witness box.

Lizzie Fleming said, 'Mr Boylan brought them.'

'How does the witness know that?' Neville asked.

'Mrs Bloom boasted about it,' Lizzie Fleming said. 'She had Mr Bloom put the flowers in a vase as soon as he came home. She refused to let me do it. She insisted Mr Bloom fetch water in the teapot from the kitchen to fill the vase while she watched.'

Mr Devereux's hand moved swiftly over the foolscap. Neville waited until the clerk had finished writing before he put his next question. 'Would the witness be permitted to tell us how Mr Bloom reacted to being allocated this task?'

'He never complained, not to me at any rate,' Mrs Fleming said. 'Mr Bloom was not the complaining sort.'

'In your opinion,' Neville said, 'was Mr Bloom aware of his wife's infidelity?'

'I'm sure he must have been,' said Mrs Fleming. 'I don't see in honesty how he couldn't have been.'

'Yet, in the months before Christmas,' Neville said, 'you observed no fits of temper, no angry words on Mr Bloom's part.'

'No, sir, I did not.'

'Would it be accurate to say, in your opinion, that Mr Bloom lived in awe of his wife?' Neville said.

'No, Mr Sullivan,' Slater intervened. 'That is a step too far.'

'In that case, I have no further questions to put before the court at this time,' Neville Sullivan said, and promptly sat down.

TWENTY FOUR

The pews reserved for members of the DMP were crowded that Monday morning. Constable Jarvis and Sergeant Gandy rubbed shoulders with Inspectors Kinsella and Machin. A row behind, Superintendents Driscoll and Smout and Assistant Commissioner A.H.M. O'Byrne followed the progress of the inquiry with interest.

After being sworn in, Constable Jarvis described his role in

the events of the morning of March 9th. At the conclusion of the
constable's account several questions on behalf of the jury were
put to him by Mr Conway but Neville Sullivan was content to
point out for the record that the division's medical examiner had
not been present.

Spruce, imposing and sober, Sergeant Gandy, no stranger to
a witness box, delivered his testimony in a voice of such authority
that the jury were almost intimidated.

If Mr Conway and his crew were happy to accept the bluff
sergeant's word for what had happened that fateful morning in
Eccles Street, Neville Sullivan most certainly was not.

'No trace of an intruder was found in the upstairs rooms?'

'No, sir,' Gandy rumbled.

'You were, I've no doubt, thorough in your search.'

'I was.'

'The garden, the lavatory, the wall at the rear of the house?'

'Searched personal, sir.'

'The door of the cellar and the basement steps?'

'Mr Sullivan, we've been through all this,' the coroner put in.
'The sergeant's answers are already a matter of record. I trust it
isn't your intention to impugn the officer's honesty.'

'Oh, absolutely not,' said Neville, demonstrating surprise that
such a thought would even cross the coroner's mind. 'On the
contrary. The sergeant's honesty and experience are irreproach-
able. For that reason, if I may, I'd like to clarify one or two
minor details for the enlightenment of the jury.'

'You may *not* cross-examine, Mr Sullivan,' Slater said. I will
not allow it. This is an inquiry not a criminal trial.'

'I'm well aware of that, sir,' said Neville humbly. 'I'm merely
curious – as I'm sure the jury are too – as to just how long the
sergeant's "thorough" search of the premises lasted.'

Sergeant Gandy's eyeballs rolled leftwards but Tom Machin
and Jim Kinsella were looking the other way.

Bushy brows knitted in perplexity, the old warrior of C Division
almost gave the game away by staring at the coroner whose
hesitation did not go unremarked by the jury.

'I think we might like to hear an answer to that, sir,' Mr
Conway said.

The coroner drummed his fingers on the arm of his chair and

took what seemed like an age to reach a decision as to the legality, if not the pertinence, of the lawyer's question.

At length, he said, 'You may answer, Sergeant.'

In Sergeant Gandy's ethical canon truth was ever flexible. He thought about stretching it one way and then the other, an oath being no deterrent, while the jury and the court waited.

At length, he said, 'A half hour.'

'A half hour,' Neville Sullivan said. 'A half hour before Inspector Machin sent you to the Orphan School to telephone for assistance.'

'Ay, about half an hour.'

'How long until assistance arrived?'

Coroner Slater said, 'If you're suggesting that the police acted improperly then I must ask you to justify your insinuations, Mr Sullivan, or withdraw them.'

'I've nothing but admiration for the Dublin Metropolitan Police, sir. However, the conditions of arrest must be addressed.'

Jim Kinsella shifted his weight on to his knees and raised an arm in the air. He waited patiently for Slater to acknowledge him, which, after five or ten seconds, the coroner did.

'Do you have something to say, Inspector Kinsella?'

'If Mr Bloom's counsel is concerned about the time scale I can clarify it for him,' Jim Kinsella said.

'Then do,' said Slater.

'Inspector Machin, of Store Street, requested the assistance of a detective by means of a telephone call. I received the telephone call from Sergeant Gandy at twenty minutes to nine o'clock at G Division headquarters in Lower Castle Yard. I travelled by tramcar to Eccles Street and reached the scene at two or three minutes after nine. The times are recorded in my notebook and also in G Division's log for the day in question.'

'There we have it,' the coroner said. 'Now may we move on?'

'One hour and ten minutes, Mr Bloom in custody but not charged. Where was Mr Bloom held in that . . .' Neville began.

'No, Mr Sullivan. We've wasted enough time on this issue as it is. Sergeant Gandy, you may stand down.'

The sergeant could not get out of the witness box fast enough. The sound of his boots thumping on the wooden steps echoed through the court room and, bent over like a man with a stomach cramp, he returned to the witness benches and, crouching, hid himself away behind young Jarvis.

However anxious he might be to save face, Roland Slater was duty bound to see fair play. It was a bold move on his part to summon Tom Machin next to the witness box.

Inspector Machin crisply recounted how he had been called to Number 7 Eccles Street and what he had found there. When asked by Mr Conway why he'd felt it necessary to enlist the assistance of a detective from G Division, Tom Machin answered, 'It was murder. Plainly murder. I felt that the ends of justice would best be served by sending for an expert investigator.'

Mr Conway said, 'To assist in questioning Mr Bloom?'

'No, Mr Bloom had not been placed under arrest when Inspector Kinsella arrived,' Tom Machin replied.

Mr Conway said, 'When was Mr Bloom charged?'

'Detained on a warrant of suspicion, you mean.'

Mr Conway said, 'Yes, that.'

'Only after the fact of death had been confirmed.'

Roland Slater sighed and said, 'In fact, I issued the warrant.'

Mr Conway said, 'Will Mr Bloom return to the witness box?'

Slater said, 'There's no obligation upon Mr Bloom to subject himself to further questioning. He cannot be forced to give evidence that might be detrimental to him in a court of Assize. However, a considerable amount of fresh evidence has come to light during the past week and will be laid out for you as the inquiry progresses. If you've finished with Inspector Machin, I propose to call Detective Inspector Kinsella to throw some light on the matter. It is the jury's responsibility to decide only if there is a case to answer, not to prove the case. That will be the lot of judges and jury in a higher court. Are we clear on that, Mr Conway?'

'We are, sir, we are,' said Mr Conway and, folding his arms, sat back while Inspector James Kinsella took Tom Machin's place in the witness box.

Jim Kinsella had served as a witness in many a High Court trial and had come prepared for all and any questions that might be put to him, not by a feral defence counsel or a ruthless Crown prosecutor but by a coroner who had something to hide and fifteen jury men uncontaminated by much knowledge of the law.

Upon the narrow ledge of the witness box he arranged his notebooks and a single file card upon which he had jotted down the order of events. He took into his right hand the Bible offered by Mr Rice, repeated the familiar oath and touched his lips to the binding of the Book. He stated his name, address and rank as an officer in the Dublin Metropolitan Police and the number of years in which he had served, then glanced at Roland Slater who, with a nod, sanctioned him to begin.

Briskly the inspector guided the jury through his involvement in the arrest of Leopold Bloom. He took them into the bedroom, described the position of the body and the condition of the room. He precluded any interjection from Bloom's counsel by stating the precise time the coroner had arrived and how, at that juncture, he had gone down into the half-basement kitchen to speak with the victim's husband.

'Speak of what, Inspector?' Slater asked.

'Cat's meat,' Kinsella answered. 'Mr Bloom was concerned about the welfare of the cat who, it seems, had not been fed.'

'The liver?'

'Yes,' Kinsella said. 'I did not interrogate Mr Bloom at this stage nor, to my knowledge, did Inspector Machin, beyond confirming Mr Bloom's story that he had gone out to buy meat and had returned to find his wife dead. I did, however, ask Mr Bloom about the front door to the house, whether it had been locked when he'd gone out. Mr Bloom said it had been left unlocked. I also observed that the fire had not been set. Mr Bloom explained that he had intended to do that when he returned from the butchers.'

'Did you ask Mr Bloom if he had murdered his wife?' Mr Conway inquired.

'No, the question was not put to him.'

Mr Conway turned again to his fellow jury members, one of whom, Tarpey, whispered something to him.

'Do you have another question, Mr Conway?' Slater asked.

'We're wondering why Mrs Bloom didn't attempt to get out of bed if there was a stranger in her room.'

'No shred of evidence has been found to corroborate an opportunistic attack by a stranger,' Roland Slater said. 'There is no

rational motive. True, a motive is not essential if we're dealing
with a mad man but a deranged person would surely have left
some trace of his presence when he broke in.'

'I may have an answer to the juryman's question,' Kinsella
said. 'After Mr Bloom had been taken off to Store Street station
I remained in Number 7 Eccles Street to conduct a more detailed
search than Sergeant Gandy had been able to do in the confusion
of discovery and arrest. The house at Number 7 is, as you've
seen for yourselves, no small property and has a number of
unoccupied rooms on the upper floors. I came to the conclusion
it would be perfectly possible for some person to hide in one of
the empty upstairs rooms and remain undetected. The front door,
however, has a metal draught board – you've seen that too, I
believe – which creates a deal of noise when the door is opened
or closed, a sound perfectly audible to any person who might be
hiding upstairs.'

'Are you saying there *was* an intruder upstairs?' Slater put in.

'No, sir. All I'm saying is that the evidence – the physical
evidence – does not rule out the possibility that some other person
was present in the house.'

'There are no witnesses to support this conclusion, Inspector,'
Slater said. 'Police enquiries in the neighbourhood have turned
up no one who saw a stranger enter or leave Number 7 Eccles
Street around the time the murder was committed.'

'Sir,' Kinsella said, 'with due respect, we don't know *when*
the murder was committed. We know from Constable Jarvis's
testimony only when the murder was reported not when it was
discovered. Dr Rule stated that the body had been dead for
upwards of thirty hours before he made his examination. In my
opinion, it's not beyond the bounds of possibility that Mrs Bloom
did *not* die between the hours of seven and eight o'clock but
several hours earlier.'

'Do you have evidence to support your claim, Inspector?'

'No, Dr Slater, no direct evidence.'

Neville Sullivan was on his feet at once. 'If the officer has no
evidence for casting doubt on my client's veracity then I suggest
. . . no, sir, I demand that his ridiculous hypothesis be stricken.
If we're going to allow half-cocked theories to be entered into
the record I'll have no alternative but to call for an immediate

adjournment on the grounds of culpable neglect on the coroner's part.'

'Contain yourself, Mr Sullivan. Contain yourself,' said Dr Slater. 'I'm no fonder of wild guesses than you are. Now, before Mr Sullivan does himself an injury, may I ask Inspector Kinsella to explain his reasons for doubting Bloom's claim that his wife was alive when he left the house for the butcher's shop?'

'I've reason to believe and will, in fact, offer proof that Mr Bloom did not spend the night in bed with his wife. In conversation with Mr Bloom, Mr Bloom declared that the cat—'

'The cat? The cat?' Neville shrilled. 'We'll be calling the damned cat as a witness next?'

'One more word out of turn, Counsellor Sullivan, and I'll have you removed from my court. Sit down at once and be silent,' Slater snapped, then, less than affably, turned to the G-man. 'When did this conversation take place? Before or after Bloom had been cautioned?'

'Before,' Kinsella replied. 'Mr Bloom told me that the cat had been fed before Mrs Bloom and he went to bed about half past ten. Mr Bloom repeated the same thing in his sworn statement to Superintendent Driscoll, a statement that's already part of the evidence.'

'What's admissible as evidence, Inspector, is for me to decide,' the coroner said, then to the jury, 'Bloom's statement *is* sworn testimony, however. Any deliberate attempts to distort the truth must be taken seriously when you come to consider a verdict. Inspector Kinsella, have you uncovered any such attempt on Bloom's part.'

'I have, sir,' Kinsella said. 'Mr Bloom's claim that he went to bed with his wife at half past ten o'clock on Wednesday evening is untrue. Mr Bloom was not in bed with his wife at half past ten. Bloom wasn't at home at half past ten, nor at half past eleven.'

The coroner waited until the buzz in the courtroom died down before he said, 'Do you know where Mr Bloom was at half past ten on the night preceding the killing?'

'In the vicinity of Nancy O'Rourke's house in Upper Tyrone Street,' Kinsella said. 'I cannot place Mr Bloom there at ten thirty but I can place him there an hour later, that is, at eleven thirty.'

'For the benefit of the jury will you explain what goes on at Mrs O'Rourke's house,' Slater said.

'It's a brothel,' said Kinsella bluntly.

'Are you implying that Mr Bloom was enjoying the company of women within O'Rourke's establishment?' Slater said.

'To the best of my knowledge Mr Bloom did not enter O'Rourke's. However, between eleven and eleven thirty he was seen on the street outside the house.'

'Do you have a statement signed by O'Rourke to that effect?'

'I question if Mrs O'Rourke would be a reliable witness,' Kinsella said. 'I do, however, have two witnesses who can place Mr Bloom in Upper Tyrone Street in the hour before midnight.'

'Are the witnesses in court?'

'They are, sir,' Kinsella said.

'Have you located a witness or witnesses to say where Mr Bloom was in the hours *after* midnight?'

Kinsella hesitated. 'I do have a witness who may shed light on Mr Bloom's whereabouts after midnight.' He paused once more. 'A witness who may, in fact, have been in Number 7 Eccles Street at the time of the murder.'

'Is that person in court today?'

'She is, sir, yes.'

'And the name of this person?'

'Gertrude MacDowell.'

'What is her connection to the case, Inspector?'

'She is Mr Bloom's friend. In fact I think Bloom intended to run off with her,' Jim Kinsella said. 'In a word, elope.'

The uproar in the court room was deafening.

Bloom was on his feet. Blazes Boylan was on his feet too, frantically searching the faces on the benches around him.

In the gallery Milly Bloom thrust herself against the rail with such force that only Dr Paterson's arm about her waist prevented her plunging into the body of the court, while Maude Boylan, motionless as a statue, stared straight ahead. Then, aided by court officers, the coroner brought the morning session to an abrupt conclusion by announcing a break for lunch.

TWENTY FIVE

Kinsella moved like shot off a shovel. He dug three half crowns from his jacket pocket and, catching Jarvis by the sleeve, slipped the coins into the constable's palm.

'The girl,' he said, 'that girl. Get her out of here as best you can. She has a friend with her, I think. Up there. The tall girl with the mop of dark hair. Take them both across to the barracks canteen and see they get something to eat. Yes, I know it's irregular but I don't want her mobbed by reporters. Keep her as cool and collected as you possibly can. Kid gloves, Jarvis, kid gloves.'

'Sir,' Constable Jarvis said and, stepping between the benches, introduced himself to Gerty and taking her by the arm led her out of the side door into a corridor already thronged with pressmen.

'Well, you've set the cat among the pigeons now,' Machin said.

'Boylan,' Jim Kinsella said. 'Put a man on him.'

'What? Do you think he's going to bolt?'

'I don't want him talking to Delaney.'

'If he chooses to go to the Belleville we can't stop him.'

'There's a sister in the gallery. Let me know if Boylan and she have any sort of conversation. Send a uniform. Make sure Boylan knows he's being watched.'

'Right. Is the jury sequestered?'

'Slater won't let them leave the building, I'm sure. He doesn't want them staggering back pie-eyed.'

'Bloom?'

'He's Sullivan's problem, not mine.'

'Is it true about the girl and Bloom?' Tom Machin said.

'It had better be,' Kinsella said, then, when a hand descended on his shoulder, turned to confront Superintendent Smout and Assistant Commissioner O'Byrne.

'Why,' said the Assistant Commissioner, 'have I not been kept abreast of developments, Inspector Kinsella? I was rather under the impression I'd made the significance of this case clear to you.'

'I submitted my daily reports as usual, sir.'

'Is that true, Smout?'

'Every detail logged,' the Superintendent said. 'The Division's books are always open, Mr O'Byrne.'

'The Commissioner will not be happy at this turn of events,' O'Byrne said. 'Unless, of course, it's a ruse to persuade Bloom to plead to manslaughter, though from where I sit that looks less likely than a finding of homicide and a full-blown trial. What else do you have up your sleeve, Inspector?'

'No more than the evidence you've heard, sir,' Kinsella said. 'How that evidence is used is for the coroner to decide. I've brought forward the witnesses I believe to be appropriate to reaching a verdict with or without a confession from Bloom.'

'This young woman . . .'

'MacDowell.'

'Yes, *is* she Bloom's lover?'

'I don't think their relationship has been consummated.'

'Odd. Damned odd. Pregnant wife having an affair and Bloom with a sweetheart on the side,' said the Assistant Commissioner disapprovingly. 'And that's not to mention whatever went on at O'Rourke's. By God, the newspapers will have a picnic when the coroner's embargo is lifted. How, in heaven's name, did you pick up on the girl?'

'Information received, sir.'

'From whom?'

'It was just a hint, sir, that's all.'

'God, you're tighter than a clam, Kinsella,' O'Byrne said. 'Still, I suppose that's what we pay you for. Where round here might a man find a decent spot of lunch?'

'The Tudor's as good as any,' Smout said.

'All right,' said Mr O'Byrne. 'The Tudor it is. Would you and Driscoll care to join me, Superintendent?'

'I would and I'm sure Mr Driscoll would too.'

'So be it. We've an hour, haven't we?'

'Slightly less, sir,' said Mr Smout and, with a nod to Kinsella, followed the great man out of the courtroom.

* * *

'You're a big chap, aren't you?' Cissy Caffrey said.

'Six feet two, eyes of blue, that's me.'

'Hark at him,' Cissy said. 'Have you got a name?'

'Constable Jarvis.'

'I'll bet that's not what your mother calls you,'

'You'd be surprised what my mother calls me.'

'I'll tell you mine if you tell me yours.'

'Don't start, Cissy, please,' said Gerty.

'Don't start what?' said Cissy. 'It's not every day I get a hand-some fella in uniform standing me a dinner.'

'Lunch,' said Gerty. 'It's a lunch.'

'If you're not going to tell me your name I'm just going to have to guess,' Cissy said. 'You look like an Algernon to me.'

'Cissy, please,' said Gerty again.

'My name's Archie,' Constable Jarvis said.

The appearance of two young women in Store Street barracks canteen created quite a stir. The catering sergeant's protests had only been stifled by Archie Jarvis's insistence that he was acting under instruction from Superintendent Driscoll, after which service at the corner table swiftly improved.

The constable was well aware that the mop-haired girl was flirting with him and he had no objection to playing along. Inspector Kinsella had told him to keep the cripple as calm as possible and not ask questions. She was very pale and frightened and, unlike her saucy chum, seemed to take no pleasure in the attention she received from the young police officers.

Miss Caffrey ate her mutton pie with a spoon. Archie saw nothing peculiar in that; his sister ate everything with a spoon. He watched Cissy crack the pie crust, dig into the meat and bring the spoon, dripping brown gravy, to her lips.

She had full lips, very white teeth and merry eyes. If Bloom had elected to run off with Miss Caffrey he would have better understood it. The crippled girl, MacDowell, was too timid, too shut in on herself to make the most of her looks. Granted she was pretty and nicely dressed but, compared to her friend, she seemed vapid. She was scared to death, of course, of what the coroner would make her say that afternoon for, being a Catholic, she wouldn't dare lie.

He said, 'Are the fishcakes not to your liking, Miss MacDowell?'

'I'm not hungry.'

'Go on,' said Cissy. 'Dig in, Gert. You'll need all your strength for afterwards. Here, we're not paying for this, are we?'

'It's on the house,' Archie Jarvis assured her.

'The house wouldn't run to a glass of stout, would it?' said Cissy optimistically. 'Quite partial to a glass at din— lunch.'

'No stout,' Archie said. 'Tea, coffee or milk only. Sorry.'

'How about puddin'?'

'Rice and prunes, or apple duff and custard.'

'Lovely!' said Cissy while Gerty lifted a sliver of fish on her fork and placed it on the tip of her tongue.

'Chew, for goodness sake,' Cissy said. 'Nobody's watching.'

Gerty closed her mouth tightly and let the tiny piece of fish slide down her throat.

'There.' Cissy patted her friend's arm. 'That wasn't so bad, was it?' To Constable Jarvis she said, 'She always eats like a bird. Surprised she ha'n't wasted away by now. She's a lovely baker, too. Her ginger biscuits are a treat. Your wife, Archie, does she bake you ginger biscuits?'

'Oh, Cissy!' Gerty scraped the breadcrumbs off a second fragment of fish. 'Leave the poor man alone. He's not interested in you.'

'I wouldn't say that,' said Archie Jarvis. 'Do *you* cook, Cissy?'

'Cook, clean, do the wash and look after the kiddies.'

'Kiddies?' said Constable Jarvis.

'Brothers,' said Cissy. 'Twins. Horrors they can be, too. Where are you from, Archie?'

Attention diverted, Gerty swallowed three tiny pieces of fish, sipped from the cup of tea that the constable had poured for her and watched Cissy weave her spell on the young policeman which, for a moment or two, took her mind off the ordeal ahead.

'Wexford,' Archie Jarvis said. 'I'm from Wexford.'

She wished she could be more like Cissy, though a lot of things Cissy did bordered on the vulgar. What she admired most in Cissy was her happy-go-lucky attitude, that and her insolence. Cissy made it clear she had a mind of her own and, while she would quite like to be a wife, she'd no intention of becoming a slave to the first smooth-talker to come along.

'We're from Sandymount,' Cissy went on. 'Tritonville Road. You ever down that way, Archie?'

'Now and then. I like the Strand when the weather's hot.'

'It's not just the weather that's hot in Sandymount.'

'Cissy! Stop it!'

'You're a fine one to talk, Gert. Didn't you first see the love of your life on the sands? You wouldn't be here now if you hadn't.'

Hastily, Archie put in, 'My father's a policeman, Royal Irish. Do you have anything against coppers, Cissy?'

'Coppers?' Cissy considered. 'Nah, not coppers like you, any roads. You should come down to Sandymount now the weather's picking up. It's only a penny tram ride from town and you never know who you'll bump into by the seashore.'

'I might just take you up on that,' Archie Jarvis promised.

'I'll be in need of a chum by then,' Cissy said. 'When Mr Bloom steps out o' that court a free man Gerty'll be off to London. Or Paris. Ooo-la-la! Paris! You can do anything you wish in Paris, be as naughty as you like.' She grinned. 'Me, I'd settle for a day out at the races. Get to wear me pretty hat, drink fizz and blow a bob or two. You ever been to the races, Archie?'

'Do you know, I never have.'

'First time for everything,' Cissy said and winked.

Gerty put down her teacup. Tea or not, a fishbone was stuck half way down her gullet. She could feel the muscles in her throat tighten, threatening a bout of the heaves.

She lifted her handkerchief to her mouth and gulped.

'What is it, dear?' said Cissy solicitously. 'What's wrong?'

'I feel sick.'

'Nerves, just nerves,' Cissy said. 'Take a great big breath, darlin',' then, to Constable Jarvis, 'We'd better get her out of here.'

Gerty crushed the handkerchief into her face and rose from the table, clattering the chair. Cheeks burning, she swung round in search of an exit. Cissy rose too and, snaring her friend by the waist, steered her towards the doorway that led to the barracks' yard.

'Hoy?' the catering sergeant shouted while the other officers in the room stared at the distressed young women and, not unsympathetically, shook their heads.

Constable Jarvis slapped two half crowns down on the table

and, grabbing up his cap, headed after the women with as much decorum as he could muster. He would be ribbed about this later, ribbed mercilessly, but right now his prime concern was for the woman he'd been charged to protect.

Gerty clung to her friend, her boot scraping the linoleum, as she stumbled towards daylight; a small defenceless creature who, Archie thought, knew little of courts and coppers or middle-aged men with scolding wives. He wouldn't take on Gerty MacDowell if she was the last free woman in Dublin, but then he wasn't Leopold Bloom, thank God. He caught the door before it closed and stepped into the yard.

Knees spread, Cissy Caffrey had Gerty draped over her forearm like a blanket while Gerty retched and retched and brought up nothing but three or four undigested bits of cod.

Cissy dabbed Gerty's mouth with a handkerchief, then, looking at Archie Jarvis, said, 'She's not well. I really should be gettin' her home.'

Archie nodded. 'If she's ill, then the coroner won't . . .'

Straightening, Gerty said, 'No, I'm going through with it.' She snatched the handkerchief from Cissy and wiped her lips. 'I don't care what they think. I'm going through with it.'

'That's the ticket, Miss,' said Archie, much relieved, while Cissy, with a sigh, retrieved the handkerchief, spat on it and, gripping her friend by the scruff of the neck, scrubbed off the last of the sick with a vigour that made Archie flinch.

Chopped egg and onion was Bloom's least favourite sandwich filling. And the tea was stewed. He applied a drop of milk from the half pint bottle that the court officer had delivered and three spoonfuls of sugar from the canister with the label, 'Property of Dublin City Council' peeling off its side.

It was all very shabby and indicative of his status in the circus that the inquiry had become. He'd been duped by the wily detective into believing that if he played along he'd not only walk out of court a free man but would still have Gerty. As for that fool, that foppish boy they'd found to defend him, he'd lost faith in him long ago. He stirred his tea with the bent spoon they'd given him and sipped, his mouth pinching with the taste of it.

He'd been left alone to stew, like the tea, in a bleak little office

at the back of the courtroom, close to the stairs that led down to
the mortuary where Molly's body had lain; Molly and the foetus
that Molly had assured him would tumble into the world wearing
a straw boater and a striped blazer and with not one drop of the
blood of the tribe of Reuben in his veins.

She shouldn't have said that, shouldn't have taunted him. She
thought that Boylan would take her on, of course, make her a
queen of song and her child, his child, a prince among men. And
if Boylan didn't take the bait then he, reliable old Poldy, would
forgive her.

The DMP officer who'd been stationed outside in case he
decided to top himself threw open the door to admit his lawyer.
Following Neville into the room was a foxy, not-quite-elderly,
little man in a morning coat, silk-buttoned waistcoat and a collar
the like of which Bloom hadn't seen since his school days. He
wore spectacles, too, nose-pinchers, that caught the light from
the room's only window and, for an instant, make his eyes sparkle.

'May I introduce my senior,' Neville Sullivan said. 'Mr Alfred
Tolland. He's taken an interest in your case since the beginning
and has one or two questions he'd like to put to you.'

The habit of courtesy urged Bloom to rise and offer his hand
but, stubbornly, he stayed in his chair, glowering over the sandwich plate while Mr Tolland drew out a chair and arranged it at
the table, facing Bloom.

Once seated, Mr Tolland peeled off his gloves, dropped them
into his lap, then, glancing up, said, 'Tell me, Mr Bloom, strictly
between thee, me and Neville here, why *did* you murder your wife?'

TWENTY SIX

S o great was the crowd in the bar of the Belleville that you
could barely find a table upon which to rest your glass, let
alone a chair upon which to rest your bottom.

Smoke from pipes, cigars and cigarettes filled the air like
ectoplasm and, hyperbole being the order of the day, the
clamour of the men of the fourth estate rose like the wail of

the damned teetering on the verge of the pit. If you wished to order a drink, express an opinion or simply greet a friend, the only way to do it was to roar at the pitch of your voice and with reporters in from Cork, Belfast and as far afield as Liverpool all doing likewise, the racket was, as Mr Flanagan put it, positively Pentecostal.

Even sharp-eyed locals were too busy ferrying booze from the bar to their corner refuge to notice that a breathless Blazes Boylan had found his way to the waterhole and, having grabbed the barmaid's attention, was hoarsely demanding service in the form of three large gins.

'Here, isn't that Gandy?' Robbie Randall said. Gesturing with a half full glass, he shouted, 'Gandy. Over there. What's he doing here? I thought he was on duty.'

'When did that ever stop Gandy,' said Charlie Palfry who, following the line of spillage from Randall's glass, had spotted the sergeant's cap bobbing above the heads of the multitude.

'Perhaps he has a titbit or two to sell,' Robbie Randall suggested. 'Who's going to stand him a jar?'

Jack Delaney had secured a bread roll filled with sausage meat. He crammed the roll into his mouth and sluiced it down with porter. 'He's here with Boylan.'

'Blazes? Where?' said Mr Flanagan.

Juggling three glasses of London Dry, Blazes elbowed through the crowd. 'Here he is, the man o' the hour,' Mr Palfry declared.

'One for me?' said Flanagan, reaching out. 'How kind.'

'Get off,' said Blazes savagely. He looked around for a ledge upon which to place the glasses but, finding none, reluctantly passed one glass to Delaney with the warning, 'Touch a drop and you're a dead man.'

He drained the glass in his right hand, as if gin had no more bite than tap water, retrieved the second glass from Delaney, drained it too and, stooping, put the empties on the floor behind a potted plant. 'God Jesus, but I needed that.'

'I'm not surprised,' said Jack Delaney. 'If I were you, though, I'd go easy on the grog, Hughie. You're in the box this afternoon and you'll need all your wits about you.'

'Particularly if Slater has a female witness who saw the whole thing,' said Charlie Palfry. 'Does anyone know who she is?'

'One of Bloom's tarts,' said Blazes.

Breathing had returned to normal but he was still sweating. He blinked, flicked away a greasy droplet from his brow and tipped back half the contents of the third glass.

'How many tarts does Bloom have?' said Randall.

'Two at least,' said Boylan.

'Who's the other one?' Mr Palfry asked.

'Martha Clifford. Christ knows who *she* is,' Blazes answered. 'I have letters from her to Bloom, so I know she exists. She's a dirty devil, too, I tell you, a spanker. Just Bloom's type. I didn't know anything about the cripple, though. He kept her dark all right.'

Sergeant Gandy loomed behind Boylan. His eyes roved hopefully from gin to stout. He licked his moustache with a thick red tongue and cleared his throat.

Blazes swung round. 'Why are you trailing me, Gandy?'

'Told you already,' the sergeant said, 'it's me job.'

'Who sent you?' said Blazes. 'Kinsella, was it?'

'Machin,' Gandy said. 'Is that Guinness you have there?'

'For God's sake, Blazes, buy him a pint,' Mr Palfry said. 'He's your man after all.'

'He is not my man,' said Blazes. 'He's Machin's man.'

'Tell you what, Sergeant, I'll spring for a pint,' said Robbie Randall, 'if you tip us a wink what Slater's got up his sleeve?'

'Kinsella thinks he's turned up a witness puts Mr Boylan with Bloom outside Nancy O'Rouke's on the night in question,' Gandy said. 'Now, what about that pint, eh?'

Flanagan said, 'What's your part in it, Jack, since you're sitting with the witnesses?'

'Buy me a drink, for God's sake,' said Gandy.

'Yes, Jack,' said Palfry, 'what is your contribution?'

'Wait and see,' Jack Delaney said.

'One drink,' said Gandy.

'Jesus!' Digging into his pocket Blazes brought out a ten shilling note and held it up between finger and thumb. 'Get yourself a pint, Gandy, fetch me another double London while you're at it, and don't pocket the change.'

He polished off the gin in the remaining glass and, stooping again, deposited the empty by the potted plant. Then he rose and confronted the *Star*'s reporter. 'It *was* you, wasn't it? You squealed. You toadied to Kinsella.'

'Did you, Jack?' said Mr Palfry.

'Ask him what he's doing on the witness benches if it isn't to see me fixed,' Blazes shouted. 'Where's Gandy? Where's my bloody gin?' He swivelled on his heel, lost balance, righted himself and cried, 'You're all the same, every bloody one of you. Licking the coppers' arses. Bugger you, Delaney! Bugger you for a squealer!'

The punch had no weight behind it.

Delaney intercepted the fist before it travelled far from Boylan's shoulder and deftly turned the blow aside.

Blazes lost balance and would have toppled to the floor if Gandy's reflexes had not been so sharp. He fended Blazes against his chest, spilling not one drop of London Dry in the process. The same could not be said for the pint of stout, the contents of which slopped over Blazes like a baptism.

'Mother o' God,' said Gandy. 'Look what you've done to yourself now, Mr Boylan,' and swiftly downing the rest of the stout and all of the gin, dragged the dandy outside to swab him down before court time.

'I don't know who's going to pay for all this,' Milly said. 'I can't possibly repay you for all you've done for me.'

'I'll take it out of your salary if it'll make you feel better,' Harry Coghlan said cheerfully. 'Penny a week for twenty years.'

Michael Paterson had steered her safely through the crowd of reporters and spectators who had gathered outside the courthouse to catch a glimpse of the villain's daughter. Michael had sent Harry Coghlan out to find a cab and bring it to the steps of the courthouse for the express purpose of whisking Milly away from the vicinity of Store Street. He said, 'In the light of what you heard this morning, Milly, may I assume you no longer wish to lodge with the Boylans?'

'No, I do not. I can't bear to look at the man.'

'Then the quicker we get you out of there the better,' Michael said and instructed the cabby to drive to the Rechabites' Hall.

In spite of her shock at the latest revelations, Milly remained convinced of her father's innocence. What riled her wasn't that her father had found himself a sweetheart or that her mother had given herself to Blazes Boylan but that she, Milly, had been stupid enough to fall for Hugh Boylan's wiles. Her anger did not lessen during the short journey across the Liffey and, if it hadn't been for Michael Paterson's restraining hand, she would have thrown herself on Daphne Boylan as soon as Blazes's sister opened the door.

'Milly? What? Is it over?' Daphne said.

'No, it isn't over. I've come for my clothes,' Milly snapped. 'Out of my way you . . . you cow.'

Daphne wore a canvas apron over a black day dress and had swept her hair up in a bun and pinned it with a comb. She made no move to close the door but allowed Milly to stalk past her and flounce down the hall while Dr Paterson, politely removing his hat, introduced himself.

'What is it?' said Daphne. 'What's wrong with the child?'

Somewhere in the depths of the building Milly tossed furniture about. Harry remained with the cab.

'Milly just found out about your brother, Miss Boylan,' Michael Paterson said, 'and what he did to her mother.'

'Oh, God in heaven! Maude should never have lied.' Cocking her head like an inquisitive parrot, Daphne said, 'That's why you're here, isn't it? To arrest me?'

'I'm a doctor, not a policeman,' Michael said. 'However, Miss Boylan, in the light of what you've just told me it might be no bad idea to put on your coat and hat and accompany us to the courthouse.'

'Maude told me to do it,' said Daphne plaintively. 'Maude told me to say Hughie was here that night.'

'And he wasn't,' Michael said, 'here that night?'

'He didn't come in until nearly six.'

'Do you believe in God, Miss Boylan?' Michael said.

'What? Yes, of course I do.'

'And anything you say under oath would be sacred?'

'I can't let Hughie down,' Daphne said. 'No matter what he's done, he's still my brother. Please, don't force me to lie for him.'

Milly marched up from the depths of the building, lugging her suitcase. Her hat was askew, her mourning dress dishevelled, her temper undiminished. She swung the case and thumped Daphne Boylan's shins. 'Out of my way, you . . . you deceiver.'

Milly swung the case again but Michael deflected it.

'Go to the cab and wait there, Milly,' he said. 'I'll only be a minute.'

He watched Milly stalk down the steps to the pavement, the suitcase bouncing behind her, saw Harry open the cab door, put the case inside and help Milly up into the cab. He felt sorry for Daphne Boylan. He couldn't force her to accompany him to court, let alone betray her brother, but he couldn't ignore the probability that her sister intended to perjure herself.

He said, 'Is that a comb in your hair, Miss Boylan?'

Her hand shot to the bun. 'What . . . what does . . .?'

'Give it to me.'

'I'll do nothing of the kind.'

'Give me your comb and you may stay here,' Michael Paterson said. 'Otherwise, I'll leave my friend to look out for you while I fetch a policeman. It's your choice, Miss Boylan: the comb or the courthouse.'

She might be weak but she wasn't stupid. She reached up and separated the comb from the bun, fastidiously picked a few fine grey hairs from the teeth and held it out to him. 'What will happen to Hughie if Maude turns against him?'

'I really have no idea.' Michael Paterson slipped the comb into his overcoat pocket. 'Whatever it is, I'm sure he'll get his just desserts.'

'That's what I'm afraid of,' Daphne Boylan said.

TWENTY SEVEN

'Of course,' Leopold Bloom said, 'I might tell you that Molly asked me to kill her and, being used to pleasing her, I caved in.'

'Surely you don't expect us to believe that she asked you to beat her to death with a teapot?' Poppy Tolland said.

'What do you know of it?' Bloom said. 'You turn up out of the blue, sit there like a great panjandrum and expect me to confess. Are you here to prepare for a trial at the Assizes, is that it?'

'No, Mr Bloom,' Poppy Tolland said. 'I'm here to see to it, if I can, that judgement is not – repeat not – carried forward to a higher court. By the by, I may not have put in an appearance before now but rest assured I've read every word of the transcript with' – a little bow towards his future son-in-law – 'a degree of perspicacity that's not yet given to my partner, due, I might add, not to his lack of application but simply his lack of experience.'

Bloom cocked an eyebrow. 'Would you care for a sandwich?'

'What's the filling?'

'Chopped egg and onion.'

'No,' Poppy Tolland said, 'thank you all the same. I'd be obliged if you'd answer my question, Mr Bloom. In somewhat less than an hour Slater will begin questioning witnesses. We have a valid line of defence based on wrongful arrest or, rather, failure to proceed with sufficient caution to afford you the protection of the law. Slater is aware of this and will do his level best to obscure procedural bungles in his summing up. However . . .'

'Yes,' Bloom said, 'I thought there'd be a "however".'

'However,' Tolland continued, 'to secure our defence we must have the truth. Now, once again, why did you kill your wife?'

'Molly begged me to put her out of her misery.'

'Assisted suicide?' said Neville. 'Utter balderdash!'

'You didn't strike her, did you, Mr Bloom? You didn't smash her mouth and gouge out her eye with a teapot,' Poppy Tolland said. 'Some other person attacked her and left her to die and you seized the opportunity to finish the job.'

'That's not how it was at all,' Bloom said.

'Tell me, Mr Bloom, what did Benson Rule miss in his examination?' said Poppy Tolland. 'How did you do it?'

'I smothered her with a bolster.' Bloom wiped the corner of his eye with his thumb. 'Given the state she was in, with her face smashed and her looks ruined, it was an act of mercy.'

'An act of mercy that freed you to run off with another woman,' Neville said. 'There isn't a jury in the land would believe what you've just told me. It also begs the question who struck her down in the first place. If I put you into the witness box with that tale, Slater will tear you to shreds.'

'What I find puzzling,' Tolland said, 'is why if she was

conscious and able to speak she didn't tell you who attacked her? Are you protecting someone, Mr Bloom?'

'Of course I'm not protecting anyone.'

'Were you even present in Number 7 Eccles Street when your wife was attacked?' Neville asked.

'I've told you a dozen times, no, I wasn't.'

'Oh, I believe you, Mr Bloom,' Tolland said. 'But it wasn't eight o'clock in the morning or anywhere near it. What time was it when you found your injured wife? Three? Half past three? No later than four, I'll wager, and still dark, which is why no one saw you at that hour, why there are no witnesses.'

'Half past three would be about the size of it,' Bloom admitted.

'Where were you until that hour?' Neville said. 'Skulking in Nancy O'Rourke's?'

'I went to O'Rourke's looking for Blazes Boylan, if you must know,' Bloom said.

'For what purpose?' said Tolland.

Bloom hesitated. 'To tell him I was leaving Dublin.'

'Are you saying you were running off with MacDowell that very night?' Tolland asked.

'That was my intention,' Bloom answered. 'Gerty – Miss MacDowell – was waiting for me in Sandymount. I'd booked passage on the boat to Liverpool. I planned to wait in the coffee shop on the North Quay until boarding. I didn't want to risk going to a hotel.'

'But instead you went back to Eccles Street,' Tolland said. 'Why would you do such a thing?'

'To warn Molly. Blazes wanted Molly to get rid of the baby,' Bloom said. 'He'd gone as far as asking Nancy O'Rourke to put him in touch with one of the women who deals with such mishaps.'

'An abortionist?' Neville said.

'Yes.'

'Surely your wife would never agree to that,' said Tolland.

'I think Molly thought she might still keep Boylan and the baby,' Bloom said. 'And if Boylan threw her over she was counting on me to stand by her.'

'Only by then it was too late,' Tolland put in. 'By then you had another woman waiting on the quayside. However, you didn't leave Miss MacDowell on the quayside, did you, Mr Bloom? That's not the kind of fellow you are. You took her with you to Eccles Street. What did you do with MacDowell while you were smothering Mrs Bloom? Did you hide her downstairs?'

'Upstairs in one of the empty rooms.'

'Was Boylan still in the house?' said Neville.

'If he was, I didn't see him.'

'But MacDowell did,' Poppy Tolland said. 'That's why you waited so long to report the crime, to give MacDowell a chance to flee the scene in the hope that you might keep her identity secret. I can readily understand why you would do that but what I can't understand is why you didn't tell the police about Boylan. It must have been obvious that Boylan had done the deed.'

'It never occurred to me that the police would arrest me,' Bloom said, 'and when Mullen refused to dismiss the charge it was too late to change my story.'

'Did you think Boylan would harm MacDowell if he knew she'd been with you in Eccles Street that night?' Tolland asked.

'I did and I still do,' Bloom answered. 'Now do you see why I don't want you to put her in the witness box?'

'It's out of our hands,' Neville said. 'Thanks to Kinsella, all the evidence is neatly laid out. Your sweetheart no longer has anything to fear from Boylan.'

'If I plead to manslaughter, you mean,' Bloom said.

'In which case your daughter will lose her inheritance,' Poppy Tolland reminded him. 'You took out a special policy to provide for your daughter because you thought something might happen to you and you didn't want your wife getting her hands on the money or, rather, Boylan getting *his* hands on your money. It's quite ironic that your wife died before you did. This I will say for you, Bloom, by your own lights you behaved quite honourably.'

'Honourably?' Neville said. 'Dear God, Alfred, he killed his wife. There's nothing honourable in that.'

'Did he kill his wife?' said Poppy Tolland. 'We don't know that. According to Rule's expert testimony Mrs Bloom died as a result of injuries received after an assault with a teapot. For all we know – and for all Bloom knows – his wife was dead when he found her and what he heard was not speech but the last gasp of breath escaping from her lungs.'

'He confessed, Poppy. He confessed.'

'Poppy?' said Alfred Tolland.

'I'm sorry. I mean . . .'

'You spoke in the heat of the moment, Neville, which is perfectly understandable under the circumstances. May not we assume that Mr Bloom also spoke in the heat of the moment? I, for one, have heard nothing approaching a confession, merely the ramblings of a man who's been treated shabbily by the law. May I remind you, Neville, that we deal only in facts,' Poppy Tolland said. 'The fact is that Mrs Bloom was attacked by an unknown assailant and died of her wounds; a fact endorsed by medical evidence already sealed by the coroner. If the unknown assailant turns out to be Hugh Boylan, as is very likely the case, then bear in mind that Boylan doesn't know what happened after he left Eccles Street. He doesn't know what went on in the bedroom. In other words . . .'

'Boylan thinks he killed her,' Neville said.

'Exactly. He is, in his own eyes, guilty. Our task now is to help the coroner prove it,' Poppy Tolland said.

'How will you do that?' Bloom asked.

'By silence and cunning,' Tolland answered. 'Your silence, Mr Bloom, and our cunning. Do you understand?'

'I do,' Bloom said. 'Indeed, I do.'

'Come then,' said Poppy Tolland, pushing back his chair, 'let's off to the courtroom, Neville, to lay out our papers and see what Mr Blazes Boylan has to say for himself, bearing in mind that the gentleman in question is the guilty party and our client, Mr Bloom, nothing more than a victim of circumstance.'

'Even if he's not?' said Neville.

'Even if he's not,' said Tolland.

Local reporters could hardly be blamed for failing to recognise Blazes Boylan's sister, the hermit of Rechabites' Hall. If Mr Cunningham had been in court he would have identified Maude at once for he knew everyone across the length and breadth of Dublin. Mr Cunningham had decided he'd had enough of Bloom, however, and had elected not to request another day off work to watch the tragedy of love, lust and betrayal reach its sordid conclusion.

Having sent Milly off with Harry Coghlan to find a cupboard in which to store her suitcase, Michael Paterson stationed himself below the staircase that led to the public gallery to wait for Maude Boylan to emerge from the ladies' lavatory.

Ignoring the pleas of the females queuing outside the cubicle, Maude squatted on the pedestal, smoked a small cigar she'd filched from Hughie's case that morning and wrestled with what remained of her conscience. Hughie had warned her that if he was summoned to the witness box then she would surely be called from the public gallery to support his claim that he was flat out drunk in bed at home in the wee small hours of March 9th and in no fit state to say boo to a goose let alone murder a big, strapping woman like Molly Bloom. But Hughie hadn't returned home that night. Daphne and she had sat up until well after midnight and his bed had still been empty when she'd looked in on him at half past four o'clock.

Six was the earliest she could honestly place him in the Hall, an hour at which she'd found him half naked in the kitchen washing a shirt and removing stains from his suit with pumice and a damp cloth. He had not been drunk: indeed, she'd seldom seen him so sober. He'd offered no explanation for his behaviour and neither she nor Daphne had asked for one.

Milly Bloom's outburst and the hints Inspector Kinsella had dropped regarding Hugh's involvement not just with Molly but with Leopold Bloom added greatly to Maude's uncertainty.

She was by nature a positive person, but being positive was all very well in the sheltered sphere in which she lived and bullying Daphne no preparation for standing up to G-men, lawyers and judges with whom a scowl and a Norfolk jacket would cut no ice. Hoisting up her tweed skirt, she dropped the cigar butt between her knees and tugged on the chain to flush it away.

Buttoning her jacket and smoothing down her skirt, she opened the door of the cubicle, shouldered past the seething throng and headed for her seat in the back of the public gallery, determined, more or less, to see it through.

'Miss Boylan?'

She recognised the fellow as Milly Bloom's man friend from Mullingar, the person the girl had been clinging to through most of the morning session. She stopped not out of courtesy but out of curiosity. She knitted her brows, stuck out her chin and said, 'Yes?'

What she mistook for a handshake turned out to be nothing of the sort. At first his hand was empty, then, like a conjurer producing a card, a comb appeared between forefinger and thumb, the same tortoiseshell comb Daphne had been wearing that morning.

Maude Boylan's blood ran cold.

'What have you done with my sister?' she asked.

'Not a thing.' He spoke softly. 'She's just where you left her.'

'You had words with her, I take it?'

'I did,' said the man from Mullingar. 'And I have to tell you that your sister is prepared to come to court and tell the truth.'

'What does this have to do with me?'

'That,' said Michael Paterson, 'is for you to decide.'

'I see,' Maude Boylan said and, plucking the comb from his fingertips, pushed him to one side and stalked out into the street, taking Hughie's alibi with her.

TWENTY EIGHT

Jack Delaney had never been in a witness box before. He was well used to sitting in courtrooms with a notebook in his lap and recording the sins of other men and women for the delectation of his readers, but to become part of the story was a new and not altogether welcome experience.

Clear eyed, clean shaven and exuding awareness of his responsibility as an upright citizen, Jack introduced himself and, with as steady a mien as he could muster, let Slater rip into him. What troubled him was not the coroner's interrogation but the sight of Alfred Tolland crouched at the defence table with his pince-nez winking and a superior smile on his foxy face.

Coroner Slater had been none too pleased when Tolland had entered court. He had pointedly enquired as to the lawyer's role, to which question Neville had answered that Mr Tolland's intention was merely to mentor and observe; and what was the harm in that?

The harm in that, Jack Delaney might have told him, was that Tolland's skill in undermining the moral authority of witnesses, nuns and priests included, was notorious. From the corner of his eye he watched and waited for Tolland to whisper in Sullivan's ear or slip notes across the table, but Tolland did neither. He remained quietly attentive, unlike Bloom who appeared to have fallen asleep.

'Are you familiar with the houses north of Montgomery Street, Mr Delaney?' the coroner said.

'I am.'

'Are you a frequent visitor to these establishments?'

'Yes.'

'What is the purpose of your visits?'

'Partly business, partly pleasure.'

Jack was tempted to trot out the tale that he was taking singing lessons from one of Nancy O'Rourke's girls, but the tension in the courtroom deterred any attempt at humour.

'Where were you late on the evening of 8th March?'

'In Upper Tyrone Street.'

'Visiting Mrs O'Rourke's house?'

'I was outside in the street.'

'At what hour precisely?'

'Close to half past eleven.'

'Tell the court what you saw outside in the street?'

'Mr Bloom arguing with Mr Boylan.'

'Were blows exchanged?'

'Not that I saw.'

'Mr Bloom and Mr Boylan arguing together at around half past eleven in Upper Tyrone Street, that is what you saw?'

'It is.'

'Both gentlemen are known to you by sight?'

'They are.'

'Had you been drinking, Mr Delaney?'

'No, sir, I was sober.'

The coroner continued his questioning without interruption from the jury foreman or Bloom's counsel. Time expanded, minutes began to seem like hours, then suddenly it was over.

'Mr Conway, do you have any questions for this witness?'

Conway shook his head. 'I don't believe we have, Mr Slater.'

Only when he dipped his chin to squint down at the defence counsel's table did Jack realise that his neck was rigid and his shoulders hunched to the point of pain. He'd expected an attack upon his moral integrity, an attempt on Sullivan's part to make him out to be not only a predator upon the flower of Dublin's womanhood but, by inference, a liar to boot.

Neville Sullivan toyed with a pencil while Tolland, lips pursed, appeared to be silently whistling a voluntary. Only Bloom raised his eyes to the reporter in the box and, with a twitch of his moustache, looked away again, more bored, it seemed, than dismayed.

The coroner leaned from his chair and asked, 'Have you anything you wish to add before I dismiss the witness, Mr Sullivan?'

'No,' said Neville Sullivan. 'Nothing.'

'Thank you, Mr Delaney. You may step down.'

Jack Delaney let out his breath, picked his way from the box and took his seat not with the other witnesses but beside his colleagues on the press benches.

'Well done, Jack,' Robbie Randall murmured.

'Five bob for an exclusive, Jack,' whispered Mr Palfry.

'I'll make that ten,' said Mr Flanagan and sniggered.

Those who knew Hugh 'Blazes' Boylan, advertising executive, impresario, seducer of women, gambler, dandy, boozer and braggart, realised at once that he was not himself as he climbed the four steps into the witness box, rested his elbow on the narrow ledge and mopped his brow with a mauve silk handkerchief.

Many things was Sergeant Gandy but a nursemaid wasn't one of them. He had sponged Mr Boylan's natty suit as best he could and had gotten him back from the Belleville to the courthouse with just enough time to wash his face and comb his hair before the court reconvened. No suitable replacement could be found for his beer-stained shirt, though, and Mr Boylan carried into the box with him more than a faint whiff of the brewery.

'Mr Boylan,' Roland Slater said, 'are you quite well?'

'Fine, fine, yes, grand, thank you, your honour.'

'Mr Rice, will you administer the oath, please.'

The oath was duly administered and the Bible kissed with not altogether appropriate passion. 'Be good enough to state for the record your full name, address and place of business,' the coroner instructed. Blazes, after pause for reflection, supplied the necessary information.

'Mr Boylan,' said the coroner, frowning, 'have you, by any chance, been drinking?'

'Medicinal brandy,' Blazes answered. 'One small snifter to calm my nerves.'

The lie slipped easily off his tongue. Confidence restored, he pulled himself together, tucked the handkerchief into his breast pocket and bestowed upon the coroner and jurymen a smile that seemed to say, 'Sure we're all men of the world, are we not now, and what's one brandy after all?'

'Your nerves?' said Coroner Slater, who apparently was not a man of the world. 'Do you have reason to be nervous, Mr Boylan?'

'I'm not used to appearing in public, your honour.'

'I am not "your honour", Mr Boylan. I'm not a judge.'

'What do I call you then?'

'You do not have to call me anything,' Slater said. 'If you insist on addressing me by a title, Mister Slater will do well enough.' He watched Blazes' smile fade and went on, 'I rather thought a concert performer would be used to appearing in public.'

'Are you going to ask me to sing?'

'No, I am not going to ask you to sing, Mr Boylan, not, at any rate, within the musical definition of the word.'

The boys on the press benches, well versed in transatlantic slang, guffawed at the coroner's remark but Blazes failed to pick up on it and, discomfited, whipped out the mauve handkerchief and mopped his brow once more.

The coroner pressed on, 'How long have you been acquainted with Mr Bloom?'

'Since back in the days when we were neighbours in Clanbrassil Street, though it was mostly Jews lived there. We moved out quick when my father's fortunes improved.'

'Did you keep in touch with the Blooms?'

'We bumped into each other when Bloom worked at Hely's, the stationers, but I can't say – no, we – we drifted apart.'

'When was the friendship renewed?'

'About a year ago.'

'How long have you known the deceased, Marion Bloom?'

'Somewhere in the region of fifteen years.'

'How did you advance your relationship with Mrs Bloom?'

'I heard her sing. I thought she was a star and would be good for a concert tour I was organising. Lovely voice, sweet as an angel's. I met with Bloom by chance, then he brought the wife along and I put it to them she might take to the platform with me.'

'Did Mr Bloom object to your proposal?'

'Not him. Molly was keen and he could no more refuse Molly than pigs can fly. Any roads, he had his mind on other things.'

'Other things?' said Slater.

'He had a woman he was seeing on the sly.'

'A woman? Is she in court today?'

'I don't know.'

'You don't know? You accuse Mr Bloom of conducting an out of marriage relationship, Mr Boylan, yet you don't know if the woman is here or not. Can you corroborate your statement with a name, at the very least a name?'

'Martha.'

'Where might this Martha woman be found?'

'Can't say. I couldn't track her down.'

'Why did you want to track her down, Mr Boylan?' the coroner said. 'Could it be that you hoped to further your own cause with Marion Bloom by inventing a mistress for Mr Bloom?'

'My own cause? Oh, you mean with Molly. Nah, I didn't need any amouses to get aboard that wagon.

'Before we allow ourselves to be lured from the facts by unfounded accusations,' Roland Slater said, 'I'd like to turn to the evidence given by Mrs Fleming. I take it, Mr Boylan, you heard Mrs Fleming swear under oath that she saw you and Marion Bloom engaged in a debauched act. I will have her testimony read out to refresh your memory if you wish.'

'Not,' said Blazes, 'necessary. I admit I was doing Molly. I mean Marion Bloom.'

'When did the affair begin?' the coroner asked, loudly enough to rise above the din of the gallery.

'June, last year.'

'Did it continue unabated until Mrs Bloom's death?'

'It did.'

'Mrs Bloom did not resist your blandishments?'

'No, Molly was always game.'

The drone from the gallery grew louder. This time Roland Slater waited until it died down before he took up the reins once more. 'You do not deny that you were engaged in an adulterous relationship with Mr Bloom's wife?'

'Why deny it? It's common knowledge.'

'Common, I think, being the word,' Slater said, then, 'Did Bloom know what was going on between you and his wife?'

''Course he did.'

'Did he confront you with the knowledge?' Slater said. 'By which I mean, did he try to deter you from continuing the affair?'

'I can't see the point in this,' Blazes said.

'Oh, can't you?' Roland Slater said. 'The point, Mr Boylan, is that a woman has been brutally murdered and it is the business of this court to determine a reason for her untimely death. Is that point enough for you?'

'I suppose it has to be,' Blazes conceded.

Slater did not rebuke Mr Boylan for his impertinence. He lowered his voice to a purr. 'Now, you have heard the medical evidence and I must ask you if you knew that Mrs Bloom was in a gravid state?'

'Dead?' said Blazes. 'I didn't know she was dead till—'

'Pregnant,' said Slater patiently. 'With child.'

'How would I be knowing a thing like that?' said Blazes.

'As you were engaged in intimacy with Mrs Bloom it's no stretch to assume you actually conversed from time to time. Did Mrs Bloom inform you that she was carrying a child?'

Blazes sucked his cheeks and declared, 'No, she did not.'

'Liar,' muttered Mr Bloom, without looking up.

'You were unaware that she was pregnant?'

'I was.'

'Liar,' Bloom once more muttered.

'Your client, Mr Sullivan, must not interrupt.'

'My apologies,' Neville said. 'It won't happen again.'

'Mr Boylan' – the coroner moved in for the kill – 'we have heard from Mr Delaney that you were seen arguing with Bloom at half past the hour of eleven in Upper Tyrone Street on the night immediately preceding the murder. What was that argument about if it wasn't about your relationship with Bloom's wife?'

'He wanted to borrow a fiver and got all hot and bothered when I refused.'

'Are you saying that Mrs Bloom's name wasn't mentioned?'

'Never a peep.'

'Did Mr Bloom tell you why he wanted money?'

'He said he was leaving Dublin.'

'Did he say why he was leaving Dublin?'

'Said it was none of my business.'

'Did it not seem obvious to you that Bloom's reason for leaving Dublin was connected to your affair with his wife?'

'He's a Jew. You never know what Jews are up to.'

Roland Slater grudgingly decided to let the answer pass without comment. 'Did you believe Mr Bloom when he told you he was leaving Dublin?'

'I thought he was trying to land me in the shi . . . soup. Look,' said Blazes, 'I was slathered. I admit it. I'd had a few too many. All I wanted to do was get on home to me bed.'

'Did you give Mr Bloom money?'

'No.'

'What did Mr Bloom do then?'

'Wandered off.'

'And you, Mr Boylan, what did you do?'

'Went home to bed.'

'How?'

'How?' said Blazes. 'Oh, cab. Yes, by cab.

'In spite of Inspector Machin's diligent inquiries no cab driver has come forward who remembers transporting you to Sefton Street.'

'Well, that ain't my fault.'

'You said, you saw no more of Mr Bloom that night?'

'Not a hair.'

'When was the last time you saw Mrs Bloom? Alive, I mean.'

'Oooo,' Blazes pondered, 'must have been the Monday afternoon before she – you know – died.'

'In the house in Eccles Street?'

'Yes, in Eccles Street.'

'Where, we may assume, an act of intimacy took place?'

Blazes grinned, 'More than one, if you must know.'

'How long did you remain with Mrs Bloom on Monday?'

'Couple of hours. No, closer to three.'

'Where was Mr Bloom?'

'You'll have to ask him. He always steered clear till Molly was good and . . . until I left.'

'Did you see Mrs Bloom again after your Monday visit?'

'No.'

'Think carefully before you answer, Mr Boylan: you were not in the house in Eccles Street in the small hours of Thursday?'

'I told all this to Kinsella,' Blazes grumbled. 'I certainly was not in the house in Eccles Street on Thursday. I was home in bed by midnight. You can ask my sisters if you don't believe me. They'll swear . . .'

'I'm sure they will, Mr Boylan.' Slater turned to face the jury. 'No doubt you have questions you are eager to put to this witness. I am, however, anxious to get to the root of the matter in respect of both Bloom and Mr Boylan's whereabouts in the wee small hours of Thursday. According to witnesses, one, other or both is patently not telling the truth. I propose to excuse Mr Boylan for the moment and allow him an opportunity to collect himself. I will recall him after we hear from the next witness when you'll be at liberty to put your questions. Does that sit well with you, Mr Conway?'

'It does, sir.'

'Good,' Slater said. 'Mr Sullivan, do you have any objection?'

'None whatsoever,' Neville said.

'Will Mr Bloom then take to the witness stand,' Slater said.

'No,' said Neville. 'Mr Bloom will not.'

'I beg your pardon,' Roland Slater said.

'Mr Bloom has chosen not to take the stand again.'

'Do you not wish your client to have an opportunity to refute the accusations made against him by the present witness?'

'There is nothing to refute,' Neville said,

'On the contrary, Mr Sullivan,' Slater said. 'If we are to give credence to the testimony of Mr Delaney let alone that of Mr Boylan then your client has been caught out in a lie.'

'Has he?' said Neville.

'Of course he has. Did he not claim to have been home in

bed with his wife at half past ten o'clock? Yet here we have two reliable – fairly reliable – witnesses who will put him in Upper Tyrone Street at or close to that hour. Does that not have the smell of deception to it, Mr Sullivan, and require an explanation?'

'I don't believe it does,' Neville said.

'In his statement . . .'

'No, Dr Slater.' Neville rose abruptly and tossed down the pencil. 'You will find no such claim in Mr Bloom's signed statement.'

'Inspector Kinsella . . .'

'Ah, yes,' Neville interrupted. 'The "cat's meat" conversation, a conversation that took place before Mr Bloom was cautioned.'

'You're hair-splitting, Mr Sullivan. In this court . . .'

'The application of the law is, it seems, selective,' Neville said.

'Mr Sullivan! How dare you!'

'My client will not take the stand to have his word weighed against that of a self-confessed fornicator. And, with respect, sir, I trust you will remember to remind the jury that no prejudice must be shown against my client or guilt implied for his decision not to put himself in the witness box.'

During the exchange Mr Devereux had sifted through the files upon his table and, without a word, handed up to the coroner a copy of the signed statement Bloom had given to Superintendent Driscoll. For an instant Roland Slater's control deserted him. He snatched the file with ill-disguised anger and, flicking over the pages with a rampant forefinger, scanned it while Neville Sullivan rocked gently from heel to toe and lightly stroked his hair.

Mr Boylan, who had not been dismissed, lolled meanwhile against the ledge of the witness box, pale-faced and sweating.

At length the coroner looked up. He hesitated, licked his upper lip and then addressed the jury. 'Gentlemen,' he said, 'it appears Mr Bloom's counsel is correct. The point was not put directly to Mr Bloom during police questioning. It is therefore not entered into evidence as sworn testimony.' A breath, a beat: 'I'm grateful to Mr Sullivan for pointing out the error and acknowledge fully his client's right to stand, without prejudice, on his original testimony. I will instruct you further in the course of my summing up. We will move on to another witness and you, Mr Boylan, may . . .'

'Wait.'

'What is it now, Mr Sullivan?'

'With your permission and on behalf of the jury, may I put a couple of questions to Mr Boylan before he leaves the box?'

'Can't it wait, Mr Sullivan? Mr Boylan will be returned to the box in due course and you may put your questions then.'

'I would prefer to put the questions now, if it please you.'

The jury members were already whispering among themselves and Mr Conway, making no attempt to silence them, was wryly shaking his head. Roland Slater knew when he was beaten. 'Very well, Mr Sullivan,' he conceded. 'Two questions only and as briefly as you can, if you please.'

At the defence table, Poppy Tolland sat up and removed his spectacles while Bloom, craning his neck, looked up at Blazes Boylan for the first time.

'Mr Boylan,' Neville began, 'you said in evidence that you were unaware that Marion Bloom was carrying a child. Is that true?'

Blazes had lost the rhythm and with it his bantering arrogance. He mopped his cheeks with the sodden handkerchief and answered uncertainly, 'It . . . it is.'

'Are you acquainted with a certain Mrs Bella Cohen who keeps a house in Upper Tyrone Street, adjacent to that of Mrs Nancy O'Rourke?'

'I . . . I've heard the name.'

'With your permission, Coroner Slater, may I jog the witness's memory?' Neville asked.

Though he would not admit it even to himself, the coroner was intrigued by Sullivan's line of questioning and, having little or no alternative now that he had ceded the floor, nodded.

Neville said, 'Mrs Bella Cohen, like Nancy O'Rourke, is the owner of a house in Upper Tyrone Street where girls may be hired for sexual purposes. I have it on best authority, Mr Boylan, that you are a regular visitor to both establishments. Is that true or false?'

'True,' said Blazes grudgingly.

'Then you do know Mrs Cohen?'

'Matter of fact, I do.'

'Have you in the course of let's say the past month engaged Mrs Cohen in conversation in respect of obtaining the services of a woman practised in terminating pregnancies?'

The din from the gallery drowned out any answer that Blazes Boylan might give. Court officers called for order and Roland Slater, with a face like thunder, stood up and remained standing until the racket died down.

'Oh!' said Blazes. 'Me, who loves kiddies and babies. I'd never do such a terrible thing.'

'In which case my information must be wrong,' Neville said.

'What information?' Blazes said then, voice rising, shouted. 'Who told you? Was it that fat bitch Cohen?' He thumped a fist on the ledge of the box. 'Damn the bitch to hell! Is she here? Have you got her here? I'll kill her, so I will. I'll kill her with my own bare . . .' The threat trailed off and he stood there, shivering a little, aghast at his outburst.

'Thank you, Mr Boylan,' said Neville. 'I have no more questions to put to this witness.'

'In which case, you may leave the box, Mr Boylan,' Slater said and waited, still on his feet, while Blazes negotiated the four shallow steps and groped for a seat on the witness benches.

'Mr Sullivan,' the coroner said, 'do you have a witness you wish me to call, a witness who is not already on my list? Mrs Bella Cohen, for instance?'

'No,' said Neville. 'I have no additional witnesses.'

Slater allowed himself the ghost of a smile and seated himself once more while Blazes Boylan, shrunken and shivering, put his head in his hands and groaned.

TWENTY NINE

'**M**r Rice,' the coroner said, 'those steps can be rather hazardous. Would you be good enough to give the witness your arm and assist her into the box.'

Gerty picked up her skirts as she'd seen it done on stage and, giving the press boys an eyeful of her ankles, allowed Mr Rice to hand her up into the witness box. From the floor of the court the box seemed cramped but as soon as she stepped into it its dimensions expanded alarmingly and she felt as if she were standing alone on top of Dalkey Hill. Leaning a little – more of a stagger, really – she peeped down at Poldy who had shifted his chair to bring her into view. He smiled and nodded and, no longer alone, Gerty lifted her head and faced the coroner.

'What is it it that you have in your hand, Miss MacDowell?' Slater asked in a kindly fashion.

'My beads,' Gerty answered.

'Ah, your Rosary,' Slater said. 'A comfort to you, I take it?'

'Yes, sir.' Gerty cleared her throat and, with another glance at Poldy, added, 'A great comfort, sir.'

'If you tell the truth, which I am quite sure you will,' Slater said, 'you have nothing to fear, young lady. Mr Rice, the oath, if you please,' and Gerty MacDowell from Sandymount was duly sworn in and, for the record, identified.

Miss MacDowell was twenty-two years old but Roland Slater insisted on treating her as if she were a child. He propped his right elbow on his left knee, brought himself as close as possible to the witness and spoke so quietly that it was all the great unwashed could do to catch the gist of the exchange.

'Do you know why you are here today, Miss MacDowell?'

'Inspector Kinsella had me sent for.'

'That's true, but do you know why?'

'Because of Poldy . . . Mr Bloom.'

'Poldy? Is that what you call him?'

'Yes.' Gerty blushed like a beacon. 'I'm sorry.'

'There's no need to apologise,' Slater assured her. 'We all have our special names. Do we not, Mr Tolland?'

'Uh?' said a startled Poppy Tolland. 'What? Yes, I suppose we do,' and hastily clipped the pince-nez to the bridge of his nose again. Used to the ways of his master, Mr Devereux prudently omitted the aside from the record.

'Mr Bloom – Poldy – is a friend, is he not?' the coroner said.

'Yes.'

'Is he a close friend, Miss MacDowell?'

Not as naïve as she appeared to be, Gerty said, 'He's not my lover, if that's what you mean.'

Somewhat taken back, the coroner uncoupled elbow from knee and sat up. 'Well, yes, I suppose that is what I mean. You're saying, are you not, that the relationship is platonic?' Gerty looked blank. 'Unconsummated, not – ah – physical.'

'Mr Bloom is a gentleman,' Gerty declared. 'He hasn't sought to take advantage of me.'

'I see,' the coroner said. 'How long have you been acquainted with Mr Bloom?'

Gerty tactfully removed their first encounter from her calculation. 'Seven months,' she said, 'and two weeks.'

'Did you meet . . . what, by chance?'

'We were properly introduced,' Gerty said, 'by a mutual friend, a widow lady, Mrs Dignam. She said it was all right for Mr Bloom and me to be acquainted.'

'In spite of the fact that Mr Bloom was married?'

'That didn't matter.'

'Did it not occur to you, Miss MacDowell, that it might have mattered to Mr Bloom's wife?'

'I never met her.'

'That,' said Slater, 'is not the point.'

'What is the point then?' Gerty spoke out. 'I love him.'

Steering away from the sticky topic of sense versus sentiment, Slater said, 'You live at home with your family, do you not?'

'Yes.'

'Do your parents approve of your friendship with a man so much older than you are, a married man at that?'

'My mother was all right with it. My father put his foot down,

but he puts his foot down about everything. I wasn't going to let
Poldy . . . Mr Bloom escape just because of my father, You don't
find many like Mr Bloom in a bunch.'

'I'm sure you don't,' said the coroner. 'May I ask what you
hoped to gain from your friendship with Mr Bloom? I mean,
what end had you in view?'

'End?'

'He could not marry you.'

'He can now,' said Gerty.

In spite of Boylan's half-cocked admission that he had a motive
for murder, Roland Slater continued to believe that the love-struck
young woman would, if given enough leeway, hand him Bloom's
head on a plate. While the court buzzed with excitement, he
pondered his next set of questions.

'Did Mr Bloom promise you marriage?' he said at length.

'He said he loved me and would never leave me.'

Ignoring the theatrical groans from cynical pressmen, Slater
rephrased the question. 'Did Mr Bloom, at any stage, indicate
that you and he would become man and wife?'

Gerty nervously fingered her Rosary. To Slater's satisfaction
cracks were beginning to show, faint cracks like those on the top
of a breakfast egg at the first tap of the spoon. She looked now
not at Bloom but up into the gallery where a tall, sallow-skinned
girl with bushy hair was making frantic signals of what might
be encouragement or, more likely, disapproval.

'Miss MacDowell, I must insist on an answer.'

In a whisper Gerty replied, 'He said he loved me and would
take care of me for all our days together.'

'Marriage, Miss MacDowell, marriage? When did Mr Bloom
promise to marry you?'

'I think it was about Christmas time. No, it was January,'
Gerty, confused, corrected herself. 'On the tram home from town.
He took me for supper at a place on O'Connell Street. It was
lovely, all lovely, with candles on the tables.'

'He proposed marriage in January, did he?'

'No, that's when he asked me to run away with him.'

'Did he promise marriage?' Roland Slater insisted.

'He told me I was his angel and my limp didn't matter,' Gerty
blurted out, twirling the Rosary beads like a little black whip.

'He said he loved me and took me in his arms and kissed me and no one had ever done that properly before.'

'Dear God!' said Slater under his breath, and then, 'Control yourself, please, Miss MacDowell.'

'I didn't want to spend the rest of my life crying in front of a mirror. When Poldy said he would take me away with him that was enough for me.'

'But did he mention marriage?'

'Who cares about marriage?' Gerty snapped.

And there it was, the transformation, passion driven and quite remarkable: Gerty MacDowell drew herself up, tossed the beads on to the ledge, stuck out her chest and said, 'As soon as we get to England we'll call ourselves man and wife, and if that's a sin before God, I don't care.'

Cheers from the gallery confirmed Dr Slater's opinion of the under class. It crossed his mind that reticence and modesty were seeping away from the world as he knew it and that in ten or twenty years his children's children, the little minim included, would be on their feet and cheering too.

Surrendering to the young woman's inexplicable appeal, he gave up trying to prove that Bloom did in his wife to marry a crippled girl-child, like a Hans Andersen fairytale rewritten by that filthy Norwegian.

'Now,' he said sternly, 'you've heard from previous witnesses that Mr Bloom was not home with his wife late on Wednesday evening, that he was in Upper Tyrone Street arguing with Mr Doylan. Where at this time were you, Miss MacDowell?'

'Packing my suitcase.'

'Are you saying it was your plan – Mr Bloom's plan – to leave Dublin that very night?'

'In the morning by the early boat.'

'Where did your rendezvous with Bloom take place?'

'He met me outside our house in Tritonville Road.'

'Your parents were asleep, I assume.'

'I said goodbye to my mother.'

'Didn't she try to stop you?'

'No.'

'And your father?'

'Drunk,' said Gerty scathingly, 'and snoring.'

'Did Mr Bloom have a bag or a suitcase?'

'A small suitcase.'

'What happened to that suitcase?' Slater asked.

'It's hid under my bed,' Gerty answered.

'We may take it that Mr Bloom's plan to leave Dublin did not work out as intended. You must tell the court exactly what you did after you met Mr Bloom at . . . what hour of the night?'

'Half past one.'

'Six hours, on estimate, before the sailing. Where did you go and what did you do in that period of time?'

'Poldy said it wasn't safe to go to a hotel. He was frightened somebody would catch up with us. He said he might be able to find a room somewhere in a house where nobody would think to look, but that fell through. He said we would wait by the dockers' coffee stall on the Quay until we could board the boat.'

'That isn't what happened, is it?'

'No. At the last minute he said he had to go back to Eccles Street,' Gerty said. 'He wanted me to wait for him on the Quay but I was frightened so he took me with him.'

'Did Mr Bloom tell you why he felt impelled to return to Eccles Street?' Slater said.

'To make sure Mrs Bloom was safe.'

'Safe?' said Roland Slater, frowning. 'Safe from what?'

'He didn't say.'

'What time did you reach Eccles Street?'

'I'm not sure. It was a long walk. We had to stop now and then because my foot . . . because I was tired. I think it would be about three o'clock or a bit after.'

'Why didn't you – Mr Bloom, I mean – hire a cab?'

'Poldy didn't want to leave a trail in case we were followed.'

'Followed? By whom?'

'I don't know.'

If Boylan's wits had been dulled by alcohol, Miss MacDowell's had been sharpened by devotion. She gave no appearance now of cracking.

'When you arrived at Number 7 Eccles Street did Mr Bloom unlock the door with his key?' Slater asked.

'No, the door wasn't locked.'

'Are you sure?'

'Poldy was surprised too, frightened, I think.' Gerty went on unprompted, 'There was a light on in the hallway. We went upstairs to an empty room. He put down the luggage and told me not to come downstairs until he called for me. I sat on the floor. I was tired and I needed to rest.'

'How long were you alone there?' Slater asked.

'About three or four minutes.'

'Did you hear anything while you waited, any unusual noises?'

'I heard a cry. More of a shout.'

'What sort of a shout?'

'Just a shout, no words.'

'What did you do?'

'I got up from the floor. I was frightened.'

'What happened then?'

'A minute or two after, Poldy came upstairs. He was shaking like a leaf. When I asked him what was wrong, he said, "Something terrible has happened."'

'Did he say what it was?'

'No. He sat on the floor and put his head in his hands. When I sat down beside him he put his arms about me. He was crying. Eventually he got up again and told me we wouldn't be going to Liverpool that morning.'

'Did you see upon Mr Bloom any sign of blood?'

'No, no sign of blood,' Gerty said. 'He told me to stay where I was then he went downstairs again.'

'How long was Mr Bloom gone this time?'

'Ten minutes, maybe.'

'Did you hear any further sounds from downstairs?'

'No, none.'

'When Mr Bloom returned . . .'

'Wait,' said Gerty. 'I haven't told you everything.'

'What,' said Slater, 'haven't you told us, Miss MacDowell?'

'I went to the middle of the stairs and looked down into the hall to see if I could find Poldy and I saw someone come out of the room at the far back of the house.'

'Mr Bloom, you mean?'

'No, Poldy was in the bedroom with the door closed.'

'This man in the hallway – I assume it was a man – did he see you, Miss MacDowell?'

'I don't think so.'

'What did he do, this man?'

'He stopped outside the bedroom door for a second then went very quiet down the hall to the front door. He bent down and put a hand over the metal thing at the bottom of the door and reached up and opened the door. Then he went outside and closed the door.'

'There was a light in the hall, you say?'

'The gas was low but it was light enough to see by,' Gerty said. 'I didn't want Poldy to think I was prying. I was scared the other man might come back so I went upstairs to the empty room again. When Poldy came for me he was crying but when I told him I'd seen a man in the hall he stopped crying. He went to the window and looked out then he took our suitcases down to the hall.'

'Was the bedroom door open at this stage?'

'Closed,' Gerty said. 'It was closed.'

'Did Mr Bloom say anything about his wife?'

'When I asked him what she'd said he told me she was sleeping. I asked him why he hadn't wakened her and he said she was sleeping too sound to waken.'

The silence in the courtroom was complete. Bloom, bent double, rested his brow on the table, eyes closed. Mr Tolland placed a hand on Bloom's back and left it there. In the gallery Milly sat up, big-eyed, her thumb crushed into her bottom lip.

The coroner let out his breath and leaned towards the witness. 'What did Bloom do then?'

'He hugged me and told me he loved me but Liverpool would have to wait. He said he had things must be done and I should go home and tell no one where I'd been. He asked me to carry the cases back to my house and keep them ready.'

'Ready for what?'

'I don't know. To leave, I suppose, when everything had been taken care of,' Gerty said.

'Why didn't you take a cab?'

'Poldy said it wasn't safe to take a cab.'

'What did he mean by that?'

'He was worried for me because of the man. He thought the man might be waiting at the cab rank. He stood with me in the hall for a while then opened the street door and looked out. He told me how to find my way home by the side streets 'cause I didn't know that part of town. He said he would wait in Eccles Street.'

'Wait for what?'

'Until the coast was clear.'

'What do you think he meant by that, Miss MacDowell?'

'Wait long enough to give me a chance to get home.'

'He was concerned for your safety, in other words?'

'Oh, yes,' Gerty said.

'It must have been difficult for you to walk so far carrying two suitcases. How long did it take you to reach Tritonville Road?'

'I did have to stop a lot. It must have been nearer six than five.'

'By which hour there would be people on the street?'

'Quite a few, and the trams were running.'

'Yet no one saw you, no one remarked on a young woman carrying two suitcases at that hour of the morning?'

'At that time of the morning nobody bothers with anyone else.'

'When you got home, were your parents awake?'

'No. I hid the cases under my bed and went to bed for I was wore out. Before I wakened up the newspapers. . . .' Gerty shrugged.

'Quite! Did you tell anyone what had occurred?'

Gerty shot one swift glance at the gallery then, facing the coroner again, stated firmly, 'I did not.'

'You kept your head down, as it were,' Slater said, 'and didn't come forward to aid the investigation into Mrs Bloom's death. Why, Miss MacDowell, did you keep silent?'

'Poldy told me to. I think he was feared the man would find me,' Gerty said. 'I think he was feared of what the man might do to me if he knew I'd seen him in the house in Eccles Street.'

'The man you saw in the house, did you recognise him?'

'No,' said Gerty, 'but I know now who he is.'

Below at the defence table Bloom lifted his head and made to rise but Neville Sullivan held him down.

'Him,' Gerty cried, pointing. 'It was him.'

'Mr Boylan, do you mean?' Roland Slater said.

'Yes. Him,' said Gerty. 'I saw him plain as day.'

*   *   *

For years afterwards Jack Delaney threatened to write an account of the affair and publish it in a book but, being Jack, he never quite got around to it. It was left to others to delve into the mystery of what made Bloom tick, why Molly Bloom had traded affection for sex with a scoundrel and why, most mysterious of all, Hugh 'Blazes' Boylan responded to young Miss MacDowell's accusation by reaching under the witness bench, fishing out his hat, sticking it on his head and leaping to his feet.

'Mr Boylan,' Slater said, 'you will be recalled in due course to answer the witness's charges. Meanwhile you must not interrupt.'

Blazes ignored the admonition. He crossed his hands on his chest and, stiff-necked, tipped his head back, the hat clinging precariously to his hair. It seemed at first as if he was about to burst into song and the court officers, led by Mr Rice, advanced upon him to put him in his place. Roland Slater waved them away.

'She wouldn't listen to me, not a word I said,' Blazes began. 'She wouldn't bend an inch and laughed when I said I loved her.'

'Mr Boylan, may I remind you that even although you have left the box you have not been dismissed and are, therefore, still under oath.'

'Love, she said, you don't know the meaning of the word. If you loved me you'd love what's in me too. God knows, I told her I had a horse at Foxrock loved me more than she did. That wiped the smile off her face. Did I think she was a horse I could buy and break? she said. Well, she said she would not be broken, not by me. She would die before she'd let some whore's lickspittle tear out the only thing she had worth keeping.'

'Mr Boylan . . .' Slater said, and then gave up.

'Your thing, she told me put it there but it's mine and mine to keep. Good luck to you then, Molly, I told her for you'll not have me to sponge off, no, nor him either. He's worth a thousand of you, she said. Then I told her, he's not coming back. She started laughing again. When I tried to shake some sense into her she told me not to be a fool, Poldy always came back. I told her again what was what with her beau ideal, and she spat in me face. Jesus, Joseph and the Mother o' God, what right had she to spit in *my* face. I'd given her the kid and surely I was entitled to have it taken away.'

'What,' Slater prompted softly, 'did she say to that?'

Blazes took his hands from his chest and clasped the nape of his neck like a prisoner surrendering to the militia. His features sagged, jowls swelling against his collar. He kneaded his neck with both hands and rolled his head from side to side. 'She'd have none of it. Poldy, he was her god and could do no wrong. Your Poldy's running away with a girl, I told her and, sitting up, she said what girl's this? I said, a girl called MacDowell who'll give him what you never could. And she said, you're a damned liar, Blazes. And I said, it's the truth. He told me so himself outside Cohen's not much more than an hour ago. You're stuck with me, Molly, but I'm damned if I'll be stuck with you when your belly's stretched like a pig's bladder and your tits are hanging to your waist.'

Mr Devereux's pen hovered over the paper. He darted a glance at the coroner but Slater was too intent on observing a star witness dying on his feet to notice.

The coroner said, 'And then?'

'She hit me,' Blazes said. 'The bitch hit me. She'd have clawed my eyes out if I hadn't . . . hadn't . . .'

'Hadn't what, Mr Boylan?'

'He was never a man to be trusted,' Blazes said.

In the gallery, without a by-your-leave, Michael Paterson clambered over Milly's knees and headed for the stairs.

'What did you do?' Slater urged.

'Lost my temper and pished it away, piddled it all away with . . . Jesus Christ . . . a teapot. I ask you, a fucking painted . . . teapot.'

In a surge of rage, Blazes tore off his hat, threw it to the floor and stamped on it. Then, gaping, he sank to his knees and, just as Kinsella reached out to support him, shouted, 'Maudie, Maudie, tell them it wasn't me,' and, with a final boozy gasp, fell dead at the G-man's feet.

THIRTY

While court officers, assisted by stalwarts from the DMP, cleared the general public from the court, Dr Michael Paterson and Dr Roland Slater, kneeling one on each side of the corpse, made futile attempts to revive it. They removed Blazes' beer-stained collar, necktie and belt. They prized open his mouth, pulled out his tongue and applied pressure to that region of his chest where his heart might be, all to no avail. Still with two fingers resting on the carotid artery, Michael Paterson looked across Boylan's chest at the coroner.

'Apoplexy?' he said. 'A fatal insult to the brain?'

'That would be my guess too,' said Roland Slater which, as it turned out, was an accurate diagnosis confirmed by Benson Rule in the autopsy room behind the mortuary the following forenoon.

There was no precedent, no protocol to guide Roland Slater through the next hour or, indeed, through the inquest into Hugh Boylan's sudden death conducted before a freshly empanelled jury on Wednesday of that same week. The hearing lasted not much longer than a couple of hours but attracted a great deal of interest from lawyers, journalists and the rabble from Trinity's medical school to whom Blazes had been something of a hero and who, collectively, were disappointed that he hadn't met his Maker while engaged in a strenuous act of copulation.

Present too at the Wednesday hearing were the Misses Boylan, Maude and Daphne, both, quite naturally, distraught. Decidedly less distraught, in fact rather irked at being winkled from his lair in Cork, was Boylan's father and the skittish young wife to whom he had been married for the best part of a year. Also present was Hugh Boylan's faithful secretary, Miss Dunne, who, brave girl that she was, managed to remain dry-eyed throughout but who, having better fish to fry by then, did not show up for the church service that preceded Blazes' interment at Mount Jerome cemetery.

A weird assortment of mourners followed Blazes' coffin to the graveside; gamblers, boxers, boozers and advertisers mainly, plus Bartell D'Arcy, two or three entertainers and a shadowy figure in a brown mackintosh whom no one ever managed to identify.

No tears were shed at the committal but the departed would have been gratified to know that several young women in Upper Tyrone Street sobbed into their knitting and several other ladies, in the privacy of their boudoirs, wept buckets at the news that such a fabulously well-endowed lover was lost and gone forever.

On that chaotic Monday afternoon, however, Hugh Boylan's transition from tipsy witness to coffined corpse was the last thing on Roland Slater's mind. Conscious of the omissions incurred in hastily bringing Bloom to book for a crime he evidently did not commit and well aware that not only was he being observed by a couple of Superintendents but by the Assistant Commissioner too, Dr Slater pulled himself together with such commendable alacrity that his impromptu decisions earned him a footnote in the next edition of 'The Coroner's Handbook'.

He began by snapping out an order to Tom Machin to dig up the medical examiner and fetch him at speed of light to the court-house while the corpse, covered with a sheet from the mortuary, remained *in situ* on the courthouse floor. Only then did he permit Miss MacDowell to be escorted from the witness box, to return not to the benches but to his private office where she would be provided with a nice hot cup of tea to calm her shredded nerves, a thoughtful gesture that proved unnecessary.

Though Gerty had never seen a man die before, she was more relieved than shocked by Boylan's dramatic exit and sufficiently in control of her emotions to touch Poldy's hand in passing, a contact that, however fleeting, sent up a little shower of sparks, at least according to Neville's report to Sarah over dinner that night, an exaggeration that Poppy Tolland, with a mandarin smile, chose neither to confirm nor deny.

All the journalists, protesting loudly, had been hustled from the courtroom together with the rest of the great unwashed, all, that is, save Jack Delaney who remained defiantly glued to his seat on the press bench and whose account of the last act of the tragic farce cost his colleagues more than one pint of the black stuff in the bar of the Belleville later that evening.

'Say what you like about the old devil,' Jack said, wiping froth from his lips with his sleeve, 'he wriggled out of trouble in the end.'

'It would have floored many a lesser man, no doubt,' Mr Flanagan agreed. 'Are we talking about Bloom here?'

'Slater,' Mr Palfry informed him. 'His neck was on the block as well as Bloom's. Right, Jack?'

'I would hardly say "on the block", but awkward questions would have been asked if the case had gone on to a higher court. Tolland would have made mincemeat of his handling before Assize judges.'

'So Bloom walked?' said Robbie Randall.

'Of course he did,' said Jack. 'What choice did Slater have after what amounted to Boylan's deathbed confession?'

'I always said Bloom was innocent, did I not now?' said Mr Flanagan. 'Now, Jack, be a good lad, tell us exactly what happened.'

'Oh, dear me, no,' said Jack Delaney, grinning ear to ear. 'If you want the lurid details, chaps, you can read all about it in tomorrow's edition of the *Star*.'

The details were a good deal less lurid than Jack Delaney led his colleagues to believe. The only colourful item in the court room was Blazes Boylan's shrouded corpse stretched out on the floor where it remained, toes up, while Roland Slater addressed the members of the jury and, waiving anything as convoluted as a point by point review, told them, more or less, how to frame their verdict and what that verdict must be.

'Gentlemen,' the coroner said, 'so far as I am aware we have now concluded our examination of the witnesses. In less unusual circumstances I would retire to review the evidence and present it to you in the form of a summing up tomorrow morning. However, I do not propose to delay you longer than is necessary and will, with your permission, bring proceedings to a close tonight. May I begin by reminding you that this is a court of record and the fact that a witness died during it must not divert you from reaching a fair verdict in respect of the death of Marion Bloom.'

At the defence table Mr Bloom and his counsellors sat quiet

as mice, though whether out of respect for the dead man at their feet or in the knowledge that Slater was heading for the door was moot.

The coroner went on, 'There is no doubt as to the cause of death: Dr Rule was specific on that point. It is, therefore, given to you to find a verdict of murder against some person or persons unknown, which means an open verdict, or to decide that one particular person was guilty of the murder of Marion Bloom.'

The pace of Roland Slater's delivery slowed, not to create tension but simply to allow Mr Devereux to catch every word of what he hoped might be a monumental decision or, if not that, at least not another legal blunder.

'It is a rule of court that the coroner does not express an opinion,' Slater continued. 'But as we have here encountered a unique situation I will take it upon myself to give you additional guidance. First, let me assure you that as Boylan had not been dismissed, his final statement was made under oath and is, thus, admissible. In other words, the fact that Mr Boylan subsequently died does not negate his testimony. What you must ask yourself is this; was Mr Boylan rational during the last few minutes of his life and was his statement tantamount to an admission of involvement in Marion Bloom's death? Was he, in fact, the intruder upon whom Mr Bloom laid blame all along?

'I cannot make your verdict for you, but' – Slater cleared his throat – 'it seems to me that whatever one may think of her decision to run off with Mr Bloom, Miss MacDowell's evidence was substantially truthful and very telling. That being the case, Boylan's account of how the crime was committed should also be taken at face value. We heard from Miss MacDowell that Bloom was anxious to protect her but, acting out of concern for his wife's safety and believing Boylan to be capable of inflicting harm, he put his own interests to one side and returned to Eccles Street when he could well have fled on the morning boat and no one any the wiser, which, I feel, goes some way to explaining Mr Bloom's reluctance to give evidence before you.

'What you cannot do is find Boylan guilty of the crime. I am categorical on that point. He was not on trial here. If the Crown Prosecutor wishes to pursue an investigation into Boylan's part in Mrs Bloom's murder then that is for him to decide. It has no bearing on your verdict. Therefore, an open verdict,' Roland Slater said, 'may be the only safe conclusion. I will express no further opinion than that. Now, I must ask you to retire and consider all that you have heard during this long and difficult inquiry.'

The jurymen went into a huddle without leaving the box while Mr Rice read them, rather superfluously, the customary oath to keep without meat, drink or fire until they had reached their verdict, a process that took all of three minutes. Mr Conway scribbled something down on a sheet of paper and rose to his feet.

'Mr Conway,' Slater said, 'do you have a verdict to give me?'

'I do, sir.'

'Do you wish to hand me your verdict in writing, Mr Foreman, or will you read it out?' Slater said.

'I will read it out,' said Mr Conway.

'Read it slowly, please.'

'After careful deliberation of the evidence submitted to us,' Mr Conway read, 'the jury unanimously agree that the evidence is too conflicting to establish the guilt of any particular person and consequently return a verdict of wilful murder against a person or persons unknown.'

'Mr Foreman, you do realise that amounts to an open verdict?'

'Yes, sir,' said Mr Conway. 'We do.'

'Thank you, Mr Foreman,' Roland Slater said.

Mr Rice formally pronounced the court closed.

And the inquest on Marion Bloom was over.

THIRTY ONE

Neville Sullivan solemnly shook Bloom's hand. Poppy Tolland, rising, gave Dr Slater a long hard look, as if to say that, thanks to Hugh Boylan's timely stroke, the coroner had gotten off lightly. Roland Slater, in turn, treated the advocate to what may have been a grin and, gathering up his papers, headed for the side door, followed by Mr Rice, Mr

Devereux and the Assistant Commissioner who, far from being peeved at the outcome, wished only to offer the coroner his congratulations on a job well done.

Tom Machin arrived with the medical examiner who, brusquely stripping the sheet from poor old Blazes, confirmed that the fellow was indeed dead, agreed to issue a certificate to that effect and instructed the constables to lug the body off to the mortuary.

By that time Michael Paterson had gone in search of Milly who had been shepherded out of the gallery and into the street with the rest of the herd and had found herself in conversation with a tall, fussy-haired young woman who introduced herself as Gerty MacDowell's best friend and seemed to think that they had something in common. Milly too had experienced nothing but relief plus a certain grisly satisfaction in watching her mother's lover drop dead. No whit of pity tainted her belief that Blazes had got what was coming to him, that Providence – call it what you will – had meted out just punishment for his gross appetites.

'Gert's all right, you know. She'll take good care of your Pa,' Cissy Caffrey said. Milly could do no more than nod while Cissy extolled the virtues of the young woman whom Papli had chosen to run off with. 'I expect he'll marry her now. No option, has he? Now our Gerty's found her man she'll never let go. She'll fatten him up, you'll see.' Cissy chuckled, then, as the courthouse door opened and a constable appeared, added, 'Nice to meet you. Got to go,' and, long legs flashing under her bedraggled skirt, darted off to waylay Archie Jarvis before he could reach the safety of the barracks.

Mr Coghlan came down the steps carrying Milly's suitcase. Behind him a gaggle of policemen and jury members emerged and then, at last, her father, the young woman, Gerty MacDowell, clinging to his arm as if her life depended upon it, which, Milly thought wryly, perhaps it had.

The crowd outside the courthouse had thinned considerably. No longer a celebrated murderer, the public's interest in Leopold Bloom had rapidly waned. Reporters rushed forward, though, calling for quotable comments on Boylan's deathbed confession, asking what Mr Bloom would do now and would he really leave Dublin, while photographers tried to snap 'the mysterious

stranger', whose evidence had blown the coroner's case right out
of the water.

In that uncertain moment, Milly longed to have the slate wiped
clean, her mother still asleep in the bedroom in Eccles Street,
Pussens in the kitchen, her father, braces hanging down his back
like a monkey's tail, standing by the sink shaving and humming
to himself, happy, she supposed, or at least contented. But no
one could put the clock back for, as Papli had once told her, time
ran on like the Liffey flowing ever into the sea.

'Milly,' said a quiet voice behind her. She felt Michael's arms
about her and rested her head on his shoulder while Mr Coghlan,
puffing a little, put the suitcase down by her side.

As if he had read her mind, Michael Paterson said, 'You can't
go back to Eccles Street, Milly. Harry and I have booked rooms
in the Imperial and one of them is for you if you want it. If your
father has other plans for you, of course, we'll understand.'

She had lost him in a sea of heads, lost her father, her first
love. He had cast her off in favour of another woman.

In spite of Michael's comforting arms, she experienced a pang
of resentment as if Papli, not Blazes Boylan and her wayward
mother, had ruined her life. And then he was with her, her Papli,
unsmiling, dark sorrowful eyes looking down at her. Behind him
she glimpsed the MacDowell woman, a pretty, dainty thing,
enjoying the attention but needy too and watching, sharp-eyed,
lest her man, her Poldy, slip away.

'Why didn't you tell me?' Milly said.

'Tell you what?' her father said.

'Everything.'

'Because,' Papli said, 'there are certain things it's best to find
out for yourself.'

'Do you love her?'

'Yes, I suppose I do.'

'More than you loved Mummy? More than you love me?'

'How can I answer that?'

'I think, sir, you'd better try,' Michael Paterson told him.

'If I don't, you'll think me a coward, I suppose.' Papli sighed.
'Well, I did what I thought was best for all of us. For you, Milly,
yes, and for me too.'

'And Mummy?'

'Most of all for Molly.'

'Are you leaving tonight for Liverpool with . . . with her?'

'No, there are too many loose ends to tidy up. Gerty daren't go home so we'll put up at the City Arms for the time being. I'll be there if you need me.'

'I don't need you. I don't need anyone,' Milly said.

'Yes, Milly, you do,' Michael said. 'We all need someone to make us complete. Am I not right, Mr Bloom?'

'How can I disagree with you when I don't even know who you are?' her father said.

'He's a doctor,' Harry Coghlan put in. 'Michael Paterson. He has a practice in Mullingar and I think I'm right in saying he's Milly's very good friend.'

'Oh!' her father said. 'What happened to Bannon?'

'He was not for me,' said Milly.

'Poldy? Poldy?' Gerty MacDowell called out.

Her father glanced over his shoulder.

'You'd better go to her,' Milly told him.

'Yes, I'd better. Do you want anything from the house?'

'The house?'

'Our house. Number 7, I mean.'

She felt tears start hot behind her lids. She pursed her lips and shook her head. He put his hands on her shoulders and held her. 'Go back to Mullingar, Milly. You have friends there now.'

'She does, Leopold, she does,' said Harry Coghlan.

'And you, Papli, will I see you again?'

'Of course you will, darling. Of course, you will.'

Milly did not believe him. He stooped and kissed her brow and then, very quickly, turned away and the last she saw of her father he was walking down Store Street with a stranger clinging to his arm and a pack of pressmen on his heels.

He sold his books at a pretty fair price and put the furniture, including the piano, to auction at Dillon's Rooms with instructions that whatever was raised by the sale be sent to his daughter at an address in Mullingar. He did not sell the bed, though. He paid Kelleher to collect the mattress, bolster and bedclothes in one of his carts and burn them in a corner of the timber yard. The iron parts, squeaky springs and rattling rings included, he dismantled and left against the wall of the jakes for the next tenant of No 7 to deal with.

Molly's clothes and Milly's 'baby' things, he packed neatly into two big boxes and had them delivered to Lizzie Fleming to launder and keep or, more likely, sell for a handful of shillings. He held back only a few trinkets that he'd given to Molly over the years and the hand mirror and silver-backed hairbrush she'd had as a girl in Gibraltar and the beads – a rosary? – that had belonged to her long lost mother, Lunita Laredo, from whom she'd inherited nothing but her good looks and full figure.

These items and four photographs, already fading, he sealed in a straw-lined box and, with almost the last of his ready cash, posted it off to Milly in the hope that when her broken heart healed she might appreciate a few nostalgic tokens to remind her of her childhood and her mother, as well as the sixteenth birthday gift from the Mercury Insurance Company to help her on her way.

Himself, he shed no tears at tackling the chores and refused to make a ritual out of it. He was, after all, a practical man, untroubled by dreams now. His only concession to revenge, and it was mild enough, was to take the vase from the bedroom and the two pieces of painted china that had been returned by the police and toss them into the Liffey before he went to have supper with Gerty in the City Arms Hotel and tuck her, chastely, up in bed. There would be time enough for satisfying his earthly desires, for breasts and bottoms and pliant young thighs, when all was squared away and he had cash and Dublin was behind them which, in fact, happened much sooner than he expected.

It was still early morning when he walked through the gates of Glasnevin cemetery carrying a small bunch of violets, wetted not with water from a painted pot but with a final tear or two.

There was no one about except two gravediggers, shadowy shapes against the ground mist, and he soon left them behind. He turned towards the section that bordered the Finglas Road, along the path that led to his mother's grave and Rudy's and the spot where Molly lay. He had ordered a stone from a carver in Great Brunswick Street and would pay that bill, and his bill at the City Arms Hotel this afternoon, for Gerty and he were sailing on the night boat to Liverpool en route to London where a man of his talents would surely find employment.

He thought of dropping by the offices of the *Freeman's Journal* but doubted if he would be made welcome and he'd be damned if he'd curry favour by buying them drink. He'd said his farewell to Cunningham, and Gerty and he had brought Mrs Dignam and Mrs MacDowell up to town for afternoon tea to say goodbye to them too.

Soon he would take a last long stroll through the streets of Dublin and leave behind all the guilt, deceptions, aspirations, disappointments and betrayals that had made him the man he was. The city would remain only in his memory and Milly and he, and Molly too, would be forgotten by all but a special few.

The wreathes had faded already and the leaves had turned brittle. He could see the wires poking through. He left them untouched on the mound of sods that had begun to settle and knit. He broke the little posy of violets into three and put a flower or two on each of the graves, the old and the new, then, kneeling, he kissed his fist and dabbed it twice on the grass beneath which Molly rested, which was the best he could do by way of farewell.

He rose then, a little stiff in the knees, looked out towards the leafing trees that sheltered the Tolka and smelled the scents of Dublin, dew-damp and fresh in the morning hour. Then, turning, he headed off to catch a tram to Grafton Street to call at the offices of the Provident Life Insurance Company and collect payment on a second policy that not even Neville Sullivan, for all his ingenuity, had uncovered: a policy made out to Leopold Bloom for three hundred pounds, the sum for which he had insured Molly's life on that monumental day last June when he had known for sure he had lost her.